Cuckoo
in the
Nest

Also by Michelle Magorian

Cuckoo
in the
Nest

Michelle Magorian

mammoth

First published in Great Britain 1994
by Methuen Children's Books Ltd
Published 1995 by Mammoth
Reissued 2000 by Mammoth
an imprint of Egmont Children's Books Limited
239 Kensington High Street, London W8 6SA

ISBN 0 7497 1756 4

10 9 8 7 6 5 4 3 2 1

A CIP catalogue record for this title
is available from the British Library

Printed in Great Britain
by Cox & Wyman Ltd, Reading, Berkshire

To

Diana Boddington, Margot Boyd, David Kelsey,
Vere Lorrimer, Julia MacDermot and
Robin Wentworth

Acknowledgements

Diana Boddington OBE, Margot Boyd, John Roffey,
Philip Wigley, Vere Lorrimer, David Kelsey,
Julia MacDermot, Robin Wentworth, Christine Evans,
The Palace Theatre, Watford, Theatre Museum,
Mander and Mitchenson Theatre Collection, Phil Robins,
Sheila Robins, Anna Robins, Rose Bruford College, Amanda
Smith, Janet Rawson, Jackie Kohnstamm and Niki Baldwin.

The author and publisher would like to thank the following
for permission to use copyright material:

The Years Between by Daphne du Maurier
Permission granted by the du Maurier Estate

A Cuckoo in the Nest by Ben Travers
Permission of the Peter Fraser and Dunlop Group Limited

Extracts from the *Kent Messenger*

Granite by Clemence Dane
Reproduced by permission of the
Curtis Brown Group Limited, London

Saint Joan by Bernard Shaw
© 1924, 1931 George Bernard Shaw
© 1951 The Public Trustee
Permission is granted by the Society of Authors on behalf of
the Bernard Shaw Estate

Hobson's Choice by Harold Brighouse
© 1916 Harold Brighouse
© Samuel French
Extract reprinted by permission of Samuel French Limited

'No suicides this week,' Aunty Win announced, laying the newspaper flat on the kitchen table.

Elsie sat with her small bony elbows on the table, picking her nose. 'Any murders?' she asked.

'Elsie, you know what I've said about doin' that. One day your brains will fall out.'

Elsie removed her finger.

'Wouldn't be able to tell the difference anyway,' scoffed Harry.

'You can talk,' cried Elsie, swinging round. 'The only reason you're in Mr Woods' class is because Miss Ferguson couldn't bear to have you for three years.'

He grinned in good humour and gave a careless shrug. 'I don't care.'

'Oooooh, Ellen, listen to this,' Win exclaimed.

Elsie and Harry's mother lifted up her head from the ironing and gave her sister a tired smile.

'Next Wednesday at St Andrew's Parish Hall there's a demonstration of electric cooking. It's at 3 p.m. You ought to go.'

'There's nothin' wrong with that range,' said Ellen.

Joan looked up from the film magazine she was reading. 'There's nothing right with it, you mean.'

'It's keepin' us warm.'

'Mum, can we have the wireless on?' interrupted Harry.

'You've already had *Dick Barton*.'

'I know but . . .'

'After supper.'

'I don't see why we can't eat ours before John and Ralph get home,' said Win with meaning.

'We spent enough time apart in the war,' said Ellen. 'We're all eating together.'

'All getting indigestion together,' muttered Win.

'What do you mean?'

'You can cut the atmosphere with a knife, when those two come in. It's a wonder they don't kill each other on the way.'

'Oh, go on, Win, give 'em a chance. It's not easy for either of them. John's missing his mates and his unit, and Ralph is missing his school pals.'

'I'm missing my friends too. He ain't the only person in the universe what's got demobbed. I'm finding civvy street hard as well. I was treated with a bit of respect in the Women's Auxiliary Air Force. Now I have to put up with some chit of a girl who can't be more than seventeen criticising the way I serve a customer or the way I organise cardigans on a shelf.'

Elsie and Harry gave each other a glance. 'We've all got our crosses to bear,' they mouthed as their aunt gave voice to it.

'Just because someone's seventeen don't make them stupid, you know,' protested Joan.

Winifred gave a sigh. 'I weren't casting no aspersions to you.'

'I've been working three years,' Joan pointed out. 'Longer than Ralph. But you treat him with more respect just because he's got a posh accent.'

'Oh, no I don't,' said her aunt. 'I treat no man with respect.'

'There you are,' said Joan. 'You called him a man, and he's only sixteen. But that seventeen-year-old, that one you called a . . . a . . .'

'Chit?' put in Elsie.

'Yeah, that's right,' agreed Joan.

'Are you sure it was chit?' added Harry.

'Yeah,' said Joan. 'Don't interrupt.'

'I thought she said something else,' said Harry grinning.

'Harry!' said his mother in a warning tone.

Elsie and Harry began giggling uncontrollably.

'Oh, none of you take me seriously. You never listen to me, ever.'

'I didn't mean to call him a man. It was a slip of the tongue,' said Winifred flicking through the newspaper. 'Oh listen, there is a murder, right here on page three. Huh! Another bigamist.'

'Does that mean he's got a big Mrs?' asked Elsie. She and her brother collapsed into laughter again.

'Don't be cheeky to your aunt,' said Ellen.

'It's hunger,' choked Harry. 'It's making me go off me 'ead.'

Ellen took the iron over to the range and swapped it for a hot one.

'Kay has an electric iron,' said Joan. 'Her kitchen is just like a film star's kitchen. It's even got a refrigerator and it's filled with so much food, she says, some days it's difficult to close the door.'

Ellen said nothing. She turned over the leg of the trousers she was ironing and proceeded to smooth a nice knife-edged crease on to them.

'If I'd been allowed to go out with Chuck, I might have been in a kitchen in America with a refrigerator.'

'With no family around you,' Ellen remarked.

'I'd have a new one, wouldn't I?'

8

'You was only fifteen,' she said firmly.

'The other girls were fifteen.'

'I promised your parents that if anythin' happened to you I'd make sure you and Kitty was all right.'

'Kitty's only three years older than me. You didn't stop her from going out with Frank and marrying him.'

'Kitty's a sensible girl.'

'And I'm not?'

'I didn't say that. But a spell in the ATS helped her grow up a bit faster, that's all. She's a bit more worldly wise than you are.'

'I've got a job which is more than she has.'

'Frank doesn't want her to work.'

'Couldn't we have the wireless on?' said Harry imploringly. 'Please.'

'Elsie's got to do her homework.'

'I've got all weekend,' said Elsie.

'If you keep leaving it all till Sunday night you won't keep up with the work. You don't want to risk being chucked out in your first term.'

'But Dad might come in.'

'That's why I told you to start earlier.'

'I wanted to hear *Dick Barton*.'

'You always want to hear *Dick Barton*.'

'He should be proud of havin' a daughter at a grammar school,' said Win. 'Any man worth his salt would be.'

'Win, please.'

'He's afraid she'll get all high and mighty like Ralph,' said Joan.

'He's not high and mighty.'

'He should stand up to his father,' said Win.

'His dad was lucky to get him work at the paper mill,' said Ellen wearily. 'It'll give him security for life.'

'So why did you go to all that trouble to let him stay at the grammar school?'

'You know why. Don't go on, Win.'

'To give him a better chance.' She rattled the newspaper with relish as if scoring a point. 'Of course, if John had been around he'd have stopped you, wouldn't he? The green-eyed monster, that's what it is.'

Harry stared at her as if she was mad. 'There ain't no green-eyed monsters 'ere. What you on about, Aunty Win?'

'Jealousy!' she said dramatically. 'That's what I'm on about.'

'That's enough, Win.'

Ellen put the iron back on the range and hung the trousers on a

9

piece of string stretched across a wall above a makeshift bed in the corner.

Outside, the yard door gave a loud slam.

'It can't be that late, surely,' exclaimed Ellen. Busily she removed the sheet and blanket from the end of the table. 'For goodness sake, Elsie,' she said urgently, picking up a small pair of spectacles. 'Put these in your room, quick. If they get broken the school won't lend you another pair.'

'And you don't want her dad to see them,' said Win. She raised her newspaper to hide her face.

There was a resounding crash from the back door. 'They've had another row,' commented Harry.

'I can't hear voices,' said Elsie. 'I expect they're still not talking.'

The door of the scullery was flung open and a blast of cold air swept into the kitchen. Standing in the doorway like a bull about to charge, stood a square-built man in his thirties with thick black hair and a red face.

He glanced round the room. 'Where is he?' he yelled. 'Where is the little tyke?'

'Who?' said Ellen nervously.

'Who do you think? Ralph!'

'You've not had another misunderstanding, have you?' Ellen began.

'Misunderstanding!' he roared. 'Is he upstairs? I'll tan his ruddy hide.'

'Didn't you meet him after work?'

'If I had I wouldn't be looking for him, would I?'

'Well, he's not here. He must be still at the mill.'

'Oh no. He's not at the mill. That's one thing I know. That fancy education you wanted for him has got him the sack.'

'No!' said Ellen in disbelief.

'I told him to keep his trap shut till he could lose that hoity-toity accent of his. If he'd just knuckled under . . .'

'But Ralph's a worker. Even in his school holidays he did farm work.'

'Oh, he worked all right but he didn't mix, did he?'

Winifred lowered her newspaper. 'If he wasn't supposed to open his mouth, how was he supposed to talk to them? In dumb-show?'

'You keep out of this. It's none of your business.'

'Oh, yes it is. I'm family.'

'And I don't want her ending up with her nose in the air,' he said, suddenly pointing at Elsie. 'One sign of it and I'm having her out.'

Elsie jumped nervously. There was a sudden snap from under the

10

table where her hands were hidden. She flushed and looked hurriedly at her mother.

'Oh, no, Elsie,' her mother whispered.

'What's that?' her father said sharply.

'Dad,' said Harry quickly, 'if Ralph's got the sack, his apprenticeship will be going, won't it?'

'So?'

'I could take it.'

'You've got to stay at school until you're fourteen,' said Ellen.

'I know but maybe Dad could persuade them to let me leave a couple of terms early, eh?'

'After today I'll be lucky to keep *my* job.'

'But I don't understand,' said Ellen. 'Why did they sack him?'

'In a nutshell, backchat, being over-qualified and reading.' He slumped down in the chair. 'I told him not to let on about that ruddy School Certificate.'

'How'd they find out?'

'He took a book with him to read in his dinner break, I ask you. Worse than that it was one of those ruddy theatre books. *French without Beer* or something.'

'Tears,' said Elsie quietly.

'What?'

'*French without Tears*. It's called a play.'

'Don't tell me what it's called, young lady.'

'She was only trying to help, love.'

'Anyway, the other boys was teasing him, but instead of shoving the book out of sight, he starts answering them back. So, one of the men snaps at him and says he can't read it. So your Ralph says, that's because bits are in French and he starts telling them what it means in English!'

'What's wrong with that?' asked Ellen bewildered.

'It was the ruddy foreman who was looking at the book. Ralph showed him up, didn't he? In front of the other apprentices, who then started calling Ralph a pansy.'

Ellen glanced quickly at Elsie and Harry. 'So what did he do?'

'Instead of socking them one, he turns to the foreman and says, "You don't seem to be able to keep your charges in order." In that posh voice of his.'

'I told you he was hoity-toity,' said Joan.

'That's what the foreman said. Anyway, they starts to take the piss out of the way he was talking. So Ralph apparently asks him what accent would be acceptable, and you know what he does?'

'He didn't hit him, did he?'

'Oh no, he only does every accent in the entire universe and then asks him if any of those will do?'

'And then?'

'He's handed his cards. And do you know what Ralph says? He says, "This must be one of the happiest days of my life." And he walks out!' He shook his head. 'Well, if he can't pay his way, he's not staying 'ere. There's boys who'd give their right arm to work in that mill. I had to eat a lot of humble pie to get him in. Especially him being so much older than the others. Ungrateful little so-and-so.'

'But where is he?' asked Ellen.

'Lying low upstairs probably.'

'We would've heard him coming in,' said Win. 'And we haven't.'

'How do I know you're not protecting him?'

'Why should I? He's as bad as you are.'

'Win, please,' said Ellen. 'You're only making things worse.'

John glared at his sister-in-law. 'You ought to be grateful you've got a home here.'

'So you keep reminding me.'

'John, don't,' said Ellen.

'And I'd like to remind you I pay my way. Even though you ain't got no carpets,' she snapped, and she raised her newspaper again.

John pushed his way forcefully past the chairs and left the room. They listened to him stamping up the stairs yelling out, 'Ralph! Ralph!'

Immediately Ellen rushed over to Elsie. Elsie lifted the spectacles. One side-piece had snapped off the joint. 'The lens isn't broken,' said Ellen relieved. 'We can fix that with some plaster. Now put them in your satchel. Quick.'

Elsie had hardly put them in the bag hanging from her chair when the door swung open and her father entered, his arms full of books.

'What you doin' with them?' gasped Ellen.

'They'll keep us warm until he gets home.' He marched over to the range.

'No!' yelled Ellen. 'Some of them's presents from the rector and his son.'

He opened the range with the tongs and threw one book in.

'Stop it!' screamed Ellen, flinging herself in front of him.

'Get out of my way!' And he gave her a shove. She fell backwards and her head caught the corner of the table.

'Ellen!' he cried. He flung the books to the floor. 'Ellen. Are you all right?'

'That's what the Nazis did,' said Win.

He swung round. 'What you on about?'

'They burnt books.'

'You calling me a Nazi?'

'Actions speak louder than words.'

'I wish Ralph had stayed in Cornwall with that vicar,' muttered Joan miserably.

'Amen to that,' added Win. 'Males give you nothing but a headache.'

Elsie gazed anxiously at her mother. Her dad was helping her to her chair. 'I'm sorry, love,' he said. 'I've had a hell of a day.'

'And now we're all having a hell of a night,' commented Win.

'Can't you keep your mouth shut for a second, woman!' he shouted.

Ellen gazed helplessly at John and her sister. She rubbed her forehead briskly as if trying to rub away the pain.

'I know you all don't think much of Ralphie,' she said shakily, 'but I do. And he's family. And right now he's out on the street somewhere by his self.'

'On a Friday?' Win quipped. 'Don't be daft. He'll be heading where he usually goes on pay-night.'

'He wouldn't have the gall,' whispered his father. 'Not after being sacked.'

'I forgot it was Friday,' said Ellen relieved. 'That's all right then.'

'Oh, what's the ruddy use,' he snapped. 'I'm off.'

'Where you going?'

'To drown his sorrows,' said Win sarcastically.

'At least I'm welcome there.'

'John, you haven't eaten.'

'Forget it. I'm not hungry.' And he flung the door open into the scullery.

Ellen ran after him but the back door was already open and all she could see was the fog outside. 'John, please!' she yelled after him.

'Aunty Ellen,' complained Joan from the kitchen, 'it's freezin'.'

Ellen closed both doors and returned silently to the kitchen. No one spoke.

'I know what would cheer everyone up,' said Harry suddenly.

'What's that, love?' said his mother in a monotone.

'We could put the wireless on!'

Act One

November – December 1946

*T*he hush in the theatre was electric. Even as the curtain hit the stage there was still a dumb silence and then it was broken suddenly by great waves of applause. Looking down at the audience from the gallery, his hands smarting with the ferocity of his clapping, Ralph could see people hurriedly wiping away their tears. The curtain sprang up revealing the cast in their Victorian costumes, holding hands. There was only one man, Basil Duke. He had played Albert Feathers, the blackmailing scoundrel of a nephew.

From below Ralph could hear cheering. He applauded with even more vigour, yelling with them. It was one of the most magical moments in the Palace Theatre for months.

Elspeth Harding, who had played the murderess, Ellen Creed, stepped forward and the audience roared their appreciation. The women in the box office had been right, thought Ralph. She did have star quality.

Basil Duke had star quality too. But of a different kind. He was the actor that Ralph most wanted to be like. He was totally different in each part he played, almost unrecognisable at times.

The actress, smiling with pleasure, indicated the cast and they all bowed again to tumultuous applause. She lifted her hand and gradually the auditorium grew quiet. 'Ladies and gentlemen, on behalf of myself and the entire company,' she began in her deep husky voice, 'we thank you for the way you have received our play tonight.'

She was magnificent, thought Ralph, quite magnificent.

'Next week,' she announced, 'we are presenting a play by Terence Rattigan entitled *French without Tears*. This charming, diverting and amusing romantic comedy is guaranteed to give an evening of pleasure in the theatre for all the family, so if you have enjoyed tonight, which I'm sure you have judging by the volume of your applause, do come again next week. We shall be here, same time, twice nightly, same place, same company in a variety of roles, so until then,' she continued, 'we all wish you goodnight and God bless.'

The Billy Dixon Trio in the pit began to play the introductory notes of 'God save the King' and four hundred and fifty seats slammed noisily back as everyone stood for the National Anthem.

As soon as it had finished the curtain came down and the theatre was buzzing with chatter. Down in the pit the three musicians had disappeared with their usual speed. Ralph stayed leaning over the railing, drinking in the red, cream and gilt of the Edwardian theatre, the nymphs and shepherdesses on the ceiling, the chandeliers, the endless rows of shabby red velvet-covered chairs. He was conscious that it might be his last Friday night here if he couldn't find a job.

'Seek and ye shall find; knock, and it shall be opened unto you,' he had heard the Reverend Collins saying in his head before the curtain rose, and he had made up his mind there and then to knock on one of those doors that night while he had some courage left.

He drew away from the railing and leapt up the steps to the swing doorway. Pausing for a moment he took a last glance back down to the stage now hidden by an immense red and gold curtain.

'One night,' he muttered with determination, 'one night I'll be playing here.' And he pushed the doors open and headed for the next flight of stairs.

Coming down into the foyer, the wide carpeted stairs were jammed with people pushing their way out into the night. Regular Friday nighters were waving to each other over the heads of others. Drifting from the open doors and up the stairway was a pea-souper fog which was now swathing itself around them.

The commissionaire in his maroon uniform covered in tarnished gold braid, was attempting to stand firm amongst the melee of pushing, chatting theatre-goers. Ralph nodded at him, thinking that after weeks of going to the theatre every Friday, the man would recognise him but he looked straight through him.

Ralph stood by the open door where some street lights still shone on the glass, and glanced at his reflection. Surveying his unruly coarse brown hair springing upwards from the short back and sides his father had forced him to have, he looked every inch a working class lad. He fiddled around with his scarf, attempting to make it look like a cravat but it looked like what it was, an ordinary khaki knitted scarf. He couldn't take it off because he didn't have a collar on his shirt. 'Mind over matter,' he muttered to himself.

He manoeuvred his way down the steps and turned round the

15

corner, heading up through the fog in the street. He hesitated at the next corner, spat copiously into his hands and then smoothed back his hair with as much muster as he could. Then he buttoned up his jacket, tucked his scarf neatly in and prayed his hair wouldn't suddenly spring up again in Stan Laurel fashion.

He peered round the corner. The stage door was open. He threw his shoulders back and stood to his full height. Shaking with a mixture of excitement and nerves he made his way towards it. Above the stage door a bright light burned a sulphurous yellow in the fog. Ralph blinked. Laughter was coming from inside. He hovered. He didn't want to appear a stage-door johnny, neither did he want to appear a sinister figure in the mist.

He stepped back quickly. Three of the women who had been in *Ladies in Retirement* came stumbling out of the back door laughing. He was about to slip in when he heard the familiar male tones of Basil Duke.

'No idea,' he heard him saying. 'I just hope it's a play set in the winter. If I have to wear summer clothes again in this weather!'

'I'm going to die next week,' said a young female voice.

'You've got your love to keep you warm,' sang Ralph's hero.

'My love will be as cold as me. At least he can wear a blazer during the performance. I'll have to keep a shawl in the wings.'

He heard an elderly voice saying goodnight.

"Night, Wilfred,' said Basil Duke.

"Night,' added a young female voice whom Ralph recognised as the maid's. And then they were in the doorway pulling their coats up against the cold and Ralph was aware of a strong smell of face powder.

'Oh my goodness, what a pea-souper!' the young actress exclaimed.

She had shoulder-length pitch black hair and was slim and lovely, Geraldine Maclaren.

To Ralph's surprise, Basil Duke was shorter than he appeared on stage. Peering at him through the mist, Ralph still couldn't decide whether he was in his twenties or thirties. He gazed at the actor's thick dark hair now slicked back so smoothly as to make Ralph sick with envy.

'I'll walk you home, darling,' Mr Duke said.

'No. Honestly. I'll be fine. I know the route with my eyes shut.'

He stared out at the fog. 'You won't have to shut them in this.'

'See you tomorrow morning then for the run.'

'And cuts,' he reminded her.

'Oh, don't. A run through and three shows! It's madness!'

'We'll survive,' he said cordially. 'We always do.'

To Ralph's amazement they gave each other a kiss. He felt embarrassed to see such intimacy at close quarters. As soon as they had gone he stepped, blinking, into the light.

An elderly man with a thick shock of white hair was sitting in a wooden cubicle reading a newspaper and sipping tea from a large stained mug. Behind him were rows of tiny pigeonholes, with letters painted roughly beneath them. Door keys hung on hooks beside them on a board with numbers on it.

Ralph stood tongue-tied. The man raised his head and glared at him. 'I'm afraid they've all gone, sonny,' he remarked in the local Hertfordshire accent. 'You're too late, best come back tomorrer night. Early.'

'But I've been waiting outside for some time,' said Ralph.

'Oh?' The man smiled at him kindly. 'Too shy to ask, that it? Leave your autograph book here and I can ask the cast to sign it for you, so's you can pick it up later.'

'But I don't want autographs,' Ralph blurted out.

'Well what do you want?' asked the man suddenly alert.

'A job. I mean, I want to work here.'

The man scrutinised his face and frowned. And then his eyes suddenly lit up. 'You want to sign up for the strike!'

'I don't think you quite understand,' Ralph said perplexed. 'I don't want to strike. I want to work.'

The man threw back his head and laughed. 'Set strike,' he said. 'Strike the set. Take it down.'

'Oh,' said Ralph, feeling a fool.

'They do it every Saturday night. But it's heavy work and long hours. They have to set up too. It can take well into Sunday. You'd best have a word with your parents first.'

'I'm seventeen!' Ralph exclaimed. 'Well, almost. I can decide for myself.'

The man leaned on both elbows and peered at him. 'Come closer, son.'

Ralph stood in front of his wooden shelf.

'You sure you want to be working backstage?'

'Yes of course,' said Ralph. 'I'll do anything.'

'You've a fine voice.'

'Have I?' said Ralph nonchalantly.

'You look more the actor type to me. You sure that's not what you really want to do?'

Ralph felt himself flush with pleasure. 'Eventually,' began Ralph.

'Ah. Look, I'll mention you to the master carpenter or stage director. Maybe they can find somethin' for you to do. Be here same time tomorrer night.'

'Thank you!'

'No promises, mind.'

'Of course not,' Ralph stammered.

'You're a bit on the small side,' he said as an afterthought.

'But I'm strong, I've done a lot of farm labouring in my time.'

'Then it'll be a piece of cake.'

Ralph backed out towards the doors. 'Good evening, then.'

'Night, sonny,' and he returned to his newspaper.

Outside, the fog was swirling more thickly. Ralph crossed the road and felt his way along the wall to the river where he had left his bicycle. It was leaning against a tree trunk a few hundred yards from the bridge, only the bridge had been obliterated. Swiftly he unpacked a pair of ankle boots from his saddle bag, removed his walking shoes, laced up his boots, crammed the shoes back in the saddle bag and put bicycle clips around the ankles of his trousers. He shoved his cap on and mounted the bike.

And then he stopped. The fog had encircled him completely. Even as he gazed out at the river it was disappearing before his eyes. He turned to look at the road but he could see nothing. He held his hand out in front of him and watched his fingers being enveloped in the strange green mist.

Standing there being rapidly swallowed up by the fog, he felt a moment of panic. He had a five mile ride home ahead of him and he would be lucky to make it to the end of the street. He took a deep breath to calm himself. The important thing was to stay put until he had found his bearings. He would have to find his way out of the town by sound. It would be too risky to go on the path by the river in case he fell in and in any case he'd have more chance of seeing street lights if he went via the High Street.

From the sound of the river behind him he knew he should be facing the back of the theatre. He stretched out his hand to the left and to his relief found the wall. Using it as a guide he reached the end of the pavement.

The blur of lights from the stage door helped him across the road. As he drew nearer he heard Wilfred talking to someone. An elderly woman answered back. At first he thought it must be one of the actresses leaving late, but the woman sounded working class.

He guided himself along the side of the theatre. In the distance he saw a vague smudge of light high up. He was hoping it was a street lamp. As soon as he felt the pavement hit the road he knew he had

18

reached the High Street. To his right were shops, a department store, two cinemas and a restaurant. To his left the road sloped downwards past more shops towards the railway station. He needed to reach the railway station and veer left to a bridge, past some bombed factories and on to the main road which would take him home. He raised his collar and dragged his bike towards the Rose and Crown. To his relief he heard the sound of men's voices, and glasses clinking, but he could still see nothing in the inky black smog.

It was going to be a long night.

TWO

There were only five habitable houses left in their street. Three on their side, two at either end opposite. The rest of the street was rubble. They were the lucky ones, his mother kept reminding everyone when they all started getting on each other's nerves when fighting for elbow room in the only warm room in the house, the kitchen. Even as he stumbled over the rubble in the fog, he still couldn't tell if it was their street or not.

His feet hit a broken pipe sticking out of the ground. Near it was the wall of a house. He felt his way along it on to the next house. Relieved, he realised he was touching his own front door. He tried to open it in case someone, out of kindness, had left it unlocked but no such luck. Slowly he groped his way past the house next to it and climbed over the rubble to the lane which led to their backyards.

He closed the yard door quietly behind him and felt his way towards the coalshed. Gently he leaned his bike against it. He had hardly let go of it when there was a clatter as it collapsed into a heap. He froze and stared at the back of the house. No lights were switched on. He just hoped no one had heard. He propped the bike up again and felt his way along to the outside lavatory. After a quick visit he headed for the scullery door. His clothes felt damp from the fog and his head ached from squinting.

For one awful moment he thought the back door was locked too, but on the second try the door clicked reassuringly open. He stepped quickly in and gently closed it behind him. Even then the fog had managed to force its way inside. Traces of it were swirling round the room. In the dark he saw the copper in the corner

19

glinting, the stone sink and wooden draining board and the mangle.

He dreaded going into the kitchen in case his father was sitting there waiting for him. He removed his bicycle clips, undid the laces of his boots and left them by the door. He turned the brass handle with painstaking slowness. Luckily the door didn't creak, and within seconds he could see by the faint light of the range grate, that his father lay immobile in his bed in a deep sleep.

He eased the door shut. There was a smell of hops in the room, and then he realised it was his father's beery breath. He edged his way carefully round the chairs on the opposite side of the room, past the dresser and towards the door which led into the narrow hall.

He was halfway up the stairs when they gave a loud creak. He remained motionless for a moment, and then carried on up to the small bedroom where he slept top to tail with Harry in a narrow bed. He slipped into the room, peeled off his sodden clothes and flung them over the rail at his end of the bed. He eased his pyjamas from under his pillow and put them on.

From the neck up he felt hot from suddenly being indoors again, but from the neck down he was chilled and clammy. He climbed gratefully into bed and was just stretching his feet down his side when he hit a tiny foot. There was a shuffling from the other side and two heads rose up.

'Elsie,' whispered Ralph. 'What are you doing here?'

'Joan was snoring so bad,' she yawned, 'she kept waking me.'

There was a creak on the landing outside. Elsie dived under the covers. The door opened. Ralph glanced nervously across the room. It was his mother. She moved hesitantly towards the bed. 'Ralphie?'

Ralph propped himself on to his elbow. 'I got caught in the fog.'

'Phone Uncle Ted's place next time. Then he can let me know.'

He nodded. 'I'm sorry if I worried you.'

'You're home now,' she said with relief and she turned to go.

'Mum,' he began, 'did Dad tell you?'

She stopped at the door and gave a nod. 'We'll talk about it in the morning. Now get some sleep. Night, love.'

'Goodnight, Mum.'

He sank back into the pillow and had just closed his eyes when urgent whispers made him look down the bed. His brother and sister's heads were raised again.

'Where you been?' asked Harry.

'Everywhere, I think,' whispered Ralph. 'It was a real pea-souper.'

'Dad burnt one of your books,' said Elsie.

'What!'

'Mum stopped him burning the rest,' said Harry.

'And Dad hit her,' added Elsie.

'He never,' said Harry. 'It was an accident.'

'Anyway,' said Elsie excitedly, 'you missed a row.'

'And *Dick Barton*.'

'But we remembered it for you. You know Snowy White had found where Dick Barton was holed up by the arch-evil . . .'

'Not now,' pleaded Ralph.

'But I might have forgotten it by the morning.'

'It is the morning. Now let me sleep. And Elsie?'

'Yeah.'

'Try not to kick. There are places on my anatomy which don't take to being kicked.'

Sounds of smothered giggling came from the other side. Ralph groaned. 'You're causing a draught,' he complained. 'Can't you laugh without moving?'

There was silence for a moment then a fresh outburst of laughter from the other side.

'I give up,' yawned Ralph. And fell asleep.

'Which one did he burn?' asked Ralph.

'Dunno, dear. You'll have to check them through.'

'Where are they?'

She glanced at Harry and Elsie who were poring over a comic. Elsie was holding her broken spectacles to the bridge of her nose and reading the captions to Harry. But he knew Elsie could eavesdrop and talk at the same time. 'I won't tell,' she said in midstream.

Ralph and his mother smiled quickly at one another.

'I've hidden them in a pile of washing in the scullery till he cools down.'

'Thanks.'

'What's in the scullery?' said Harry suddenly alert.

'Do you want to know what happens next?' interrupted Elsie.

'Yeah.'

His mother handed Ralph a plate of fried bread and dripping and a mug of tea. 'What are you going to do, then?' she asked. 'You can't go back to school, love. He won't hear of it.'

'I don't want to now. I'll find a job. I won't scrounge off you, don't worry.'

'It's not that.'

'You've done enough for me.'

She reddened. He loved it when she blushed. She looked pretty again.

'It was the rector,' she began embarrassed, 'he persuaded me.'

'I couldn't have done it without you, Mum.'

'Oh, go on. You worked hard for it. Now eat that up before it goes cold. I've got things to do.' And she disappeared into the scullery.

A newspaper was lying at the end of the table. He reached over for it and flipped it open at the job advertisements.

'No time like the present,' he said and he crunched his way through the fried bread. He was starving and the bread only whetted his appetite. He gulped down the hot tea.

'Mum,' he said casually, 'there might be a chance of a job just for tonight.'

She appeared in the doorway. 'Oh yeah?' What kind of job?'

'Well, um,' he said slowly, 'every Saturday night at the Palace Theatre, they have to take down the set.'

'What's a set?' asked Elsie.

'Scenery, nosy parker.'

'Just wanted to know,' she said returning to the comic. 'Watch out, yer yellow-livered hombre!'

'Sometimes they need extra hands,' he continued hesitantly. 'I saw a man backstage there and he suggested I pop round after the show. He's going to put in a good word for me.'

'I see. But won't it be late?'

'Later than late, Mum. All night.'

She came into the kitchen and sat down beside him. 'I don't know, love. I don't like to think of you out all night. And your dad . . . It was bad enough last night.'

'But I wouldn't be out. I'd be cycling back in daylight. I'd be even safer than coming back from the theatre on a Friday.'

'Talking of which,' she said biting her lip. 'I don't know if your father will let you go any longer. He's dead ashamed of you doing it.'

'He's ashamed of me breathing,' commented Ralph. 'He only has to see me and I make his blood boil. I only have to open my mouth and the steam starts coming out of his ears.'

Elsie began to giggle. He gazed affectionately at her. She was such an appreciative audience. She peered owlishly at him, her glasses juddering on her nose. Though eleven, she was so small and skinny she could pass for being nine. She grinned mischievously at him.

'How are you going to pay for a ticket?' asked his mother.

Ralph sighed. 'I don't know. And I must go. It's the one thing that keeps me from going insane.'

'What does insane mean?' said Harry suddenly interested.

'Barmy,' said Elsie.

'Mum, what about tonight?'

'He'll be that mad.'

'I don't mind him being mad with me, as long as you don't get hurt.' And he leaned over and touched the cut on her forehead. She blushed again.

'I slipped.'

'I don't want you "slipping" again,' said Ralph, not believing.

'He wouldn't hurt me for the world, Ralphie, honest. But it's difficult with your Auntie Win here and . . .' She stopped.

'She says males give you headaches,' said Harry.

Ralph laughed. 'I can believe it. Look, Mum, if I do this job, it'll mean I'll be out of the way part of the evening. That'll give him more time to cool down.'

'Not if he knows where you are.'

'I don't know what he thinks is going to happen to me. I'm not suddenly going to turn up for breakfast in silk pyjamas, a Chinese dressing-gown and a cigarette in a long cigarette holder, am I?'

'You try telling him that.'

'At least it'll show I'm trying to look for work.'

'That's true. But even if you did get it, what about the rest of the week?'

'I'll find something.'

She gave a nod. 'I better get a move on. If I don't queue up at the butcher's soon we'll have carrot stew again.' She picked up his empty mug and plate and left him to scour the paper.

Searching the advertisements, everybody seemed to want girls, either to be trained as nurses or child nurses or as maids or cooks. There were a few light engineering apprenticeships going but he would only come up against the same problem. Slowly he looked down the small ads again. His eye fell on the word 'Winford'. Another 'housemaid wanted' ad probably. 'Gardener and odd job,' he read out surprised. 'Youth wanted.'

The yard door gave a slam and was followed by the whirring sound of a bicycle chain. There was only one other person who had a bicycle. His father. 'Come on, Harry!' said Elsie, folding the comic and rising.

'What you doin'?' he protested.

'We need some fresh air.'

'You gone daft?'

'Out!' she ordered.

'Don't boss me!' he started.

'I ain't.'

'Yes you are.'

'I'll be Snowy White again.'

His eyes lit up. 'You're on.'

'Not that way,' she said grabbing his darned sleeve. 'We'll go out the front.'

'We ain't visitors,' he said. Just then they heard the sound of hobnail boots stomping up the yard. 'Oh yeah, I get. Good idea, Elsie,' Harry stammered and he and Elsie fled out of the door.

A sick feeling crept into Ralph's mouth. He looked down quickly at the paper and read: Trained and untrained mental nurses and attendants. Male and female required. 'Now there's a possibility,' he murmured attempting to make himself laugh. He didn't think his father would find it amusing though.

The back door slammed.

'Is his lordship out of bed yet?' he heard his father demand.

'He didn't get back till this morning.'

'He shouldn't have been out. Ruddy pansy.'

'John. Don't say that.'

'Where is he, then?'

'In the kitchen. Looking for jobs in the newspaper.'

'He don't want work. He just wants to lay about reading pansy books.'

By now Ralph's fear had disappeared. Anger had replaced it. The door was flung open. His father attempted to tower in the doorway, his stocky frame stretched to its ultimate.

'This is between him and me, Ellen,' he said over his shoulder. 'No more hiding behind his mother's apron.'

Ralph rose furiously to his feet. His father slammed the door shut. 'Don't think you're too old for a hiding, lad.'

'Go on then. Hit me. But I'll hit you back.'

'You what? I could wipe the floor with a little toe-rag like you.'

'And that's what you'd like to do, isn't it? You've been dying for an excuse to do it ever since I came back home. So why don't you get on and do it?'

'That's a lie. I've gone out of my way to help you. I got you a job for life. Steady, stable, with one of the best companies around. Good hours, good pay and a pension scheme. But oh, no, that's not good enough for you, is it? Well, I wash my hands of you now. You're on your own. You find your own work.'

'I didn't resign, Dad. They fired me.'

'I know they fired you. For reading a pansy book.'

'No!'

'You answered back.'

'I answered, that's all. I forgot I was supposed to keep it secret I could speak French.'

'Don't give me that. You wanted to show off.'

'No. Funnily enough, this week was the first time in months that I started to feel more relaxed. That's why I was off guard.'

'Relaxed! You're there to work.'

'In the lunch break.'

'Dinner! We don't need your lah-di-dah names round here.'

'Dinner then,' he said exasperated. 'I tried to hedge round it, but in the end the foreman got it out of me, that I had School Cert.'

'Clever enough to get a ruddy book exam, but not clever enough to keep your trap shut.'

'I was shocked too, Dad. My work was as good as anyone's. I worked hard. They just had it in for me.'

'I wonder why,' he said sarcastically. 'You must think I was born yesterday. I heard what you said to him about it being the happiest day of your life.'

'He asked for it. He looked so smug when he gave me my cards. He said that the manager didn't think it fair that someone with my qualifications should take an apprenticeship away from someone who hadn't. And I'd only cause trouble later on when I got bored. He was delighted, Dad. That's why I said it to him.'

'You didn't have to dance around.'

'I had to, to make it convincing, otherwise he would have thought it was sour grapes. I wanted to make sure I rubbed that satisfied smirk off his face.'

'You did that all right. Everyone knows now that I've got a rotten apple for a son.'

'I'll find a job.'

'You'd better, because if you don't pay your keep, you don't eat here. You don't sleep here. Joan's been paying her way for three years now. She ain't going to carry you, sonny. Neither am I or your Aunty Win. And I know that you've already spent part of your last pay on that pansy theatre of yours. That'll have to stop too.'

'If I work hard, I'm entitled to spend some of it on something I like, or is there one rule for everyone else in this house, and another for me?'

'Don't tell me what you're entitled to. You're entitled to nothing till I see you muck in like the rest of us. You've got away without bringing in a pay-packet for two years! But not any longer. You bring in a pay packet and you can join us at the table. Otherwise you can stay in your room and read your precious books.'

'All but one!'

'Oh, yeah, you heard, did you? Well, you can thank your ma that I didn't tip the rest in.'

'Let's hope it wasn't a library book, Dad. If it was they'll be sending you a bill.'

'Oh, no, sonny. If it was a library book it'll be out in your name.'

'You'd let me pay for you damaging it!'

'You brought it into the house.'

'It was in my room.'

'In *my* house,' he pointed out. 'And I say what comes in 'ere and who comes in 'ere.'

'So why were you so keen to get me back from Cornwall? I was happy where I was.'

'Looks like I rescued you in time. You're working class, and don't forget it. Family is the most important thing in the world. You lose family, you lose everything. That's where your first loyalty is. So you can drop that accent.'

'Which working-class accent would you like me to speak, yours or Mum's?'

For a moment his father stared dumbstruck at him. 'Hertfordshire or London?' Ralph continued.

'I dunno!' he said angrily. 'Don't twist my words.' There was silence between them.

'I did try,' said Ralph eventually. 'I'm sorry.'

'So am I,' his father said bitterly.

'Look, I've seen a job advertised. I'll go and ring up about it now.'

'What is it?'

'Gardener and odd job.'

'Odd job! You wouldn't have a clue.'

'I can learn.'

'If you phone they won't even bother to see you. They want a local lad. Your voice will put them off.'

He was right. 'I'll put on an accent, just to get me an interview.'

His father grinned triumphantly. 'Which accent?' he said.

Touché, thought Ralph. He hated this man so much, yet he was annoyed that he couldn't bring himself to hurt him and say Hertfordshire. But if he said London to please him, he'd hurt his mother. And then he knew. 'Cornish,' he said simply.

THREE

*I*t was a towering Gothic-style Victorian house with odd wings sticking out of it. A large ornate gate, wedged between high hedges, led to a wide path to the front porch. There was a small gate at the side to a tiny path which, Ralph presumed, led to the tradesman's entrance.

He opened it and wheeled his bike towards what appeared to be a dilapidated conservatory at the side. Peering in, he could make out bedraggled dead plants on shelves, and beyond, the kitchen door. Swiftly he sneaked past it to take a look at the back garden, and gulped. An enormous, unkempt lawn with waist-high grass sprawled past two sheds, trees and overgrown shrubs down to the river. The owners didn't need a gardener, he thought, they needed a combine harvester.

At the back of the house was a large room with french windows in the centre and a bay window on either side. Outside it was a long veranda with a glass roof, covered in ivy which had reached there from ornate pillars supporting it. Stone steps covered in moss and weed led down from it to wide overgrown borders of what appeared to be mostly convolvulus.

He was returning to the kitchen door when a young man came flying out. He was about nineteen, taller than him, strong looking, muscular. Yet he couldn't seem to get out of the door fast enough. Ralph watched him fly down the path like a frightened rabbit. He stepped into the conservatory and peered in through the window. A skinny disgruntled woman in an apron was moving around a large kitchen. Ralph took his cap off and knocked on the door. The woman glanced round and opened it.

'Come for the gardener job?' she asked in the local dialect.

Ralph nodded. He decided not to talk unless it was absolutely necessary.

'The last victim,' she muttered.

Ralph indicated the direction the youth had fled, opened his mouth, remembered his code of silence and then closed it again.

'Yes,' said the woman. 'He's just been to see Mrs Egerton-Smythe. And I don't think he'll be coming back.'

A bell above the door rang. She gazed sorrowfully at him. 'You're wasting your time, lad. She'll 'ave you fer breakfast. If you want to leave now I can always say you didn't turn up.'

Ralph shook his head.

'Don't say I didn't warn you.'

They walked out into an oak-lined hallway, with a massive hallstand along the wall by the kitchen door. Ralph gave an appreciative whistle. The woman grunted. 'You don't have to polish these floors. I tell her, she should get linoleum. Linoleum is the thing now. Give it a quick swab down and bob's yer uncle.' She led him to one of the doors. 'Knock,' she said, and then abandoned him.

Ralph knocked as hard as he could. 'Think nineteen,' he muttered to himself. 'Think mature.'

'Come in!' yelled an irritated voice from the other side.

Ralph swung open the door and found himself in what appeared to be a library. Glass cabinets with shelves of books stretched up to the ceiling. Two leather armchairs stood solidly on either side of the laid, but unlit fireplace.

A handsome middle-aged woman of medium build in a tweed suit and brogues was standing by a massive table in the centre of the room. Her chestnut hair was gripped untidily back from her face. She looked tired and angry. Ralph's first instinct was that she didn't belong in the room. She scowled at him as if challenging him. 'So you're Mr Hollis,' she snapped, looking him up and down. 'More like Master Hollis to me. Still I did say gardener's *boy*.'

She strode over to him. 'Bend your arm,' she commanded. He did so.

'Oh,' she said surprised. 'There is muscle there. The strong wiry type, eh? Seen the garden then? Had a quick pry before you came in?'

He nodded.

'Now I like *doers*, Master Hollis. I haven't the time nor the energy to check that people are *doing* what I ask. When someone says they'll do something, I expect them to *do* it. I've had enough of encouraging people to get on with it. Now Master Hollis, are you a *doer*?'

Ralph nodded again.

'Another silent type, eh? How wearisome.' She began marching up and down the carpet as if a thorn had found its way into her clothes and was sticking into her. 'Hollis! Hollis! Hollis!' she muttered. 'Doesn't sound very Cornish to me. Is it Cornish?'

Ralph shook his head.

She stared at him. 'Well!' She paused. 'Elucidate.'

Goodbye job, thought Ralph. Still it was only his first interview. He cleared his throat. 'I'm from round here actually. But I was evacuated to Cornwall during the war. I put on the accent because I knew you wouldn't interview me otherwise. And if you're worried about me not being physically able to cope, I must point out that I worked on local farms in my school vacations.'

Her jaw dropped. 'You little fraud!' she roared. 'This isn't some Saturday job for a middle class schoolboy. Now clear out of here and don't waste my time!'

'I'm not a schoolboy. I had a job until yesterday when I was told I was over-qualified. In fact I might as well lay all my cards on the table. I have School Cert. And I didn't get it by sucking eggs and counting clouds out of the window. It was hard work.'

'Got quite a little temper, haven't we, Master Hollis.'

'Yes, we have, Mrs Egerton-Smythe!'

She pursed her lips. 'Well I'm afraid holiday harvesting is not required here. You've been reading too much . . .' She waved her hand as if searching for the right name.

'A.G. Street?' he suggested.

He could see that he had guessed right, but it was obvious he had little chance of a job. 'If you want me,' he stated firmly, 'which I doubt, you can tell me what you want me to do. If I don't know how to do it, I'll find a way of doing it. I'm not witless, you know.'

'Are you playing truant?' she demanded.

'No. I told you. Yesterday I was sacked from the paper mill. If you don't believe me you can contact them. I'm sure they'll send you the worst letter of recommendation you're ever likely to read.'

'Paper mill?' she exclaimed. 'What the hell were you doing at a paper mill?'

'My father took me out of school and got me a job there.'

'He's a bloody manager, isn't he? Is this some kind of character-building experiment?'

'No,' said Ralph wearily. 'Look, I need a job, but I want it on my terms now. I'm not spending any more time pretending I'm something I'm not.'

The faintest flicker of amusement passed her eyes. 'Oh, lucky you. You know who you are, eh?'

Ralph opened his mouth, and then to his astonishment he burst out laughing. The woman strode across the room to a long velvet cord which she pulled. And Ralph couldn't stop himself. It was as if the last four months of awfulness had finally taken their toll. He knew she was calling for the maid to take him back to the kitchen and out. And he was beyond caring. He had no job and he had ruined his first interview for one. He hadn't had a conversation about any of the things he loved, like plays or the theatre or books or ideas, for months. His brain was atrophying and now he suspected he might be going insane. He took out a handkerchief

29

and wiped his eyes.

The door opened and Queenie entered.

'Queenie, Hollis will be staying for tea.' She turned to him. 'You have no further appointments this afternoon have you?'

Too surprised to speak, he shook his head.

Queenie held the door open for him. He was about to move when Mrs Egerton-Smythe raised her hand. 'No, Queenie, Hollis will have tea with me. In here.'

Queenie gasped. 'But, madam!' she protested.

'Hollis and I have a lot to talk about,' and she turned sharply to Ralph, 'haven't we?'

Ralph nodded again, amazed. The door closed.

'Now, sit down, and we'll discuss what we're going to do with that jungle out there.' Ralph just stared at her. 'Or have you decided to look for work elsewhere? Don't worry, it's quite common. I seem to scare the living daylights out of most people who work here. I don't know why.'

'You mean I've got the job?'

'Don't be an ass, boy. Of course you have. Now do as I say and sit down. I want to interview you a little more.'

He lowered himself into one of the leather armchairs opposite her and grinned. 'You mean, interrogate me.'

'Exactly. Now where shall we start?'

It was already dark when Ralph wheeled his bicycle out through Mrs Egerton-Smythe's small gate. He stopped for a moment to gaze back at the large forbidding house. He had a feeling Mrs Egerton-Smythe's brusqueness was caused by some kind of pain but, in spite of her irritability, he liked her. He gave a broad smile.

As he cycled away, his spirits were so high that he found himself singing a Brandenburg Concerto. He headed towards the wide tree-lined road which led off Mrs Egerton-Smythe's avenue. Once he reached the High Street, he turned left past the department store on the corner where his Aunty Win worked and the little dress shop a hundred yards further on where his cousin Joan worked, past two cinemas, a jeweller's, a shoe shop, a butcher's, past the tower with a clock on it which stood in the centre, past more shops until he was outside the Palace Theatre. He pulled on his brakes and glanced up at the hoarding advertising *Ladies in Retirement*. Next week, it announced, *French Without Tears*. 'Charming, Amusing, a Delight!'

He mentally crossed his fingers and skimmed downhill towards the railway station and bridge.

The family were all sitting round the table when he arrived home. Several arguments were going on which were being refereed by his mother. His father was polishing his boots, a sign that he was going out.

'You're not old enough for the Saturday thriller, Elsie,' his mother was saying. 'You'll have nightmares.'

'I won't,' she insisted. 'I know it's just a story.'

'It's for grown-ups.'

'So's them books Aunty Win reads out. You let me listen to them.'

'You're not supposed to be listening.'

'Mavis White's allowed to go out to Saturday dances with her friends,' interrupted Joan. 'And meet boys there. He said that's where he'd see me, and I promised.'

'You had no right. If he wants to take you out he can come here and pick you up hisself. Elsie, clear the table.'

She turned and winked at Ralph. ''Ow d'you do?' she mouthed.

'I got it.'

'Oh, Ralphie!' And to his surprise she flung her arms round him, and then suddenly broke away blushing.

'What's that?' said his father, looking up.

'I got the job.'

'Regular, is it?'

'Occasional.'

His father gave a snort.

'It's a start,' said his mother.

'And if I do well she might spread the word to her friends.'

'Gardener!' he scoffed. 'What kind of job is that?'

'Mum,' began Elsie, 'couldn't I listen to the first bit of it?'

'No.'

'What if I met him at the Odeon?' pleaded Joan.

'What's wrong with him meeting you here?'

'It'd scare him off. He'd think it was serious.'

'It is.'

'You know what I mean.'

'Elsie, clear the table!'

'Hello,' said Aunty Win into her newspaper. 'There's another bigamist in here.' She tutted and shook her head. 'I dunno.'

Because they had only six chairs, it was Harry's turn to sit on Dad's bed at supper, but he accidentally spilt some gravy on it in the middle of his exciting rendition of the previous night's episode of *Dick Barton, Special Agent*, which made his father almost hit the ceiling, since it was the one place in the house he could call his own.

He was only to have slept in it temporarily but it had stretched to six months because Aunty Win didn't feel she should share a room with her nieces. Ralph volunteered to change places, but his father said he didn't want no slackers sitting on his bed. Elsie said Harry could share her chair and so they spent the rest of the meal giggling as one or other kept pitching to the side. After the meal, his Uncle Ted, a large portly man in his fifties, from two streets away, called for his dad. He had persuaded him to go greyhound racing with him. His father wasn't interested in greyhound racing, but he told Ralph that he thought it was better for both of them if one of them wasn't at home.

Sometimes Ralph wondered if there was something he had done when he was little to cause so much hostility between him and his father, because try as he might, he rarely got a smile out of him.

While Elsie and his mother washed the dishes in the scullery, Joan arranged to go to the cinema with a friend of hers. And still Ralph didn't mention going back to the theatre. He watched his mother spread out a blanket and sheet at the end of the table and iron a dress for Joan whilst Aunty Win read aloud an announcement of carpet sales from the newspaper and then began the third chapter of her Margery Allingham detective novel. It constantly surprised him that two sisters should be so unalike. Both in their thirties with five years between them, his aunt, who was the younger, appeared five years older. A head taller than his mother, she was robust, with a face which seemed to gather into a point, and fiery blue eyes whereas his mother was slight with wavy chestnut hair and soft dark eyes. Constantly on the move, she rarely sat down.

As he gazed at her methodically ironing, he felt a deep fondness for her. But her illiteracy still embarrassed him. No one suggested she should learn to read. How she managed to shop for food amazed him. Even the letters she wrote to him, when he was in Cornwall, were dictated to his aunt or Joan or Elsie while his mother was busy with something else, so she said. Elsie read to her. Even Joan read to her. Yet she seemed to show no shame. Aunty Win read her thrillers, Elsie her children's books and Joan her women's magazines or film magazines.

He waited till Joan had gone out and Elsie was in bed. Harry had been allowed to stay up for the thriller and had promised to tell Elsie every detail the next day. It was while his mother began ironing shirts for Sunday best, that he broached the subject of the set strike. 'Mum,' he began, 'I won't need that shirt in the morning.'

'Oh?'

'Remember? The set strike. It's all night.'

His aunt stopped reading. 'What's this, Ellen?'

'Another job he's hopin' to get. Ralphie, I don't think it's a good idea. Your father will take the belt to you. You know what he thinks of the theatre.'

'He's out. He doesn't have to know.'

His mother glanced at Harry who was listening with rapt attention to the wireless. 'He's going to notice you're not here in the morning.'

'He won't. After a night out with his brother, he'll sleep through all of us having breakfast,' Win commented.

'Ralphie,' said his mother quietly, 'the rector would be very upset if he thought you was missing church.'

'I can go to Evensong. I prefer it anyway. It's simpler than the morning service.'

'Ellen, the more he's out of the way, the better,' said his aunt.

'Thanks, Aunty Win,' said Ralph sardonically. 'I'll go without a night's sleep and get up with everyone. And go to bed early tomorrow. After church.'

'I don't like keeping secrets from yer dad, Ralph.'

'Mum, please,' begged Ralph, 'I've got to find some way of getting my foot in the door.'

'Why?' said his aunt. 'You don't want to spend too much time there, you know,' she added significantly.

'Not you, too,' said Ralph wearily.

'Don't talk to your aunt like that.'

'I'm sorry, but where's the harm?'

'I don't like it, Ralph.'

'I might not even get the work and it's only on Saturdays.'

'What do you think, Win?'

'Work's work when all is said and done, I s'pose. And he might as well be hung for a sheep as for a lamb.'

Ralph caught his mother's eye. 'So can I go?'

His mother gave a sigh. 'I don't want you out in the dark with no lights.'

'I've checked my dynamo.'

'I'll leave the front door open so you don't disturb him. But don't forget to lock it afterwards.'

'Mum,' protested Harry, 'I can't hear.'

'Thanks, Mum,' said Ralph.

Half an hour before curtain down, Ralph stood awkwardly outside

33

the stage door not knowing quite when to make his presence felt. He walked back down the road towards the High Street and stood in front of the brightly lit foyer. At the first glimpse of the Saturday nighters flooding down the staircase he ran back down the road and hovered by the door again.

Peering in he could see Wilfred sitting in his cubby-hole. Nervously he stepped in. He was about to speak when he realised that he didn't know the man's surname. The old man looked up and frowned. 'Yes?' he said. 'What you doin' in 'ere?'

'I came last night, sir, about a job?'

'Oh,' he said, slapping his forehead. 'Sorry, sonny, I completely forgot. I ent seen Mr Johnson or Mr Walker all day.'

Ralph's heart fell.

The man looked sorry for him. 'Stand over there,' he said pointing to a notice board.

Ralph walked over to where a large skip was wedged up against a wall and leant against it. He heard a door being opened at the top of the steps and voices.

'So when do you think you'll be back?' said a female voice he recognised as belonging to one of the batty sisters in *Ladies in Retirement*.

'I don't know,' said the dark voice of Elspeth Harding. 'Before Christmas, I hope. I need the money!'

'Money? What's that?' quipped the younger actress.

'Oh, don't,' said Elspeth Harding in mock despair.

As soon as Ralph saw them appear at the foot of the steps in their hats and coats he stood to attention.

'Well, we're off, Wilfred,' said Miss Harding.

'Not fer long, I 'ope.'

'Tell that to the producer,' she laughed.

'You'll be snapped up by the West End.'

'That's what I keep telling her,' said the younger actress.

'Right now all I can think about is catching the train, getting home and cooking myself a meal.' She glanced aside at her companion. 'I envy you, Annie, living so near.'

More footsteps were making their way down now. Ralph looked up expectantly. Geraldine Maclaren appeared. She was flicking through a playscript. 'Oh, bliss,' he heard her breathe. 'Only one costume.'

She looked dazzling in a red jacket with padded shoulders and red skirt with navy piping. A red hat was perched to one side on her black wavy hair. Ralph was shocked to see how heavy her make-up was at close quarters. In the corners of her eyes were dark red flecks. It looked almost as if she was wearing a mask. 'Is Bəsil down yet?' she asked Wilfred.

'Not yet, Mrs Maclaren.'

At that moment Ralph's hero came leaping down the steps with his script.

She swung round. 'Have you had time to have a look?'

'Yes, I'm playing a real sod,' he said cheerfully. 'And I can wear my evening dress all through.'

'Lucky thing,' she said. 'I think I'll try to get hold of a cape from somewhere to keep me warm.'

'You could wear long johns underneath.'

'I don't think so somehow.' She smiled. 'I'm looking forward to this, I've only been in one Priestley play before and I loved it. Oh, hell! I wore my white dress for *Moonlight over Athens*. The audience will recognise it. Unless I wear a coloured sash perhaps?'

Ralph returned to sitting on the skip and tried to make himself sink into the surroundings as they shook hands with Wilfred and disappeared into the night. Finally a tiny elderly woman bustled up to Wilfred with a small bundle. 'Not much washing this week,' she said, 'it being a costume drama. Next week's going to be busy though. Lots of whites.' She caught sight of Ralph out of the corner of her eye.

'He's looking for work,' Wilfred explained.

'Call boy?'

'Strike.'

Ralph pushed himself away from the skip. 'They've got everyone they need,' she said.

'I know,' he whispered. 'But I didn't want to disappoint the lad. Anyway he can hold a ladder, can't he?'

'Listen, lovey,' said the old woman to Ralph. 'There ain't much hope but I'll take you backstage and you can ask Jack Walker. 'E's the master carpenter. He and Mr Johnson, the stage director, are in charge of hiring and firing.'

'Thanks awfully,' he said.

'But don't get in the way or they'll have my guts for garters.'

As they stepped up the stone stairway he felt the old adrenalin returning. On the first landing to his right there was a door. To his left there were more steps leading upwards. 'The other dressing rooms is up there,' she said noticing him glancing up at them. She pushed open the door.

He found himself in a long corridor. As they walked along it they passed a dressing room with a door open. It was just as he had imagined it, with light bulbs round the mirrors. Hanging on a rack

35

were Victorian dresses above pairs of button boots. Next to the room was a dilapidated kitchen-cum-sitting room and another dressing room. He hovered in the door. There was the ulster Basil Duke had worn as Albert Feathers when he had walked over the marshes in the rain in flight from the police. Scattered in front of the mirror were sticks of greasepaint and small round tins. He was astounded to see so much make-up.

'You coming, love,' said the old woman.

'Yes, of course, sorry,' said Ralph, startled.

'Those are the number-one and number two dressing rooms,' she said over her shoulder. 'The more important you are, the nearer you get to the stage.' She looked at him quizzically. 'It ent your first time backstage, is it?'

'Yes.'

'Funny that, you look like you've bin 'ere before. Look at home.'

'I feel it,' he said shyly.

'This way,' she said and she pushed open a black door.

Ralph was surprised to find himself standing in the wings. On his left the doors to an enormous shed adjoining the stage were open. Stacked in corners and along walls were piles of furniture, painted scenery and boxes. On long worktables were pots of paint and glue and props. There was a strong pungent smell which seemed to cause his nose to retreat into the back of his head.

The painted flats on his immediate right had been removed, leaving the rest of the set and auditorium exposed. Most of the furniture had been removed from the house, and the flagstone floor which looked so solid from the gallery, he discovered, was only painted canvas. Two young women were staggering towards him with a Georgian sofa. Behind them on-stage right, a young man with wavy hair and a large muscular man in his forties, were carrying the piano where the retired dancer had been strangled by Ellen Creed whilst playing Tit Willow.

Ralph turned to ask the old lady who he should ask about work, only to find that she had disappeared.

'Isla!' called out the young man. 'Could you shove those chairs out of the way?'

'Hang on a minute, Robin,' said one of the young women. She lowered her end of the sofa and began clearing a couple of heavy dining-room chairs out of the way. Feeling desperately empty-handed, Ralph lifted her end of the sofa.

'Oh,' said the other young woman. 'Where did you spring from?'

Isla appeared at their side, chairs in hand. 'Marvellous,' she said. 'Helena will show you where to take it.'

Dumbfounded by this easy acceptance of his presence he found himself backing with the girl called Helena towards the shed.

Helena was small and strong with untidy short blonde hair and grey eyes. She was wearing a threadbare navy jersey underneath maroon dungarees. She pointed with her chin to a stack of furniture in the corner.

'The sofa goes there,' she explained.

'What can I do now?' Ralph asked after they had carried it to the pile.

'Didn't Jack Walker tell you?'

'Well I haven't exactly asked him yet,' he began.

'Helena!' yelled Isla from on-stage.

'Stay here,' said Helena. 'We've got to finish clearing the props. They can't clear the set until we do. Is it your first strike?'

Ralph nodded, but before he had time to explain, she was already dashing towards the stage, her small mercurial figure whirling round the set, grabbing any props in sight.

As the two young women came towards him, their arms filled with nineteenth-century bric-a-brac, Isla came directly to him. 'Look,' she said. 'Now is not the time to ask Jack what he wants you to do. I should just keep out of the way for the moment till he needs you.' She looked at the heap of props around the table. 'What a mess!'

'Want me to sort it out?' he asked.

The two girls glanced at each other and smiled. 'Rather,' said Helena.

'Why not?' laughed Isla. 'It'll save us having to do it on Monday.'

'And I can go and help with electrics,' said Helena beaming.

As soon as Helena had left them, Ralph found Isla giving him a penetrating stare. Like Helena she, too, was wearing a jersey under a pair of dungarees, only her jersey was brown and her dungarees green. Unlike Helena she was attractive in a striking buxom sort of way. She was the same height as Ralph, with huge almond-shaped brown eyes, short glossy chestnut brown hair, and a wide full-lipped mouth. To his embarrassment he found himself blushing. She gave a deep warm laugh.

'Come with me,' she said.

Ralph followed her to the pile of *Ladies in Retirement* furniture.

'Grab hold of this,' she said, and she flung a sheet at him. 'We need to cover this all up until we can return it to people who have lent it to us.' She glanced at him curiously. 'You're not going into acting, are you?'

Ralph found himself nodding.

'Poor fool,' she said looking a little sad. 'So you're learning a bit before going to drama school?'

Drama school! Ralph hadn't even thought about drama school. He found himself nodding again and hated himself for lying to this stunningly beautiful young woman.

'How on earth did you manage to persuade Mr Johnson to let you help on a strike? Or do you know Jack Walker?'

Ralph opened his mouth to answer but no sound emerged.

F O U R

'*L*ook out!' she yelled suddenly.

Ralph swung round. Helena, who was carrying a china mandarin with a nodding head, was about to go flying over a statue of a Madonna and child.

'Thanks,' said Helena.

'I'll be glad when all these antiques are back at Parker's,' said Isla. 'I've been sweating buckets during *Tears* rehearsals. Every time someone makes a grand gesture I've been expecting to hear the tinkle of shattering Ming.'

Helena gingerly put the mandarin on the table. Isla was removing a list from underneath some imitation seaweed.

'Wrap anything on this list with a "P" beside it, and put it in here,' she said, pointing to one of the packing cases.

Ralph took the list and she and Helena dashed back on to the stage.

'Oh, well, here goes,' he whispered.

Methodically he unpacked the props which had been thrown willy nilly into one of the other packing cases, picked up the ones from the floor and spread them out on the long table. Then piecemeal, he put all the props with 'P' beside them at one end.

Out of the corner of his eye he observed a dishevelled-looking man in his thirties in dirty overalls standing next to a youth who appeared to be painting dark-green fleurs-de-lis on sea-green wallpaper. The youth was feverishly painting the ones at the bottom while the man stood on a ladder painting the top ones.

On-stage a workman was hauling on heavy ropes. As he pulled, the painted ceiling of the Tudor farmhouse was lifted into the flies and two burly men carried the flats which had been underneath it into the scene dock, and stacked them next to the *Ladies in Retirement* furniture.

Ralph placed the borrowed props in the box and ticked them off the list. He noticed there was a 'T' placed against other props on the list and began sorting those out.

'How're you doing?'

It was Isla. He handed her the list.

'The snuffbox is probably in the jacket of one of the actors' costumes. You'll find it in dressing-room two. The shepherdess is over there,' she added gloomily. She pointed to a headless porcelain woman with a crinoline, on one of the worktables by the wall. 'I'm not looking forward to returning her.'

Before he could speak she had run back on-stage again. He had to tell her, had to tell someone that he was there under false pretences. One of the men carrying the flats past him must be the boss. If only he knew which one!

He heard a large burly one say to the painter, 'We can't do anything till the lamps and panatrope are cleared and the stage swept, so keep painting.'

Ralph realised *he* must be the master carpenter. The man turned and gave him a puzzled look.

Ralph walked swiftly towards the stage, out through the door into the corridor, and towards dressing room two. Once inside Basil Duke's dressing room he closed the door and leaned against it, sweating profusely. He knew he was being ridiculous. He had to ask the master carpenter for permission to stay and the longer he left it, the worse was his crime.

He glanced at the dressing room table. Make-up had hastily been put into a box at the side, with a grubby towel flung half over it. A round tin with Crow's removing cream lay beside it. Ralph gingerly prised it open. It smelt vaguely like lard. Peering under the towel into the box he could see a tray with sticks of used greasepaint of every shade. He was about to look under the tray when he noticed an enormous Victorian book of magazine stories. Perhaps Basil Duke had used it to look at pictures of Victorian men or do a bit of research. He picked it up and began flicking through the pictures. Suddenly something furry leapt out. With an alarmed yell he dropped it. As it fell to the floor he could see other furry things.

'Oh, my goodness!' he whispered. 'They're his moustaches.'

He put the book back on the table and glimpsed inside. Sure enough, moustaches of every size from a small clipped one to a walrus one were pressed into the book. At the back of them was a hard residue of white stuff which looked like dried glue. Gently he picked up the escaping moustaches from the floor and carefully replaced them between the pages, hoping that Mr Duke didn't have an index arrangement to them.

He found the silver snuffbox in the pocket of the checked suit. He slipped back out into the corridor and headed back to the door. Everyone was on stage busily untying the ropes which were connected to the ceiling canvas, now lowered to just above floor level. Head bowed, he returned to the prop table, wrapped the snuffbox and placed it with the other Parker props and ticked it off.

Hurriedly he left the scene dock and walked into the area on-stage where the flagstoned floor was being rolled up. Ralph shyly joined the end of the line of people and helped push it along.

As men carried it off into the scene dock Ralph stood awkwardly in front of the footlights not knowing what to do next. He spotted Helena attempting to move two boxes in the stage right wings. Cables trailed from two turntables on them towards two speakers on either side of the footlights. She was removing a gramophone record from one of the turntables and placing it carefully in its sleeve.

Isla was picking up cigarette ends. 'Can I help?' he asked.

'Yes,' she said. 'The brooms are over there.' And she indicated the widest brooms he had ever seen, leaning up against the back wall of the stage. 'This whole area has to be cleared.'

Relieved to be doing something, he grabbed one and swept with gusto. Out of the corner of his eye he observed a private exchange between the master carpenter and a stage hand and a small envelope passing hands.

Then the master carpenter turned on his heel, headed straight for Ralph and towered over him with his hands on his hips.

'Now then,' he said abruptly, 'mind telling me who you are and what you're doing here?'

The silence seemed to last for hours. 'Well?' said the man impatiently.

'I meant to ask,' he began. 'I mean . . .' he stammered.

'Sorry, Jack,' said a voice from behind, 'he's a friend. He's learning. I meant to ask you but I clean forgot. And when I remembered I couldn't find you.'

'Isla, you know the rules! If he ain't on the payroll and a spot bar falls on his head, we'd be in serious trouble. He ain't insured.'

'Yes, I know. I'll make sure he stands to one side. But can he help me mark out first while Helena makes the tea? I'm sure no lights will fall on him.'

He frowned.

'We can all get home earlier,' she added.

'I suppose so. But don't go telling Mr Johnson.'

Ralph, Isla and Helena watched him head for the scene dock where two workmen were waiting to be paid.

'Thanks,' said Ralph quietly to Isla. 'I tried to tell you . . .' He paused. 'How did you guess?'

'It was the putrid colour you turned.'

'Oh.' And he laughed.

'Give us a hand with the stage cloth will you? Then we can mark up.'

Ralph, Helena and Isla spread it out on to the stage and tautened it with weights. Then they carried a long roll of green felt and unrolled it on top, smoothed it down and fixed the weights at the edges.

Helena went to wash the mugs and make tea. 'They can't put up any of the flats till I get this marked up,' said Isla. She unrolled a thick piece of paper from a small table on the left side of the stage next to the curtain, which she called the prompt corner. Beside it on a wall were all sorts of switches for lighting and sound cues. On the piece of paper was a ground plan. She laid it out on the floor.

'These are the walls of the set,' she said pointing to the outer lines, 'and these rectangles are where the different bits of furniture are set. I take a measurement from this line here,' she explained drawing her finger down the centre.

'So you have to measure and mark up the back flats first, is that it?'

'No. And by the way we call the back part of the stage, upstage and the front part of the stage going down towards the floats, downstage.'

'What are floats?'

'The footlights.'

'But why does the furniture have to be a precise length from the centre?' he said. 'Can't you just set them roughly?'

'Not when you're dealing with timing a move or a line.'

'How often have you to do this?'

'Every day once the moves have been set. And I have to put back the furniture for the evening show on their marks. Only snag is that sometimes I have to measure up and mark for that show all over again in the afternoon.'

'Why?'

'Because of this,' she said pulling out a piece of chalk from her pocket. 'Some of the marks I've made get rubbed off during morning rehearsals so . . .' She shrugged and pulled out a bundle of string. 'I think we'd better get on with it.'

With a tape measure, chalk and knotted string it took them three-quarters of an hour to measure out where the walls and furniture for *French without Tears* would be set. Helena appeared with mugs of tea for them and took two more to the painters in the scene dock.

'Don't usually get to have a cuppa during a strike,' said Isla, smiling. 'Helena and I usually leave Judy to make it for the others but she's always too busy painting to do it.'

'Judy? Oh, is she the youth painting?'

Isla nodded.

'Oh. Sorry. I didn't mean . . . It's just I couldn't see under her hat that she was a girl.'

'And the fag hanging permanently from her mouth doesn't help, does it?'

'I didn't expect there to be so many girls back-stage.'

'It's the best way of getting acting work. I'm ASM, that's assistant stage manager, and I get to play small parts occasionally.'

'I thought I'd seen you. Oh, you're good!' Ralph felt himself redden again.

'Tell that to my father,' she added sardonically.

'Doesn't he think you are?'

'Nope. Mind you, I'm beginning not to care.'

'So he wants you to stop acting, is that it?'

'Oh, no. He just wants me to be better at it. Well, as long as I don't overshadow him. He's Geoffrey Leighton.'

There was an awkward pause.

'I'm sorry,' began Ralph. 'I'm not very good at names.'

'It's refreshing,' she said airily and she gave a broad smile. 'It's quite funny really. Most ASMs are bursting to get on to the stage. Here we are in a good rep with an ASM who can take it or leave it and Helena, who's general dogsbody, who's changed her mind.'

'Is that true? That you can take it or leave it?'

'Yes,' she said brightly. 'Still, I'm not much good at anything else, except walking dogs. So this will have to do.'

Just then Helena reappeared. She didn't look like someone who was changing her mind. She looked positively jaunty.

'Is it true for you too?' he blurted out.

'Is what true?' she asked, scooping up the mugs.

'That you're changing your mind about acting. You look so happy.'

'I am happy. But to be honest, I am not a very good actress.'

42

'But she's superb at sound,' said Isla. 'She can hit the right band on a record blindfolded. She has nerves of steel. Correction. She has *no* nerves.'

'I like it. That's all.' She leaned forward confidentially. 'Arthur is going to let me help him set up the lights on Monday.'

'Arthur's the chief electrician,' explained Isla. She stood up. 'Now I suggest you stay in the scene dock while the flats are being put in. You can help with the furniture downstage once the walls are in.'

'Do you want me to set them on the marks?' he asked eagerly.

'We can't really do that while Sam and Judy are still painting. We'll have to keep dustsheets on the floor till they've finished. Anyway, best to stay out of sight in case Mr Johnson decides to leave his office and pop in.'

Helena laughed. 'His office is the Rose and Crown,' she explained.

Ralph found some glue near the table where the shepherdess had been dumped. It was congealed in the bottom of a paint tin. With a small stick he pasted it on the shepherdess's neck and gently pressed her head back on to it. The join was just visible, but with a bit of paint or a ribbon around the neck he was sure it wouldn't show. Suddenly Isla and Helena came dashing out from one of the flats on stage.

'Can you give us a hand with the props!' yelled Isla. Ralph leapt up as if in a dream.

'Some of them need to go on the set,' Isla explained. 'The others can go on to the prop table.' She brought out two lists. 'These tell you what goes on-stage and what's set in the wings. I'll do the on set props, and you can help Helena with the prop table.'

'Wonderful,' said Helena. 'At this rate we might get home before light!'

'Personal props will go this end,' said Helena pointing to the end of a long table in the wings. 'And the rest at the other end.'

'What are personal props?' asked Ralph.

'Things like a cigarette case, or a particular book an actor has to enter carrying, or spectacles or a watch.'

As he and Helena busied themselves setting up the prop table Isla walked past them and disappeared behind the set with armfuls of books and ornate French lamps. And then she was by their side.

'Slight problem,' she said. 'The French lesson books haven't been done.'

'I'm sorry, I thought Judy was doing them,' said Helena.

'She's been so busy she forgot. We'll have to carry a dozen books

43

back to our digs and cover them there.'

'Why can't you cover them here?' asked Ralph.

'Because there's no time to do it tonight.'

'I can cover them.'

'There's white paper by the glue table,' said Helena.

'We'll still have to take them home and write something French on them.'

'No one will be able to read them from the audience.'

'The fur brigade will.'

'Who are the fur brigade?' asked Ralph bewildered.

'People who always sit near the front in their furs,' she said.

'Why can't I write in French on them?'

They stared at him in amazement. 'Can you speak French?' they chorused.

'Well, School Cert standard.'

'Marvellous. Helena can you show him where everything is? Judy and Sam are working on the left flats now. We can start setting stage right.'

Back at the glue table Ralph settled himself down with a dozen books, and covered each book as carefully and speedily as he could. And then he had a brainwave. After years living in the rectory surrounded by theology books he began to paint on the spine of the book in italic writing. To his horror the paint ran in rivulets and he had to tear off the cover and put another one on. He found a pen and a bottle of black ink and supporting each book with one hand, spine upwards, he was relieved to find that the ink didn't run. Swiftly he wrote *Le francais pour aujourd'hui vol. I.* and drew a small fleur-de-lis underneath. He lined the books up next to one another to make sure the writing and the fleurs-de-lis were level with one another.

Behind him, from the stage there was the sound of general banter and laughter and banging of nails, and in spite of sitting on his own he felt a sense of belonging he hadn't felt in years.

He was busily working when he heard footsteps. Out of the corner of his eye he saw Jack Walker approaching. He looked down hurriedly, aware of his fingers trembling. The master carpenter stood behind him and said nothing. Ralph began to sweat. As delicately as he could he finished the fleur-de-lis on the eleventh book and propped it up next to the others.

'Ain't you got a home to go to, lad?' the man barked.

Ralph turned, feeling his face reddening. 'I told my parents I'd be going to a strike.'

'Did you now?' He peered at the books. 'French speaker, eh?'

'Well, schoolboy French.' He added modestly, 'I only just scraped by.' And then he cursed himself for saying schoolboy.

'You ent gonna get paid for this, you realise that?'

'Yes, sir.'

'I don't usually allow stage-struck youngsters to help and neither does Mr Johnson. We got enough to cope with. But you're certainly a good worker. Let's say you got away with it, shall we?'

Ralph nodded.

'For tonight, that is. I s'pose you want to come next week?'

'Yes, please!'

'I'll ask Mr Johnson. As long as you're out of our way it should be all right.'

He gave him a curt nod and walked away. Ralph was about to start on the last spine when there was a loud 'Oi!'

Ralph swung round again. 'Yes?'

'Any good at making tea?'

'Yes, sir.'

'When you've finished you can wash up the mugs and make us a fresh cuppa. That'll be seven cups, including you.'

The kitchen was a tiny room with old chairs and armchairs along two walls under shelves stacked with props and scripts. At the far end, pots of paint and brushes were stuck higgledy-piggledy round a sink. On the wooden draining board was a tray with dirty mugs on it and a grimy gas ring. A huge kettle, a tin of dried milk, a bowl of damp sugar and a tea caddy were on the table beside it. Peering inside the kettle he discovered a mound of tea leaves waiting to be restewed. He added water to it, put it on the gas ring to stew and set about washing the mugs.

He pushed the door open with his foot and sidled into the wings. Edging his way behind the upstage flats, he carefully avoided the weights and entered through a pair of open french windows which were upstage right. Blocking his way was a stepladder. Isla and Robin had hung a huge pair of pink and white curtains up and were now attaching a pink and white pelmet above it. Matching sashes were draped over the steps. 'Excuse me!' he said.

'Oh, you angel,' gasped Isla.

Helena was up another ladder placing leather-bound books on shelves in the alcove in the upstage centre wall. 'Jack says the books look very good, which is something, because he rarely gives praise. Let's hope Sam Williams likes them.'

'Who's he?' asked Ralph anxiously.

'The designer.'

'Its beginning to look like a living room,' Isla said with relief.

45

'It's supposed to be in a villa in a small seaside town in the South of France,' explained Helena.

The stage was nearly set out except for an armchair, a small table and more ornaments and pictures. They were to go on to the downstage left wall which was still being painted. Jack Walker appeared suddenly.

'Home, you lot,' he commanded. 'Come in Monday, usual time, and finish setting up then. Lighting will be at nine. Dress rehearsal at two.'

After Ralph had helped Helena carry her ladder back to the scene dock he returned to the stage. He wanted to have a last look at his books in the bookcase.

Robin had already gone and Isla and Helena were chatting in the corner. He said goodbye but they didn't hear him. He hesitated for a moment and then made his way backstage to the wings. He was about to open the door to the corridor when he heard a voice call after him. It was Isla.

'You can't go out that way. The stage door's locked,' she said. 'Wilfred went home ages ago. We have to go out by one of the side doors. Come with us.'

'Thanks,' said Ralph shyly.

He followed the two girls out through a door by the prompt corner and found himself in the stalls. Isla led them through another door at the back of the auditorium which led into the foyer. They then turned down a small corridor at the side and Isla opened another door which opened out into a small alleyway round the corner from the High Street.

'Where do you live?' asked Isla.

'Braxley,' he said.

'That'll take you for ever,' exclaimed Helena. She turned to Isla. 'Do you think Mrs McGee would put him up for the night?'

'I have a bike,' he interrupted. He stared awkwardly at them for a moment in the dark. 'Thanks for covering up for me, by the way.'

'I like people who are a bit cheeky,' said Isla. Ralph enjoyed the look of admiration she gave him so much that he felt a slight fluttering sensation in his chest and a tightening in his throat.

'So it's fine about next week?' he ventured.

'It depends what Jack Walker says to Mr Johnson.'

'If you turn up and make the tea, that'll win them round,' said Helena.

'I'll be seeing the play on Friday,' he said to Isla. 'Are you in it?'

'Oh, no, the parts are too big.'

'I thought you might be playing Jackie.'

'You dark horse! You know the play.'

'Coincidence,' he said embarrassed. 'If you wait for me to get my bike, I'll walk you both home.'

'Thanks,' said Isla, 'but we're staying in the same digs, so we'll protect one another from any dragons we might come across.'

'Poor Judy,' said Helena, 'she has to paint until she finishes.'

'All three of us share a room,' Isla explained.

'It's like being drama students again,' laughed Helena.

He watched them walk away until they were out of sight and then ran with excitement down the dark alleyway to the road at the back of the theatre and across it to the one which led to the river.

His bike was still where he had left it. He leapt on to it, switched on his dynamo and began pedalling wildly along the river path towards the railway bridge. He had done it! He had actually walked into the very heart of the Palace Theatre and helped behind the scenes. And with any luck he would be returning. Suddenly he had a vision of a girl in dungarees with dark eyes and a deep throaty laugh and he began to shake with the sheer exhilaration of it all. 'Yahoo!' he yelled. 'Yahoo!'

FIVE

*H*e could just make out the dark outline of the trio of houses which stood defiantly between the piles of rubble and gutted houses on either side. He hauled his bike over a broken segment of wall, wheeled it over loose bricks towards the lane at the back of the houses. As he carried his bike into their tiny yard, he spotted his father's own bike leaning up against the coalshed and he suddenly realised that his father must have noticed the absence of his bike. He quickly brushed his anxiety to one side. He would have to deal with that, if and when it arose. He slipped back out of the yard and went round to the front of the house.

The front door gave a loud click as he turned the handle. He froze, waiting for footsteps and the sudden exposure that light flooding through the coloured-glass windows at the top of the door would give. But there was silence. With a relief that almost made him weep, the door eased open. Quietly he shut it behind him. He was halfway up the stairs when he realised he had forgotten to lock it.

Cursing he crept back down the stairs and retrieved the key from a little shelf. He was about to insert it in the lock when the most tremendous grunting sound came echoing through the hall. Startled, he dropped the key. Luckily there was a mat to catch it. He listened out for footsteps again, but none came. There was another grunt followed by a loud drone. He smiled. It was coming from the front parlour which was now a bedroom for Joan and Elsie. Suddenly he had a vision of Joan lying under a white satin eiderdown in a four-poster bed draped with veils and chiffon, Hollywood style, like the American films she was forever going to see. Her hair was coiffured, her lips dark red and bow-shaped, and as the dark handsome figure of Errol Flynn gazed at her beauty, Joan would begin to snore like a pig. He pressed his hand against his mouth, to smother his laughter, shot up the stairs into his room, stripped off and dived under the covers.

Luckily there was only one pair of feet that night, although if Joan continued her trumpeting, Elsie would soon be joining them again. There was a creak on the landing.

'As I thought,' he muttered, full of sympathy.

The door opened slowly. Ralph peered over the covers. By the dim grey light of dawn he saw his mother. He watched her make her way to his bed. 'Everything all right?' she whispered.

He propped himself up on one elbow. 'Sort of.'

'Did you get work there?'

'Yes and no.'

'What does that mean?'

'I helped out, but I didn't get paid.'

'Why not?'

'Because I hadn't asked the stage director or the master carpenter for permission to be there. In fact I would've been out on my ear if it hadn't been for one of the ASMs. That's an assistant stage manager. She made out I was a friend who had come to watch and learn and that she had forgotten to ask permission. She even got ticked off for it.'

'Young, is she?'

'No. She's about twenty.'

'Very old. Walk with a stick, did she?'

'You know what I mean.'

'Too old for you.'

'Mum! It's not like that!' But he could see that his mother was smiling. 'Anyway,' he said firmly, 'in the end the master carpenter said he'd put in a good word for me so I can do it again next week. They still won't be paying me but I'll learn a hell of a lot if I help.'

'She must be a good looker.'

'Mum!' he said exasperated, but he found that he was blushing and he laughed.

She touched his hair. 'It's good to see you happy again.'

He sighed. 'Not for long, I expect. Fireworks to face soon enough, I suppose. Did he say anything?'

'We was all in bed before he came back.'

'Was he drunk?'

''Course not.'

'How do you know if you weren't up to see it?'

'Just 'cos a man smells of beer it don't mean he can't handle his drink, love. Now get some sleep. You must be done in.'

So must you be, he thought.

'And you'll have to get up same as everyone.'

'I know.'

He watched her move back to the door. 'Mum,' he whispered.

'Yeah?'

'You shouldn't have waited up for me.'

'Who says I did? I just happened to hear the door. Anyway Aunty Win's like a donkey in the night. I'm black and blue. I don't know what she dreams about but she's kicking the hell out of somebody.'

'Dad, I expect,' said Ralph sardonically. 'Or a bigamist.'

'Oh, Ralphie, don't start me up,' and she smothered a laugh and fled from the room.

It seemed as though he had only closed his eyes for a second when he felt himself being torn apart by small insistent hands. He woke to find Elsie and Harry rocking him from side to side. He yawned and promptly fell asleep again.

'Push him harder!' he heard Elsie mutter urgently. 'I got to use me other hand to keep me specs on.'

'I'm pushin' him as hard as I can.'

'Sit up, Ralph,' he heard her say and he felt a small thin arm encircle itself round his neck and yank it forward. 'You'll get Dad in one of his moods if you don't get a move on!'

That seemed to motivate him. He hauled himself out of bed and allowed his brother and sister to shove him out of the bed and lead him to his clothes.

'Do you mind!' he said when he realised that Elsie was attempting to pull his pyjama trousers off. 'I've seen it all before,' said Elsie nonchalantly.

'Well, you haven't seen my all, Elsie,' he said, hanging on to the trousers, 'and I don't intend you should.'

Elsie gave the sort of exasperated sigh one would give to a small

49

child and stomped to the door. 'Mind you make him dress, Harry,' she said waving an admonishing finger at him.

Ralph smiled. His tiny sister's bossiness with Harry amused him.

'I can remember how to dress myself, Harry. You can go if you want.'

'You're joking. I ain't going nowhere till you're washed and dressed.' He pointed to the large jug which was standing in a china bowl on the table. 'Your water's there.'

'You mean our water.'

'I don't need to wash. I'm clean enough.'

Ralph stood in his trousers, his braces dangling down the sides of his legs. He poured the icy water into the bowl and proceeded to wash his face and hands. 'Sure you don't want any of this?' he said, flicking some at his brother.

'Gerrof!' Harry protested.

'Its not acid, you know. It won't burn you.'

He rubbed his face vigorously and then stopped. His skin felt slightly rough. He touched it gently with his fingertips.

'Harry,' he said, 'can you see any stubble?'

Harry peered at him in the gloom. It was a dismal day outside and it permeated the room.

'Nah.' He grinned. 'Spots, mebbe.'

Ralph flicked some more water at him. He rubbed himself vigorously with a towel. He was freezing. Still the water had woken him up a bit.

He grabbed the clean white shirt his mother had left out for him, tucked it in and hauled his braces over his shoulders.

'You can go now,' he said to Harry.

'I'll wait till you've done your buttons up.'

'She's really got you under her thumb, hasn't she?'

'I let her think she has,' said Harry airily.

Ralph grabbed his collar which was dangling over his end of the bed, held it in his hands like the murderess Ellen Creed and advanced towards him. Harry gave a shriek and crawled hastily over the bed to the door with Ralph after him.

'Glad to see *someone* in good spirits,' said Aunty Win in the kitchen, 'though I don't know why.'

Ralph and Harry gave each other a glance. Ralph noticed that his father's bed was made up and sounds of water were coming from the scullery. His mother was frying bread over the range. A large bowl of dripping was in the centre of the table.

'So you got home,' she added.

'Win, *please*,' said Ralph's mother urgently. 'I couldn't take another row.'

'On your own head be it,' said Aunty Win. 'But don't say I didn't warn you.'

Ralph grinned. In spite of his aunt's gibes he was happy. His sudden jolt into a world of insecurity left him feeling strangely liberated. At the paper mill he knew which direction the rest of his life was going to take. The pension at the end of it had not made him feel secure, but as if he was living in a coffin. Instead of the dullness he had felt for months, his wits felt sharpened. From now on he would have to take each day as it came. He looked round the room with renewed interest and everything seemed intensified; the black range, the white sheets and shirts, grey trousers and pale cardigans hanging over them, the red rug over his father's narrow bed, the window at the end of it which looked out on to the yard. Even the whorls in the scrubbed wood table seemed vivid. He took in the smell of frying bread, the floral apron on his mother's slim frame, her hair dishevelled, her face pink. The door opened and Elsie and Joan came in in their Sunday best.

'Aunty Ellen,' whined Joan, 'I don't feel so good. Can't I stay at home?'

'It's only once a week,' said Ralph's mother.

'If we went to the later one we could get extra sleep.'

'If we went to the later one we'd have dinner late.'

'It's best to get it over with,' said Elsie.

'And then me and Dad can get to the allotment quicker,' added Harry.

Their mother put the plate of fried bread on the table and began pouring tea. 'Now eat up quick,' she said.

The scullery door opened and Ralph's father stood in the doorway, his coat and cap on.

'It ain't that late, is it?' cried Ralph's mother in alarm. And then she froze. 'Where's your collar?'

'I ain't going to church. I'm going down to the allotment.'

'Now?' interrupted Harry eagerly.

'John,' pleaded Ralph's mother.

'I ain't standin' next to him,' he said, glowering at Ralph.

'I'll go to Evensong,' Ralph said quickly.

'Wait for me, Dad,' said Harry. 'I got to get out of this clobber.'

'I'm going on me own,' he snapped.

'But, Dad, you promised to take me with you.'

'I'll see how I feel this afternoon.'

51

'John, please come with us. It's one of the few things we can do together as a family.'

'Don't kid yourself we're a family,' he said angrily. 'You've made it perfectly clear whose side you're on.' He stopped as if too overwhelmed to speak. 'I need some fresh air,' he said in a choked voice, and with that he slammed the door.

Ralph watched his mother stand at the window, dazed and silent, the teapot still in her hand. When she turned, her face was drained of all colour. 'Eat up,' she said, looking tired. 'Or we'll be late.'

SIX

*R*alph lowered his head and pedalled faster. His first day as a gardener and the rain was streaming down his face under his sodden cap in rivulets. He headed for the road which would take him to Winford and further away from the tense atmosphere of his home. Instead of Sunday having been wonderful because of his father's absence, it had been a day of gloom. Harry had been miserable because he had been looking forward to spending time on the allotment with his father and Elsie was upset because Harry was upset and also because her father hadn't offered to take her with Harry.

In the end they went out to play amongst the bombed-out debris of the street. Most of their friends in the street had been moved on or killed. They didn't play with the children in the other streets because they were from another street and therefore arch enemies.

Joan spent the day in her room with a girlfriend where they had experimented with hairstyles from film magazines. His mother prepared Sunday dinner, cleared up after it and rolled out dough in the afternoon while his aunt read aloud the next chapter of a Margery Allingham. At least his aunt chose a better class of detective story, but the sight of his mother being read to still embarrassed him.

When she had spotted him writing, she had said 'You have such a nice way of putting things, Ralphie. I loved opening your letters and reading them.' And he had wanted to say, 'It's all right, Mum. You don't have to pretend. I don't mind that you can't read.' But to his shame he knew that he wouldn't be able to make it sound convincing.

His father had returned when it was dark, flushed from a day's digging and planting. For his mother's sake Ralph had gone up to his room to avoid another confrontation, but when he came down to supper he was accused of being lazy or too hoity-toity to stay in his family's company. Whatever he did, he couldn't win.

As he turned the corner he sped through an enormous puddle which drenched him from head to foot. But he didn't care. He just wanted to cycle away his fury at having to live in the presence of his father. At least he wouldn't have to cycle to work with him any more.

He saw the railway station ahead, rode over the bridge and towards the High Street, juddering over the tramlines past the shops. He slowed down and paused for a moment opposite the Palace. Outside, a poster announced: Opening night. *French without Tears*. The stage electricians would be setting up lamps by now, and Helena would be wanting to help them. He smiled. Only four more days and he would be seeing the play. He set off again. Until then he must put all theatrical thoughts aside and think only of Mrs Egerton-Smythe.

The woman in the kitchen stared at him as if he had come from another planet.

'Don't you move,' she shrieked. 'I just cleaned this floor!' And she slammed the door.

Through the window he watched her dart out of the kitchen. Within minutes she returned with Mrs Egerton-Smythe, who looked as irritable as ever. He watched her storm over to the door and fling it open. 'You silly fool,' she snapped. 'What the hell are you doing here?'

'I'm sure there's plenty I can still be doing,' he said quickly.

'Belt up, Hollis,' she interrupted. 'I mean, what are doing standing out in this! You look like Niagara Falls. Come in.'

'But the floor . . .' pointed out Ralph.

'Damn the floor! The floor can't catch pneumonia.' And with that she dragged him into the kitchen. 'Stand in front of that Aga while I get you some dry clothes. Queenie! Follow me!'

Ralph was so stunned that before he could protest she had slammed the door behind him.

'The master's clothes, it will be,' muttered Queenie disapprovingly over her shoulder. And she followed Mrs Egerton-Smythe out of the kitchen.

By the time Queenie returned he had begun to shiver.

'Mrs Egerton-Smythe says you're to take off your boots and socks 'ere and come with me,' she said and she pressed her lips together tightly.

He pulled off the boots with some difficulty and then peeled off the socks. Standing barefoot on the scrubbed flagstone floor, a sock dangling from each hand, he felt rather foolish. Queenie stared at him with her arms folded and then produced a clothes horse from the wall, opened it out and placed it firmly in front of the Aga. Ralph hung one sock from one bar and the other on the opposite side, fighting down a desire to laugh.

'This way,' she commanded. And Ralph followed her out into the hallway, his trousers clinging soggily around his legs.

He was taken up to an enormous bathroom on the first floor. A huge white bath with claw feet stood under a window overlooking the garden. A large sink with blue designs under the taps was on the wall alongside it. A tall green basket with a lid stood near a dark mahogany cabinet. Someone had draped a threadbare white towel across it. On a seat of a wicker chair were several pairs of trousers, a leather belt, woollen shirts, pullovers and socks.

'I'm to wait outside for your clothes,' said Queenie eyeing his soaked garments disparagingly, ' so's I can dry 'em before you goes home.'

As soon as she had left the room, Ralph bolted the door and avoided standing in front of the keyhole. The clothes were good quality in spite of being worn. He chose a plain blue shirt, a thick navy blue jumper, grey flannels and socks. The flannels were so large he had to turn the legs up half a dozen times, and use the belt round them. He decide to leave his underwear on. He wasn't going to let Queenie contemplate them in the kitchen.

He had hardly unlocked the door when Queenie snatched the bundle of clothes from his arms. 'I dunno,' she said turning. 'I dunno.'

Ralph followed her as she rapidly raced across the landing and down the wide staircase to the main hall. They had just reached the kitchen when Queenie stopped. 'Mrs Egerton-Smythe wants to see you in the garden room. It's that door there,' she said pointing to one opposite, further along the hall.

'I've got to get my boots.'

'There's wellingtons on the veranda. Mrs Egerton-Smythe will show you.' And she opened the kitchen door and slammed it in his face.

Ralph slid across the polished floor in his stockinged feet and knocked tentatively.

'Come in!' yelled a voice.

Ralph's first impression of the garden room was whiteness. All the furniture was covered in sheets. Mrs Egerton-Smythe was standing by the french windows facing him. He hung in the doorway while she stared angrily at him.

'Thanks for these,' said Ralph after an awkward silence.

'They're not yours to keep,' she stated. 'They're my husband's, on loan, until Queenie has dried what you came in.'

'Yes, of course,' said Ralph.

'I expect you already know he's dead by the kitchen grapevine.'

'No, Madam,' said Ralph, stunned. 'Would you prefer it if I took them off.'

'No!' she barked. 'Now, you can't cut the lawn today, but I can show you the garden shed. It will be your domain from now on.'

She opened the french windows and stepped out. He could hear the rain drumming loudly on the glass roof of the veranda. As he moved across the room he gazed around at it. He loved the bigness of it, in spite of its dark and miserable appearance. It let him breathe easy again. It was what he missed about not living in the rectory.

'Splendid!' he whispered.

'Oh, you approve, do you, Hollis?' she remarked wryly.

'Very much,' he said stepping quickly outside.

'Boots are there,' she said indicating the pair of wellingtons by the wall. 'What size are you?'

'Eight.'

'They're nine. They'll have to do. And help yourself to one of the oilskins, or sou'westers.' She pointed to a large shed halfway down the garden at the side. It was half-hidden by trees. 'That's the garden shed. There's a woodshed further down. Get to know it. Queenie will ring a bell when it's lunch.'

Ralph stepped into the large boots and picked out a sou'wester and the smallest oilskin. It came down to his ankles, but he was glad of it as it protected his legs as he waded through the wet grass towards the shed. He fumbled with the lock on the door with his cold hands and glanced quickly back at the house. Mrs Egerton-Smythe was standing by the french windows observing him. He looked hastily away and pushed open the door.

It took him a while to get accustomed to the darkness. It was obvious that no one had been in the shed for a long time. In the gloom he saw a large motor-mower covered in cobwebs. Tools, boxes and spades were scattered loosely around the wooden floor and, on shelves on the walls, empty dusty flowerpots stood with the remains of dead plants hanging over the sides. A big window, now covered with grime and cobwebs, looked down to the jungle of high grass, trees and the river beyond. He hung his oilskins on a hook behind the door, picked up an old rag and bucket and took it outside to the small stand-up tap he had noticed just outside the door. He placed the bucket underneath and turned it on. He was about to turn it off when it suddenly began to shudder and a burst of water came gushing out.

The first thing he did in the shed was to wash the window. Anything to let a little light in. And then he grabbed a broom and went on a cobweb hunt. 'Shelves next,' he muttered. As he divested the shelves opposite the window of pots and empty seed boxes he found, to his alarm, dust all down the jersey and trousers. Frantically he beat it off and looked around for some overalls. He found some tossed into a heap in the corner. He held them out at a distance and then, screwing up his nose, he stepped into them. They stank of years of dampness.

It was with some surprise that he heard a school bell ringing. At first he ignored it, but then remembered Mrs Egerton-Smythe mentioning the lunch bell. He pushed open the door. Queenie was standing under the veranda roof swinging a large bell up and down. As soon as she spotted him she disappeared. He threw the oilskins on and made a quick sprint through the rain and up the steps to the veranda. The french windows were open. He hung his oilskins on the hook and stepped out of the boots. He noticed, as he entered the room, cobwebs at the sides of the doors and a long line of dark dust. It looked as if they had been closed for a long time.

A few nondescript pictures remained hanging on the walls, but there were light squares where other pictures must have once hung. Even the large mahogany mantelpiece above the fireplace was empty. He stepped on the old blue carpet and made his way to the door.

Lunch was a bowl of vegetable broth with a hunk of grey bread.

Queenie sat at the opposite side of the table and watched him suspiciously. ''Ow come you speak with such a posh accent?' she said suddenly.

'I went to a grammar school.'

'Did they teach you to talk proper there, then?'

'No. But I suppose I picked it up by osmosis.'

''Ow d'ya mean?'

'From the teachers and some of the other boys. It was that or Cornish.'

'Why?'

'Because it was in Cornwall.'

''Asn't done you much good,' she commented, 'all that education.'

56

Ralph shrugged. He spooned the last mouthful of soup into his mouth. 'That was splendid.'

A flicker of a smile spread across her face, and then it was gone.

'If that's your way of trying to get a second helping, you're wasting your time,' she said sulkily. 'There's rationing, you know,' and she whisked the bowl away from him.

'How are my clothes doing?' he said after an awkward silence.

'Oh don't worry, they'll be dry. You won't be going home in the master's clothing.'

A mug of tea was slammed on to the table. Ralph bit into the bread.

After lunch he returned to the shed. The cobwebs were gone, the shelves were swept clean and the tools were either on the shelves or leaning neatly against the wall. The motor mower was brushed down, with bits of it he had discovered lying beside it. He now sat on the floor and stared at it. Years of Latin grammar and algebra had not equipped him for this. Hours later when he heard the bell ringing again, he blinked. He had been so absorbed in fiddling with the machine that he had merely squinted when the light had begun to fade.

He stuck his head outside. It was still raining. He ran across the grass in his oilskins again. He found his clothes lying folded on one of the dustsheets in the garden room. Hastily he pulled off the navy jersey.

When he was dressed he carried the armful of borrowed clothes to the kitchen. Queenie was peeling potatoes. She glanced up at him.

'Put them there,' she said indicating the table. 'Your boots are by the door. So's the mac.'

On the hook behind the door was a beige trench coat, the kind every detective wore in a thriller.

'On loan,' she said imperiously. 'To be returned.'

'Thanks.'

'Don't thank me. I just work 'ere.'

'Do I say goodbye to Mrs Egerton-Smythe?'

'I dunno. No one tells me anything.'

He laced up his boots and attempted to hide the tremor of excitement he felt at doing up the raincoat.

'I'll see you tomorrow, then,' he said at the door.

'Prompt', said Queenie.

He hovered outside the stage door. He wanted to be seen in the raincoat. He hoped his hobnailed boots didn't spoil the effect too much. He removed his cap, held it behind his back and stepped in. Wilfred was sitting in his cubby-hole reading a newspaper. He looked up and frowned. 'I just came to thank you,' said Ralph hurriedly.

The man's face unfolded. 'Oh, it's you. I didn't recognise you. 'Owd it go?'

'It went well. I didn't get a job, but I hope to be allowed to attend the strike this Saturday.'

'Good,' he said, and he returned to his newspaper.

Ralph gazed awkwardly at him. 'Well, cheerio, then.'

Wilfred looked up again. He gave a wave. 'Cheerio, lad.'

Ralph cycled home disappointed. He had wanted the man to leap up and down and say, 'Well done, lad! You'll go far. Mark my words.'

It was pitch black when he wheeled his bike into the street. A tiny slip of light was shining across the pavement from Elsie and Joan's room. He ran round to the yard and leaned his bike by the wall. His father's bike was not there. Relieved he ran to the back door, flung it open and ran straight into a damp sheet.

Of course, it was Monday. The room was still slightly warm from the copper's being stoked all day. He wiped his feet and opened the scullery door to the kitchen. Elsie was sitting at the end of the table, head down, scribbling at tremendous speed as if her life depended on it. Harry sat near her with a dog-eared comic. His mother emerged from under the cascades of washing which were hanging from a wooden clothes rack from the ceiling. Months ago he had been embarrassed at the sight of male and female underwear swinging amongst sheets and shirts and petticoats. Now he took it all in his stride.

'Ralphie!' she began, and then gaped at his trench coat.

At that moment, the door behind him swung open and Aunty Win entered. The two women gazed at him stupified. Ralph grinned.

'It's on loan,' he said. 'Till it stops raining.'

'What *do* you look like?' said his aunt.

'Inspector Gideon of the Yard,' said Harry in awe.

'It's soaked,' said his mother, feeling it. 'You'd better hang it up.'

She lowered the wooden clothes rack. Ralph hung the raincoat over the end and watched his mother haul it up. 'Where's Joan?' said his aunt.

'In her room,' said his mother, 'changing. You'd better get out of your togs too,' she said looking at his aunt's sodden coat. 'So how

58

did it go, Ralphie? I kept wondering what you were doing in all this rain.'

'Getting to know the garden shed.'

There was a sound of a whirring bicycle in the yard. Suddenly Elsie gathered up her books and Harry grabbed her satchel. In seconds they had gone. A waft of cold air billowed in.

'Shall I disappear too?' he asked.

'You'd best face the music sooner than later,' she sighed.

His Aunty Win draped her coat in front of the range and rolled up the sleeves of her cardigan as if to do battle. His mother, noticing this defiant gesture, turned away hurriedly to look at the supper.

Harry returned and sat on his father's bed, bouncing up and down.

The scullery door opened and his father slumped in, visibly smaller. Ralph gazed helplessly at him. Harry shot off the bed and stepped towards him grinning. 'Well, Dad?' he asked excitedly. 'Did you ask? Did you ask about me?'

His dad looked startled. Harry could hardly contain himself with excitement. 'What did they say? Did you tell them I only got a few months to do?'

He made school sound like a prison sentence, thought Ralph.

'Harry, sit down,' said his mother. 'Can't you see your dad's tired.' She glanced up at Ralph. 'Can't you all sit down. It's crowded enough in here as it is,' she said. 'Elsie, lay the table.'

'Elsie's not 'ere,' said Win.

His father then looked at Ralph with such hatred it frightened him.

'Bad, was it?' his mother said softly.

'It'll pass,' snapped his father.

'It's not your fault,' she said.

'No,' he said. 'It's yours.'

'Mine?'

'You shouldn't have let him go to that grammar school. He don't belong 'ere.'

'Thanks,' said Ralph sardonically.

'Don't give me none of your lip.'

He turned swiftly to Ralph's mother. 'He hand over his wages last Friday?'

'Course he did.'

'You hand over the same wages this Friday, lad, and no more fancy visits to that theatre.'

'Joan goes to the cinema three times a week. Are you going to ask her to hand over all her wages?'

'Joan works hard.'

'So do I.'

'Did, lad, did.'

'Dad, they didn't sack me because I wasn't working hard enough.'

'Don't give me that. They need good workers.'

'I'll be a good worker, Dad,' said Harry eagerly.

'I was that ashamed today,' he said angrily.

'Why?' argued Ralph. 'Why didn't you stick up for me? Isn't that what real fathers are supposed to do?'

'Are you telling me I'm not a real father to you when I get you a plum job?'

'Doing what I hated doing!'

'This is real life, sonny. Work's work. You're lucky to have it with so many ex-servicemen hunting for jobs.'

His mother began laying the table.

'Elsie should be doing that,' he said. 'Where is she?'

'In her room.'

'I'll get her,' said Harry hurriedly and he dashed out.

There was a stony silence. His aunt sat back in her chair with a look as if to say, 'Men, didn't I tell you, Ellen?'

His mother stood helplessly, the cutlery still in her hand. The door opened suddenly and Elsie appeared. She looked pale. 'What you bin doing?' roared her father. 'You know you're supposed to be helping. I'll not have two layabouts in this house.'

'Sorry, Dad,' she said quietly, and she took the cutlery from her mother.

'You still haven't answered my question.' Elsie looked up startled. 'I'll ask you again. What have you been doing?'

'Talking to Joan. She's got another letter from Kay.'

Ralph groaned inwardly. That would be another evening of Joan looking like a wet weekend because she could have been living the life of a movie star like her friend, instead of selling ladies' clothes in the High Street.

Elsie hastily finished putting out the cutlery.

It was when they were sitting round the table eating that his father noticed the trench coat. His father, as usual, sat at the end of the table near the hallway door. His mother at the other end, by the range. Ralph sat on the wall side by his mother and his aunt. Harry and Joan opposite. Elsie was sitting on the bed. True to form, Joan had been playing the ill-done victim to the hilt, while Harry chatted to his father, ignoring the atmosphere while his father ignored him.

60

Then Ralph saw his father suddenly look up and his face change. 'Where the hell did that fancy raincoat come from?'

'Mrs Egerton-Smythe lent it to me,' said Ralph quickly.

'Well, you can take it back.'

'I will be, Dad.'

'I 'ain't havin' you being a parasite to other people.'

'She lent it to me, Dad, because it was raining.'

'Well, do without until you can buy your own.'

'How can I if I have to hand over all my money?'

'You can wear your grammar school raincoat,' he said sarcastically.

'I've grown out of it.'

There was a moment's silence.

'So have they put anyone in Ralph's place?' insisted Harry.

Ralph had to smile. Persistence was his brother's middle name.

'Will you leave me be. A man's entitled to eat his meal in peace.'

There was another silence.

'John,' began his mother tentatively, 'ain't you going to ask Ralphie about his new job?'

'Job?' he exploded. 'Job! Go on then, surprise me.'

Ralph knew his mother wanted to help, but he'd much rather talk to her about Queenie and the shed and the room with the dust covers, later.

His father sat back in his chair and gloated. 'He can't think of anything.'

'Ralphie, why won't you tell your dad?' asked his mother, coaxing him.

'Because anything I say, he'll find fault with.'

'You won't, will you, John?'

But his father remained silent.

'Is my blue cardigan nearly dry?' whined Joan.

'I'll shove it in the oven for a bit,' said Ralph's mother. 'That'll do it.'

'I expect it will,' she said sadly, and she sighed. 'If only we had radiators.'

'Like Kay,' chorused Elsie and Harry and burst into fits of giggles.

'That's not funny,' she protested.

'I s'pose you'll be wanting to borrow my umbrella,' said Aunty Win.

'Can I?'

'As long as you don't leave it at the pictures. Who's going with you?' she added suspiciously.

'Dolly.'

'No hanging around outside,' said Ralph's mother.

'What do you take me for,' she exclaimed.

'I know Dolly,' said Ralph's mother.

'She likes anything in trousers,' said Aunty Win.

'Not everyone likes being a spinster,' said Joan crossly.

'Joan!' exclaimed Ralph's mother. 'Don't speak to your aunt like that.'

'You're all men haters! You just want me to end up in a monastery.'

'A nunnery,' said Ralph.

'Oh shut up, toffee nose.'

'You're only seventeen,' said Ralph's mother.

'Like Kay,' chorused Harry and Elsie.

'Leave off,' said Ralph's father. 'Have a bit of respect for your cousin.'

Joan turned to her uncle and blushed.

'Ellen, don't you think you're being a bit tough on her?'

'No,' said Ralph's mother firmly. 'Now, you promise you'll come straight home, or I won't finish drying off this cardigan.'

'I promise,' said Joan sulkily.

Suddenly Ralph's father pushed back his chair. 'I'm off, then,' he announced.

'But, John,' said Ralph's mother.

'I'm meeting Ted.'

'Oh,' said his mother, looking disappointed.

'I need a drink, especially after today.'

Harry placed his hand on his father's arm. 'Dad, don't forget to ask about me apprenticeship tomorrow.'

'Don't give me orders. I'm asking no one nothin'.'

And with that he pushed his way violently past the chairs and walked out into the scullery.

'Don't get downhearted, Harry,' said Elsie in a motherly way. 'It'll take him a bit of time.'

Ralph caught his mother's eye, and they smiled with amusement. 'I better go and get ready,' said Joan leaving the table.

Once the two had left, the atmosphere in the room was visibly lighter. Ralph's mother placed a large teapot on the table and sat down. 'Now, Ralphie,' she said eagerly, 'tell us. What was it like?'

The door flew open again. It was Joan. 'Don't forget it's the blue cardigan,' she said, and slammed the door behind her.

His mother stood on a chair and pulled the blue cardigan down. 'I don't know why she's so fussy about what colour she wears,' said Aunty Win. 'Who's going to see it in the pictures?'

'We'll wait till she's gone, love,' said his mother. 'Then we can have a proper talk.'

'Can we have the wireless on?' said Harry.

'Why not?' said Ralph's mother.

'Now where's my cup of tea?' said Aunty Win.

SEVEN

R alph climbed into the smelly overalls and peered out of the window. It was now clean enough for him to make out the river more clearly. It had stopped raining and there was a field of lawn to cut. He dragged the motor mower out through the door and attempted to get it to go but the motor still wasn't responding. With a heavy heart he knew he would have to tell Mrs Egerton-Smythe that he had failed to get it working. He went back to the kitchen entrance and knocked on the door.

Queenie was washing up at the sink. She scowled when she saw him and took her time drying her hands. 'What you want?' she snorted.

'I need to talk to Mrs Egerton-Smythe.'

'I'll get her. Stay there,' she ordered, glancing at his overalls with disdain.

Ralph gazed back towards the mass of swaying grass. It was windy and leaves were being flung into the green undergrowth.

'Good God!'

Ralph turned, startled. It was Mrs Egerton-Smythe at the doorstep. He opened his mouth to speak.

'You smell like a rotting cabbage dump! Where the hell did you find those!' she exclaimed, waving at the overalls.

'In the shed. I didn't think you'd mind,' he began.

'My God, there's mould on them!'

Ralph flushed slightly. After years of living in an environment where it was blasphemous to use God's name in vain, he was aware of feeling vaguely alarmed.

'Aren't they damp?'

He nodded.

'Ass! Why didn't you say? Is that why you want to talk to me?'

'No. It's your motor mower. I can't get it to work.'

'Oh, God!' she exploded and she stormed past him. Ralph

63

glanced upwards waiting for a flash of lightning from the powers that be to strike her, but nothing happened. Feeling awkward he followed her.

She knelt down in the long grass and examined it.

'I'm sorry,' he said. 'I spent ages slotting bits together. I really thought it would work.'

She rose up in front of him, her hands on her hips. 'Petrol,' she said.

'Petrol?'

'Petrol. That ingredient that used to be a grey-black colour but has now been changed to pink and is commonly known as pool.' Suddenly she marched off in the direction of her garage. She turned and glared at him. 'Are you going to stay there like a mildewing statue?'

He ran to join her. She waited outside for him. There was a massive door at the front but she opened the side door. Ralph stepped in after her. There was a smell of petrol, engine oil and leather. She pulled a cord and a swinging light bulb lit up the gloom.

Ralph gasped. Standing jacked up was a large dark green car with a low bonnet. The massive spoked wheels were red. Dazed, Ralph walked round to the front. There on the front of the bonnet, rising up from the radiator cap was an eagle, its wings outstretched and below its feet a triangle with 'Alvis' written on it in silver.

'She's beautiful!' he breathed. Tentatively he touched the two enormous headlamps. They stuck out prominently above two medium-sized lamps and a pair of trumpet-like horns in front of the radiator.

'Glad you approve, Hollis,' Mrs Egerton-Smythe remarked and she suddenly looked sad.

'Why is she jacked up?'

'No point in having it on the road with petrol rationing, and my husband and other son weren't interested in driving it anyway. It belonged to my eldest son. He was killed in '44. He left it to me.'

'Gosh!' Ralph exclaimed, still unable to take his eyes off it. 'Lucky you.'

'Yes. Lucky me,' she said quietly. 'One day I shall learn to drive her,' she added, picking up a bucket. 'Now let's see if we can bleed her.'

'Bleed her?' asked Ralph, alarmed.

'Of petrol, you fool.' She stuck a small hose into the petrol tank and to Ralph's astonishment she began sucking it, pushed it away quickly and shoved the end into the bucket. When it was half full, she whipped the hose out of the bucket, held it up and drained back the remaining petrol into the tank.

'Hold this,' she commanded, handing him a funnel and a tin can. After she had poured the petrol into the can she walked briskly out of the garage. Ralph had hardly stepped outside when he found she had already disappeared into the house. He had a feeling that she had said more than she had intended.

Throughout the course of the week his days took on a routine. He would arrive at the shed, grab what he needed and return to widening and shaping the borders. He stacked the turf he had cut in case he got cold feet and wanted to put it back.

In the middle of the day he would hear a bell being rung. He'd wash his hands at the tap outside and go into the kitchen where he would eat vegetable broth and bread and be glared at by Queenie. Then he would work in the afternoon until it grew dark, go home, quarrel with his father who would then leave in high dudgeon, and would then attempt to relate the day's events to his mother who was always too busy to listen.

On Friday the rain swept across Winford in great gusts. Dry clothes and a towel were waiting for him in the bathroom on his arrival. When he came out he found Mrs Egerton-Smythe waiting for him at the top of the staircase above him.

'Feeling strong?' she called down to him.

'I suppose so,' he answered, mystified.

I want you to get a chest down from the loft. I have some more gardening books there. We could have a look at them.' She turned tail and disappeared. This was obviously her signal for him to follow.

The staircase was wide. He let his hands glide along the huge mahogany rails and gazed up at the magnificent high ceilings and white empty walls.

'I used to have pictures hanging there,' came a voice from above him. But that was all she said and Ralph didn't feel he could ask her to elaborate. At last they reached the top of the house. In the ceiling of a huge landing was a trapdoor.

'Stay there,' she ordered.

She disappeared into a nearby bedroom and re-appeared with a chair and placed it under the trapdoor.

'There's one of those pull-down steps just inside. I'm not tall enough.' She sounded rattled.

He climbed up and stretched upwards. He gave the trapdoor a quick push. It fell with a crash to one side. Fumbling around the sides his hands touched something hard and cylindrical-shaped. He gave it a tug. A small collapsible stepladder swung over and on top of him. He leapt off the chair. She pushed the chair aside and pulled the ladder down to the ground.

'There should be an oil lamp near. See if you can find it.'

Ralph didn't say anything for he noticed she was growing more agitated by the second. At times she glanced nervously down the stairs as if she expected someone to appear at any moment.

The stepladder was covered in dust. Like the shed it had obviously not been used for years. As his head emerged through the trapdoor opening he was amazed to find that the loft was in fact a huge attic room at least thirty feet long with several windows. The rain was pattering noisily on the roof and the dour sky didn't cast much light. But it cast enough for him to spot the lamp. A box of matches had been placed near by. Within minutes the lit oil lamp had transformed the vague shadows around him to recognisable objects.

'Are you still alive up there?' Mrs Egerton-Smythe shouted up to him.

He peered down at her. 'It's marvellous up here,' he exclaimed.

'Did I ask for your opinion, Hollis?'

Ralph smiled. 'No, madam.'

'Right, let's see what's what.' And she began climbing the ladder.

Ralph stood back with the lamp as she searched among boxes and furniture.

'I'll take that,' she said hurriedly.

It was a portrait of a young man in a blazer. Handsome, hair swept back. For a second her face softened and then she suddenly tossed her head. 'Right. Let's look for some gardening books,' she said quickly.

Ralph had just placed the lamp on an upturned trunk when he caught sight of a huge creature in the corner. He gave a frightened yelp and nearly knocked the lamp over.

'What the hell!' yelled Mrs Egerton-Smythe. 'What's got into you?'

'There!' he shrieked.

'Where?'

'There, in the corner.'

She turned to where he was pointing. 'It's only a bear.'

'A bear!'

'Don't worry. It's stuffed. It's been in the family for years. My parents used to have it in our hall when I was a child. My father used to put his hat and scarf on it when he came in. Ah. That's the one,' she said, and she pointed to a small tin chest in the corner. 'Think you can manage it?'

It weighed a ton but he found that if he balanced it on his shoulder with his right hand, and guided himself down the ladder with his left, it was quite easy. To his surprise she came swiftly after him, carrying the painting. 'We'll come back for the rest later. I want this in my room as soon as possible.'

He heaved it back on to his shoulder and followed her with speed down two flights of stairs and along a corridor. She threw open a door and beckoned him in with agitated gestures.

'Shove it under there,' she commanded, pointing under a huge, mahogany bed. Ralph did so, glancing round the room. Everything was dark wood, sombre colours, dark velvet curtains.

'Quickly!' she urged.

He followed her out, padding silently along behind her. He hauled down two suitcases, another larger chest and a stack of books on painting and sculpture and photography. And all the time he noticed a sense of growing urgency in his employer's manner. As soon as they had finished he put the lamp out, stood on the chair, pushed up the stepladder and replaced the trapdoor.

'Now,' she said, 'you'd better collect your wet clothes from the bathroom and take them downstairs for Queenie to dry. I'll call you when I need you. Oh, and Hollis, I wouldn't mention our little venture to her.'

Ralph nipped down and had just taken his clothes out of the bathroom and on to the landing when he froze. From the hallway he could hear Queenie using the telephone, but in such a secretive manner that he knew she wasn't meant to be. Intrigued, he sat on the stairway and eavesdropped.

'Just now,' she said, 'I heard them.' Pause 'She's got this new gardener's boy and she asked him to go upstairs. And he's wearing some of Mr Egerton-Smythe senior's clothes because his got wet.' Pause. 'That's what I thought.' Pause. 'I can't but I can have a look in her room when I dust up there.'

Ralph was horrified. It sounded as if Queenie was conspiring with someone to steal.

'Not at all, sir. It's my pleasure,' she said, sycophantically. 'So you'll be calling tonight, sir.' Pause. 'Oh no, I won't breathe a word, sir.' Pause. 'Well, I had to do what's right, sir. I knew you'd want to know.'

Ralph sneaked quickly back to the lavatory next to the bathroom, pulled the chain and made his way noisily down the stairs. He heard a muffled whisper and the light clunk of the receiver being replaced on its cradle.

By the time he reached the kitchen, the door was closed. He knocked.

Queenie opened it and glanced disapprovingly down at the bundle in his arms and up at the clothes he was wearing. 'Mrs Egerton-Smythe said I was to ask you to dry these.'

She grunted and snatched the clothes. 'Wangled your way into those clothes again I see,' she said. The bell rang. 'That'll be for you, I s'pose. 'That's the study

He knocked at the door. When he entered, his second impression of the room was similar to the first. Cold masculinity, but not a masculinity he could identify with. When he looked at the endless shelves of glassed-in books he was surprised to find they were all law books.

'My husband was a KC,' she commented and her voice took on a lifeless quality. 'Law students come here to read them. They'll be popping in and out next week. It's their half-term at the moment. Now, these books look far more interesting.'

On a small table in front of him were some of the books from the loft. 'Pick what you want. Do you have a saddle-bag?'

'Yes, madam.'

'Good. Take them home. Peruse and digest.'

'Thank you.'

There was a creak outside the door. Ralph looked up at Mrs Egerton-Smythe but she hadn't noticed. It was probably nobody. Just the house shrinking with cold. There was still no fire in the grate. She caught him glancing at it.

'I only keep it going for the students. When it's half-term I don't because . . .' She paused. 'Actually that's my business, Hollis.'

After lunch it stopped raining. It was too soggy to work on the lawn so he decided to dig over the earth in the borders. At the end of the day, the bell was rung, and his dry clothes were handed to him. He changed in the bathroom, left Mrs Egerton-Smythe's clothes folded neatly on the chair, as he had been instructed, and then returned to the study to collect his first pay-packet. It was in an envelope on top of the gardening books he had selected.

'Well, Hollis, you've almost impressed me. Better keep it up, though.'

'Yes, Mrs Egerton-Smythe.'

'What are you going to do with your new-found wealth then?'

He was about to say 'That's my business' when she gave one of her slight smiles again.

'It's all right, you're not obliged to tell me.'

68

'*French Without Tears*', he blurted out and then wished he hadn't.

'The Terence Rattigan play?'

He beamed. 'Yes, do you know it?'

'I saw it once, years ago, with my eldest son. Off you go. I'll see you on Monday morning.'

As he approached the door he heard footsteps in the hall outside. He swung it open only to catch the kitchen door just closing. Enough was enough, he thought. Swiftly he shut it again.

'What now?' she asked impatiently.

'Madam, there's something I must tell you. It's about Queenie.'

EIGHT

She didn't speak for some time. She stared for what seemed an eternity at the bookcases and then said very quietly, 'Thank you, Hollis.'

Ralph felt awkward. 'I hope you don't think I'm being a sneak,' he stammered.

She looked at him in surprise as if she had forgotten he was there. 'I expect you know which side your bread's buttered on.'

Ralph flushed with anger. 'It wasn't that at all!' he exclaimed.

For a fraction of a second her face softened and then she quickly frowned and the old angry look returned. 'No, that was rude of me. I apologise. You'd better go now.'

Ralph gave a nod. He was just about to open the door when she suddenly said, 'Enjoy the Rattigan.'

Up in the gallery, listening to the Billy Dixon Trio in the pit, he mulled over her words. He had the strange feeling that she would have liked to have come too but he couldn't have asked her even if he had wanted to.

He longed to know what the surprise visit was all about and if Mr Egerton-Smythe was the other son she had mentioned. Whoever he was, Mrs Egerton-Smythe would not be able to move those trunks by herself if she wanted to hide them.

The auditorium grew dark. The music died down. The curtains rose to a living room in France with its walls of sea green, and pink and white striped accessories. The sun was flooding through the french windows. The table was laid for breakfast and there in the centre of the alcove on one of the shelves was a row of white books with his italic writing and fleur-de-lis design on them. Somewhere hidden from the audience were Isla's chalk marks. She would probably be watching from one of the wings now. The thought of her produced a glorious ache which suffused his entire body.

A young man appeared through the french windows, gazing in despair at a textbook. The play had begun and Ralph felt himself being drawn into another world where men wore white flannels and blazers, fell in and out of in love, had civilised arguments and everything came all right in the end.

When the play was over he made his way back to the stage door and hovered for a moment as if hoping to catch some drift of conversation coming from a dressing room window somewhere. He had broken his usual Friday habit. Instead of going to the second show after having supper at home he felt it would be wiser to go to the first show before his entire pay packet had been removed from him by his father.

Suddenly he decided to return to Mrs Egerton-Smythe's house. He collected his bike from the wall near the river and headed back through the High Street.

There was a chink of light in the library curtains downstairs. He stood on the opposite side of the road still not knowing quite what to do. He heard footsteps coming down the side of the house. He saw Queenie walking away in the opposite direction.

Swiftly he wheeled his bike over the road, through the gate and hid it behind the hedge. He leapt up the stone steps to the arched porch and stood in front of a heavy black door with its ornate brass knocker and knob. There was an iron ring at the end of a chain. He gave it a hearty yank. The bell rang from inside. He glanced around to see if there were any visitors' cars. He found himself sweating at the sound of footsteps. A light came on in the hallway. There was the sound of a heavy latch and the door swung open.

To Ralph's relief it was Mrs Egerton-Smythe. When she saw it was him she looked relieved too.

'Have you forgotten something?' she asked.

'No.' He hesitated. 'Look, it's none of my business but if you want any of those trunks moved to where they can't be found, I'll help you.'

To his amazement, she gave an amused smile and then hauled him in looking hastily around. 'You're a man after my own heart, Hollis,' she remarked.

They hid one trunk in the boot of the Alvis which she then locked.

70

A smaller trunk was hidden in the corner of the garden shed under sacking and flowerpots. They moved swiftly and silently, hauling boxes and cases from her bedroom and down the stairs and hid them in the coal cellar. They had just finished when Ralph remembered something.

'Hell!' he exclaimed. 'You must have something around otherwise he'll wonder what you *did* get out of the loft and he'll smell a rat.'

'Of course. Good thinking, Hollis.'

'The gardening books! They're in my saddle-bag. I'll bring them back in.'

Just then there was a knock at the door. 'Doesn't waste time, does he, my son,' she said wryly.

'My bike is round the front. Can you leave the kitchen door unlocked? Then I can sneak the books in round the back.'

She nodded and they separated. As he dashed into the kitchen, he heard her yell out, 'Just coming!' That was all Ralph heard before he was flying down the side of the house. From the corner he saw the light from the house flooding down the front path.

'Charles! This is a surprise,' he heard Mrs Egerton-Smythe say loudly. 'And Mr Patterson, what brings you here so late?'

'Just passing this way,' said a rather pompous voice.

Ralph held his breath. As soon as the door closed he sprinted down the path, across the pavement, through the front gate and dived behind the hedge, where he fumbled nervously with the buckles of his saddle-bag. He piled the books high in his arms and ran back along the side path to the kitchen.

He had hardly dumped the books on the table when, to his horror, he heard voices just outside the door. He noticed the broom cupboard was open. He dived into it and held the door as close as he could to himself. There was a sound of a switch and a chink of light filtered into the cupboard.

'It's all right, Charles, *I* can make you a cup of tea.'

'Where's Queenie, then?'

It was the voice of the man Ralph had heard in the porch.

'I sent her home early.'

'What's this?' he barked.

'Gardening books. Hollis helped me get them out of the loft today. He's the new gardener.'

'A new gardener? Why wasn't I informed?'

'Why should you be? It's my garden.'

'And I think we should keep it the way Father wanted it.'

'Why?'

'In his memory, of course. I'll put these back in the loft for you.'

'No, thank you, Charles,' Ralph heard Mrs Egerton-Smythe say firmly.

'But they're filthy. Look at the state of them.'

'That's why I put them in the kitchen so I could sponge the covers.'

Ralph grinned.

'You're not serious about this, are you?' The voice was different now. It had a warning tone in it. There was a silence.

'I don't know,' Mrs Egerton-Smythe said, but her voice had lost its firmness. 'I can at least daydream, can't I? Or is that not allowed in this house, either?'

'There's no need to get hysterical, Mother.'

'Charles, if I scratched my nose you'd say I was hysterical.'

'I don't like you being up in that loft. It's not healthy.' He paused. 'You didn't bring anything else down, did you?'

'Like what?'

'You know damned well what.'

'Your brother's things?'

'Well, did you?'

'How could I?'

'You said there was this Hollis chap with you.'

'He's a boy. He'd hardly be able to carry trunks. Anyway, what would be the point? Since you and your father padlocked them I wouldn't be able to get inside, would I?' she added with bitterness.

'We did it for your own good,' he said. 'If you'd let me get rid of then I wouldn't have needed to.'

'Why should I? Are you afraid of a little bit of him in the house?'

'Don't be ridiculous, Mother. He's dead and I think you should accept that. Better to get rid of his belongings and forget about him.'

'And start fresh, so to speak?'

'Of course. That's what I've been saying for two years, Mother.'

'Perhaps you're right.'

Ralph wanted to burst out of the cupboard and say 'No, no, keep them as long as you like.' But he was pleased he hadn't, for Mrs Egerton-Smythe was holding her trump card.

'Of course I'm right.' He sounded delighted.

'That's why I've been thinking about your father's books.'

'What on earth do you mean?'

'I think you should get rid of your father's law books to the university.'

'I've never heard of anything so absurd!'

'But you've just been saying that one should get rid of . . .'

'That's a little different,' he said, the sarcasm rising in his voice. 'Laurie wasn't my father.'

'Ah,' she said wryly. 'One law for your father. One law for Laurie.'

'Well of course,' he snapped. 'Father was a genius.'

'A dead genius.'

There was a shocked intake of breath. 'Mother! You're his wife.'

'*Was* his wife.'

'You're just tired. His books are staying here. That's what Father would have wanted.'

'Perhaps if there was no fire in the library the students wouldn't be so interested in using them.'

'Mother, if you dare do that I shall employ someone to do the fires myself and deduct it from your . . .' He stopped.

'Wages?' she added.

'Don't be ridiculous.'

'Well, I feel like a curator here. Keeping guard on some mausoleum or monument to our national heritage.'

'You are, in a sense. You should be proud to keep his memory alive.'

'I'd like a home, Charles.'

'This *is* your home!' he said, exasperated. 'What are you doing?'

'Putting the kettle on. You did say you wanted some tea. And your friend must be freezing to death in the library.'

'Why isn't there a fire in there?'

'It's half-term, remember?'

'You could at least keep the room warm. It'll take ages to get it warm again next week.'

'I can't afford it. Keeping that fire going all day is an extravagance. Perhaps if the university could donate something towards the cost.'

'I give you enough, don't I?'

'Only just. Fuel is very expensive. It's also getting hard to find. It means I can't light a fire anywhere else in the house.'

'But you don't need to. You have that as a sitting room in the evening.'

'And the daytime?'

'I assumed you sat and supervised in there.'

'Did you?'

Ralph could hear the tinkling of cups and saucers.

'Mother, there's no need to do that. I'm only making a passing visit.'

A passing check-up, Ralph thought.

'Charles,' began Mrs Egerton-Smythe, 'this really is too big a house for one person. I've been thinking of taking in lodgers.'

There was an audible gasp. 'Have you lost your senses?'

'If I took lodgers,' she continued, 'I wouldn't be dependent on you.'

'You aren't dependent on me. It's Father's money. I'm just delegated to give it to you when needed.'

'I would have preferred it to be a solicitor.'

'I am a solicitor.'

'Outside the family.'

'And let them take payment for it?'

'Of course, if it had been left to me.'

'You would have spent it in the first six months!'

'You think I would. I've always done the household budgeting, remember?'

'It's hardly the same thing.' He was beginning to sound bored. 'Look, I must go. We're expecting people. Sandra will wonder where I am. Now, if you'll excuse me.'

'I could take law students,' she went on. 'Surely your father would approve of that.'

'Law students! Living here?'

Ralph heard the door open.

'You make it sound as if they'd be sleeping on an altar.'

The cupboard was suddenly dark and Ralph heard the door close. He stepped out cautiously and sprinted across the room.

NINE

*H*is mother flung back the scullery door and dragged him into the kitchen. 'Where have you been?' she demanded.

His aunt and Joan were sitting at the kitchen table. Joan gave him a cursory glance before returning to her magazine. His aunt sat back on her chair and folded her arms. 'I went to the theatre. It's Friday.'

'Does his breath smell?' asked Aunty Win.

'Don't be silly, Win. He's too young.'

He pulled out his pay packet and presented it to his mother.

'It's been opened,' noted his Aunt.

'I took out a shilling for my theatre ticket.'

'He still hasn't told us where he's been.'

'Yes I did. The theatre.'

'For both shows?' his mother asked.

'I stayed on a bit to help Mrs Egerton-Smythe.'

'Mm,' said Aunty Win, suspiciously.

His mother placed one piece of bread, a potato and a nub of cheese on to the table. 'I'm sorry, it's not much, love.'

Ralph drew up a chair.

'She tried to save you some stew, but your dad said if you couldn't be bothered to turn up for supper, you didn't deserve any, so he ate what was left,' his aunt said.

His mother turned away and hurriedly brought him out a mug of tea from the pot on the range.

'Thanks, Mum,' he said quietly.

She smiled and pushed the cup across the table.

'Aren't you having one? You look like you could do with a sit down.'

'Don't mind if I do,' she smiled, and she poured herself one.

She had hardly sat down when Joan glanced up. 'I'm a wage earner too,' she said scowling. 'How come I don't get one?'

Ralph's mother gave him a 'what's the point' shrug and was about to give her cup to Joan when Ralph caught hold of her arm.

'No you don't,' he said. 'Joan's got legs. She can pour herself one.'

'I didn't notice you pouring yours out,' she objected.

'I've only just come in. I bet you've been sitting there for hours.'

'It's no trouble,' said his mother rising. 'I don't want Joanie thinking I'm favouritising.'

Ralph sighed and got on with eating. His Aunty Win raised her newspaper. Within seconds there was a loud tutting noise from behind it. 'Good show, was it?' asked his mother when she eventually sat down again with another cup of tea.

'Splendid,' said Ralph.

His aunt lowered her newspaper. 'Don't I get a cup?' she said affronted.

Ralph lay back in the dark mulling over the conversation he had heard. No wonder Mrs Egerton-Smythe was angry most of the time.

The bolster under his head had gone flat. He raised his head, plumped it up and sank back into it again, but he couldn't sleep. He felt uneasy, not turning up at the house till Monday. He didn't trust Charles Egerton-Smythe. He was more than a stuffed shirt. His voice was ruthless and condescending. From downstairs he heard faint noises and guessed it must be his father returning from the pub. He didn't know which was worse, his being home in the evening with the tension between them or going out and leaving his mother sad and quiet. He knew he was the cause of all the friction but felt impotent to make matters better.

'Ralph,' came a sleepy voice from the other end.

'Yes,' he whispered.

'Keep still, will ya. You're making me cold with all the draughts.'

'Sorry.' Ralph closed his eyes. 'I must do something,' he whispered to himself.

He decided to go to the tradesman's entrance as usual. He rang the bell, but no one answered. He peered into the kitchen – there was no sign of Queenie. He rang again and waited. He was about to leave when he noticed that the door to the garden shed was slightly ajar. He knew he and Mrs Egerton-Smythe had closed it. Maybe she was in there trying to open the small tin trunk.

He ran across the grass, and hesitated. He could hear movement from inside. He knocked at the door. There was a frantic shuffling. He waited again. 'It's me, Mrs Egerton-Smythe,' he said politely, 'Hollis.' The scrabbling stopped. Ralph pushed the door aside and found himself face to face with Queenie. Her face was bright red and Ralph, at a glance, could see she had been at the sacking in the corner. 'What are you doin' 'ere?' she snapped.

'I should be asking you that question.'

'Don't you be saucy, young man. If you must know, Mrs Egerton-Smythe sent me here to look for somethin'.'

'Oh, can I help?' he asked innocently. 'I know where everything is. I've reorganised it, you see. I expect that's why you're having a problem.'

'I ain't havin' a problem,' she said ruffled. 'I found what I wanted.'

'Oh?' he said looking at her empty hands. 'What was it?' Her face reddened again. 'It's not big enough,' she stammered.

'Maybe I could find a bigger one,' said Ralph enjoying himself. 'I'll have a look. Just give me a clue.'

'Hedge cutters,' she said after a pause.

He took a pair from the shelf nearest the window. 'Will these be big enough?'

'Oh! There they are!' she gushed, acting so badly that it was all Ralph could do not to laugh.

'Good job I was here, eh?'

76

'Yes. Yes,' she said hurriedly.

'Now which hedge did she want cut.' She looked startled. 'Or shall I ask her?'

'No!' she screamed. She backed out of the shed. 'She won't remember anyway. Her memory's not so good now. She's got a lot on her mind.'

He watched her fly back to the kitchen.

'I'll just start on the ones near the river, then,' he called after her.

He had been standing on a stepladder clipping a huge hedge for about an hour when he saw a familiar figure striding towards him.

'You're not supposed to be here till Monday,' she hollered.

'Weather forecast said it would be raining all day on Monday.'

He sat on the ladder and watched her approach.

'Liar,' she said. 'What's the real reason?'

'Couldn't keep away, could I? Wondered if you'd had time to look at those gardening books?'

'And?'

'Queenie said you wanted the hedge cut. I found her in the potting shed. She knows where that small tin trunk is now.'

Mrs Egerton-Smythe paled.

'It's none of my business, madam, but maybe you ought to unlock them and put whatever's in them somewhere not so easy to find.'

'I can't,' she said quietly, and she hastily looked away.

'Oh. Have you lost the keys?'

She swung round. 'Yes.' He could see she was lying and he wanted to help her lie even better. 'I thought so. Having been up there so long.'

'How did you know that?' she said sharply.

'From the dust.'

'Oh yes, of course.'

'May I make a suggestion, madam?'

'Out with it then.'

'I break the locks for you.'

'Thank you, Hollis, but I'll probably want to lock them up again.'

In case Mr Egerton-Smythe checks up on you, he thought.

'I can get ones that match from the High Street.'

She smiled. He knew she had agreed.

'We'll have to move fast,' he added.

'Why?'

'Just a feeling,' he said.

'Queenie?'

'Something like that. We'll have to get rid of her.'

'Yes. She's probably on the phone right now.'

'The butcher's!' said Ralph. 'My mother says the queues are always a mile long there. Tell her you've heard there's a special offer of tripe. Then wave to me from the french windows when she's gone.'

'Where do you get all these ideas? From the theatre?'

'My Aunty Win reads green Penguins out to my mother. Margery Allingham, Ngaio Marsh. You name it.'

'How nice for your mother.'

Ralph shrugged uneasily. It was then that he noticed Queenie hovering at the end of the garden.

'What are you going to say about me hedge clipping?'

'I'll pretend I forgot and thank her for remembering. That do, Hollis?'

He grinned and carried on snipping.

Half an hour later, he was pushing his bike back down the road, the pockets of Laurie Egerton-Smythe's large sports jacket bulging with new identical looking padlocks.

He was about to take a detour so that he could avoid the part of the High Street where the butcher's was when he saw Queenie coming round the corner and heading in his direction. Swiftly he crossed over the road. Ahead of him was the stage door of the theatre. He flung his bike on to the pavement and dived in between the doors. Wilfred was talking to a tall man with white hair and a flushed complexion. He spotted Ralph as soon as he walked in. Ralph walked boldly over to him and said very firmly, 'It's me again. I thought I'd just pop in to see if there was any chance of me seeing Mr Johnson before the strike tonight.

'You're in luck. Mr Johnson, the lad I was telling you about.'

Ralph looked upwards and found Mr Johnson staring down at him from a great height.

'I'm Isla's friend,' he gulped. 'I expect she's mentioned me.'

The man continued to stare at him. 'Young Isla thinks you can do things back to front, lad. You shouldn't have been anywhere near the strike last week.'

'Oh,' he said feebly.

'But,' he went on, 'the master carpenter told me you made yourself useful.' He frowned at Ralph and then eventually gave a weary sigh. 'You toe the line. Whatever Jack Walker says, jump to it. Understand?'

'Yes, sir. Thank you, sir.'

Ralph was so exhilarated by this stroke of luck that he quite forgot that he was hiding from Queenie until he leapt out into the street and spotted her at a public phone box. Luckily she had her back to him. He wheeled his bike swiftly round the corner and hopped on to it, cycling down an alley past the second-hand clothes shop he had discovered actors from the rep frequented.

As soon as he hit the High Street he pedalled as fast as he could.

With relief he saw there was no car outside Mrs Egerton-Smythe's house. He leapt off his bike, ran with it up the side of the house, rang the bell and dumped his bike by the wall.

Mrs Egerton-Smythe flung open the kitchen door. He pulled the padlocks out, sweat pouring down his face. 'Have you emptied them?'

'Yes,' she said.

'Buckets!' he panted. 'Buckets! Earth!'

'Hollis, what are you talking about?'

'Fill the trunks,' he gasped. 'Queenie telephoning from the box.'

For the next quarter of an hour she and Ralph shovelled earth into buckets which they carried upstairs. They filled the large trunk and suitcase and repadlocked them. Then, between them, they pulled the stepladder from the loft down and hauled them back up. Ralph slid them across the floor. 'Two up and two to go,' she declared. They filled the suitcase which had been in the car boot and returned it to the loft. They were shovelling earth into the one in the shed, when Ralph suddenly said, 'Queenie will have told him about this.'

'Oh lord,' said Mrs Egerton-Smythe. 'Got any similar tin trunks?'

'There's one in the garage. It's filled with tools.'

They dashed conspiratorially across the grass, smothering their laughter like a couple of schoolchildren. They had just swapped the trunks and carried her son's one through the garden room into the hall when the bell at the front door rang. Through the coloured glass was a silhouette of a man. Horrified, the two of them gaped at one another. Ralph nodded his head upwards, frantically. With incredible speed they ran swiftly up to the top of the house with the trunk. The doorbell rang again. 'He'll use his key if I don't answer it,' she said.

'I can do this on my own,' said Ralph.

As she ran down the stairs, he heard her calling out loudly, 'Just coming.'

Ralph swung the trunk on to his shoulder and staggered up the tiny steps. To his alarm he heard heavy footsteps coming up the stairs. 'Really, Charles, this is too much! I told you yesterday I merely brought down a few books. I think you're overstepping the bounds of duty. Charles!'

As quietly as he could, Ralph pushed the trunk gently into the loft, pulled up the ladder and slid the door over it, just as the footsteps reached the landing.'

'I merely want to look at the roof, Mother. We've had a lot of heavy rainfall and I want to check that there are no leaks.'

'There aren't.'

'That's convenient,' he heard Charles say. 'The chair's still there.'

'Yes, I forgot to put it back in the bedroom.'

'Fortuitous.'

To Ralph's horror he heard him step on to it. Quickly he turned around looking for somewhere to hide. And then he saw a figure looming in the shadows. The bear! Praying he wouldn't cause any creaks he moved stealthily towards it, pulled it forward and squeezed in behind it. He heard the trapdoor being flung aside and was aware of a spill of light casting shadows along the roof. A beam of torchlight went scurrying along the walls like a small ack-ack light. He listened to the sound of the padlocks being handled.

'Found any leaks?' said a voice from below.

'Not yet.'

'What are you doing up there?'

'I bumped into some trunks. Really, Mother, his things ought to be cleared out. Let me deal with it.'

'They don't belong to you, Charles. Neither did they belong to your father. So I shall keep them for as long as I like.'

'Why? It'll only upset you. It's just too sentimental for words, keeping all this rubbish. I mean, look at that bear. Completely useless.'

Ralph shrunk down, willing him not to come over and check it for moths.

'Have you finished looking for leaks, Charles?' There was a slight pause.

'Yes,' he said at last.

'Good.'

'But I think I'll stay for a while and see what's been done to the garden.'

The loft was plunged into darkness again. Ralph slipped out from behind the bear and crept back towards the trapdoor.

He was ashamed of his feeblemindedness at not opening it and climbing down. It was only a little jump from the ladder to the floor. If he had moved immediately after Charles Egerton-Smythe had gone downstairs, he might have been able to pretend he had just come in from the garden, but he also might have been caught on one of the landings. And how would he have explained his being there? He would lose his job and Mrs Egerton-Smythe would have no ally.

As the hours passed, his stomach began to gurgle loudly. He was going to miss the Saturday strike! If he didn't turn up they might think his parents had stopped him and see him as a boy and not want him around again.

He found an old rug and wrapped it round himself to stave off the cold but he was so chilled he began to feel slightly sick. And then he heard a car draw away. He had hardly moved towards the trapdoor when there were footsteps on the landing. Someone was whispering. At first he couldn't make it out, and then to his relief he heard the word 'Hollis'. Gingerly he moved the trapdoor and peered down but there was no one there. There was more whispering from one of the rooms.

'Here!' he whispered back urgently. He heard a hurried tread of shoes and Mrs Egerton-Smythe came into view.

'Up here!' he repeated.

She looked up. 'My God, Hollis. Have you been up there all this time?'

'Yes,' he answered, his teeth chattering.

'You must be frozen.' He nodded. 'Look, I know this is a lot to ask, but could you hang on for ten more minutes. Queenie is due to leave then.'

He nodded again, covered the trapdoor and lay down. He must have fallen asleep because he was startled to feel the trapdoor moving underneath him. He crawled backwards. The trapdoor was pulled aside and hands reached up for the ladder.

'What time is it?' he said through his clamped jaws.

'Ten.'

'Morning or night?'

'Night.'

'Saturday or Sunday?'

She gave a sudden snort. 'That bad is it? It's Saturday.'

'I haven't missed the strike then.'

81

'Oh, lord, you're delirious. Come on down before pneumonia or *rigor mortis* sets in.'

She had drawn the curtains in the library so that no one could see in. The embers from the fire were still warm. She insisted he sit in one of the leather armchairs as close to the fire as he could. To his embarrassment, she brought a tray of food in for him. He stood up and protested, but she only told him to shut up and do as he was told.

The combination of hot food and warmth was making him drowsy. He longed to lie down on the hearth and go to sleep but he resisted. He would miss the strike if he shut his eyes.

'Now,' she said, when he had finished eating, 'what's all this nonsense about a strike?'

'They strike the set every Saturday at the Palace Theatre.'

'And you help?'

'I did a bit last week. But really I'm supposed to keep out of the way.'

'So why are you going again?'

'To learn and also because I want to get my foot in the door.'

She gazed at him steadily. 'That important, is it?'

'Very.'

'You want to work backstage?'

'No.' He took a deep breath. 'I'm going to be an actor.'

He had said it. Not even 'I *want* to be an actor', but 'I'm *going* to be an actor'.

'I see,' she said slowly. 'And what do your parents think?'

'They don't know. I hadn't really dared say it till tonight. My father would probably shoot me.'

'And your mother?'

'She'd be worried, but . . .' He paused. 'She'd probably get used to the idea.' He smiled. 'I feel so relieved to have admitted it!' And then he stopped. 'Oh. Will this put you off employing me?'

'I think I can cope,' she said wryly, 'but I wouldn't let Queenie know.'

'Rogues and vagabonds, and all that?' said Ralph.

'Exactly. Now, young man, you'd better get a move on.'

He removed Laurie Egerton-Smythe's jacket.

'Do you want to borrow it?'

It surprised him that she wasn't upset to see him wearing it. 'No. I'd better take my own one.'

'Yes, it is rather large.'

'It's not that. I don't want to mess it up at the strike.'

It was while she was letting him out that she brought up

something which was so obvious he wondered why he hadn't thought of it himself.

'Have you asked to play any parts there?'

'No,' he said surprised. 'I've had no training.'

'And you've done no amateur dramatics?'

'Only at school.'

'Any good?'

Against his will he found himself smiling. 'People seem to think so.'

'You can mention that in a letter, can't you? To the producer?

'I suppose so.'

'You're small. There might be a young part going. You're local. The producer can only say no.'

Ralph stood in the doorstep feeling slightly dazed.

'You'd better go, Hollis,' she said at last.

'What?' he said, suddenly remembering where he was. 'Oh. Yes, madam. Goodnight, madam.' He was about to leave when he realised what she was doing. 'Are you sure you should be encouraging me?'

'Be a waste of time discouraging you, wouldn't it?'

'Yes,' he said happily. 'Yes it would.'

'I'll see you Monday then.' And she closed the door.

ELEVEN

Only a month to go before the panto season, Ralph thought. Only a month of Saturday strikes. He peered down into the dress circle and stalls. The Billy Dixon Trio were playing a stirring and romantic piece with gusto. And then it was over. The lights dimmed. The audience stopped talking and the curtains rose to darkness. Suddenly there was the sound of a revolver being fired. A woman screamed and then there was silence.

'There!' said another woman's voice and the lights came up on the sophisticated 1930s drawing room Ralph had watched being set up almost a week ago. A tall fair-haired woman in her late twenties was standing by a light switch near the mantelpiece. Two women were sitting in armchairs. The one downstage right was drawing on a cigarette from a long cigarette holder. A small blonde girl was sitting on a settee, looking petulant. They were all wearing long evening dresses. Geraldine Maclaren's was white with a sky blue sash. The others were pale pink, blue and mauve.

Ralph leaned over the gallery rail and smiled. The play had begun.

He stumbled over the rubble in his street. In spite of the raincoat he was soaked. Gale force winds had made it impossible to ride his bike and in the middle of it all there had been a violent hailstorm which had buffeted viciously against his skull through his cloth cap. Everything about him streamed or clung wetly to his body. He staggered into the yard and carried his bike in to avoid the sound of the bicycle chain waking his father. To his alarm he noticed there was a light on. He already felt like a punch bag that had been pummelled about. If his dad hit him he would just fall over.

He was about to go in and get the confrontation over with when, through a chink in the curtains, he noticed someone else in the kitchen walking up and down in agitation. For a moment he thought it was his mother. He stayed still, listening, but the rain drowned their voices. And then, to his amazement, he realised it was Joan! It didn't look like the kind of conversation he wanted to walk in on. He decided to try the front door.

To his relief, he found it unlocked. He slipped into the tiny hall and eased the door to a close. In the dark he could hear the drips from his raincoat hitting the wooden floor. He moved stealthily to the foot of the stairs, his hand outstretched for the banister rail. He was halfway up the stairs when he heard Joan's voice. 'I know I could make you happy,' she said. 'I understand what you're suffering. I do. Honest!'

Ralph was riveted. Joan and his father! But he was twice her age. If he so much as laid a finger on her he would sort him out. He clenched his fists.

'Joanie, you're a lovely girl,' he heard his father say gently, 'and I'm chuffed you feel like that about me, but it's not on.'

'But I thought . . .' she began. 'But you've been sticking up for me and that, when she's been against me.'

'She's not against you, love. She just worries a bit.'

'But Uncle John, I feel so sorry for you, having a wife like her. She don't even try.'

'What do you mean?' His father sounded rattled now.

'Look at her hair. She don't make no effort for you. I can see that. And then there's you down 'ere, all alone and . . .' She paused. 'So I knows why you goes out so much.'

'Sit down, my girl!'

Ralph froze. There was a scrape of a chair followed by an ominous silence.

'Now you listen to me,' he heard his father whisper angrily, 'there's no one in miles can hold a candle to your aunt.'

'But, Uncle John . . .'

'That's enough.' There was another silence. 'The reason your Aunt Ellen don't have time to do her hair, as you put it, is 'cause she's spending all of it running this house, and looking after us lot. She's taken your Aunty Win in, and she took you and Kitty in. Not out of duty but because she's kind-hearted. She's too kind-hearted for her own good.'

'But I thought you and 'er was . . .' Her voice trailed away.

'Was what?'

'Well.' She faltered. 'It's just that you don't seem like a . . . well . . . married.'

'Well, we are. And we're staying that way.'

There was another long pause. 'Do you want me to pack me bags, then?'

'Course I don't.' There were sniffing sounds by now. 'I stick up for you, like a dad does, see. If your dad had been alive he would have done the same thing.'

'He wouldn't. He'd be worse than Aunt Ellen.'

'There you are, then. 'Ere, have this.'

There was a sound of nose blowing.

'Oh, Uncle John, you won't say nothin', will you?'

'Course not. It's just a little misunderstandin', ain't it?' Ralph heard his father give an embarrassed cough. 'It's good we've been able to sort it out.'

'Yeah,' said Joan sounding relieved. 'That's right. A misunderstanding.'

'Now you get back to sleep.'

At this point Ralph didn't wait to hear any more. He crept swiftly up the stairs and sneaked into his room. A distant street lamp lit up the rivers of rain that were dribbling rapidly down the window. He had hardly started to peel off his clothes, when he felt a spot hit his head. 'That's all I need,' he moaned.

He draped his clothes over the bars at his end of the bed and groped around in the dark for the towel on the washstand. He rubbed his hair vigorously with it and then spread it over the pillow. He was so chilled he ached. He stretched his icy feet down past Harry's feet and rested them on a warm knee. But it had no effect. He was shivering so uncontrollably, the bedsprings were squeaking. He lay with his damp hair stuck around his face, no nearer to sleep. Gradually the warmth from the bed penetrated his frozen limbs and sleep overtook him.

The bed was empty when he woke up. He rolled over to look through the bars and came face to face with his sodden clothes. He raised himself and peered over them. The rain had stopped. He listened out for footsteps downstairs. Being Saturday, Joan and Aunty Win would be at work, but if there was no sound of Harry and Elsie, they would have already left for their Saturday cinema club. He slipped out of bed and opened the door. He couldn't even hear the wireless but then his mother didn't like to have it on too much because it would need recharging too often. He would have to hang his clothes over the range. It was the trench coat he was worried about. In spite of spreading it out carefully, it was all crumpled. He opened his drawer and pulled out a pair of his grammar school flannels. To his surprise they were loose around the waist. He did them up and glanced down. They barely reached his calves now. He pulled on a shirt and pullover, gathered his belongings together and made for the landing.

His mother was rolling out pastry on the kitchen table. She burst out laughing when she saw him.

'Do I look that bad?' he said smiling.

'Yeah!'

'Sorry I got up late,' he said. 'The winds were so bad.'

'Good show, was it?'

'Splendid. Really gripping. Basil Duke was foul.'

'I thought you liked him?'

'The character he was playing was foul. It all started out fairly innocently. Then gradually, as layer after layer kept being lifted off, it turned out that everyone had been having secret affairs with everyone else.'

Just then there was a whirring sound from the yard. 'I thought he'd gone,' he said alarmed.

'Give him a chance,' his mother said, and she hurriedly began rolling the pastry.

'But I've got Mrs Egerton-Smythe's trench coat here!'

And then he remembered his pay packet. Hastily he put the damp envelope down on the table.

He heard the door of the scullery opened. 'Put your clothes over the horse,' she commanded. 'And put the irons on the range. I'll iron it after I've done this and dry it on the clothes rack. She ain't in no hurry for it to go back, is she?'

At this juncture the door swung open. Ralph dumped the clothes at the end of the table, grabbed the clothes horse from near the range and opened it out. He didn't look at his father. He was just aware of a silence as he put the irons on the range. It was only when he turned to pick up his clothes that he caught his eye.

'Decided to get up, eh?' said his dad.

To Ralph's surprise he looked slightly nervous.

'Storms held him back,' said his mother into the dough.

'Didn't hear you come in,' he said. Ralph watched him shift uneasily. And then the penny dropped. His father must be worried that he had overheard the conversation in the kitchen between him and Joan. If he said he had come in through the hall, Mum would be for it for leaving the front door unlocked. He busied himself with his clothes to give him time to come up with an answer. 'You were asleep,' he said quickly.

'But I stayed up late last night,' his father said.

'Did you, love?' said his mother. 'Why was that?'

'I was thinking.'

'What about?'

'Oh, this and that. You must have been very late.'

'I was. It was too windy to ride. I had to wheel the bike.'

'All the way from Winford?'

'Yes. And I couldn't walk very quickly either.'

He noticed his father give the raincoat a glance. 'I thought I told you not to bring that into the house.'

'Mrs Egerton-Smythe ordered me to. She doesn't want me off sick.'

'Good job he did have it, love,' said his mother quietly. 'He would have got pneumonia otherwise.'

There was a pause.

'So I was out for the count, then,' said his father, 'when you come in?'

'Well and truly. I even knocked over a chair and it didn't disturb you.'

His mother gave him a warning look. He always had a tendency to exaggerate when he lied.

After a breakfast of bread and marge with a sprinkling of sugar and a large mug of tea, his mother cleared the table and began pressing the hot irons into the trench coat. The rising steam almost camouflaged her. His father, he noticed, was pretending to read a newspaper. It was strange having him around. He wished he would go away, so that he and his mother could continue their chat about the play.

While the trench coat was drying on the overhanging rack, his mother ironed his damp clothes. 'You could do with some new clothes,' she said. 'You're growing out of everything so fast.'

'I'm nearly as tall as Basil Duke,' he said, and then wished he hadn't spoken.

His father lowered his newspaper. Ralph waited for 'And who the hell is Basil Duke?' To his amazement he said, 'That your pay-packet?'

'Yes, sir.'

His father looked equally surprised at being called 'sir'. It was a slip of the tongue. Before Ralph could take it back, his father glanced at his mother.

'If he brings in enough,' he said, 'mebbe we should let him put a bit aside for trousers, that sort of thing.'

Ralph gaped at him. Even his mother looked stunned and then realised she had been holding the iron in the same place for too long and removed it.

'There's a second-hand clothes shop for men off the High Street,' Ralph said casually.

'Been in it, have you?' his father asked.

'No. Just looked through the window.'

'Perhaps you should take a gander in there this afternoon, then. See what their prices are like.'

Not a hope, thought Ralph. He couldn't walk in dressed in the clothes he had, and then he remembered the trench coat.

'Of course, you'd have to give up this Friday theatre lark. That would put more money towards it.'

So that was it, thought Ralph. He took a deep breath. 'I won't buy trousers,' and he picked up his old ones.

'They're still damp!' his mother protested.

'They'll dry on me,' he said. 'Once I'm on my bike.'

Ralph snatched the rest of his clothes and the trench coat. He glared at his father. 'You can never give without taking away, can you, dad?' And with that he stormed out of the room.

Yards from the second-hand clothes shop he changed from his ankle boots to his walking shoes. He noticed they were tight. Even his feet were growing now. His mother had managed to slip some of his pay-packet back to him before he left. With shame, he had accepted it gratefully. He wouldn't have the chance of wearing the raincoat too many times. Outside the town he had pinned a collar to his shirt, stuffed the woollen scarf into his bicycle bag and tied his grammar school tie around his neck. He hovered by the window. Through the overcoats and suits, Ralph could see rows and rows of striped blazers and white trousers, breeches, Norfolk jackets, dinner suits and sports jackets. Up on shelves were hats and scarves.

An elderly man was busy with some shelves at the back. As soon as Ralph opened the door a large bell rang, sending him whirling round.

'Good afternoon, sir.'

'Good afternoon,' said Ralph, startled.

'Can I help you?'

'Do you have a selection of cravats?' asked Ralph, deepening the pitch of his voice. He had noticed many of the rep actors wearing them.

'Yes, indeed, sir. Any particular colour?'

He swallowed. 'I haven't decided yet.'

The man took out two drawers from underneath the counter.

'Thank you, sir,' said Ralph.

The cravats were wonderful. Most of them had a paisley design on them. After gazing at them for some time he was torn between choosing one he liked or one which would go with the few shirts he had. He whittled it down to three and laid them on the counter. He was just going through the agony of which one to choose when the bell above the door rang. Ralph glanced briefly aside and then felt himself reddening. It was Basil Duke.

Ralph looked hastily back at the cravats.

'Good afternoon, Mr Duke!' beamed the shopkeeper.

'Just a fleeting call to make sure everything is fine for Monday.'

The shopkeeper went over to one of the racks where an old coat was hanging. 'Is this rough enough for you, sir?'

'It's perfect, Mr Gutman.' 'And the price of the evening scarf will cover it?

'Yes, sir. Well, it's silk, as you know.'

'I might not be able to get it back before the dress rehearsal,' he said. 'The dresser doesn't bring back our laundry till the half.'

Mr Gutman waved his hand. 'I'll make out the usual IOU, sir.'

'Good. I'll pop in for the coat on Monday morning then and bring back the scarf later in the afternoon or Tuesday.'

'Take it now if you like.'

'Oh, could I? That would be marvellous.'

'After all, sir, you're hardly likely to . . .'

'Emigrate,' he finished for him.

The two men laughed. It was obviously a joke they shared many times.

Mr Gutman scribbled out an IOU note and handed it to him with the overcoat. 'I did like your performance this week, sir. Mesmeric. Full of evil undertones.'

Basil Duke gave a delighted smile. 'Thank you, Mr Gutman.'

'A strange piece, if I may say so, sir.'

'Oh, I agree. But compelling.'

'Oh, yes, sir. Very.'

Ralph was so riveted by this interchange that it took him a few seconds to realise that Basil Duke was looking at him.

'Can't make up your mind, eh?'

'What?' said Ralph, embarrassed at being caught eavesdropping.

'I don't blame you,' said Basil Duke. 'I think the three you've chosen are the nicest designs.'

Ralph watched him walk to the door and then, just as he laid his hand on the handle, he swung round.

'Haven't we met?' he asked Ralph suddenly. 'I'm sure I've seen your face somewhere before.' And then his face lit up. 'You were leaning on a skip one Saturday night underneath the notice board.'

Ralph couldn't stop himself from smiling. 'Yes, that's right.'

'Are you in the business?'

'Not yet, sir, but I hope . . .' He heard his voice dwindle.

'Good.' And Basil Duke waved his hands towards the cravats. 'I should choose the . . .' and then he stopped himself. 'No, you must choose it. Cheerio!'

Ralph watched him fly across the alley, the old coat on a hanger.

'Wonderful actor,' said Mr Gutman.

'Yes,' breathed Ralph.

'And now, sir, come to any conclusions?'

Ralph glanced down at the three cravats. The green and brown design would probably suit his complexion better, because of his eyes, and the grey and blue would look smart with a white shirt, but what really aroused his excitement was the midnight blue with the red paisley design. He knew it was loud, but he loved it with a yearning which almost made him sick. He picked it up.

'Would you like to try it on in front of the mirror? All our regulars from the Palace do.' And he gave Ralph a broad smile.

'I think I'd better come clean,' Ralph began.

'You've never tied a cravat before?' the man finished for him.

'No.'

'I should be honoured to be the first to instruct you.' Ralph undid the tie in front of the mirror, his fingers trembling. Slowly he watched himself pull away his schoolboy stripes from underneath the collar of his shirt and he released the top button. As Mr Gutman placed the silky cravat around his neck, Ralph felt he had taken another step towards manhood.

TWELVE

There were two sets for *Almost a Honeymoon*, a lounge and a bedroom in a flat in Mayfair. The play was set in 1930.

Ralph sat cross-legged on some dyed hessian which from a distance looked like a carpet. The flats and curtains for the lounge were up and the chalk marks were down.

The fly-man, stage hands and chief electrician had gone home. The props for *Dangerous Corner* had been sorted out and Ralph was sitting with Isla and Robin, drinking mugs of tea which he had made. Helena was working surreptitiously behind them, replacing the red gels from every third footlight, with pink ones. The amber and blue ones she left alone. 'Isla, are you sure you don't want a hand with the props?' asked Robin. 'You look awfully tired.' Ralph overheard him quietly add, 'Is it an awkward time?' Appalled he should ask such an intimate question Ralph felt his face burn. But Isla didn't seem embarrassed.

'No. And no thanks. We've got Hollis.' And Ralph felt her hand on his shoulder. He was aware that he wanted her to leave it there and felt slightly bereft when she removed it.

When he had arrived wearing his cravat, he had been disappointed that she hadn't said, 'Oh, don't you look handsome' or 'What a lovely cravat'. But by the time he was busy dealing with the props he realised it meant that he didn't look out of place wearing it.

'Hollis.'

He turned towards her slowly as if in a dream. She did look tired, but the tiredness only enhanced the huge ovalness of her eyes.

'Will you help me set the furniture and then help Helena with the props?'

Hearing her name mentioned, Helena joined them. 'It's a very proppy show,' she warned Ralph.

'The proppier the better,' he said airily.

He was hardly aware of time passing with Isla. He wouldn't have minded if they had set up five times if Isla hadn't looked so unhappy. He had tried to make her laugh with the few jokes he knew, but she only smiled out of politeness.

When he had finished helping her they walked down-stage and gazed at the curved tree designs that wound their way up the flats. The flat was a strange mixture of gay 1930s and old-fashioned antiquity. All the furniture appeared Georgian except for the lamp, rug and sofa. It was while he was laying out the bedroom props with Helena in the wings, that he found out the cause of Isla's sadness. 'Hollis, there's still a hell of a lot of furniture to set here in the wings, for the second act.' she whispered. 'Could you help me stack them, only Isla's feeling a bit down.'

'What's wrong with her?' he asked quietly. 'Is she ill?'

'In a manner of speaking. She's love-sick.'

It was as though someone had hit him savagely across the face. For a moment he was too stunned to speak. 'Anyone in particular?' he asked, attempting to hide the tremor in his voice.

'Her fiancé.'

'I didn't know she was engaged,' he said shakily.

'No reason why you should,' said Helena surprised.

'Is he in the cast? Have they had a tiff?'

'No. He hasn't been demobbed yet, and it was in the papers yesterday about the hold-up. Some MPs have been protesting about it.'

'But shouldn't that please her?'

'That's what I told her, but it's only confirmed there are delays.'

'Is he in the business?' he asked nonchalantly, using the new slang.

'No. He wants to be a farmer in the Isle of Wight. That's where his family live. Shush. She's coming.'

'It says two powder bowls, one mirror and one puff should be on the dressing table in the second act. Isn't there a danger of them falling off and breaking during the scene change?' asked Ralph hurriedly.

'Put them in one of the top drawers,' said Helena loudly. 'They can be set after the dressing table's been placed on its marks.'

'How are you getting on?' asked Isla.

'Slowly, but surely,' said Helena cheerfully.

'I suppose you'd better get the bedroom furniture organised. We must make sure it doesn't get in people's way.'

'Ralph and I are going to do that,' said Helena.

'We're going to have two very quick scene changes,' Isla sighed. 'I think the trio will have to have some extra music up their sleeves,' and she gave a laugh, but Ralph saw, to his anguish, that she was trying to put on a brave face, and he felt helpless to console her.

The journey home was a painful blur. He had been aware that he found Isla attractive, but he did not realise how deep his feelings for her were. It was as though someone had taken his heart out, smashed it into pieces and shoved it back in again without putting it back together, so that everything hurt and jangled around inside him. Repeatedly he relived the sensation of her slender fingers lingering on his shoulder. And then he was home and back to creeping up the stairs again. He was in such a daze that it took him a while to realise that there were two heads at the end of his bed and they were both raised.

'Elsie,' he whispered. 'What the hell are you doing up here?'

'Waiting for you,' she said urgently. 'Hurry up and get in bed, we've got loads to tell you.'

'You've missed the biggest row ever,' added Harry.

'I doubt it,' said Ralph wearily. He folded his cravat carefully and put it in his drawer.

'What's that?' said Elsie sharply.

'For someone who's as blind as a bat, you see an awful lot.'

He saw her tiny shoulders shrug. He draped the trench coat over the end of the bed and undressed behind it into his pyjamas.

'You look ever so posh in them,' said Elsie.

'So you keep telling me,' said Ralph with a grunt, and then got into his end of the bed.

Elsie gave a sudden squeal.

'Shush,' said Harry. 'You'll wake everyone up.'

'It's his plates of meat. They're freezin'!'

'Are you really going to stay here all night?' asked Ralph. 'I'm tired. I've been working.'

'You can't go to sleep yet,' squeaked Elsie.

'And, anyway, the night is nearly over,' said Harry.

'So what have I done now?' said Ralph.

'It's not about you,' said Elsie.

'I'll tell him,' said Harry.

'Nah. I want to. You leave bits out.'

'I don't.'

'You do.'

'Could we get this pantomime over with?' said Ralph exasperated. 'Sharing a bed with you two is like sharing a bed with a music hall double act.'

They dived under the covers. Smothered giggles came from underneath. He waited for the covers to stop shaking. In time the two heads emerged again.

'Elsie, you go first,' said Harry.

It was a good job that any light there was, was behind Ralph, because it was all he could do not to laugh. Elsie was like a tiny electrified wire. Even her short hair seemed to take off. Beside her, genial and large, was Harry. Elsie, the brains to his brawn. It was like gazing down at the mutual admiration society.

'So?' Ralph said at last.

'Are you ready?' Elsie asked eagerly.

Ralph groaned.

'It's about Dad,' she said.

'And Mum,' added Harry.

'What about them?'

'Dad took her to the flicks,' said Elsie.

'The matinée at the Odeon,' said Harry.

'*On their own*,' Elsie emphasised.

'They didn't tell no one,' said Harry with espionage in his voice.

'Then how do you know?'

'They didn't let on *before*,' said Elsie exasperated. 'But they did afterwards.'

'Aunty Win was ever so narked,' said Harry.

'And Joan went all quiet.'

I bet, thought Ralph.

'Aunty Win was liver,' explained Harry.

'Livid,' said Elsie.

'She says, "You might've waited".'

'And dad says, "If a man can't take out his own wife without a third degree it's a poor lookout".'

'That shut 'em up.'

'Then it went a bit quiet and Dad says, "Why don't you go tonight, the two of you?"'

'And they went all huffy.'

'I'll treat you,' he says.

'So they did.'

'Joan went out with Aunty Win on a Saturday night?' said Ralph in disbelief.

'Yeah,' breathed Harry. 'Funny, ain't it?'

'And then there was this electricity cut.'

'Mum says the government has to ration it 'cos there ain't enough coal.'

'Are you sure it wasn't something else?'

'Nah. Aunty Win read it out from the papers. To get us prepared, like.'

'Anyway Mum lit a candle and we all played cards.'

'Just the four of us.'

'Dad didn't go to the pub?' Ralph asked, amazed.

'Nah. Uncle Ted came and Dad said he was stayin'. And Uncle Ted thought he was ill.'

'So did I.'

'But he weren't.'

'And it were ever so nice.'

'And Mum was laughin'.'

'And guess what I saw?'

'You didn't.'

'I did. I saw Dad hold her hand under the table.'

'He never.'

'He did so,' said Elsie triumphantly. ''Cos when the lights come up I saw him let go of it and Mum's face was as red as a tomato.'

Ralph was alarmed. The thought of his father touching his mother made him feel uncomfortable. He would have to make sure he was around more often in case she needed his protection.

'Thanks for letting me know,' he said quietly.

'Our pleasure, ain't it, Harry?' There was silence. 'Harry?'

But Harry's head had sunk on to his pillow.

'You best get some sleep too, Elsie.'

'Yeah,' she said yawning.

Ralph watched her settle.

'It were ever so good,' he heard her murmur.

Ralph listened to the steady rhythm of his brother and sister breathing and for some strange reason he suddenly felt very lonely.

'The bit I liked best was when they were both sleeping in the same bedroom but they didn't know it,' said Ralph, wrapping the pink lid of a fluted glass perfume jar. 'I didn't realise how much I needed a good laugh.'

A week had passed; a week of rain, wind and floods. Ralph had spent it dragging driftwood up the lawn from the river, stacking it to dry in a corner of the woodshed, and doing odd jobs round Mrs Egerton-Smythe's house. Although he knew there were law students in the library he never saw them. He arrived before they did and they left early.

At home his father spent more time with the family, which made his mother happier for a while until everyone began to tread on each other's toes in the crowded kitchen and Ralph's mother was caught in the crossfire, which was usually between him and his father. The thought of his Friday visit to the theatre was the only thing which had kept his spirits up. That and the Saturday strike.

'Basil Duke is very good at comedy.'

'They both are,' said Helena.

'Yes, although Geraldine Maclaren is pretty.'

'What's that got to do with it?'

'I always used to imagine that in order for a woman to be amusing she had to appear grotesque.'

'You haven't seen the Lunts.'

'No. They work a lot with Noel Coward, don't they?'

'Yes.'

He sighed. 'There's so much I want to see. Money, that's what I need.'

'Cheer up. You'll have enough for tickets, one day.'

'When I'm old and grey,' he said. 'And by that time, people like John Gielgud, and Laurence Olivier and Noel Coward will be dead.'

'Have patience,' she remarked. 'Has Mr Neville replied to your letter yet?'

'No. Nor my second one.'

'He's been very busy with the play.'

'When he acts in a play, does he produce it too?'

'Not usually. There are two other producers who come in sometimes. Arnold Swann and Geoffrey White. They're actors too. But don't bother writing to them. Mr Neville is the one.'

'I'll drop in another letter this Monday,' Ralph said.

Helena laughed. 'One minute you're as pessimistic as hell, the next ridiculously optimistic.'

'How's Isla?' he said, picking up a pink-backed hairbrush and mirror and turning away so that Helena wouldn't see his face.

'Not too wonderful, I'm afraid. It's been a foul week weatherwise and she's been walking from pillar to post, getting soaked, trying to find props for this next play. It's set in the eighteen hundreds in what was the kitchen of a twelfth-century castle on Lundy. Mr Neville wants a mixture of hundred-year-old props and the odd twelfth-century one. Judith has been doing her best, making some of the early props but . . .'

Ralph didn't hear any more. He glanced at Isla who was walking past him looking desperate.

'Yes, she's still feeling miserable,' Helena commented.

Ralph turned. 'I'll make some tea, shall I?'

'Wonderful!'

Out in the kitchen, rinsing out the dirty mugs, he could hear the rain still falling. He glanced down at his trousers. He was soaked from the knee down. The kettle began steaming. He grabbed a dishrag and poured the water into a enormous teapot. He approached the painters with the tray first. Isla was standing by Judy who was still painting as usual, her hair tucked up into a cap stuck on her head, a cigarette attached to her lip.

Isla was waving her list in an agitated manner. Ralph hung back.

'But I didn't say I definitely could,' said Judy exasperated. 'I told

96

Sam I didn't have the time.'

'Where the hell am I going to find one before Monday?' Isla asked with a catch in her voice.

As Ralph stepped forward with the tray, he saw tears rushing down Isla's cheeks.

'Couldn't they do without it?' said Judy through her cigarette.

'No, Mr Neville has got this bee in his bonnet about having one.'

'Here,' said Ralph quietly passing her a mug.

She took it, not noticing him. 'Everything will be closed tomorrow,' she continued. 'And I won't have any time on Monday.'

'Isn't there an old pub or a museum that might have one?'

'Oh, lord,' said Isla wearily.

Ralph put Judy's mug by her knees. 'Can I help?' he asked hesitantly.

Isla wiped the tears from her face. 'Don't mind me,' she said and she forced herself to smile. 'I'm just a bit tired.'

'I could ask my employer to give me Monday morning off,' he said. 'And do some searching for you.'

'I don't think you'll have any more luck than me,' she said. 'I've looked everywhere.'

'For what?'

'You'll never believe it,' she sniffed. 'A bear. A bloody great stuffed bear.'

Salvation, thought Ralph. 'I can get you a bear,' he said casually.

THIRTEEN

Ralph and Mrs Egerton-Smythe dragged the bear down the last flight of stairs to the hallway. They propped it against a banister and stood for a moment to catch their breath. 'Good job Queenie isn't here,' gasped Ralph. They were trying desperately to keep quiet, not wanting to alert the law students to what was going on. 'We'll have to give the old chap a bit of a dusting down,' said Mrs Egerton-Smythe, gazing up at the mountainous frame of brown fur.

'We could vacuum clean him,' suggested Ralph grinning.

'Splendid idea.'

'I wasn't being serious.'

'I am. I think it's a damn good idea. We'll take him into the garden room. There's a socket in there and it's out of hearing. You'll find the Goblin in the kitchen cupboard.'

'The Goblin!' said Ralph in disbelief.

'The vacuum cleaner. Goblin is its brand name.'

'Goblins and bears,' he spluttered, and he collapsed into a heap on the bottom stair.

'If you want to get this to the theatre on time, you'd better get a move on!'

'Oh, lor,' he said, leaping up, and they grabbed the bear and pulled it across the hall floor.

After they had vacuum cleaned it they paused to stare at the rain which was pounding noisily on the veranda roof. 'My father's oilskin raincoat, and his trilby. He'll have to wear them.'

'Who?'

'The bear, you fool.'

'But I can't carry him in a trilby and raincoat!' said Ralph aghast.

'Got any other suggestions? He'll get soaked otherwise. You can hardly carry him and an umbrella, or are you hoping he might hold one in his paws?'

'I see your point. Oh, hell! What if the students look out of the window, they'll see his head sticking out above the hedge.'

'I'll go in there and deal with the fire,' she said. 'That'll keep their eyes fixed down into their books.'

The only way he could carry the bear, which was a head taller than himself, was to throw his arms around the waist, haul himself upwards so that the bear's hind paws hovered somewhere above his ankles, and shuffle. He struggled out of the kitchen door into the driving rain and waited. Mrs Egerton-Smythe had loaned him a sou'wester. With the trench coat he now felt like a cross between a deep-sea fisherman and his brother and sister's hero. He counted slowly to twenty, reckoning that by then Mrs Egerton-Smythe would be safely sticking a poker into the library fire, and began to manoeuvre himself towards the hedgerow.

Everything was quiet as he walked down the long avenue. Not that he would have seen anything beyond his brunoesque friend. It wasn't until he turned into the street that led to the High Street that he was conscious of the distant murmur of voices. He propped the bear on to his feet and rested his dripping forehead against the back of the bear's raincoat. He had just clasped the bear's waist again when he noticed someone staring out of a window at him. He heaved the bear upwards and staggered round the corner. A strong gust of wind sent him reeling. He gripped the bear more firmly and moved nearer the shops for shelter.

He was aware of the sounding of car horns, but he didn't think it was anything to do with him, until he reached the High Street. He stopped at the next corner, rested the bear again on his feet and peered round. Blinded by both rain and the bear it wasn't an easy journey.

'Oi!' yelled a man from a car window. 'The picnic's that way! Just bear right.'

'Ralph smiled politely, wrapped his arms round the bear and lifted him up. He didn't have to worry about people getting out of his way. They could see him coming for miles, though there were two women who had been chatting with such absorption they didn't notice him until he was almost on top of them. They gave such a shriek that Ralph nearly fell over. He apologised profusely but the two women were laughing so hysterically they didn't hear him.

'There's someone holding him,' said one of them.

'Well, of course there is, Doris. You didn't think it was moving of its own accord.' And they stared at him as Ralph struggled past them.

Progress was grindingly slow and not helped by a host of amateur comedians. Aside from the horns, he had to put up with endless puns about bears. Each time he stopped for a rest, some joker would inevitably yell out, 'taking a paws for breath, eh,' or 'Just a little more forbearance needed, sonny,' and endless 'Bear lefts' and 'Bear rights'. He hoped to pass the shop where Joan worked, unseen, but he saw her head framed in the window, first smiling and then looking shocked when she realised who was causing the disturbance. Ralph shuffled faster, mentally patting himself on the back at every side road that he passed. The ringing of bicycle bells and car hooters persisted and Ralph's face ached from forcing himself to smile.

'Hold it!' said a voice.

'Not another pun,' muttered Ralph wearily.

'You moved. Hold still,' said the voice.

Ralph peered round the side of the bear to look at the new joker and was immediately greeted by a flash of light. He blinked and saw a man in an old raincoat with a camera. 'I'm from the *Winford Observer*,' the man said, cheerily. 'Can you give us another one?'

'Yes, of course,' said Ralph.

'Turn the front of your sou'wester up so we can see your face.'

Ralph hung on to the bear by the belt of the raincoat, leaned it against him and with his free hand, attempted to fold the rim back.

'Splendid,' said the man, and there was another flash from his camera. By now, a small crowd had gathered round. The man took a tatty notebook from his pocket.

'So where are you taking your furry friend?'

Ralph beamed. He suddenly realised that this was an extraordinary piece of luck. Publicity for the Palace. 'The Palace Theatre,' he said eagerly. 'They're opening a new play tonight. It's called . . .'

'*Goldilocks*!' yelled one of the crowd.

'And he's playing the romantic lead,' said another.

'*French without Bears*,' said a woman.

'*Almost a Honeyjar*,' yelled another female voice.

'Who does he play?' asked the reporter.

'No one,' said Ralph attempting not to lose his temper.

'What, no lines?' said the first heckler.

At that the crowd gave a sympathetic 'Ahhh!'

'Please, sir,' said the reporter, raising his hand. 'Let the lad speak.'

'It's set in the last century in a farmhouse kitchen which was a twelfth-century castle, on an island in Scotland. The bear is part of the scenery. It's a thrilling play!' he emphasised.

'A comedy thriller, eh?'

'No. It's very dramatic.'

'And the name of the play, sonny?'

'*Granite*,' he said loudly. 'You mustn't miss it.'

The man scribbled something down. 'And your name?'

'Hollis, Ralph Hollis.'

'Thanks, sonny,' and he gave a wave and walked away.

Ralph was about to lift up the bear again when he suddenly remembered something. 'Sir!' he yelled. '*Winford Observer* man! Will it be in by *this* Friday? If it isn't it will be old news.'

'If we get a decent photo, yeah.'

Exhausted he staggered on through the High Street, and the rain continued to pelt down. Gradually he grew immune to 'What, no spats?' 'Detective Inspector Pooh, I presume' and the odd joker asking the bear for a light. When he arrived at the corner of the street which led to the stage door of the theatre, he let himself enjoy a last rest of bear on feet. He could hear the roar of the river at the end of the street and could see waves crashing over the banks.

'Not long now!' he gasped, and he hoicked up the bear and stumbled across the road.

Luckily the stage door was propped open. He squeezed the bear through, staggered towards the notice-board and leant the bear against it.

'You look done in,' said Wilfred. 'Wait there.'

Ralph gave another nod. He closed his eyes and listened to the sound of Wilfred's boots clumping up the steps. He wondered if he would ever feel dry again. For the last fortnight he seemed to have spent every day being drenched or damp. He hoped he wasn't beginning to smell of mildew. He heard light footsteps coming at great speed down the stairs. He opened his eyes and stood upright. Isla's face appeared around the bear.

'Oh, Hollis,' she yelled. 'He's wonderful! He's just perfect! Oh, thank you!' And to Ralph's amazement she flung her arms round him and kissed him on the cheek. 'You're a real treasure,' and she laughed. 'This will cheer up old mothballs up there. Mind you, knowing him, he'll tick the bear off for being late,' and she giggled slightly hysterically from relief. She stood back and gazed at the bear. 'This does come off?' she said, tugging at the raincoat.

'Oh yes,' said Ralph reassuringly. 'It's only on because of the rain.'

'You clever thing.'

'Well . . .' he began, but instead of telling her that it was Mrs Egerton-Smythe's idea, he fell silent. Anything to keep her beaming at him.

'He'll still be wet in places,' he said, 'especially his face.'

'Helena and I will rub him down with a towel.'

They undid the raincoat and removed the trilby.

'Looks like you've got the wrong hats on by mistake.'

'I know,' said Ralph, untying the sou'wester, 'but if I'd worn the trilby it would have fallen off in no time.'

She tousled his hair and he loved it. He wanted to catch hold of her hand and keep it just where it was, but instead he just smiled and smiled and smiled.

Ralph took the bear's head and backed up the stairs, and Isla took hold of his feet.

'Are the actors on stage?' asked Ralph in the corridor, noticing that dressing rooms one and two were lit.

'No! the dressing rooms are being cleaned out and Florrie will be hanging all the costumes up and checking they don't need mending.'

'Won't the cast know that already?' said Ralph puzzled.

'No, the costumes only arrived today. They're hired because it's a period piece. That's why the cast love doing old plays. Anything

101

from the 1920s means they have to race around getting clothes themselves.'

'But what if they don't have enough money to get them?' asked Ralph astounded.

'They beg, borrow, or just try to draw on their own wardrobe.'

'But what if they don't have a wardrobe?'

'Oh, you must. It's in your contract,' she said. 'Of course, you wouldn't know. Look, let's get the bear into the scene dock and I'll explain.'

Within minutes of being with Isla, Ralph had swung from ecstasy to despair and he didn't know which was more painful. It seemed as though every entrance into the theatre was barred to him for one reason alone. Not talent, not experience, not training, but money.

Without money he knew he couldn't go to drama school. Even if he worked hard towards a scholarship it would probably only pay his fees. Or there was the equivalent of an 'apprenticeship'. The theatre would employ an ASM who would slowly learn the ropes, going from general dogsbody to the odd line in a play and upwards. But one of these 'apprenticeships' was usually funded by a sympathetic father who would give the theatre a hundred pounds. From this the theatre would pay the ASM two pounds per week for the year. If that wasn't bad enough, it appeared that even if by some miracle he did manage to get into the theatre, he would also have to provide a wardrobe for himself, make-up, and photos.

He walked back from the theatre to Mrs Egerton-Smythe's in a daze, the sou'wester tucked in his pocket. As soon as he arrived, she looked at him sympathetically and declared, 'You need a tonic. Go and tinker with the Alvis.'

And it had helped. Temporarily. That is until he passed the theatre. At least depression had made the ride home pass quickly. He was hardly aware of the journey at all.

FOURTEEN

Dear Mr Hollis,

Thank you for your three letters making absolutely sure I know you are local and willing should there be a suitable part for you.

I am, of course, delighted you wish to join our company, but one of the reasons why we retain such a high standard is that we only employ actors and actresses who have been to drama school and/or who have had professional experience.

If you are still eager to join the profession, I suggest you apply for auditions at London drama schools and contact me for an audition after your training.

Ralph folded the letter and stuck it in the trench coat pocket, feeling sick.

When he arrived at Mrs Egerton-Smythe's he stood for a moment to gaze at the vast garden before him. 'No floods, no gales, no fog,' he said.

He changed into the large socks and wellies and walked down the river to see if there were any other bits of driftwood he could pick up before beginning the gargantuan task of weeding.

That night he arrived home later than usual. His father's bike was already in the yard. With relief he realised that at least he wasn't wearing the trench coat. He washed his hands in the scullery and opened the door into the kitchen. To his surprise everyone was already eating supper.

'Sorry, Mum,' he said. 'I didn't realise it was that late.'

'This isn't a hotel,' said his father curtly.

Ralph decided to say nothing. Elsie moved over to Harry's chair leaving one free for him.

'Thanks, Elsie,' he murmured, lowering his aching limbs into it.

'Like to tell us where you've been?' asked his dad.

'Mrs Egerton-Smythe's.'

'All this time?'

'Have to make the best of the good weather. Couldn't do much last week, but she still gave me a full wage. I want to make it up to her.'

'Oh, you've a conscience. You do surprise me.'

Ralph gave a weary sigh and shoved a spud quickly into his mouth. He was weak with hunger and if he could stave off a row until after he had eaten, he might manage to finish it before being sent from the room.

'I noticed you got a letter this morning,' said his mother cheerily. 'Was it from the rector?'

Before Ralph could lie, Joan blurted out, 'It had a Winford stamp on it.' Ralph took a mouthful of stew. It stuck in his throat for a moment.

'Why would he have a letter from Winford?' asked his aunt.

'That's what I thought,' said Joan. 'Perhaps someone saw – '

Ralph gave her a warning look. Joan reddened. There was silence.

'Ain't you goin' to tell us, then?' said his aunt. Ralph scooped another forkful of food when suddenly the plate was whisked away from him. His father had removed it.

'Answer your aunt when she speaks to you. Or didn't they teach you any manners at that rectory?'

'It's not important,' said Ralph.

'Perhaps you'd like to show us the letter so we can make up our own minds.'

'I haven't got it any more.' It was true. He had left it in the trench coat.

'So what was in it?'

'Nothing.'

'Don't lie.'

'All right,' said Ralph angrily. 'If you must know, I've been trying to get an interview for a job, but they don't want to know.'

'Over-qualified?' he asked sarcastically.

'Under-qualified.'

'What's it for? Brain surgery?'

'It doesn't matter, does it,' Ralph answered miserably. 'They won't see me, so stop being so bloody sadistic.'

'Don't you use language like that in this house. And in front of women. I'll have no swearing in this house.'

'God, I hate you.'

To Ralph's amazement his father looked genuinely shocked. He stared at Ralph as though winded.

'Ralphie,' said his mother, 'that's a terrible thing to say to your dad.'

'Why? Everyone knows he hates me. But that's acceptable, I suppose.'

There was a dreadful, dreadful silence. No one moved.

Ralph felt awkward and miserable, but he had no intention of apologising. 'Never wanted me back,' he mumbled incoherently.

'I fought to get you back,' his father said quietly.

'Ralph,' began his mother, 'you've upset your dad.'

His father gave her a dismissive wave. 'Now you know why I don't want Elsie at that hoity-toity grammar. One day she'll be saying the same thing to me.'

Ralph stared at the table. His father pushed Ralph's plate towards him. He took a fork to the food, but didn't have the heart to lift it to his mouth. He heard the sounds of his family eating, but in spite of his hunger he couldn't swallow another mouthful.

'I thought you might be wanting this back,' said Mrs Egerton-Smythe, handing him the letter. 'I hope you'll forgive me but I had to open it to find out what it was.'

'Thanks,' said Ralph quietly.

'It's not no.'

'Isn't it?'

'They have scholarships at drama schools, don't they?'

'Yes.'

'There you are. You'll be seeing the friend you delivered the bear to. Ask her what she did to get accepted.'

'Her father's famous. She's grown up in the theatre.'

'Oh.'

'There's Helena,' he said suddenly. 'I could ask her.'

'I'm sure this other girl had to audition too, in spite of her father.'

'Audition. I'll need to work on some speeches.'

'Some light at the end of the tunnel, Hollis?'

'Yes.' And he smiled. 'Thank you, madam.'

For the rest of the day and for the rest of the week he weeded with a rapidity he wouldn't have thought himself capable of. His back and legs continued to ache and his fingers were permanently stained. He was racing against the gusts of fog that had begun drifting over the garden and occasional bouts of frost. By the end of the week, the hard physical labour had helped work out a lot of his anger and misery.

He and his father hardly talked now. Aunty Win still scoured the newspaper for any bits of gossip from the outside world, meaning Winford and the surrounding area and the vaster regions of Kent, and his father still went out with Uncle Ted but, Ralph noted, not so often. Often he would sit by the range hacking bits out of a piece of wood with a knife, something he apparently used to do when he was in the army. Elsie still managed to do her homework secretly and Harry continued to hang on to his father's every word.

When Friday morning came, Ralph could hardly contain his excitement. Isla was playing the part of a fifteen-year-old servant girl in *Granite* and he would be seeing her perform that night.

A low fog hung over the street so that he had to ride with his dynamo on and keep ringing the bell. He skidded several times. Frost on the roads had made them slippery. The air hung damp and heavy about him. He knew he would be spending all day in it, weeding, but the prospect of Isla and a play that night filled him with renewed energy. He ran through the crisp frost-bitten grass to the shed. He had just changed into his overalls when there was a knock on the door. It was Mrs Egerton-Smythe with a newspaper. She held it out to him.

'I think you should look at the front page,' she said.

He unfolded it. Under the headline 'BEAR WITH ME!' was a photo of Ralph holding a bear. He glanced up at her. 'Read it,' she said.

"Bear with Me. That was the cry of Mr Ralph Hollis as he struggled through shoppers and storm winds and rain to deliver his companion to the Palace Theatre for their new play, *Granite*. 'A good night's entertainment. A comedy thriller,' he said."

'I never,' Ralph protested. "You mustn't miss it," he continued. 'Well, at least that bit's true and they'll have some publicity. Do you think the producer will be pleased?'

'He might,' said Mrs Egerton-Smythe, 'but certain members of my family might not see it in that light.'

With horror, Ralph remembered the conversation he had overheard in the cupboard.

'It might be a good idea if we keep this from Queenie.

'She's bound to want to see the paper,' said Ralph. 'She looks at the job section every Friday.'

'Really? Oh dear.'

'Wait a minute,' said Ralph. 'Has she ever seen the bear?'

'No.'

'So if she sees the photo, she might not connect the bear to here?'

'No, but she knows you, and if she happens to mention to a certain person that the gardener's boy has been seen behaving in a manner not fitting for an employee of the Egerton-Smythe residence, and he sees the photo of the bear — '

'He'll put two and two together and I might get the sack.'

'It's a possibility. How soon can you get it back for me?'

'Dawn on Sunday morning?'

'Better not risk it. You might bump into churchgoers.'

'I could stick a collar on it backwards.'

'Thank you, Hollis, I think not.' She sighed. 'We'll just have to play it by ear.'

'So this might be my last week?'

'I doubt it. It's very difficult to find help nowadays. Cheer up. You do take quite a good photo.'

Ralph gave her a sardonic look. 'Ralph?' she said. 'Nice name,' and she disappeared into the fog.

Ralph stared at the newspaper, rereading and rereading it. 'The front page,' he murmured. It must do the Palace some good. He wondered if Isla would see it.

He tore out the piece and stuffed it in his jacket pocket. He then threw the paper on to the floor and crumpled the rest of the front page with his foot. Hopefully Queenie would just think it had been damaged by the delivery boy.

The pea-souper had enveloped everything in its yellowy green fug. He groped his way towards the kitchen and knocked at the door. Through the window he saw Queenie coming towards him. She flung open the door.

'Yes?' she said.

'Thought you might be looking for this,' he said, waving the paper.

'What you doing with it?' she asked suspiciously.

'I found it in one of the flower-beds. I'm afraid it's taken a bit of a bashing. Half the front page is missing.'

'Don't suppose there was much interesting on it,' and she snatched it. 'Ta.'

'I suppose there's no chance of a cuppa, is there?'

'You're not tramping over my kitchen. I'm making the Christmas pudding and cake today.'

'I can take it with me.'

'You ain't working in this?'

'I'll chop wood,' he said, 'till it clears.'

She drew in her mouth again. 'I'll see what I can do.'

'Thanks.'

'I didn't say I would.'

'I'll be in the woodshed.'

Ralph couldn't wait till the second show. He was too excited. He bought his ticket at the box-office and sprinted up to the gallery. To his surprise he found there were already people seated. Usually he was one of the first to arrive. More men, too, he noted. He turned his head aside and seated himself with his programme, keeping his head down in case anyone recognised him. He had never heard so many people cramming into the gallery, and he could only conclude it was because of the publicity with the bear.

The Billy Dixon Trio appeared in the pit in their tuxedos and soon dramatic sea music battled with the chatter in the auditorium. The lights dimmed, the music changed to a haunting Scottish air, poignant and sad. The curtain rose exposing a vaulted room with stone walls; a twelfth-century castle kitchen. It was an incongruous mixture of two centuries, with curtains on the spyhole windows, overlooking the sea, prints on the walls, and Windsor chairs. A young man and young woman dressed in early nineteenth-century clothes were seated at a table downstage right staring at each other. Also seated, in an inglenook, was a stoutish man. He was elderly, his face expressionless.

To Ralph's surprise there was rapturous applause from the gallery. They must be pleased to see a certain member of the cast back, he thought. At that moment, Isla entered in a long dress, carrying two candlesticks. Ralph watched mesmerised as she set them down on the stool by the fireplace.

For some inexplicable reason, everyone about him was laughing. They were obviously seeing something in Isla's performance that he was missing.

He watched her drift shyly over to the dresser, stage right, pick up the lighted candle there, and make her way to the stairs, past a row of hooks with oilskins, and coils of rope hanging from it, and the six-foot bear which now took pride of place at the foot of them. She had hardly taken one step when a comic from the gallery yelled, 'What, no cuddle?'

This was greeted by an 'Ahhh!' from his mates, and 'He's behind you!' Isla carried on up the steps to raucous laughter, and then she was out of sight. Ralph was even more perplexed.

The elderly stout man lit the two candles, watching the young man and young woman as he did so, and then suddenly said, 'Bed!'

'Who's going to carry Teddy!' yelled one prankster, two rows behind Ralph.

'Go on,' said Geraldine Maclaren.

'That's about all,' the young man replied shyly.

'Tell me another story!' she insisted.

'*Goldilocks and the Three Bears*,' shouted the same man.

'One bear,' added someone else.

Horrified, Ralph realised that the source of their mirth had not been Isla's performance but the massive hairy creature at the foot of the stairs, and he, Ralph Hollis, had been the cause of it. He was about to turn round and tell them to keep quiet when he realised that he might be recognised. He groaned inwardly. He was even thinking in bear puns now.

The actors ignored the comments and continued to play the scene but unfortunately, having got into the wrong frame of mind, the audience were finding bear *double entendres* everywhere. Ralph buried his head in his hands in anguish.

It was nearly dawn when he reached his street. Exhausted, he wheeled his bike into the yard. Being Friday he had no key, but he decided to try the front door, just in case his mother had slipped down to unlock it in the night. And it was unlocked. It felt like the only good thing to have happened to him all day. And then he remembered it was another day.

Once in his bedroom he peeled off his damp clothes and, as usual, spread them out at the end of the bed, in the vain hope that some miracle draught would dry them. He fumbled under his pillow, but his pyjamas had disappeared.

'I've got them,' whispered an urgent voice at the end of the bed.

Ralph dived behind the bed to cover himself.

'Elsie! You've got your own room.'

'Yeah, I know but . . .'

'Let Joan keep you warm.'

'Harry don't snore.'

He sighed. 'Are you wearing my pyjamas?'

She giggled. 'Course I ain't. I just thought I'd warm 'em for you.'

'Oh,' said Ralph surprised. 'Thanks!'

He watched the lump moving at the end.

'Harry!' Elsie demanded. 'Move over. He's lying on them,' she explained. 'Harry.'

Ralph heard a grunt, and after a firm yank, the striped articles came flying across the room to where Ralph caught them. Shivering, Ralph pulled them on rapidly. 'They feel wonderful, Elsie,' he said and he climbed into bed.

Elsie gave a shriek.

'Sorry,' said Ralph, moving his cold feet to one side.

He was just settling down when he heard a lot of hissing. 'Oh, Elsie, what now?'

'Ain't you gonna tell us, then?'

'Tell you what?'

'About you being a star.'

Ralph raised his head. 'What are you talking about?'

'You! On the front page of the paper.'

He had completely forgotten that his Aunty Win bought the *Winford Observer* every Friday after work.

'Did Mum see it?'

'Yeah. She's ever so chuffed. Uncle Ted's been round. He thinks that Dad's been keeping it a secret.'

'Oh, no! Damn!'

'We had people popping in all last night. It were ever so exciting. Aunty Win says we've never had anyone famous in the family.'

'What did Dad say?'

'Not much. He couldn't get a word in anyway.'

'How am I going to explain?. He doesn't know about the strikes, does he?'

'What strikes?' Elsie asked innocently.

'Elsie, you're the best eavesdropper I know. The Saturday strikes.'

'Oh,' she said nonchalantly. 'You mean when you nip out after Dad's gone to the pub and nip back after he's asleep. No.'

Mind you, thought Ralph, if his father did stop him going, that would be wonderful, he wouldn't have to face Isla. His feet began to tingle. Circulation was returning.

'How does it feel?' Elsie asked urgently. 'Did people ask you for your autograph?'

'No.' And he smiled.

'Joan has been quite nice about you,' she said surprised. 'I think she thinks it's like living with Errol Flynn.'

'Elsie, I hardly think Errol Flynn would stumble down Winford High Street wearing a sou'wester and carrying a bear.'

'Don't bear thinking about, do it.' she giggled.

'Elsie!'

'Yeah.'

'Promise me something.'

'What?'

'No bear puns. I've had a bellyful of them tonight.'

'What's a pun?'

'A sort of word joke.'

'I'll *bear* it in mind,' she said, putting on a posh accent.

'Elsie!'

'All right! All right!'

There was a creak on the landing. They fell silent. The door opened. 'Ralphie!' It was his mother. She moved to his end of the bed. 'Ralphie.'

'Yes,' he whispered. 'Sorry I didn't phone Uncle Ted, I couldn't find a telephone box.'

'That's all right, love.'

'Thanks for leaving the door open.'

'There's a lovely photo of you in the *Winford Observer*. Ever so funny. Have you seen it?'

'Yes.'

'And that headline, "BEAR WITH ME!" I expect you could hardly *bear* to read it,' she said.

The bed began to shake and sounds of smothered giggling came from under the covers.

'Elsie! Is that you?'

There was silence for a fraction of a second and then the giggling began again. 'She's fleeing from Joan's nose,' said Ralph.

'Oh, really,' she said. 'Her snoring can't be that bad.'

'It is,' Ralph stated. 'In fact when I got lost, I kept listening out for it to guide me home by.'

'Ralph, that's not kind.'

'But true,' came a muffled voice.

His mother gave a sigh. 'Elsie, go to sleep.'

'Yes, Mum.'

'Now, look, Ralphie, your father couldn't go to the pub, the fog was that bad, so he knows you ain't had much sleep. It was his idea to leave the front door open.'

'*His* idea!' said Ralph astounded.

'So he won't mind you sleepin' in.'

'Thanks, Mum.'

He watched her tiptoe to the other end of the bed and pull down the covers. 'Elsie, I want a word with you later.' There was silence. 'And don't kid me you're asleep. I can see you smiling.'

Ralph laid back and closed his eyes. As he drifted into sleep he could hear the sounds of the hecklers in the gallery ringing in his ears. If only he could grow a beard.

FIFTEEN

His clothes were still damp. He pulled a pullover over his pyjamas, bundled them in his arms and hopped barefoot over the freezing floorboards.

The kitchen had all the appearance of the *Marie Celeste*. There was no one there. He suddenly realised that he had never experienced being alone in the house. Even when people were out, his mother was always around in the kitchen or scullery, or hanging washing in the yard if the weather was fine. But there was no sign or sound of her. He assumed she had gone shopping, but when he looked on the shelf above the wireless the family's ration books were still piled there.

A neat pile of new newspapers was stacked at the end of the table. He recognised the top one immediately. The *Winford Observer*. Last night's. With a familiar photograph and that familiar headline. Amazed, he sat down at the table and went through them. There were about a dozen of them. His aunt must have bought every copy in Winford. He noticed the kettle on the range. The lid had begun to rattle. He was about to hunt for the cloth his mother used for lifting the kettle off the range when he heard a creak on the upstairs landing and his mother's foot on the stairs. For once he would have a chance to have an uninterrupted chat with her and pour out the ghastly side of the newspaper business. He was holding the empty teapot in his hand and smiling when the door swung open. But it wasn't his mother. It was his dad.

Without being able to stop himself he knew he must look disappointed but instead of his father looking angry, he reddened. 'Beaten me to it,' he mumbled, staring at the kettle.

Steam began billowing all around Ralph. He turned quickly.

'Don't touch it!' said his father abruptly and walked swiftly across the room, grabbed the cloth and picked up the kettle. Astonished Ralph watched him make a pot of tea. His father caught his eye.

'I done my share of tea making in the army,' he stated.

'Where's Mum?' Ralph asked.

'She's upstairs,' his father answered evasively. 'I thought I'd make her tea.'

'Is she ill?'

'No. Just thought she could do with a lie-in.'

Ralph was puzzled. He'd never known his mother have a lie-in. 'Shall I take her tea up to her?'

'She'll be down in a minute.' There was a creak on the stair. 'That'll be 'er now.' He picked up a couple of mugs. 'Want one?'

'Yes,' he said, still self-conscious. 'Thanks.'

The door opened and his mother stood in the doorway. She looked different. Flushed. Younger. Softer. In her hands, bundled up, was a summer dress. It was awash with pink and pale blue flowers. Her hair was tousled and she gave a shy smile.

'I'm glad you managed to have a lie-in,' said Ralph.

'Oh?' said his mother growing bright red and she caught his father's eye. 'Yes. I needed it,' she said quickly. She caught sight of the teapot and mugs, and went to pour.

'No, love,' Ralph's father said quickly. 'You sit down.'

She hesitated and then pulled up a chair. 'I feel like a queen,' she laughed.

Ralph stared at his father. It was then that he realised that he looked younger too. Almost callow. They both looked embarrassed about something. And then he guessed. The *Winford Observer*!

'I suppose you've seen it then,' he commented awkwardly to his father.

They both stared at him. He glanced at the pile of newspapers. 'Yes, it is a bit embarrassing,' he admitted. 'I never thought it would get on the front page.'

'You was doing an errand for Mrs Egerton-Smythe, weren't you?' said his mother.

'Yes.' It was near enough the truth.

'I'll just go and put this in to soak,' she said, and she rose and left the room.

Ralph and his father were left facing each other at the table while sounds of running water and swishing sounds emanated from the scullery. His mother reappeared. 'I might as well use the hot water,' she said, picking up the kettle and disappearing back in the scullery.

'She can't sit down for a moment, your mother,' said his father.

There was an uncomfortable silence. 'Look, Dad,' Ralph began hesitantly. 'I'm sorry about the other night. I never meant . . .'

'All forgotten, lad,' his father mumbled into his mug. 'Gets a bit crowded here. Tempers get short. You know how it is?'

'Yes,' said Ralph, awestruck at this sudden change in his father.

'Heavy, was it? The bear?' he asked politely.

'Very. I couldn't see where I was going either.'

'Your tea's getting cold, Ellen,' shouted his father.

'I'll be back in a minute,' she shouted back. 'I might as well do this now before Elsie and Harry get back.'

Ralph grabbed his mother's tea. It was a bit unnerving not having his father scowling at him. 'I'll take it to her,' he said hurriedly.

His mother was squeezing the dress out.

'It's pretty,' said Ralph putting the tea on the wooden draining board. 'I haven't seen it before.'

'Not much cause to wear it,' she said, and she turned sharply away and took a gulp of tea. ' Ta, love.'

She fed the dress through the mangle and turned the handle.

'Won't it be too cold to wear?' Ralph asked.

He noticed she turned away to drink her tea again.

'I really needed that,' she said, smiling awkwardly.

He followed her back into the kitchen. His parents glanced at one another and gave a little smile and it went quiet again. As his mother draped the summery dress on the clothes-horse in front of the range there was another silence.

'Look,' said Ralph at last. 'It hasn't gone to my head if that's what you're thinking. It's only the *Winford Observer*. I'll be forgotten next week.'

His mother turned. 'We won't forget, love. We've never had anyone been in a paper and on the front page.'

'Joanie is going to send a copy to Kay,' said his father suddenly.

And Ralph laughed. And it was so extraordinary that his father had made him laugh. And his mother laughed, and then his father was laughing too. And he had forgotten what they were laughing at after a while. It was like a safety valve for the past few months. When they had recovered they talked easily, the awkward silences gone. And for a fraction of a second he felt part of the family.

'What are you going to do with yourself today?' his mother asked eventually.

'I think I ought to go into Winford.'

'See if people recognise you?'

'Sort of,' he lied. 'Get it over with before Monday.'

'What's happening on Monday?'

'I have to take the bear back.'

That wasn't the real reason he was going into Winford, of course. He decided he had to see Isla as soon as possible to apologise for being the cause of the previous evening's nightmare performance. He parked his bike in the usual spot, changed into his shoes and cravat, smoothed back his hair and headed for the stage door. Wilfred was reading the *Winford Observer*. He looked up smiling and then his face fell. 'Your face is mud, sonny boy,' he commented. He held out the paper and indicated the front page.

'I know, I've seen it,' Ralph mumbled.

'People 'ere ain't too pleased at your comments.'

'But I didn't say that!' Ralph protested. 'He just wrote what he wanted to write. I suppose he didn't believe me. He just didn't think a bear would be in a serious play.'

'Especially when they're wearing an oilskin raincoat and trilby,' Wilfred added.

'I had to keep him dry!'

'I know that. Isla knows that, but . . .'

'Isla!' said Ralph reddening. 'Then she's not angry with me?'

'I'm afraid she is. She don't take kindly to publicity hunters.'

'But I didn't do it on purpose. He took my photo before I knew what was happening.'

'If you'd told her she could have asked the theatre to ring up the *Observer* and put a stop to it. Why didn't you tell her? Was it supposed to be a surprise?'

'No. I was so relieved to have got here with the bear it slipped my mind.'

'That's not how she sees it.'

'I've got to explain.'

114

'Not now, sonny. It's Saturday.'

'I know it's Saturday. What's that got to do with it? Please, I must see her.'

'Saturday,' repeated Wilfred, as if speaking to someone with a mental problem. 'They're running *Sweet Aloes* now, ready for Monday night's opening. Then the cast who's in *Granite* are given their cuts so's they can fit three shows in today. They don't leave this theatre until curtain-down.'

'But they must break for tea.'

'No. Isla usually goes out and gets food for them.'

'I could see her then.'

'She's in *Granite*. I doubt they'll let her go. It'll be Robin.'

'This is terrible.'

'You could say that. Mr Neville's none too happy either. So I should keep clear of this building if I was you.'

'I've got to face the music,' he stated dramatically. 'Some time.'

'Not today. Look, you'll be helping with the strike tonight, won't you?'

'Do you think they'll let me?'

'Dunno. But apologise, or give your explanation then, why don't you? Saturday ain't a good day. After a week of twice nightly, Saturday just about flattens everyone.'

'Could you tell her I was here?'

'No. I don't want to upset her with three shows ahead of her.'

'No. Of course not,' Ralph said quickly.

'I'll see you tonight then,' said Wilfred.

Ralph nodded miserably. He was about to leave when he noticed several large wicker baskets with labels hanging from them. 'New lot arriving from the North,' Wilfred explained. 'They're early. The rest are coming on Monday. Panto rehearsals begin next week. That's going to raise a few sparks. Legit and variety working together.'

'Is it?' said Ralph puzzled. 'Why?'

'Ask Isla later. Right now I think you ought to scarper.'

'Yes, of course,' he murmured.

'Cheer up. It ain't the end of the world.'

'Yes, it is,' he remarked mournfully, and he thrust his hands into his pockets and stuck his fingers through the holes in the lining.

He stood outside the stage door feeling suicidal. He needed to do something which would cheer him up, and then he remembered Mr Gutman.

Through the second-hand clothes shop window, he could see that Mr Gutman was alone. He had his glasses on and was sitting on a stool at the counter sewing a button on to a jacket. Ralph stepped in nervously. Mr Gutman peered over his glasses, and then he beamed. 'Beautiful, sir,' he said.

At first Ralph was entirely flummoxed until he realised Mr Gutman was commenting on the way he had tied his cravat. The compliment was like a heady draught of warmth. Much needed.

'Now, sir. What can I do for you this time?'

'Could I just look? I don't have any money today, but I'd like to get some idea for when I do.'

'Perhaps I can help?'

'Evening dress,' he began, 'a dinner jacket, morning dress . . .' He paused. 'There's more but I can't remember. It's what I'd need if I was given a contract. I can dream, can't I?'

Mr Gutman gave an amused smile. 'It's a good start.'

'So you'd let me look, even though I haven't any money at the moment.'

'Actors never have any money.'

Ralph smiled at the reference.

'Might I suggest something first though, sir?'

'Yes, of course. I need all the advice I can get.'

'Then allow me to take your measurements.'

As Mr Gutman approached him with the tape measure, Ralph could already feel his spirits lifting.

'Broad shoulders, trim waist. Ah, youth!' Mr Gutman sighed.

He was wheeling his bike back from the river when he spotted Helena leaving the stage door. 'Helena!' he yelled. 'Helena!'

She turned, surprised, and then put her hands on her hips. 'Oh, no!'

'My name is mud,' he finished for her. 'Listen, you must tell Isla I didn't say what he said I said.'

'Honestly?'

'Cross my heart and hope to die.'

'And you weren't seeking publicity for yourself?'

'No. The only thing I was thinking of was getting the bear to the theatre in one piece. The weather was foul, remember?'

'But why didn't you tell us?'

'I forgot. That's how little it meant to me. There was a moment when he was photographing me when I actually thought it might help bring extra people in.'

'It did,' said Helena. 'But they were expecting something more in the variety line, not legit.'

'That's the second time I've heard that today. What does it mean?'

'I'll tell you tonight. I must get some food for the cast.'

'Yes, of course. Oh,' he said suddenly, 'so you think it will be all right for me to come to the strike tonight?'

'We need you. The prop list is a mile long and there are two sets.'

She was about to go when he took hold of her arm. 'Will you explain to Isla?'

'If I find the right moment, yes.'

'Thanks.'

It was evening when he wheeled his bike into the yard. Through the lighted window he saw his aunt and Joan looking slightly dazed. It was such an unusual sight that Ralph stood for a moment and stared at them. Then, curious, he walked briskly into the scullery.

'What's the problem?' he heard his father say. 'You said you wanted to stay in this evening.'

'I expected to have my sister's company,' he heard his aunt protest.

'I'd like her company too,' remarked his father.

Ralph was riveted. He wished he could eavesdrop longer, but he knew he must have been heard coming into the scullery. He opened the door. 'Hello!' he said casually.

He made little impact.

'But you're not really going to go,' Joan stammered, white-faced, 'are you? It's a joke, ain't it?'

'No,' Ralph's father said. He was sitting on a chair whittling away at his piece of wood. His mother was standing with her back to everyone and stirring something in a saucepan. She was looking embarrassed. Her hair was in curlers and bundled up into a headscarf. She glanced up at him and gave a shy smile.

His Aunt gave a snort. 'At her age!' she said disdainfully. 'It's disgusting.'

'Thirty-six is hardly old age,' Dad pointed out, swiping his knife along the wood.

'Ellen,' said his aunt, 'you're not really going, are you?'

Ralph was completely mesmerised. So too were Elsie and Harry. 'What's going on?' he asked.

'I'm taking your ma out tonight,' his father said.

Ralph looked at him aghast. 'Tonight? To a pub?' The thought of his mother in a place like that horrified him.

'Worse,' said his aunt. 'He wants to take her dancin'.'

Ralph stared at his mother's slim back. Then he remembered the

117

dress she had washed. He glanced at the clothes rack. It was gone. This was disaster. He wouldn't be able to go to the strike. How could she go tonight, of all nights! And then he remembered Aunty Win would be in the house. His father was not to know he wasn't in bed when he came back. It was only when this relief hit him that he realised his father was actually going to spend an evening with his mother.

Then Elsie suddenly said, 'So we won't be playing cards again?'

'You can play with Aunty Win and Joan.'

'I'm going out,' said Joan sulkily, 'to the flicks.'

'I'll play cards with you,' said Ralph, but there was no response.

'Lay the table, Elsie,' said his mother.

'So I'm going to be left here alone with your three nippers on a Saturday night! After I've worked hard all week. It's a liberty! But then what can you expect from a man. No thought.'

At this Ralph's mother turned round. 'It's John's home too,' she pointed out.

'He don't have to work on a Saturday, do he?'

'Elsie!' repeated Ralph's mother. Elsie stood up quickly as if waking up from a dream and pulled out the cutlery drawer at the end of the table.

Hardly anyone talked during supper. As soon as the meal was over his Aunt and Joan went their separate ways into their own rooms. Elsie went out to the scullery to help them with the washing-up. Ralph's father drew out a green canvas suitcase from under his bed and pulled out a dark blue suit with stripes.

'That's new,' Ralph gasped.

'It's my demob suit,' said his father. 'Thought it were a bit too fancy for wearing so I kept it in 'ere.' His father proceeded to pull down his braces and unbutton his flies. 'Interesting, is it?' he remarked. 'Me getting undressed.'

Ralph made head swings up to the ceiling at Harry. 'What you doin'?' said Harry.

'Thought you might like to look at my books,' said Ralph.

Harry stared at him as if he was mad. 'Why?'

'You might be interested.'

'No, I won't.'

'You might,' said Ralph with meaning.

'I don't like books.'

'I've got some trousers I've grown out of. Perhaps you'd like to try them on.'

118

'It's too cold up there.'

'Harry!'

'Oh.'

Upstairs they sat on the bed.

'They're really going out, aren't they?' Ralph said.

'So they say.'

'They must be. Dad's getting dressed up.'

'She won't go,' said Harry matter of factly.

'Do you think that's why she was so quiet. She hasn't plucked up the nerve to tell him?'

'Nah. Aunty Win will stop her. She'll have hersterics.'

'Hysterics,' Ralph said.

'No she won't,' as if to an imbecile. 'Men have hysterics.'

'Harry!'

'What?'

Ralph sighed. 'Never mind. So what makes you so sure?'

'Before you come back from Cornwall, Dad tried to take her out somewhere. Dunno where. But she never went because . . .'

They heard footsteps on the stairs and up to the landing.

'That's Mum,' said Harry.

They slid off the bed and pressed their ears to the door.

'Five seconds,' said Harry.

'Five seconds to what?'

'One, two, three, four, five.'

At this point Ralph heard his aunt's voice, pleading and shouting.

'See,' said Harry. 'Nah. She won't go out.'

'Well, that's a relief,' said Ralph, not liking the thought of his mother being pushed around by his father.

'Remember, I'm the one who's paying for Elsie's uniform,' he heard his aunt say. 'She wouldn't be able to stay at that posh school without me.'

'That'll get her,' said Harry.

'But that's blackmail,' whispered Ralph. 'Surely Mum doesn't need to be blackmailed?'

'And my money buys in extra comforts in this house. And it's not as if I live in luxury 'ere. I'd like to have a carpet.'

Ralph and Harry looked at one another.

'Do I mind? No, I've stood by you. Helped you with Kitty and Joan.'

'She only got demobbed six months before Dad,' said Harry. 'What's she on about?'

'I had a good life in the WAAF. I could have stayed. But no.' There was a pause. 'Ellen! Ellen! I'm warning you, Ellen.'

'Have you noticed something?' said Ralph. 'Mum isn't saying anything.'

'She'll be sitting on the bed,' said Harry like a man of the world. 'Aunty Win will go down in a minute, tell Dad Mum ain't feeling well, and that'll be that.'

After a tirade of shouting they could hear weeping. Because of this, their aunt's speech became so garbled it was difficult to decipher what she was saying.

'If you care about your family staying together,' she burbled. 'you'll stay in with your family.'

'That'll get her,' said Harry.

The bedroom door opened and slammed.

'Don't tell me,' said Ralph wryly. 'That's her exit line.'

'Yeah. Good, ain't she?'

They waited to hear if their mother would follow but there was silence.

'We might as well go down and get warm,' said Harry. 'Mum won't be coming down now.'

They opened their door quietly and crept down to the kitchen. They met Elsie creeping out of the front room.

'All over,' said Harry airily to her, and he threw open the kitchen door. 'Blimey!'

'Well, come in,' said their father. 'You're causing a draught.'

But it wasn't Aunty Win standing in the kitchen with him. It was their mother, wearing the dress she had washed that morning, with stockings and polished shoes. Her hair was waved up into three rolls round the side of her face and hanging down softly, and she wore a touch of lipstick.

'Mum,' breathed Elsie. 'You look so pretty.'

She smiled and Ralph was overcome with such a feeling of tenderness for her that he was furious with her father for forcing her to go on with this charade. He was suddenly aware of his father's rough square hands and his bulky square body, and he wanted to protect his mother yet he felt helpless to do anything.

He heard the scullery door open and within seconds Uncle Ted burst in. Everyone stared at him. Usually his uncle had a permanent smile on his ruddy face, but his face fell. He glanced from one to the other looking startled.

'John, you ain't bringing . . .' He paused. 'I don't think it's quite the place for ladies. Bit rough, don't you think?'

'We're going dancin', Ted.'

'Dancin'! You're 'aving me on!' And then his smile vanished. 'You are, ain't you?'

120

'No. Can't stop. Got a bus to catch.' And Ralph's father lifted Ellen's coat from the chair and held it out for her.

His mother still hadn't said a word. Something dreadful was happening and Ralph could do nothing to prevent it.

'Mum?' said Elsie.

'Yeah,' she said softly, looking a little sad.

'Can I listen to the Saturday night thriller?'

She smiled. 'Oh, Elsie! You never miss a trick, do you?'

'Can I? Please.'

'You'll have to ask your Aunty Win. She's in charge tonight.' And she thrust an arm into the waiting coat.

'You don't have to go!' Ralph blurted out.

His mother looked puzzled. 'I know, love. I *want* to go. I've been looking forward to it all day.'

After his parents had gone, Ralph decided to leave soon after for the theatre. He suspected Win might manacle him to a chair. Anything to get her own back on someone, particularly a male.

When he arrived at the stage door he found Wilfred and the elderly dresser having a cup of tea in the cubby-hole.

'Here he is, Florrie,' said Wilfred.

The elderly woman looked up from her chair. 'You're brave,' she said.

'I don't feel it,' said Ralph. 'Sir,' he said, turning to Wilfred, 'do you think it would help if I wrote a letter of apology to Mr Neville explaining things.'

'Dunno.' He turned to the dresser. 'Florrie. What d'you think?'

'Wouldn't hurt, I suppose. Then again he might have forgotten by next week and it might just stir him up again.'

'Forgotten!' cried Ralph in disbelief.

They were interrupted by the distant sound of applause. 'Curtain down,' Wilfred remarked.

'Oh, hell,' said Ralph, and he suddenly felt sick.

'If you stays where you are, you'll be spotted, sure as eggs is eggs,' said Florrie.

'Go and wait over there,' said Wilfred, pointing to the notice-board.

Ralph sat on one of the skips. He could hear talking and laughter coming from above. He turned up the frayed collar of his jacket and stared at the cast list for *Sweet Aloes*. The two actresses who played the elderly dotty sisters in *Ladies in Retirement* were back, as was the elderly actor he had seen play the vicar in the summer

121

production of *The Importance of Being Earnest*. Helena, Isla, Robin, Geraldine and Raymond Maclaren, and Basil Duke were also in the cast.

Upstairs, the first clattering of feet was on the steps. Ralph leaned further forward, covering his face with his hand, as members of the cast walked past him chattering and saying their goodnights.

'Son,' said Wilfred calling out. Ralph slid off the skip. 'They've all gone now. You can go up.'

Florrie was opening a little door at the side of the cubby-hole. 'You can come up with me if you like.'

'Thanks,' said Ralph. 'Perhaps they won't strangle me if you're around.'

She lumbered and swayed up the steps while Ralph followed her like a condemned man climbing the scaffold. As soon as he had opened the door to the wings he bowed his head and made straight for the pile of props which were now crowding the prop table and the scene dock. He picked up the prop list. It had *Granite* written above it, a play which would remain permanently etched into his brain, and began rapidly to sort out the props. Jack Walker, the stage hands and Robin carried the castle walls past him at a steady and intense pace. There was a tap on his shoulder. It was Helena.

'Can you give us a hand with the table?'

Ralph moved numbly towards the stage where he could see Isla waiting at one end of a massive piece of furniture. She was looking serious. Dismayed, Ralph took hold of the other end. 'It was all a ghastly mistake!' he stammered. 'I'm terribly sorry.'

And then he noticed Isla's mouth twitch and suddenly she burst into uncontrollable laughter and collapsed on to the table. She was laughing so much that Jack and the others noticed and winked at Ralph. 'Oh,' she gasped.

'But I don't understand,' said Ralph. 'It was awful. I was in at the five o'clock show on Friday.'

'Awful?' spluttered Isla. 'It was hell!' and she and Helena both laughed.

'Did Helena explain, then?'

'Yes. And it all made sense then. But next time anyone takes a shot of you – '

'I'll let you know,' said Ralph.

Isla picked her end of the table again. 'Has Helena told you what we're in for?'

'Yes.'

'It's the last show of the season before the panto, so they're splashing out.'

'I read the cast list,' said Ralph, backing with the table. 'I see you're in it.'

'Yes,' she groaned.

'Aren't you pleased?' he said astonished.

'No. I have to black up. It'll take me ages to get off, which means even less sleep.'

As they carried the table into the scene dock, Ralph caught sight of a familiar hirsute figure stuck in the corner. 'I need to get his nibs back as early on Monday as I can,' he said. 'How early can I come?'

'Nine. That do?'

He nodded. It'll have to, he thought.

They dumped the table in one corner. Isla pointed to two piles of props for *Sweet Aloes*. 'That Victorian lot of furniture is for Act One. That 1933 lot is for Acts Two and Three.'

'Thanks, Isla.'

'Whatever for?'

'For not being angry with me.'

'At least I know your name now. I always thought Hollis was a funny Christian name.'

SIXTEEN

Ralph cautiously opened the door which led into the wings. It was dark. He crept past the prop table only to discover the doors to the scene dock were closed.

'Bring up your batten one ambers to a half,' he heard a man say from the auditorium.

'Right ho, sir,' yelled a voice from above.

Ralph glanced upwards. On a small platform just below fly floor level, the chief electrician was standing in front of a large metal dimmer board. 'Plot it,' said the voice from the auditorium which Ralph now guessed belonged to the producer.

'Put a deeper blue in the flood outside the window, Chalky. No. I've changed my mind. We can get that effect by just taking it down a bit.'

Isla was sitting at the prompt corner next to a set of switches, looking intently down at a large open book.

'Arthur, we need some surprise pink in this act. I want the ladies to look their best. They'll look anaemic in this light.'

Ralph edged closer.

'That's it. Next cue please.'

'Isla!' whispered Ralph.

Isla swung round startled. 'Gosh, you gave me a fright. Where have you been? I expected you ages ago.'

' I'm sorry. I overslept. Can I take the bear?'

'Yes, quick,' she said, 'while Helena's shifting the lamp.'

The bear was leaning against the door of the scene dock, fully kitted out. Ralph backed swiftly with it but, in his haste, the bear's hat fell off. He laid it on the floor and had just managed to yank the hat over the bear's ears when he heard two men speaking on stage.

'Quick!' Isla whispered urgently. 'It's Mr Neville.'

Horrified, Ralph threw himself at the bear and had just managed to stagger with it to the prop table when a door from stage left opened, sending a beam of light from on-stage, directly on to the bear. Behind the bear Ralph listened to a tirade of expletives which would have made even Mrs Egerton-Smythe blush. What made it more extraordinary was that every vowel and consonant was crystal clear.

There was a pause.

'Well, are you coming out? I know this bear is incapable of standing by itself.'

Ralph peered round. 'Good morning, sir,' stammered Ralph. 'Mr Neville, I believe?'

'I am he,' roared the producer. 'Now would you mind telling me what the hell you're doing?'

'Retrieving the bear, sir.'

'Incognito, I suppose!' he quipped, indicating the bear's attire.

'It's to keep him dry,' said Ralph hoarsely.

'And why now? I don't know if you had noticed, but we are attempting to light a show which opens this evening.'

'I couldn't take it back after the strike,' he began.

'Strike? What the hell do you know about the strike?'

Ralph felt himself reddening.

'Robin!' yelled the producer. Robin and Isla appeared instantly. 'He's been helping with the props during the strike,' explained Robin.

'Well, not exactly helping,' said Isla quickly. 'He's allowed to observe from a distance and make tea.'

'Yes, that's right,' agreed Robin hurriedly.

'He wanted to learn.'

'This is not a drama school, Isla. Now, can you organise this to be delivered to its owner at a more suitable time. I do not want a repeat performance of last week's fiasco!' He wheeled round to

Ralph. 'Because of your attention-seeking, young man, we had to remove the bear from the remaining performances. But that still didn't stop a few complaints from members of the audience who had come especially to see it!'

'I'm sorry, sir,' said Ralph. 'Honestly, I never meant . . .'

The man waved his hand, indicating that the conversation was at an end. Ralph watched him turn abruptly away. 'Now, let's get on with the rehearsal, shall we?'

Ralph speedily lifted the bear up and had almost reached the door when he was stopped in his tracks by another roar from the producer.

Ralph balanced the bear on his feet and peered round again.

'Will you leave that ******* bear alone!'

'But the owner needs it as soon as possible. I'll be in terrible trouble . . .'

'You're in terrible trouble already, laddie. Isla!'

'Yes, Mr Neville?'

'Take this bear away from him!'

'But, Mr Neville,' Ralph pleaded.

'That's enough, Mr Whatever your name is.'

'Hollis, sir,' said Ralph helpfully.

'Well, Mr Hollis, give Isla the address of the owner and it will be delivered as soon as possible.' He was about to enter the upstage-left door again when he swung round. 'Hollis?' he repeated. 'Ralph Hollis? The young letter-writer?'

Ralph nodded, even though Mr Neville pronounced his Christian name 'Rayfe'.

'I was about to send you another one apologising, Mr Neville.'

Mr Neville sighed. 'Apology accepted,' he said. 'Now listen to me, what you do in the scene dock is the master carpenter or stage director's business. But what you do on the stage is my business. Understood?'

'Yes, sir.'

'Good morning.'

'Sir?'

'Now what is it?' he said exasperated.

'May I continue dropping you the odd letter,' he asked. In the background he was aware of smothered giggles coming from Isla. 'By all means, but you'll be wasting your time,' and he left. Ralph propped the bear in the wings, and went over to where Isla was standing with her back to him, her head bowed. 'You don't give up, do you? Now give me the owner's address.'

'I don't like you being out in weather like this,' said his mother in the kitchen over breakfast.

'I've got to go in, it's pay-day.'

'I don't mean that. At least it's daylight when you're workin'. It's being out at night I don't like. Couldn't you go to the theatre next week?'

'There isn't a play next week. The theatre's closed till *Cinderella* opens.'

'What do you think, John?'

'Don't bring me into it. I don't like him going anywhere near there.'

'I've got back the other times,' Ralph said.

'There's people fallen in the river in those pea-soupers,' she said.

'And they scream their heads off as much as they like,' added Aunty Win. 'But it ain't no use 'cos no one can see 'em.'

'Cheerful lot, aren't you,' said Ralph.

By the time he reached Winford he was beginning to think his mother was right. Not only was the fog obliterating everything, but the roads were icy. The traffic jams were so bad that he pushed his bike along the pavement, wheeling it gingerly round pedestrians, who only emerged from the fog when they were almost on top of him. Around him he could hear horns blaring and smell the exhaust from cars stopping and starting.

When he finally reached the Egerton-Smythes he still could not see the house, but as he drew nearer the kitchen door, he managed to make out a glint of glass from the little conservatory which stood outside. He wheeled his bike into it so at least he would be able to find it again later, and then stepped outside and edged his way along the wall towards the garden.

He stood on the veranda and stared and stared. There was nothing but fog. No borders. No trees. No sheds. Nothing.

He backed towards the kitchen again and peered in.

Looking through a window, it was a relief to be able to see something. The room was empty. He knocked. There was no answer. After several more fruitless knockings he tried the handle. It was unlocked. He stepped in, the fog swirling in after him so that it seemed to begin enveloping the large scrubbed table and chairs. Hastily he shut the door as if beating the fog back. The kitchen was cold. Propped against the jug on the table was a note folded over. It said 'Queenie' on the outside. Ralph opened the door into the hall. There was silence. It was almost as if he was the only person left in the house. He turned back to the kitchen and opened the note.

Dear Queenie,
   Have gone to fetch Jessica.

Who was Jessica? he asked himself. Perhaps she was an elderly aunt or sister.

Have no idea what time we'll be back because of the fog. Could you make up a large saucepan of soup, from any scraps you can find. Have left ration book out should you be able to make it to the shops, though prefer you not to venture out as I am expecting the chimney sweep. He has been asked to do the chimneys for two rooms, the library and the dining room.
   His money's in the jug. Tell Hollis I have left instructions for him in the shed.

Celia Egerton-Smythe.

Ralph folded the note and propped it back against the jug. She had obviously written the letter before the fog had swallowed up the shed. He walked over to the range. It was cold. He could only suppose Queenie had been trapped in the fog too. He opened the drawer at the base of the range and began looking for something to empty the ashes into. It was about an hour later when there was a knock at the front door. He washed his sooty hands quickly under the kitchen tap, wiped his hands on the backs of his trousers, and ran into the hall. Three young men were standing in the porch.

'Yes?' asked Ralph.

'We've come to study,' said one of them.

'But you're on holiday, aren't you?' said Ralph.

'Yes,' said another, 'but Mr Egerton-Smythe has given us permission to come here during our vacation.'

Queenie arrived when Ralph was on the floor, attempting to clear up the burnt bits of newspaper which had caught fire when he had been trying to light the range.

Before he could hide what he was doing he heard the door open and looked up to find her standing over him.

'And what, might I ask, is goin' on 'ere?'

'Mrs Egerton-Smythe is out.'

'I would have done it, thank you very much,' she snapped. And then Ralph remembered what kept people happy through a Saturday strike. 'Actually you've arrived just in time,' he said. 'I've just made a big pot of tea. Fancy a cuppa?'

Queenie stood in her coat, hands clasped tautly together, lips pursed.

'You look like you could use one,' he added.

'I might,' she snapped.

'Sit down,' said Ralph. 'I'll bring it to you.'

'Don't think you can get round me like this.'

Ralph quickly turned his back on her to hide his smile. By the time he had poured her a cup she had unbuttoned her coat.

'How did you find it, then, getting that range going?'

'Dreadful!' said Ralph. 'Can you show me how to do it?' he asked, pouring himself another cup.

'Why?' she asked suspiciously.

'In case you're caught in another of these pea-soupers. It took me about three hours to get it started.'

Queenie cupped the tea in her hands, the mistress of the kitchen once again. She gave a mysterious smile. 'I might,' she said airily.

By the beginning of the afternoon, the fog had lifted and the garden and sheds were visible again.

Ralph told Queenie about the three students and how he had had to light a fire for them in the library, but he kept quiet about the chimney sweep's visit. In the shed he found a note from Mrs Egerton-Smythe. It was brief.

Garden looking alive again. Do what you will.

Mrs Egerton-Smythe.

He knew that meant getting the fork out and digging. He took his jacket off, climbed into the overalls and jauntily balanced the fork on his shoulder. He felt a wave of satisfaction coming over him and a mild feeling of possessiveness about the garden. He stuck the fork upright into a border and strode down to the river. There was something else he needed to do before beginning work. Down at the tiny jetty he lay on his stomach and picked up two pieces of driftwood. More had washed up on the bank. This scrimmaging along the bank had become a daily ritual. He had seen the state of Mrs Egerton-Smythe's coal cellar. With rationing growing ever stiffer, there was a possibility she would be left with no fuel at all.

He leaned all the dripping driftwood on one wall, and then, after quickly drying his hands, he felt along some of the other driftwood, selected those he thought had dried and piled them on the other side of the shed where he would chop them up later. He was beginning to make quite a pile. Then he returned to his digging. As soon as the smell of freshly dug earth hit his nostrils, he felt the old adrenalin surge through him. For the rest of the afternoon he dug with a vengeance, rarely glancing up at the house. When he reached the part of the border which went from the shed to the river, he began to shape it into a curve. He had visualised growing shrubs round to an opening which would lead to that part of the lawn. An arch. There were enough trees bundled together there. He was aware of the sky darkening but he continued to dig with urgency, before anyone could rush out and prevent him from changing the look of the garden. And then he realised that it wasn't the dark that was making him screw up his eyes. Familiar green wisps of fog were whirling round his feet. He bumped into the woodshed. Slowly he took several sideways steps and then walked carefully forward until eventually he found the garden shed. He peeled off his overalls and slipped his jacket on. The soles of his boots were caked in their usual deep platform of wet earth. He sat on the steps outside the shed and proceeded to prise it free with a trowel. He was just starting on the sole of his second boot when he heard light classical piano music coming from somewhere.

It was so extraordinary to hear any sounds at all, except the river and a few birds, that he thought someone must have left a wireless on near a window. But the music wasn't being played by a professional because they kept stopping and going back.

He quickly trowelled off the rest of the mud, stood up and stared into the fog, in an effort to gauge where the music was coming from. With slow movements he worked his way carefully through the swirling mist. His foot hit the veranda. The piano music was louder now. He stepped underneath the ivy covered roof towards the french windows and peered in.

Seated at a piano, the white dust-sheet thrown carelessly in a pile on the floor, was a young girl. She had bright red hair which hung in thick plaits and she was wearing a school hat and coat. He knocked on the window. She looked up, startled, and then indicated the door. It was unlocked. When he stepped inside he could see that her face was covered in thousands of huge freckles. As she smiled he noticed that her two front teeth overlapped each other slightly.

'Hello,' she said brightly. 'You must be Ralph Hollis. I'm Jessica.'

SEVENTEEN

'C lose the door. It's freezing enough in here already.'
'Sorry,' he said quickly, and he slammed it shut. She laughed.

'You're surrounded in fog.'

'Yes, it's awful how it follows you in.'

He paused. 'Look, I'm terribly sorry, but I still don't know who you are and why you're here.'

'I'm Mrs Egerton-Smythe's daughter.'

'Daughter?'

'I broke up today. I'm at boarding school.'

The door opened suddenly. It was Mrs Egerton-Smythe. 'Ah. You've met. You'd better stay to supper.' And she was gone.

'Very bossy, my mother,' said Jessica and then her smile dropped for a fraction. 'Sometimes.'

'It's nice to see one of the dustsheets off,' Ralph said politely.

'I'd like to pull the whole lot off,' she said vehemently. 'It looks so grim in here, but I suppose it protects the furniture,' and she sighed. 'It's my favourite room, but once the cold weather comes, my mother covers everything up.'

'Why?'

'Can't afford to heat it. The library and kitchen swallow up all our coal. I'd like to spend Christmas here, but everyone thinks I'm mad.'

Ralph found himself very much at ease with her. She was a nice kid. You didn't have to squeeze blood out of a stone to persuade her to speak.

'I think it would be grand to have it in here,' he said.

'Do you really? Oh, you're humouring me!'

'No, I'm not. It's private back here and you look out at the garden, and if there's any sun it floods in.'

'I know. It's glorious, isn't it?'

'So what's to stop you putting up decorations?'

'What's the point? It's still too cold to stay in here. Once the holidays start at least we can light a fire in the dining room instead of having to keep one going in the library.'

'That's what you think.' He told her about the three students. 'Oh, he can't,' she cried. She frowned. 'I know what he's up to. He wants us to go early to his house. It's bad enough having to spend Christmas Day there, but he'll want me to look after his priggish wife. She's expecting a baby. The way she's behaving, you'd think she was dying from consumption.'

'You're not very fond of him, I take it?'

She looked at him guiltily as if she had said too much. 'Not much. I'm hoping the fog will get worse so that he can't call round. He always does on my first night home, to read my school report. Some welcome.'

'But surely that's none of his business.'

'It is when he's paying the school fees.' She paused. 'Well, it's not exactly him. It's my father's money, but he's in charge of it. He even . . .' She bit her lip suddenly. 'I'm sorry. I'm talking too much.'

'If you change your mind, I'll help you decorate. After all, you'll still be coming in here to play the piano, won't you?'

'True. If only we could light a wood fire here,' she said. 'I started collecting wood from the river last summer, but when I found there was a bird's nest up in the chimney I gave up.'

'There isn't one there now.'

'Oh? You mean you've managed to get rid of it?'

'Sort of.'

'Thanks for the thought, but the chimney hasn't been swept for years. Even when my father was alive, he wouldn't let us be here in the winter. He said it was a summer room.'

'Are you going to let me speak?' said Ralph.

'Sorry,' she said. 'Go on.'

'What if I told you the chimney was swept today?'

The girl stared at him, uncomprehending. 'Don't tease me,' she said at last.

'I'm not,' Ralph protested. 'When the chimney sweep arrived he couldn't sweep the one in the library. So I told him to sweep the one in here.'

'So we can use the fireplace,' she breathed. 'Does my mother know?'

'Not yet.'

'Oh, I wish, wish, wish . . .'

Suddenly they were plunged into darkness. 'Oh, hell,' she said. 'The fuses have gone.'

They groped around in the dark laughing until they found the door. They were standing in the hall when the kitchen door opened and Mrs Egerton-Smythe came through with a candelabra with four lighted candles on it.

'Electricity cut,' she explained. 'The latest thing to be rationed by the government. We're eating in the kitchen. It's warmer.'

'Charles will have a fit,' giggled Jessica.

'And Queenie will have a dozen fits,' muttered Ralph.

'Mother sent her home early as soon as she spotted the fog.'

'The students,' he said alarmed. 'They're not still in the library, are they?'

'They're on holiday,' Mrs Egerton-Smythe reminded him.

'Three turned up today, I had to light a fire for them. Mr Egerton-Smythe gave them permission to come in their vacation.'

By the light of the candles he saw how pale she had become. 'Before the chimney sweep came.'

'Oh, no, really,' she protested. 'So he could only sweep one chimney?'

'Not exactly,' said Ralph slowly.

'He didn't come?'

'Oh, yes,' said Ralph. 'And he did clean two chimneys.'

She stared at him puzzled. 'The garden room,' said Jessica quietly.

'Hollis,' said Mrs Egerton-Smythe, 'I want a word with you, but first I'd better check the library.'

She opened the door. They had gone.

'The lazy so-and-so's,' Ralph exclaimed, staring at the grate, and untouched coal. 'They couldn't even be bothered to keep it going.'

'Right, Jessica, will you excuse us?'

'I might as well come too. I'll only eavesdrop outside.'

'I'm sorry,' said Ralph. 'I suppose I lost my temper and it seemed such a sweet revenge.'

'How? Revenging whom?'

He shrugged. 'I couldn't bear to see them taking over your home.'

'That's my business.'

'Yes, madam, I realise that now. Is this the sack?'

'No. Now you'd better give me your parents' phone number.'

'They don't have a phone. Look, please don't complain to my father. He'll kill me.'

'I'm not going to complain, you silly ass. I'm going to tell them you won't be home tonight.'

'What do you mean?'

'We're kidnapping you,' giggled Jessica.

'Belt up,' said her mother. 'You're staying because of this fog.'

'But you don't understand. I'm going to the theatre. It's Friday night.'

'Dear, you'll be lucky if you make it to the end of the drive. Go tomorrow instead.'

'But it'll be the cut version on Saturday.'

'Don't say they ration shows as well as electricity now,' she said drily.

'They do on Saturdays. It's the only way they can fit in three performances, and this is the last play of the season. It's very kind of you to offer, but I *must* go.'

Mrs Egerton-Smythe was right. He got lost in the drive. When he returned to the warmth of the candlelit kitchen he noticed there were three bowls on the table.

'Now,' said Mrs Egerton-Smythe smiling, 'whom do I phone?'

'My Uncle Ted,' said Ralph. 'I only hope he can get to their house to tell them.'

After supper Mrs Egerton-Smythe disappeared upstairs leaving Jessica and Ralph to chat about the garden room and Christmas.

'What I don't understand,' said Ralph puzzled, 'is why you and your mother are expected to go to your brother's and not the other way round. I thought most people came to their mother's. Kitty, my cousin, and her husband Frank are coming all the way from Kent to have Christmas with us.'

'It's harder them coming here,' said Jessica. 'They have warmth.'

'But why can't you both stay here? Just you and your mother. Or does she want to spend it with your brother and his wife?'

'No fear,' said Jessica.

'Am I missing something?' said Ralph bewildered. 'This is your mother's home. If she wants to spend Christmas in it, she should.'

'That's just the point,' said Jessica. 'It isn't her home, not exactly. You see when my father died he left the house to Charles, but he stipulated in his will that my mother should live in it until she dies. So it is her home while she lives, but she doesn't own it. Also he's in charge of my father's money so he hands it to her like pocket money, if she toes the line.'

'And if she doesn't?'

'He *forgets* to put it in her bank.'

'But isn't that illegal?'

'Oh, he's got lots of legal cronies. They'll just assume my mother is being unreasonable and not able to handle the money he gives her and say, "Isn't it lucky he's in charge."'

'So he's got power over his own mother until she dies?'

'In a nutshell, yes.'

'And you?'

'At the moment, but I'm working at . . .' She stopped. 'I haven't told anyone yet. I'd rather keep it to myself. Do you mind?'

'Course I don't. You hardly know me.'

'Doesn't feel like it,' she said surprised. 'It feels like we've known each other for years.'

'Me too,' said Ralph. 'Do you mind if I keep asking questions? You don't have to answer them.'

'Fire away.'

'Has your brother always been like that? I mean, bossy?'

'No. He's got worse. He's getting his own back.'

133

'For what?'

'For not being my mother's favourite. Well, it isn't exactly true that Laurie was her favourite. It was just that they were more in tune and anyway someone had to stick up for him. Also because Laurie was the eldest my father tended to concentrate on him following in his footsteps. Laurie wasn't willing and it caused arguments. Once Laurie died, my father began to notice he had another son. Charles didn't have the same mind as my father, but he worked hard and qualified as a solicitor.'

'Is that why Charles had Laurie's stuff locked up?'

She looked shocked for a moment. 'How d'you know about that?' she breathed.

'I broke the locks for your mother, filled the chests with earth and fixed new padlocks on them.'

'You didn't,' she said, awestruck. 'So Laurie's belongings are *out*!'

'Yes.'

She leapt off the chair and did a strange kind of ecstatic jig all around the kitchen.

At that moment they heard footsteps coming down the stairs. Jessica slid quickly on to a chair.

'I'll explain about the chests later,' she said.

Mrs Egerton-Smythe opened the door, bearing a huge pair of men's pyjamas and a dressing gown.

'Sorry, Jessica,' she said, 'they're Laurie's. I hope you don't mind, but these are the only men's nightclothes I have.'

'Of course I don't mind.'

'I'll sleep in my underwear,' said Ralph. Jessica giggled.

'In this weather!' Mrs Egerton-Smythe exclaimed. 'Now, do as you're told.'

'But I'm off duty, aren't I?' he said cheekily.

'Watch it, Hollis. Or you'll go without a hot-water bottle.'

'A hot-water bottle!' he exclaimed, and he pulled an imaginary forelock. 'Yes, ma'am. No, ma'am. Three bags full, ma'am.'

Jessica was giggling more than ever. She was a good audience. 'Bed, you two,' said Mrs Egerton-Smythe.

'But it's too early,' protested Jessica.

'I agree, but I ought to start watching our coal supply now and I can't let this range burn indefinitely.'

She filled three hot-water bottles from the kettle, wrapped their nightclothes round them and dumped them in their respective arms.

'Stick these in your beds,' she said. 'Jessica, show Ralph where Laurie's room is. Unless you have any objections.'

'Course I don't. But we don't have to go to sleep, do we? I'm too excited to go to sleep.'

'Do what you want but don't complain of being cold because you've been in each other's rooms.'

'We won't, will we, Ralph?'

Ralph smiled.

Jessica was so extraordinary. Even her mother seemed different since her arrival. Softer. They shut the kitchen door in the vain hope that some warmth would be retained for the morning, and then made their way through the icy hallway and up the stairs to the second floor.

Ralph was sleeping in the room next to Jessica's. She said their rooms overlooked the garden, but glancing out of the window you wouldn't have been able to tell.

They shoved their bottles deep into their beds and took their candles back down the corridor and down the wide staircase to the bathroom. They met Mrs Egerton-Smythe on their way up. 'I'm afraid you'll have to use your finger to clean your teeth, Hollis.'

'Oh, don't keep calling him Hollis,' Jessica protested.

'See you two in the morning,' she said, ignoring her daughter's remark.

Ralph and Jessica stood at the sink, the two candles propped precariously in front of them.

'Jessica,' he said quietly. 'If you don't like me sleeping in Laurie's room, I can easily sleep downstairs somewhere.'

Jessica, her mouth full of toothpaste, shook her head and spat it out. 'I'm pleased you're in Laurie's room. I'm sick to death of pretending he never happened. Hurry up and clean your teeth and then come into my room and I'll explain.'

They tiptoed back upstairs. After Ralph had folded back volumes of material on Laurie's pyjamas he slipped the dressing-gown on. It trailed along the floor behind him. He edged the door open, candle in hand, crept to Jessica's room and knocked gently on the door.

There was a pad of feet on the floor. She stood shivering in her pyjamas and a thick pullover. 'Quick!' she urged, beckoning him in. 'I'm freezing.'

He followed her in. Around the walls he could see shelves of books, a gramophone and records.

'Climb in under the eiderdown at the other end,' she commanded. And then she started to smother her laughter.

'What's so funny?' he asked.

'You! You look drowned in Laurie's things.'

He lifted up the eiderdown and they sat upright, the eiderdown

135

up to their chins facing each other.

'So tell me about him,' Ralph burst out. 'Why are his things locked away?'

'The day we heard he'd been killed, my father began to haul everything out of his room and anything that was his around the house. He was going to throw it all away or have it burned.'

'But why?'

'I suppose that's how some people cope with grief. They get rid of all the person's possessions as quickly as possible.'

'How did your mother manage to stop him? From what I've heard he sounds . . .' He stopped.

'Dictatorial?' Jessica finished for him.

'I didn't quite say that,' Ralph said.

'It's true though. Well,' she said, leaning forward conspiratorially, 'this is the strange thing. Laurie left a very simple will. Leaving everything he had to my mother. My father looked for loopholes but couldn't find any. But he locked all Laurie's things up in trunks. My mother was terribly upset. She said she wanted to see his things around. So did I. But my father said she wasn't facing facts. It was war. He was killed. We must forget him and move on. If she was neurotic enough to keep them in his house she could, but they would be locked up. Clever, eh?'

'The tyrant!'

'One day I asked my mother why she wanted to keep them. She said she didn't want to keep everything. Laurie had asked her to do what she wanted with it, but it's up to her to decide what she wants to give away, and when. She said that until she had looked at them and touched them she couldn't grieve properly. Does that sound mad to you?'

'No,' said Ralph. 'My two cousins, Kitty and Joan, were buried for hours and hours when their parents' house was bombed. Kitty was buried the longest. They were the only two survivors. My mother said she appeared to be fine after the ordeal. In fact she joined the ATS as soon as she was old enough. But it wasn't till the war was over and she was married to Frank, that she started reacting. They lived with us for a while and we could hear her screaming. Poor Frank. We thought he was beating her up so he had to explain and that's how we knew. It was as if, while the war was on, she had to put her reactions aside. Being with Frank helped her have the courage to remember. She used to have the most terrifying nightmares, all about being buried alive.'

'I don't think my mother will have nightmares,' said Jessica.

'No, but she might cry.'

'What made you say that?' said Jessica startled.

'I don't know,' said Ralph surprised. 'It just came out.'

'Fancy you knowing she didn't cry. Least, I don't think she did. She just went all quiet and buttoned up and bad-tempered.'

'You mean she hasn't always been so snappy? Oh. Sorry.'

She laughed. 'Oh, she's always had a bit of a temper. I've got one too.'

'How did *you* cope after Laurie's death?'

'I used to go into the garage and stare at his Alvis, and remember all the drives he had ever taken me on. I miss his music though. He had loads of records. By the time I arrived from school my father and Charles had already stashed everything in trunks and had stuck them in the loft. If they could have got the Alvis up there they would have done. Luckily, nobody wanted it so they couldn't give it to anyone for 'safe keeping', if you know what I mean. My mother says that as soon as petrol rationing is over she's going to learn how to drive and teach me. That's a secret. You won't tell, will you?'

'Of course not.'

She sighed. 'Oh, I wish we could have Christmas here.'

'You could have both,' Ralph suggested. 'If you really have to spend Christmas Day there, you could pretend it's not your real Christmas and have your own private one here.'

'Oh. If only,' she said.

'Do it,' he urged. 'I told you I'll help you. I can cut holly and stick it round the room and I'm good at fires.'

'Modest too,' she teased. 'Right,' she said with determination. 'I've told you all our family secrets. Now I want to know all yours.'

'I don't have any,' said Ralph.

'Liar! My mother's told me all about you. Come on.'

'I still don't know what you want to know.'

'About the theatre!' she said exasperated. 'About you wanting to be an actor!'

EIGHTEEN

'You've got it going!' exclaimed Mrs Egerton-Smythe. 'Well done!'

They were gathered in the cold kitchen, shivering round the range.

'I am impressed,' said Jessica.

'Don't be,' said Ralph. 'I made a pig's ear of it yesterday. Queenie gave me some invaluable tips.'

'How did you manage to persuade her?' said Mrs Egerton-Smythe in disbelief.

'Tea and flattery.'

Queenie had managed to find her way to a phone box to say she wouldn't be coming in. The fog was so bad that the trams were at a standstill.

They were just settling down to tea and toast when there was a knock at the front door. For a moment they looked at each other puzzled.

'Charles!' said Jessica in alarm. 'Oh, hell, we're eating in the kitchen.'

'With me,' added Ralph, 'a servant.'

'Laurie's dressing-gown and pyjamas. They'll still be on the bed!'

There was another knock.

'I'd better answer it,' said Mrs Egerton-Smythe. 'Jessica, go upstairs and hide any evidence.'

Jessica leapt from her chair and, while Mrs Egerton-Smythe walked into the hall, Ralph stayed by the door, eavesdropping.

'Mrs Egerton-Smythe,' he heard a voice say.

'Yes?'

'We're looking for Master Ralph Hollis. He never returned home last night. I believe he works for you.'

'He's here,' said Mrs Egerton-Smythe surprised. 'Do come in.'

Ralph backed away from the door. Mrs Egerton-Smythe entered with a police constable who was holding his helmet in his hands. 'This the boy, ma'am?' he asked, glancing at Ralph.

'Yes, constable.'

'You've caused your mother a lot of worry,' he began.

'But I rang his uncle last night, so that she wouldn't,' Mrs Egerton-Smythe interrupted. 'A Mr Ted Hollis.'

'Well, he hasn't been in contact, ma'am. Are you sure you're not covering up for the boy?'

'Certainly not. Why don't you ring Mr Hollis yourself. Goodness!' she said suddenly. 'Maybe he's the one you should be looking for. Perhaps he got lost in the fog last night.'

'Perhaps,' said the constable. 'May I use your phone, ma'am?'

'Of course.'

They went out into the hallway. Ralph hovered by the door. 'May I speak to a Mr Ted Hollis,' he heard the constable say. 'Ah. Good. I'm Constable Hughes from Winford Police Station. I'm ringing concerning a message you might have received about your

nephew, Master . . .' He stopped. 'So she did contact you?' Pause.
'May I ask why you didn't inform his parents?' Pause. 'Your
opinion is of no concern to me, Mr Hollis. Do you realise because
of your behaviour you have wasted valuable police time?' Pause. 'I
think you'd better change your tune, Mr Hollis. You could be put
on a charge. The boy's parents have been worried sick.' Pause. 'I
see. Thank you, sir.' Pause. 'Yes, that's all.' Ralph heard the
receiver clunk on to the cradle.

'He didn't pass the message on,' Ralph heard Mrs Egerton-
Smythe say.

'I'm afraid not, ma'am.'

'His poor mother!' she exclaimed. 'Was it because of the fog?'

'No, ma'am,' said the Constable slowly. 'He appears not to be on
very good terms with the boy's parents. He also didn't take kindly
to being thought of as a messenger boy. I won't repeat . . .'

'Yes. Yes, I see. Is there any way his mother can get to a phone?'

'His mum and dad are at our police station. Perhaps?'

'Oh, please do.'

Ralph listened appalled. He was touched that his parents should
care enough about him to report him missing but furious that they
were treating him like a child!

'Hello, Sarge. P.C. Hughes speaking. I've found the Hollis boy.'
Pause. 'Oh yes. Safe and sound. His employer kept him home
because of the fog. Are his mum and dad still there? Mrs
Egerton-Smythe would like to speak to them.'

Ralph stood in the kitchen, wishing the ground would swallow
him up. Once she heard his parents' accents, she'd be so shocked at
her daughter chatting to him, he knew she would insist that she and
Jessica had breakfast in the dining room while he remained alone in
the kitchen. He heard footsteps coming down the stairs. 'What's
wrong?' he heard Jessica ask.

'I'll explain in a minute. Go and keep Ralph company.'

Ralph! She called him Ralph! Not for long though, he thought.
Jessica came in and, like him, left the door ajar. 'Have you been
listening?' she whispered.

He nodded.

'What's been going on?'

'Hello. Is that Mrs Hollis?' he heard her mother say in the hall.

'Shush,' said Ralph urgently, and they crept over to the door.

'Yes, he's fine, Mrs Hollis. I'm sorry this has happened. I left a
message with a Mr Ted Hollis, but he declined to come and tell
you.' Pause. 'No trouble at all. I'm pleased to have been able to
help. But the fog was terrible.' Pause. 'Really? No wonder you were

worried.' Pause. 'Yes, of course you can. I'll go and get him.'

Jessica and Ralph shot across the room, dumped themselves into chairs and nonchalantly began drinking tea.

'Your mother wants a word.'

'Oh,' said Ralph. He went into the hall and picked up the receiver. 'Hello, Mum.'

'Oh, Ralphie,' cried his mother and she burst into tears. 'I'm that relieved!' and then she became incoherent and he heard his dad's voice.

'Your mother's been worried sick!'

'Uncle Ted didn't pass on the message, Dad.'

'May I?' said Mrs Egerton-Smythe. Ralph handed her the receiver and returned to the kitchen.

Mrs Egerton-Smythe didn't make any comment about his parents, and, he noted, she continued to call him Ralph.

The second surprise of the day was when she brought a pile of books into the kitchen and dumped them on the table. 'I thought you might be interested in borrowing these,' she said. 'They were Laurie's.'

'But what about Jessica?'

'It's all right. I'm more interested in books.'

Ralph stared at her puzzled.

'Novels,' she explained.

And then he caught sight of one of the titles. '*Arms and the Man*! George Bernard Shaw!' And he scrabbled frantically through them. 'J.B. Priestley! Terence Rattigan! Noel Coward! Ben Travers! Shaw! You really mean I can borrow these?' He stopped. 'My bedroom ceiling leaks. They might get wet.'

'Don't put them under the leaks then,' said Mrs Egerton-Smythe.

That afternoon the three of them removed the dustsheets in the garden room and Ralph carried the scuttle of coal from the library, and lit a fire.

The fog continued to surround them like an impenetrable blanket and, because of this, he knew what Jessica and Mrs Egerton-Smythe wanted to do. He helped them carry all Laurie's belongings down to the room and while Jessica listened to his records and Mrs Egerton-Smythe read through papers and letters by the fire, he sat on the settee and read *Flare Path*.

'How is it he had so many plays?' Ralph asked in the middle of Act II.

Mrs Egerton-Smythe looked over her reading glasses. 'He loved the theatre. We used to go regularly to the Palace.'

'Why didn't you say anything?'

'One doesn't discuss family matters with a servant,' she said wryly.

'Oh!' said Ralph. 'That definitely means I'm sacked, then.'

'No. But while Queenie is about I shall continue to call you Hollis. Behind the scenes,' and she smiled at this theatrical reference, 'I shall call you Ralph.' And she returned to her reading.

Before Ralph left for the theatre, he refilled the coal scuttle from the cellar and placed two of the candelabras on the mantelpiece because there was the possibility of another electricity cut.

The fog still surrounded the house, but it didn't seem quite so thick. At least, that's what he told himself. Mrs Egerton-Smythe didn't protest too much. She seemed to understand how important it was for him to be there and Ralph knew he could return any time he liked.

Also, he had a feeling that Jessica and her mother had a lot of talking to do.

'Cheer up,' said Helena as she and Isla and he sat round the mound of *Sweet Aloes* props. 'You look as though your best friend has just died.'

'I won't be here for any more Saturdays,' he said. 'Not for ages.'

'True,' said Isla, 'but there's always the night before Christmas Eve.'

'What's happening then?'

'We'll be setting up for the panto.'

'There won't be anything for him to do,' said Helena. 'Don't raise his hopes.'

'He could make tea for us, and Judy might need some finishing off work done to the coach or pumpkins, or whatever.'

'Does that mean you'll be working at Christmas?'

'Oh, no,' said Helena. 'We get Christmas Day off.' 'We just have to be back first thing Boxing Day morning for setting up the lights, doing a dress rehearsal and performing two shows.'

'We'll be finished early tonight,' said Isla beaming.

'Oh, don't,' groaned Ralph. 'I can't understand why you're so cheerful.'

'Panto time is wonderful. You have no rehearsals in the morning and just two performances a day. It's like being on holiday! And the theatre is packed.'

'And backstage,' said Helena, smiling, 'it's chaos. We've got children and older girls coming from two local dance academies and variety-hall performers coming too. It'll be a real mix.'

'Variety and legit,' said Ralph to himself.

'Yes?' said Isla, puzzled.

'What does it mean?'

'Variety is more in the music-hall tradition. Comedy acts and gags, passed down from father to son, or ones invented and honed over the years. Legit is plays, three-acters. You know.'

'Oh, I see. But Wilfred said something about them not mixing.'

'Oh, everyone is always afraid of that. The rep lot that stay for the panto think the variety lot are going to be rough, wander round with beer bottles in their hands and give them a hard time. And the variety lot are worried that the rep lot will be snobbish and standoffish and then they're always surprised at how well they get on.'

'I think that's all we can do now,' said Helena, looking at their prop list.

With a heavy heart, Ralph walked out of the pass door into the stalls with them and walked through the auditorium.

Outside, the fog was still there, but Ralph could just make out the pavement and lampposts.

After a dismal 'goodbye', which made Isla and Helena laugh, he collected his bike from the side of the river and headed for home. It wasn't easy.

The roads were icy. He rode, slid, hopped off, pushed, rode and slid again. He wheeled his bike into the yard, stuffed as many of the plays as he could into his jacket pocket and headed round to the front door. He had just relocked it and had put the key onto the shelf when he heard footsteps in the kitchen. Before he could flee up the stairs, the door was swung open. Standing in the doorway in his long johns was his father.

'This way, lad,' he commanded. 'I want to know what's going on. I can't get any sense out of your mother, so I'd better get some sense from you. Neither of us are going to bed until I do,' and he stood back and held the door open for him.

NINETEEN

They sat face to face at the kitchen table, a candle between them as there was no electricity. Ralph did not speak. He stared at his father, attempting to fathom out how much he knew. 'Well?' said his dad.

142

'What do you want to know?' Ralph asked.

'What do you mean, what do I want to know? Where the hell have you been?'

'The theatre. I couldn't go and see the play last night because of the fog.'

'There was fog tonight.'

'But not as bad.'

'And after that?'

'What?'

'Oh, come on. You must take me for a fool. At first I thought you'd been seeing some girl. And then before I could say anything, I noticed your mum was a bit cagey. Then I found out she left the front door unlocked. She's a terrible liar, your mother. Not only that, she hates doin' it. So if you have any thought for her, you'll own up so she can stop avoiding my eyes every time I ask her about it.'

'Ask about what?' Ralph asked casually.

'These Saturday night jaunts. I've heard you come in late.'

'I can't tell you.'

'What do you mean, you can't tell me?'

'If I do, you'll take it out on Mum and stop me from . . .' He hesitated.

'Stop you from what?'

'Helping out.'

'Helpin' out? At what?'

'Does it matter? I'm not working. I'm learning. I'm not doing any harm.'

'Oh, I see, you're getting a bit of extra money on the side, only you don't want to let on because you know I'd expect you to hand it over.'

'I don't get paid.'

'You work all night and you don't get paid,' he repeated. 'You ain't making any sense, boy.'

'I told you. I'm learning. And getting my foot in the door.'

'What door?'

'I can't tell you.'

'We're going round in circles here. Right, let's start again. Does Mum know where this so-called work is?'

Ralph did not answer.

'I take it she does then, so it can't be a brothel.'

'Dad!'

'So why would I stop you?'

'Because you wouldn't approve.'

'I don't approve of you deceiving me,' he pointed out.

Ralph looked away. Outside he was presenting a calm front, but inside he was frantically trying to find a way of telling half a lie or breaking the truth gently.

'If you don't tell me, I'll have to keep an eye on you every Saturday night. There'll be no more sneaking out.'

'I'm not doing anything wrong. Why is it so important?'

'I'm your dad. I've got to do right by you until you leave home and get married.'

'But I can't win with you. If I work it's never the right kind of work.'

'That ain't true. I didn't think much of this garden lark. But I've come round.'

There was another silence.

'Look, Dad, I'm tired.'

'So am I.'

'Couldn't we talk about it in the morning?'

'It is the morning.'

Ralph was horrified to find tears welling into his eyes. Just the thought of telling his father left him feeling bereaved because he knew it would be the end of helping on the strikes. He turned sidewards and propped his head with one hand so that his father couldn't see his face.

'I help out at the Palace,' he said, his voice quavering. 'They have to strike the set every Saturday night and put a new one up. I make them tea and mend any broken props and sort out the ones that need to be returned, sweep the stage, that sort of thing.'

His father said nothing and Ralph kept his face covered.

'All men, is it?' his father asked awkwardly.

'No. I usually work with two of the ASMs. That's assistant stage managers. They're female.'

'That's something then,' he heard his father say with relief.

This response puzzled Ralph but he still kept his hand where it was.

'"ow come you don't get paid, then?'

'They can't afford it.'

'So why do you stay?'

'To learn.'

'What for?'

'I want to.'

'Ralph, what's the point of workin' and not getting paid?'

'You don't get paid for keeping an allotment.'

'I do that for the family. Puts food on the table.'

Ralph lowered his head even further.

'What are those books?'

'Plays. Mrs Egerton-Smythe lent them to me.'

'What you wanna read that stuff for?'

'Because it's alive. Because it opens doors to another way of life. Because it's about people and conflict between people. Because it makes me feel angry or makes me laugh or think in a new way. I don't know.'

'You don't need to read books for that!' his father remarked. He sighed. 'And these girls, they don't mind you hangin' around?'

'No. It means they can get home earlier.'

'You ain't hoping to get paid work there?' he asked tentatively.

'Yes, but don't worry. There's no chance. We don't have enough money. You have to be middle or upper class to get into the legit theatre,' he said bitterly. 'Legit means plays. Repertory. That sort of thing.'

'Now I'm completely stumped. To get paid work you got to have money? Sounds Chinese to me.'

'You either go to a training place where you have to pay fees, unless you get a scholarship, which I won't . . .'

'Why not?'

'Because I'd have to pay for coaching.'

'You don't need coachin'. You've got a brain. What's the other?'

'Your father gives a hundred pounds to the theatre and they pay you two pounds a week to learn the ropes.'

His father gave a whistle. 'A hundred quid! I see what you mean.'

Ralph suddenly realised that he and his father were having a conversation and not a shouting match. He turned slightly and peered through his fingers. And for a moment his father looked almost likeable.

'That's that, then,' his father said with finality. 'No point in still doing it.'

'Well, that didn't last long, did it?' Ralph muttered angrily.

'What?' said his father.

'Nothing.'

Neither of them moved.

'So?' said Ralph at last.

'I ain't got nothin' more to say.'

'Well, I have!' said Ralph swinging round and leaping up. 'I'm going to go on helping for as long as I possibly can. There's nothing for me to do now it's the panto season, but as soon as the next season of plays starts, I'm volunteering again. It was hard enough getting in . . .'

145

To Ralph's amazement his father suddenly burst out laughing. Ralph was furious. Here he was, about to give the most dramatic exit of his lifetime and his father was laughing at him. 'I don't see what's so funny,' he said offended.

'I understand now!' his father yelped and he began shaking his head from side to side. 'You was helping at the *theatre*, not Mrs Egerton-Smythe.'

Ralph stared at him as if his father was losing his senses.

'Dad, you spoke to her on the phone! You've seen the dirt under my fingernails. She pays me!'

'I know all that!' his father choked. 'But the bear!' he chuckled. 'The bear trip! It was for the *theatre*. You weren't doin' no favours for Mrs Egerton-Smythe. That's why everyone was so secretive about it!' And he slapped his thighs.

'Actually it was Mrs Egerton-Smythe's bear,' said Ralph stiffly. 'In fact, the trilby and oilskin raincoat belonged to her dead husband.'

They glanced at each other for a second of seriousness before they both collapsed. Above their heads the floor creaked.

'Oh, oh, oh,' wept Ralph's father. 'And they was all so solemn about it! Oh, oh, oh. I can't bear it.'

'Please, no bear jokes!' gasped Ralph. 'Oh! I can't take any more.'

By now there were light footsteps on the stairs and in the hall. The door swung open. His mother stood in a nightdress, her hair fanned out around her face in tangles and waves. She looked at them in astonishment and gave a perplexed smile. 'What's goin' on?' she asked. 'I had to come down. Win's started to grind her teeth.' She hurriedly closed the door and began to shiver.

'Come on, love,' said Ralph's father and he held out his arms.

To Ralph's amazement, his mother sat on his father's lap.

'Mum!' he exclaimed, embarrassed.

The two of them beamed at him.

'Oh, Ralphie!' she laughed. 'We are married you know.'

Ralph stepped out of the second-hand bookshop, a pile of books in his arms. Instead of having soup and bread in Mrs Egerton-Smythe's kitchen at midday, he had cycled into Winford to do some Christmas shopping. There were still nine days to go but he had grabbed the chance in case there were more fogs. His father had let him keep some of his pay packet and he had bought everyone in his family a second-hand book except his mother. Aunty Win had a detective novel, Joan a film annual, Elsie a girls' boarding school adventure, Harry a comic annual, his father a book on vegetable growing and Kitty and Frank a book of tips on how to make furniture out of boxes. He bought Isla a collection of love poems by John Donne, which he hoped she wouldn't open till Christmas when she was at home, and got Helena an old *Punch* book of stories and cartoons.

He stuffed the books into the basket on the handlebars of his bike and wheeled it quickly to the alley next to the theatre where there was an old junk shop often visited by Isla when looking for props. He had been there earlier but had asked the man to put his purchases aside because they were breakable, a record for Jessica, a rather ornate wine glass for her mother, and a cup and saucer for his own mother, with red roses on it and gold rims.

He propped the bicycle outside. Through the grime and dust, half hidden in an alcove, the shop assistant, an elderly man in slippers could be seen sitting on a chair reading. He peered over a pile of boxes when he heard Ralph open the door and staggered to his feet. 'I put them in a box,' he said, 'with a bit of paper round them. You'll need some string to tie the box on the back of your bike though.'

'Damn!' said Ralph. 'I haven't any.'

'There might be some lying about,' said the man vaguely. 'Have a look round.' And he disappeared into the alcove again.

Ralph had just found an old canvas bag and some dubious-looking bits of string which he knotted together, when he noticed something tarnished and black sticking out of a pile of battered ankle boots. He swallowed, his heart thumping rapidly. Hastily he pulled the boots aside and drew it out. It was a candelabra for four candles. He turned it over. It was silver. He pulled out his money. His father had given him extra to buy his own Christmas present from the family since, he explained, he and his mother didn't know what to get him.

He strolled casually towards the alcove. The man peered out again. 'You find some, then?' he said gazing at the knotted string and bag. He glanced at the candelabra. 'Don't tell me you want that. It's a filthy old thing.'

'I know,' shrugged Ralph. 'But with all these electricity cuts . . .' and he left the rest of the sentence dangling in the air.

'Tuppence,' said the man. 'That do?'

'Tuppence,' said Ralph, matter-of-factly, hoping that the man had not picked up the excitement in his voice.

Outside, he tucked the canvas bag around the wooden box and tied it firmly to the back of his bicycle. The candelabra he wedged

147

in the middle of the books so that it wouldn't fall out. It stuck out black and beautiful from under the lid of the basket. He hopped on to the bike and headed back to Mrs Egerton-Smythe's, suppressing a strong desire to yell for joy, till he had turned the corner at the end of the alley.

He had hardly leant his bike beside the woodshed and strode out towards the river when he heard shouting. It was Jessica. She was leaning out of her bedroom window waving. 'I'm coming down!'

'But it's freezing out here,' he yelled back.

'It's freezing in here,' she answered.

He watched her close the window, took his fork towards a border and began to turn the earth over. Within minutes he heard Jessica's feet pounding down the lawn. Steam was erupting from her mouth like a whinnying horse and her plaits were flying up sideways next to her green woolly hat, giving the appearance of moving handlebars.

'Aren't you cold without a coat?' she gasped.

'This warms me up,' he said shoving the fork back into the ground.

'I wondered where you'd got to.'

Poor kid, he thought, she must be lonely.

'I wanted to get my Christmas presents before another fog descends.'

'Did you see *Sweet Aloes*?'

'Yes. It was *so* good!'

'What was it about?'

He hesitated. 'I don't think your mother would approve of me telling you.'

'So it can't be about a murder,' she said. 'It must have something to do with an indiscretion.'

'That sort of came into it.'

'Involving bedrooms.'

'No,' he said slowly.

'But am I getting warmer?'

'Jessica!'

'I shan't give up.' She stuffed her hands in her pockets. 'By the way,' she added, casually, 'how old do you think I am?'

He glanced aside at her in her school coat and black wellingtons. The freckles seemed even more startling against her pale frozen face.

'Thirteen?'

'I thought so,' she sighed. 'It's these freckles.'

'How old are you then?'

'Fifteen.'

He stared at her amazed and then realised he was being rude.

'So I think I'm old enough to be told the plot of *Sweet Aloes*.

'No,' he laughed. 'But I'll have to tell you anyway.'

The two of them carried on chatting, Jessica hopping from one boot to another with her scarf up to her ears, shoulders hunched up, while Ralph kept turning the earth over. And to Ralph's surprise he found he was telling her everything; about how he was in love with Isla but it was hopeless because she was in love with someone else, and about the row with his father and how it had ended up with them laughing.

And Jessica told him how she had been working extra hard at school so that she could take her School Cert a year early at fifteen. She was brighter than her brother Charles and she had a feeling he would have her out of school before she could achieve any academic success. And then she told him her secret. She wanted to go to art school. Her dream was to be a sculptress.

'My only chance is a scholarship,' she said, 'or getting a job and paying for the fees as I go along. Charles would never agree to it of course, so *please* don't breathe a word or he'll remove me even earlier and send me off to some awful finishing school to finish me off, well and truly,' she added dismally.

'I promise,' said Ralph. 'Does your mother know?'

'Yes. Luckily she's all for it, and I have a lovely housemistress I can talk to and she's been having chats with the headmistress and my mother.'

'Quite a conspiracy.'

Jessica giggled. 'Yes it is rather. You went to a grammar school, didn't you?'

'Yes.'

'Did you stay long enough to take School Cert?'

'Yes.'

'And?'

'I got it.'

She smiled. 'That's wonderful.'

'Apart from my mother, you're the only one who's looked so pleased.'

'Wasn't your father pleased?' she asked astonished.

'No. But that's another story.'

'Which you're going to tell me.'

'Of course,' he laughed, resigned, and he threw his fork into the next section of border and began to do just that.

149

Christmas Eve fell on a Tuesday.

He cut masses of holly from the garden and he and Jessica decorated the garden room. Later they painted strips of paper and glued them together to make paperchains and she showed him how to make paper lanterns and stars for Elsie. He cleaned up the candelabra and it was like new, sumptuous and elegant. At Mrs Egerton-Smythe's request he dug up two small pine trees from the garden. Mrs Egerton-Smythe insisted that he take one tree and some holly home with him. She gave him a khaki great-coat which Mr Egerton-Smythe Senior had worn in the Home Guard, a Christmas bonus in his pay packet and a dozen candles.

Jessica and her mother were going to have their Christmas dinner at Charles's home, but had persuaded him to let them stay the night in their own home and for once he seemed quite ready to accept this. Ralph and Queenie were to have Christmas Day and Boxing Day off.

Ralph was let off work early, so that the dusk was only beginning to fall when he pushed his loaded bicycle towards the High Street. He parked it in its usual secluded place and took out the presents for Helena and Isla. To his surprise he found that his legs were shaking with nerves.

Light was spilling out across the snow from the stage door. He paused for a moment. It felt as though he had been away from the building for years. Wilfred was sitting as usual in his cubby-hole, reading a newspaper. He didn't see Ralph at first. Ralph stood shyly in front of him unnoticed. Finally he cleared his throat. Wilfred glanced up, gave Ralph a surprised look and then leapt to his feet.

'I wonder,' began Ralph, holding out the two parcels, 'would you put these in Helena and Isla's pigeonholes?

'Are you afraid of heights?' Wilfred asked excitedly.

'I don't think so. Why?'

'Stay there!' he commanded. 'Don't move.'

Bewildered, Ralph remained at the cubby-hole still holding the parcels. After a few minutes the sounds of hurried footsteps came down the stairs. It was Wilfred returning with Mr Johnson. 'You're not afraid of heights, are you?' Mr Johnson enquired.

'I already asked him,' said Wilfred.

'No,' said Ralph.

'We need someone on the limes.'

'Limes?' asked Ralph puzzled.

'One of the lights in the auditorium. It's a follow spot. You follow the actors with it. It'd be two shows a day, six days a week.

150

Afternoons and evenings. Two shillings a night. That's twelve shillings a week.'

Ralph thought quickly. He would have to ask Mrs Egerton-Smythe if he could work mornings only, perhaps make up the work on a Sunday.

'Now I know you're keen to get onto the stage, lad,' said Mr Johnson, 'but doing this job won't make any difference to you getting an acting job later on.'

That's what you think, thought Ralph.

'Well?' said Mr Johnson. 'That's the wage I'm offering. Take it or leave it.'

'I'll take it,' Ralph said.

Act Two
December 1946 – March 1947

ONE

*H*e decided to climb the long narrow ladder to the scaffolding platform and the spotlight, before the house was open to the public. He was trembling with nerves and he had a feeling that if members of the audience were around to watch him, his legs would be shaking so much, he might fall.

It was Boxing Day, the first matinée, and it seemed as if the last forty-eight hours had been a lifetime.

After Ralph had accepted the job, he had pushed his bike home in a trance. Nothing, not even the worst quarrel at home, could penetrate the wall of happiness which seemed to well up inside and surround him. When he had stuck holly, paper chains and paper lanterns round the kitchen, his mother, Harry and Elsie loved it. Joan was indifferent, and his aunt and father had poo-pooed it. It was the first time he had seen them agree about anything. The tree was unanimously crowed over, except for his father, who suddenly accused Ralph of trying to usurp his position. Ralph had never meant to cause offence. Disappointed, he noticed his father growing more bad-tempered as Christmas approached. Unable to understand why, he refused to let himself be drawn into an argument.

He and Elsie placed the tree in a tin bucket, packed earth round the roots and stood it on the cupboard reserved for the wireless. They painted bits of paper, rolled them into balls and hung them on bits of cotton in the branches. Then they put all the parcels round the base.

On Christmas Day Ralph watched in anticipation as they opened them. Everyone seemed pleased with their presents. He kept his one until last.

His mother had looked quite overwhelmed. 'Oh, it's beautiful, Ralphie,' she gasped.

'Our money never bought that,' said his father, suspiciously.

'It did,' said Ralph. '*And* I had money left over. And he told them how he had spotted them.

'What you want a lah-di-dah thing like that for?' complained his father.

'It's not lah-di-dah,' Ralph had said, determined not to rise to the bait.

'Well, they ain't being used here, I can tell you that,' stated his father firmly. 'You'll be wantin' champagne next!'

But there was an electricity cut and it was so dark outside that the candelabra with four candles was put centre-table and it added a certain magic to the meal.

Ralph kept his news about the theatre job until Boxing Day. Sensing his father's mood he didn't want to spoil Christmas Day for everyone else. Joan and his mother had already been upset that Kitty and Frank had not been able to join them. Heavy snow in Kent had made travelling impossible. Instead they would be sharing Christmas in the Nissen hut with the other squatters.

Over breakfast the following day he had said casually, 'I'm working today.'

'Oh, Ralphie,' exclaimed his mother. 'I thought Mrs Egerton-Smythe was giving you today off.'

'She has done. It's other work.'

His father had suddenly looked alert, but Ralph felt so exuberant that his father's glowering face still didn't touch him.

'What other work?' asked his mother.

'I hope it's not what I'm thinking,' said his father.

'Oh?' said Ralph innocently. 'What's that?'

'Playing around in that theatre for nothin'.'

'Oh, no, it's paid work, Dad.'

'Doing what?'

'Lighting. I'm on one of the follow-spots for the panto.'

'I don't want you mixing with that theatre lot.'

'I've already accepted the job.'

'Tell them you can't.'

'It's an emergency. The chief electrician has had an accident on the ice and he's lying in hospital with his leg up in a sling, so the assistant has to work the switchboard which means that someone needs do her job. You wouldn't want to spoil the pleasure of hundreds of children, would you, Dad?'

It was soon after this, that everyone seemed to need to go to their rooms, or the scullery, leaving him and his dad to have yet another shouting match, ending in his father saying he never wanted to see his face again and Ralph cycling off to Winford in a fury.

Luckily Mrs Egerton-Smythe and Jessica were delighted with his news. Work in the mornings would be fine, but he need not come on a Sunday, but when Jessica said, 'Oh please let him!' Mrs Egerton-Smythe relented. Though Ralph had a feeling with Jessica around he wouldn't get much work done.

'Everything in order?'

The manager was standing in evening dress at the foot of the stalls. He had been calling out to each section of the house.

'All in order, sir,' he heard the senior usherette call back.

'The house is open,' the manager declared.

Ralph knew this was the signal for the commissionaire to release the safety bar at the main doors.

With a flutter of excitement Ralph sat on the crossbar of wood, his boots resting on a small platform, and attemped to make himself comfortable behind the spotlight. But not too comfortable. It was a long way down. Not the sort of place to drop off to sleep. He checked he had everything he needed; tongs for changing the carbons, canvas gloves, the card with his cues on and two gels.

Gradually he heard the high-pitched chatter of children and the raised voices of their mothers asking them if they wanted to go to the lavatory. Most of them were carrying rugs. The theatre had suffered from the electricity cuts too and there was no heating.

Immediately below him he watched a woman empty a flask of hot water into a hot-water bottle and tuck it underneath a large rug which was spread out along her family's knees. From the movement under the rug they were all taking turns with it.

Ralph went over the panto in his mind. They had had a dress rehearsal that morning. And apart from the green gel getting stuck twice it hadn't been too bad. He had two gels, one red and one green. All he had to remember was white or open for the fairy godmother, Cinderella and the prince, green for the ugly sisters, and red for one of the comic scenes between the broker's men. Once he had slid in the appropriate gel he had to follow the actors with the spot.

He glanced at the card with the cues written on it. With its strange list of abbreviations and instructions, it looked daunting. 'PU means pick up,' he whispered to himself. 'PS means prompt side. Follow till DBO means follow till dead black out.'

Suddenly the house was full. Latecomers were climbing over laps as people stood awkwardly, clutching their blankets, to let them pass. Ralph spotted the Billy Dixon Trio enter the pit with a fourth musician. The latter sat at a set of drums with hooters and coconut

154

shells and other stage props surrounding him.

Ralph opened the metal box in the spotlight and slid in two carbon rods as thick as a fountain pen, opposite one another. He left enough space between them for the electric current to leap across the gap, and switched on the power. Suddenly there was a brilliant light. It reminded Ralph of the spark trains made on wet points. He turned away quickly as the carbons hissed into life and a waft of smoke began to rise from the box.

He tilted the spotlight and swivelled it round so that it pointed centre-stage. He pulled off the scarf Jessica had made for him for Christmas and stuffed it in his pocket. The follow-spot was already throwing out quite a heat. On the other side of the circle he could see Helena operating her follow-spot.

The house lights dimmed. There was a roll of drums followed by a rousing overture from the trio. The audience began to chatter excitedly in low voices and the curtain rose and there was silence. Crowding on to the stage, outside Harduppe Hall, Baron de Brokes home, were Mademoiselle Woods' Academy girls and the Gladys Winston Young Ladies, dressed as villagers. The audience gasped and broke into applause.

It was Act Two and the Mademoiselle Wood Girls had almost finished performing their military tap-dance across the stage, all eyes and teeth. A few spun round holding one leg high in the air and then the number ended with salutes from the girls in the back and the front row of girls jumping into the inevitable splits.

Just a short reprieve and soon Isla would enter as one of the young men. He could feel himself growing excited already. He had seen her costume in the dress rehearsal. Over tights and black shoes with buckles, she wore a close-fitting tunic in blue and white, down to the top of her thighs. Having seen her so often in dungarees or a skirt, he had never realised how shapely she was. He had adored girls from afar before but it was the first time he had experienced such a strong physical desire for someone he was in love with.

The reprise of the tap-dance was over and there she was, upstage centre, resplendent, beautiful and dazzling, and he swung the spot on, for him, the star of the show.

There was less than an hour before the 6.30 p.m show. Ralph wasn't sure what people would be doing between the shows for food. He had to see Helena to check that he had used the spot correctly. Liar! It was Isla he had to see. He hadn't found the right moment to ask her if she liked the book he had given her for

Christmas and she still hadn't said anything. He had no regrets at having given it to her, yet ever since, he had felt excruciatingly embarrassed every time he saw her. He longed for her to say something yet dreaded it too.

He waited till the last member of the audience had left before climbing down the ladder. In spite of his shaking legs, adrenalin took him effortlessly leaping up the stairs to the swing doors, through red and white passages with their framed photos of past productions on the walls, down the passage behind one of the boxes in the dress circle on to the pass door and into the wings.

He found Isla and Helena already setting up the props on the prop table for the next show. He hovered, his hands in his pockets and strolled nonchalantly towards them.

'Would you like me to make tea for the cast?' he asked.

Isla whirled round. 'Oh, would you?'

'Of course,' and he wandered off to the door which led to the corridor behind the stage.

He was about to swagger through it when Helena called out to him, 'Any problems with the lighting?'

'I don't think so,' said Ralph. 'How did it look?'

'Fine.'

'Phew,' said Ralph and to his relief they laughed.

The Academy Girls and Gladys Winston Young Ladies were crammed into the dressing rooms at the top of the theatre. They didn't need tea as their mothers had organised their own refreshments. The ugly sisters, played by two music hall men, were in dressing room one and Cinderella, Dandini and Prince Charming in dressing room two. Buttons and Baron de Broke shared dressing room three on the next floor and the two broker's men were in dressing room four. Isla shared dressing room five with another actress on the next floor opposite dressing room six where the fairy godmother had a room of her own.

The speciality dance duo changed underneath the stage.

Ralph ran around the rooms with mugs of tea on a tray, knocking on each door, to be greeted by men and women in various states of nakedness, or with tatty silk dressing gowns wrapped loosely around them, their stage make-up as garish as coloured masks. It was the first time he had seen it on men at such close quarters. It shocked him at first but after a while he hardly noticed it.

By the time he came down with the tray, the kettle was boiling again. Helena and Isla entered the kitchen and collapsed on the threadbare chairs.

'I forgot to ask you,' said Ralph. 'Should I make tea for the fly-men and the stage hands and Arthur?'

'No,' said Isla. 'They'll go to the pub for bread and cheese and beer.'

He poured out three cups for them and then sat opposite them and pulled out a package from his trousers. Suddenly he was conscious of its contents. He hesitated for a moment and then too hungry to care, he drew out a rather squashed piece of bread and dripping.

'Like a bit?' he said smiling.

'Bread and dripping!' exclaimed Isla. 'Oh, yes. Oh, no. You won't have any left for yourself.'

'I'll have supper waiting for me when I get home,' he lied.

He shared the bread out in lumps and everything was fine again, but there was still no talk of their Christmas presents. He sipped his tea slowly.

'Did Wilfred give you your presents?' he asked casually.

They stared at him puzzled. 'What presents?' asked Isla.

'Did you give us presents?' Helena began.

Ralph nodded.

'This is awful!' said Isla. 'I'm so sorry. We had no idea, did we, Helena?'

'No.'

'Well, things were a bit hectic,' Ralph saaaid, feeling his face growing warm. 'What with one thing and another, I expect he forgot.'

Helena sprang up. 'I'll get them.' she said excitedly. Before he could stop her, she ran swiftly out of the door. Ralph cleared his throat. 'I'd better go and drink this in the wings,' he muttered.

'Why?' said Isla. 'Don't you want to be here when we open them?'

'No,' he said. 'You might not like them and then it would be embarrassing for you.'

'Don't be silly.'

Ralph sat on his chair as stiff as a rock and stuck his nose in the mug. As soon as he heard footsteps coming along the corridor, he dropped his mug into the sink and grabbed the tray.

'I'll just go and pick up the empty cups,' he said quickly and he collided in the corridor with Helena who was clutching the two parcels.

'Where are you going?' she asked.

'Off to collect any empties,' he said.

By the time he came back, the parcels had been opened. He had hoped that Isla would have been on her own, but instead, the two of them were reading.

They glanced up and smiled. 'This is perfect,' Helena said. 'I haven't got time to read novels nowadays and I need something to wind me down before I go to bed. And I love a laugh. It's ever so kind of you.'

Ralph shrugged his shoulders as if to say, 'Oh, it was nothing.' He found he couldn't bear to look at Isla.

'And I love mine,' she breathed. 'How lovely of you to give me a book of love poems. Philip will love these too. I know he will. I'm going to choose some, write them out and send them to him.' And she laughed. 'You're so thoughtful.'

On the outside Ralph was smiling, but inside it was though someone had taken a crowbar to his insides. Forcing himself to smile was making his head ache so badly he wondered if he was beginning to look like a gargoyle.

'Glad you liked them,' he said casually and he piled the cups into the sink ready to wash for the interval.

'Oh lord,' said Isla, looking at her watch. 'It's the half.' And she fled.

'Need a hand?' said Helena, and she came and stood by his side.

From outside the number one dressing room he heard Isla knock at the door. 'Mr Butler, Mr Higgins, this is your half-hour call. Your half-hour call, please.'

Thirty-five minutes to curtain-up, thought Ralph, staring at the murky water surrounding the cups. Everything had five minutes added on before the show, he had discovered. The quarter was twenty minutes before curtain-up. The five-minute call meant you had ten minutes, and beginners call, five minutes. It was to make sure that all the actors for the opening scene were ready in the wings five minutes before they were needed.

'Being in love tends to make some people insensitive,' said Helena suddenly.

Ralph glanced down at her.

'She misses him so badly that everything reminds her of him whenever she's not working. It doesn't occur to her that someone else could be feeling just as badly for her.'

Ralph blushed. 'You won't say anything, will you,' he begged.

'Course I won't. And you won't take it out on her on-stage, will you?' she added, jokily.

'How do you mean?' said Ralph.

'Not putting the spot on her when needed.'

'But I couldn't do that,' he exclaimed. 'That's my job.'

She smiled. 'You're quite an old pro already, aren't you?'

'It's not that,' he said. 'I've made her happy, that's what counts.'

She nodded and gave his arm a squeeze. 'I wish I could find the right words. But every time I think of something, it's a cliché.'

'Honestly,' said Ralph, 'I don't need to be consoled.'

He wanted to say, just being in the same building is enough, but much as he liked Helena, he found it too intimate a thought to express. Perhaps it was because she was so much older than him. He would see Jessica in the morning. He'd tell her. He could tell her anything.

True to his word he did put the spot on Isla when it was needed. A lump still came into his throat every time he saw her, throwing her arm expansively out to the audience, standing there with her shapely legs astride, her hands on her hips, and her wonderful, wonderful smile which seemed to melt into every bone in his body. But something stronger than his feelings forced him to concentrate. The show. And it was hard because he felt such conflicting emotions, love, despair, anger at this Philip chap she had mentioned, and pain, pain, pain.

What helped him were the antics of the broker's men. The rep actor played the straight man who gave the feed lines to the music-hall performer, a stout man in his fifties, who made the audience laugh with his punchlines. They had already added a couple of new gags and there was a running gag about a sack of flour descending from the flies which brought the house down.

By the interval he felt almost normal again. He rested his chin in his hands and gazed up at the massive glass chandelier on the ceiling and the nymphs and shepherdesses. It was impossible to feel too unhappy in a theatre, he thought. He had heard of actors going on stage in terrible pain which disappeared while they were on stage. Dr Greasepaint, he had heard someone call it. Perhaps emotional pain was numbed too.

The lights dimmed, the drums rolled and the second act music began. Ralph stretched out his hand and rested it on the follow-spot.

TWO

He paced up and down his bedroom whispering Iago's speech, pounding his fist into his hand, leaning towards an imaginary audience in a fury. He stopped again. Something was

159

wrong. He could feel the bitterness and hate in the man, feel his sense of ambition, but the accent still didn't seem right. He sighed.

'One more time!' he muttered to himself.

He watched Roderigo leave and then when he was sure he was out of earshot, he stepped forward conspiratorially.

> *'Thus do oi ever make moi fool moi purse,'* he spat out,
> *'For I moine own gain'd knowledge should profane*
> *If oi would toime expend with such a snoipe*
> *But fer moi sport and profit. Oi 'ates the Moor;*
> *And it is thought abroad that 'twixt moi sheets*
> *"E 'as done moi office.'*

He carried on, feeling his neck tauten with venom, his face grow hot, and his voice break. And then he was at the closing couplet.

> *'Oi have't; it is engender'd. Hell and noigt*
> *Must bring this monstrous birth to the world's loight.'*

And with a flourish he swept an imaginary cloak before him and stepped off into the inky darkness.

He was going to look at his *Saint Joan* speech when he had finished the Iago piece but decided to leave it till the next day.

He had been working on both of them on and off for two weeks, thinking about the two characters as he shovelled in Mrs Egerton–Smythe's garden, or cycled to and from Winford. He hoped, that way, the characters would seep into his bones.

'Sorry I'm late' he said to his mother in the kitchen.

"Ave a good lie in?' she asked nonchalantly.

'Sort of. I've been working a bit too.'

'Oh, yeah?'

He hesitated for a moment. 'Rehearsals start for *Dear Octopus* on Monday,' he said. 'Mr Neville is producing it.'

'Oh, yeah?'

He watched her peel off a slice of bacon and the sight of it made his mouth water. She threw it into the frying pan with two slices of grey bread.

'So I thought I'd work on a couple of audition speeches, just in case I can persuade him to see me.'

'Is that what all that walking up and down up there is about?'

He laughed. 'Yes. It helps me think.'

'Oh,' she said suddenly, and she stretched up to the mantelpiece. 'These come for you yesterday.'

She threw two envelopes on the table. He recognised the writing. One was addressed to 'Miss R. Hollis' in Jessica's handwriting, and one to 'Master R. Hollis' from Cornwall. Jessica's had been opened.

'Who did this?' he exclaimed angrily.

'Elsie. She thought it was hers. She thought it must be Miss E. Hollis.'

'Did she read it?'

'Nah. Soon as she read out "Dear Ruth," I told her to read out who it was from. When she said Jessica, I guessed it were for you. What's the idea of calling you Ruth?'

'She's not allowed to write to boys. She has to put that in case one of the mistresses checks.'

'Does her mother know?'

'Yes, of course. Well, I think so.'

'You've taken quite a shine to her,' her mother commented, and she turned the bacon and bread over.

'It's not like thàt all,' Ralph cried indignantly. 'You're always jumping to conclusions.'

His mother flung the fried bread and bacon on a plate. 'Still the older woman, is it?'

'Mum!'

He was furious because he could feel his face burning. 'No! And Jessica and I are just friends.'

'That do?' said his mother, sliding the plate over to him.

'Looks marvellous,' said Ralph. 'I'm starving.'

'Who's the other one from?'

'Mr Wickham. He's a teacher in the Sixth. He directs most of the school plays. He's been very helpful to me. And I'm grateful but . . .' He sighed.

'Helpful? How?' she said and she sat down quickly beside him. Ralph suddenly noticed how pale she had become.

'Mum, are you all right? You've gone an awful colour.'

She waved her hand dismissively. 'I ain't been sleepin' so well lately. This cold weather keeps making me want to get up in the night. And then I'm so cold it takes me a while to get warmed up again and get back to sleep. Go on. You were saying?'

'I told him I had an audition and that I was going to work on a couple of speeches. Anyway he's told me what would make the best impression. It's just that the two pieces he's selected are deadly serious and I enjoy comedy best.'

'I thought you had to be able to act every kind of part at the rep. Serious and funny.'

'You do. But Mr Wickham thinks they won't take me seriously if I do a funny piece as well as a straight piece. He's also suggested I

161

do Iago working class, and as I know the Cornish accent like the back of my hand, that's the accent I should do it in. And I'm doing it. It's just I feel that the accent hasn't grown naturally from the character. It feels like it's been added on.'

'This older girl at the rep, have you told her?'

'No. I don't want to bother her. She's been a bit browned-off lately. She's missing her fiancé.'

'Oh.'

'Anyway I want to surprise her.'

'Your breakfast is getting cold. Eat up.'

'Is Dad at his allotment?'

'Yes. It's heartbreaking for him. Most of the veggies he's planted have been hit by this weather.'

Ralph glanced up at the window. The lower half was already piled high with fresh snow.

'They say there'll be a blizzard tonight,' she said anxiously.

'I'll be all right.'

'I hate you coming home so late in this weather.'

'It'll only be for another week,' he said dismally. 'Then I'll only be late one night a week.'

'You think they'll still let you help?'

'I hope so. I've proved to Jack Walker that I'm reliable. He should put in a good word for me.' He sighed. 'There's going to be a new ASM working there from Monday.'

'Girl or boy?'

'Girl. Helena's leaving at the end of the panto. She's been offered a terrific job with a number one touring company, doing sound and lighting.'

He stared miserably down at his plate.

'I can't keep up with you, Ralphie,' said his mother. 'Don't tell me you're soft on her too.'

'Mum! No, it's not that. It's about this new girl coming in.'

'She might be very nice.'

'That's not the point. She hasn't been to drama school, which means she'll be doing a sort of apprenticeship for a year.'

'And you'd been hoping a hundred pounds would drop from the sky and you could be the new ASM.'

'Something like that.'

'You'll be all right,' she said. 'You've got determination.'

He smiled. 'Thanks, Mum.'

After breakfast he read Jessica's letter. It made him laugh.

He was just folding it up when there was a crash from the scullery.

'Mum?' he said.

But there was no answer. He sprang up from his chair and ran to the door. He found her lying on the stone floor with the plate smashed beside her.

'Mum!'

He raised her to a sitting position. She gave a groan. 'Is it time to get up?' she murmured.

'Mum,' said Ralph. 'You fainted.'

She opened her eyes. 'What am I doin' 'ere? Oh, Ralphie,' she wailed, 'I've broken a plate!'

'Damn the plate!' he said. 'Put your arms round my neck.'

'Don't fuss.'

'Put your arms round my neck,' he commanded. He scooped his arm under her knees and picked her up. To his surprise she was quite light. He carried her into the kitchen and put her on a chair nearest the range. 'Now stay there,' he said. 'You're having some hot sweet tea.'

'Oh, Ralphie!' She smiled weakly. 'Honest, I'm fine.'

'I'm ordering you,' he said.

She looked at him amused. He poured her out tea from the pot on the range and dumped some sugar in.

'Go easy on that. That's rationed, remember?'

'And you've probably been giving your ration to everyone else,' he said.

He sat beside her, concerned. She had gone a waxen colour.

'Oh, that feels good,' she said, sipping the tea. And then suddenly she dumped the tea on the table and ran into the scullery.

Ralph followed her to find her vomiting in the sink.

'Get me a towel, will you, love?' And she turned on the tap. The pipe gave a rumbling sound. Ralph prayed it wouldn't burst. His father had lagged every pipe in sight, but with everyone else's pipes bursting around them it seemed they were living on borrowed time. At last the water spluttered out and he left his mother to wash her face.

Back in the kitchen he insisted that she get into his dad's bed. 'It's warm in here,' he said.

'I've got dinner to get,' she protested, but she allowed him to tuck her up. 'Oh, Ralphie,' she said, 'I've got a bit of a pain.'

'Where?'

'Down 'ere,' and she patted her stomach. Then to Ralph's alarm she burst into tears and sunk her face into the pillow.

He stayed beside her stroking her head until she fell asleep. He didn't want to leave her, yet he didn't know when his father would be back. Elsie and Harry had gone to the cinema club and Joan and his aunt were at work. He wanted to fetch a doctor, but he didn't want her to wake up and find no one there.

He scraped some potatoes and carrots, put them in a saucepan and shovelled more coal in the range. And then he sat and watched her. As soon as he heard the sound of boots tramping through the snow he sprang to his feet and looked out of the window.

'Dad!' he murmured. 'I never thought I'd be pleased to see you.'

He closed the scullery door behind him and opened the back door to the yard. 'Dad!' he cried. 'Mum's ill!'

His dad thrust Ralph aside and dashed into the kitchen.

Ralph found him staring down at her and it was then that he realised, from the expression on his father's face, how much he loved her.

'I know it'll cost money,' Ralph whispered, 'but, please, can't we get the doctor to come?'

'Blow the money,' he said. 'I'll find it somehow. I'll phone from Ted's.'

'If he's not in, I can call in on the way to Winford,' said Ralph.

'Good lad.'

Ralph sat beside his mother while his father ran to phone the doctor. 'You'll be all right now, Mum,' he said softly.

The house was only half full, which was unusual for a Saturday night, but as soon as Ralph stood at the stage door after the performance was over, he understood why. The weather forecast had been right. There was a blizzard. He stepped back to the skip where he had propped his bike. Most of the cast were gathered round Wilfred's cubby-hole. It was then Ralph discovered that it was not the keys that the cast handed to him on a Saturday night, but a shilling each and he realised that this Saturday tipping was some kind of theatre etiquette. He looked away, not wanting Wilfred to notice that he had seen.

As Ralph stood hunched in his greatcoat, plucking up enough courage to brave the elements, the Academy Girls and Gladys Winston's Young Ladies crowded by the stage door with their parents and then ran out, their heads bowed. Eventually Isla came down the stairs. She was chatting to Helena.

'Oh, lor,' she said, seeing the crowd. 'Is it bad?'

'That's the understatement of the century,' commented the fairy godmother, who had been collecting her script of *Dear Octopus* from Wilfred.

Ralph stepped forward. 'Would you like me to walk you to your digs?' he asked.

'No, you've got much further to go than we have. You're not going to try and ride that home?' she exclaimed noticing his bicycle.

Snow was now whipping in a frenzy through the doors.

'Ent there somewhere near where you can stay?' interrupted Wilfred.

'Yes,' said Ralph.

'Then stay there,' he said. 'You'll never make it to Braxley in this.'

Ralph nodded, but he had no intention of staying at Mrs Egerton-Smythe's. He had to know how his mother was. He had only been out in the street for five minutes with his collar up and cap pulled well down over his eyes when he was almost tempted to struggle back to the theatre and sleep there. As soon as he hit the High Street, the wind was so powerful that it bowled him over and he fell into a pile of snow, his bicycle sprawled across him. He struggled to his feet and attempted to clamber back on to it. By the time he had reached the railway bridge he realised that he would have to go on foot and push his bike. He made his way to the road leading to Braxley and stared ahead. It was covered in snow. Alongside were high hills of it where men had been shovelling it in heaps for the last few weeks.

There was no one except him. Ahead of him the road was untouched by footprints or tyre marks. Surrounded in a whiteness which whirled into his face and both pierced and numbed him, he trudged, still wondering whether he had made the right decision, but as soon as he thought of turning back he knew it was out of the question. He had to know if his mother was at home or in hospital. He swayed and stumbled, lifting his bike, pushing it against the snow, tripping and falling and hauling himself up, not even bothering to dust off the heavy layers of snow which now caked his greatcoat.

The snow looked so soft that several times he was tempted to give up and lie down, but then he remembered stories of people dying in their sleep in the snow and he staggered on. He was too exhausted even to feel exultant at recognising his house. Ironically it looked almost pretty. With the remaining two houses on either side it stood like a country house planted in the middle of Lapland. He fell forward and watched his hands and knees disappear. Pulling himself up laboriously, he dragged his bike sideways towards the alley which led to their backyard.

As he went to pull the door to the yard open, a bank of snow tumbled against him and knocked him over. He scrabbled around, digging away at the cold icy mass until he had freed his bike. At last the door opened. All he had to do now was put his bike away in the shed, make his way to the scullery door and let himself in. He had just dragged himself towards the shed when a powerful gust of wind sent him reeling to the ground and his bike went crashing into the door. He lay in the snow, too tired to move.

To hell with it, he thought. Enough is enough. I'm going to sleep.

THREE

Someone was trying to disturb him. He struggled to push them away but he couldn't move and the wind was dragging him forcibly through the snow. He never realised that wind could feel like hands gripping. He dreamt he could hear a voice repeatedly calling his name and then the wind lifted him like a sack of coal. And it was quiet. There was no more howling, just fingers wrenching at his overcoat buttons. He wanted to cry out, 'Leave me alone!' but he was too exhausted to speak. He felt himself falling and then being caught by something strong. The same force lifted him up and laid him on a flat hard surface. He would sleep here then, he thought.

But the hands had yanked him upright, and as much as he tried to protest he was unable. Gradually he began to feel a piercing pain in his eardrums, and something wet trickled from his head and down his face.

The wind was dragging his overcoat off, but he was beyond caring. A rough substance was being rubbed violently round his face and hair and then was stuck in a lump under his head. It felt soft. When he woke next, his boots and socks had been taken. Let them have them, he thought and he fell back to sleep. Each time he drifted into consciousness, his body was being dragged from one place to another and wet clothes were being peeled from his limbs.

And then he noticed the smell of candle wax, and warm cloth being pulled up his legs. Just as he was about to drift back to sleep he was yanked about again. But he felt warmer and the pain in his ears grew less intense. There was a moaning noise. He tried to make out where it was coming from, but after a few minutes he realised it was coming from him. He was hauled up to a sitting position and something hot touched his mouth. He opened his eyes.

Swimming in front of him was a chipped cup and beyond it the

166

dark outline of the range. It was then that he was aware of a firm arm holding him up. He forced himself to raise his head and found his father holding a cup out to him.

'Drink this, lad, it's got something strong in it to warm your insides.'

'How?' he began.

'We'll talk about it in the morning. I'll 'old it fer you.'

Ralph sipped at the proffered cup and the warm liquid hit his chest and stomach with startling rapidity.

'Mum?' he started.

'We'll talk about it when you've had some sleep.'

'Don't want to worry her,' he gasped.

'She don't know. She thinks you're staying at Mrs Egerton-Smythe's, which you should have done, but I knew you wouldn't. Too fond of yer mum to do that. That's why I waited up for you.'

Ralph nodded. He wanted to ask something else, but he couldn't remember what it was.

'No more questions,' his father said, and then fatigue overtook him again and as his eyes closed, he felt himself being lifted up and his cheek resting into someone's neck and he could smell his father's sweat, warm, familiar, and he was back in another time. He was eight years old with the measles and he had got up too soon and had fainted, and his father had caught him and carried him back to bed. And it was as though he was being rocked in a travelling cradle.

The next thing he heard was his father giving someone instructions.

'Warm him up,' he commanded.

'He's freezing,' said Harry.

'We'll warm him, won't we, Harry?' said Elsie.

And then his head was on a pillow and two small bodies nestled in on either side of him and as their warmth suffused into him, his arms and legs drifted out of reach and he was glad to be shot of them.

Elsie and Harry were building a huge snowman with his mother and father. Ralph stood at a distance watching them, feeling lonely and left out.

'Can I join in?' he asked, but before they could answer Joan needed help from his father and Aunty Win ran up and needed help from his mother and they turned to Ralph and said, 'There's no room.'

And then his father had said, 'But I could do with some help, lad,' and Ralph felt a terrible sense of loss, because he didn't want to help. He wanted to play, and he knew it was too late, that the time for playing was gone, and he woke up to a coldly lit room. Instead of lying with his head touching the tail end of the bed, he was touching the head of the bed. From downstairs he could hear voices coming from the kitchen.

He remembered walking home in the blizzard and arriving in the yard but everything else was a jumble of sensations. His pyjamas felt different. He glanced down only to find that he was wearing a pair of his father's long johns. As he lay in bed thinking, he realised his father had stripped him as naked as a baby. Suddenly he remembered it was Sunday.

'Mrs Egerton-Smythe,' he cried, and he flung back the covers.

He made for the chest of drawers in the corner. He guessed that his wet clothes were downstairs. All he had left to choose from were an old pair of school flannels which almost came up to his shins, and a school shirt and jumper. He decided to keep the long johns on. At least they were warm. Hauling socks over them and his flannels, he tucked his shirt in.

He picked up a stone at the side of the washstand and went through the morning ritual of breaking the ice in the jug before pouring the water into a bowl for washing.

He crept quietly out of the bedroom, easing the door gently to a close. For a moment he hesitated on the landing, staring at his mum's and Aunty Win's bedroom, wondering whether to knock or to go downstairs first. From the kitchen he heard muffled sounds of distress. He nipped quickly down the stairs feeling tiny splinters sticking to his socks.

When he hopped through the kitchen door he was greeted by a strange sight. Elsie was sitting pale and puffy-eyed at the table, her hands covered in soot. Harry was sitting equally pale-faced by her side. At the other side of the table, Joan sat, pouting. His aunt was scowling at Elsie who was sniffing and wiping away a steady stream of tears.

'What's going on?' asked Ralph.

His aunt's head shot round. 'So you've decided to get up, have you?'

Ralph gave a weary sigh. He was sick of having to remind her that he didn't get home until late from work. He ignored her. 'Elsie?'

She gazed up at him, but when she tried to speak she was sobbing so much, she was incoherent.

'She can't get the range going,' said Harry quietly.

168

'Stupid girl,' her aunt snapped. 'Her dad's right, grammar school's no preparation for a girl.'

'Mum never showed me,' Elsie wept.

'What about you two?' Ralph said with icy politeness.

He had guessed by now that his mother was still in bed.

'It may have escaped your notice,' said Aunty Win, in an angry whisper, 'that I work in the top department store in Winford. It ain't going to go down well if I turn up with dirty fingernails.'

'It's the same for me,' said Joan. 'Anyway I have enough to do.'

'I'll get the range going,' said Ralph.

'You?'

'Queenie showed me how to do it. I don't mind showing you.'

'Show Elsie,' said his aunt. 'It's her responsibility until your mum's better.' And she stalked out of the room.

'You'll want to know, won't you, Joan? In case Elsie's ill,' but she was already following his aunt. To his surprise it sounded as if they had both gone into the front room.

'Why is Aunty Win going into your bedroom?' he asked his sister. 'Has she been told not to disturb Mum?'

Elsie nodded. Ralph drew a handkerchief from his pocket and handed it to her.

'It's been terrible,' whispered Harry. 'Last night me and Elsie was sent upstairs and there was all this shouting and cryin' coming from downstairs.'

'We tried to listen on the landing, but we couldn't make out what was wrong,' Elsie stammered. She stared at him, her hands clasping the handkerchief. Ralph could see she was shaking.

'They ain't tellin' us everything,' she whispered. 'Oh, Ralph, do you think she's going to die?' and she burst into tears.

Harry stared helplessly at her. 'Can you find out?' he asked Ralph.

'I'll do my best.'

Elsie sniffed. 'In the end Dad called us down to the kitchen. It were ever so quiet.'

''Orrible quiet,' added Harry.

'Where was Mum?'

'In bed, upstairs. The doctor said she was to go up there away from us lot. He was 'ere when we got back from the flicks.'

'It were ever such a good picture,' enthused Harry. He looked down. 'Sorry. I'll tell you about it later.'

'Anyway,' said Elsie tearfully, 'Dad carried Mum upstairs then.'

'She looked ever so white,' added Harry.

'And the doctor says to us, "You'll have to help a bit now. Your mum's to stay in bed and rest and not be upset."'

'Didn't he tell you anything else?'

'I asked him, but he just said, "If she rests, there's a good chance . . ." and then he went.'

'So what happened after you and Harry were called down to the kitchen?'

'Well, Dad says, for now, I got to go back into your bedroom. If it don't work out, he'll move the bed in 'ere up there.'

'We'll cope,' said Ralph smiling. 'But hold on, where would Dad sleep if he moved it up?'

His brother and sister glanced at each other and then back at Ralph.

'Where he slept last night,' said Elsie quietly.

'Up there,' said Harry pointing to the ceiling.

'With Mum?' asked Ralph, aghast.

They nodded. 'That's what one of the rows was about,' said Elsie. 'Dad told Aunty Win to move all her stuff out and move in to our bedroom with Joan.'

Ralph gave a whistle.

'Dad said, Mum needed peaceful nights, and that Aunty Win was a vestless sleeper,' said Harry.

'Restless!' giggled Elsie.

'Yeah. Anyway she kicks her a lot, that sort of thing.'

'And Aunty Win said it was better than what he did to her,' Elsie said. 'Dad's been ever so nice to Mum lately. He's always doin' things for her now. So what did Aunty Win mean?'

The two of them looked at him with such innocence that he knew it wasn't the right time to explain. What disturbed him was that his mother would no longer have the protection of his aunt. And then he remembered his father's look of tenderness when he had stood in the kitchen gazing at her and it left him feeling confused.

'You know Aunty Win,' he said. 'She's always exaggerating.' The look of relief on their faces made him want to hug them. 'Now then, about this range?'

'Dad says me and Aunty Win and Joan are to do Mum's jobs.'

'I bet that didn't go down well,' Ralph commented.

'Only they're leaving it all to Elsie,' Harry burst out.

'Does Dad know?'

'No. I don't want him getting upset,' said Elsie quietly. 'And anyway he wouldn't understand.'

'She's got to light the range every morning,' said Harry. 'And cook breakfast before going to school, and do the supper at night.'

'Why?'

'Because Elsie gets home before they do.'

'But I usually do me 'omework then,' said Elsie.

'I see how Dad wouldn't understand.'

'Aunty Win says she ain't going to help Elsie with her uniform no more. Or her school books,' said Harry.

Elsie then buried her head in her arms and burst into tears. 'Dad says it's all for the best.'

'I bet he did,' said Ralph grimly. He put his arm round his sister. 'Elsie, your uniform is pretty large, isn't it?'

She nodded.

'I bet it will get you through at least three years.' She looked up at him, tear-stained, but alert. 'It's got enormous hems,' she hiccuped.

'There you are, then. By that time I'll have saved up enough to help you with the next uniform.'

'But what about things like pens and protractors?'

'I'll find a way, I promise.'

'Oh, Ralph,' she hiccuped. 'But how am I going to do me homework?'

'I'll ask Queenie to give me some easy recipes.'

'But I got to do the ironing as well,' she said. 'I 'ave to get the copper goin' today so's I can do our week's washing, then do a bit of ironing at a time every night.'

'But what about Aunty Win and Joan?'

'They said they'll have been workin' all day,' said Harry.

'They don't count school as work,' said Elsie.

'I'll sort it out. Don't worry. Now. Let's get this range going.'

His dad found the three of them huddled round it. The kettle was standing on top. They turned round in unison.

'How's Mum?' Ralph asked.

'Tired.'

'Elsie told me how she's got to rest.'

'Yeah. Doctor says she's exhausted. She's to stay in bed until . . .' He stopped. 'Until he says its right for her to get up again.'

'I suppose we have been a bit of a handful,' Ralph said quietly. His father said nothing for a moment.

'Elsie, you get the range going?'

Elsie reddened.

'I did,' said Ralph. 'I've shown her and Harry how to do it, in case I can't do it one day.'

'You? You're always up last with these late shifts of yours.'

'Only this week. Until then I'll clean it out and lay it when I come in. Then all Elsie needs to do is to light it. She'll have enough to do

171

with cooking breakfast and supper and doing everyone's washing and ironing,' he added pointedly.

He and his father stared intently at one another.

'So that's how it is?' he said quietly.

Ralph nodded.

'Can you get the copper going before you go to Mrs Egerton-Smythe's?'

'Yes.'

His father cleared his throat. 'And you'd better show me 'ow to do it an' all,' he said shortly, 'just in case.' And he waved his hand.

He looked sternly at Elsie. 'Come 'ere.'

Elsie startled, stepped forward, her eyes wide with fright.

'Until your mum's better, I'm going to wash my clothes, Harry's and Ralph's.'

'You're a man,' gasped Harry.

'Who'd you think did our dhobi when we was in the army?'

'I thought they 'ad women do it for you,' said Harry. 'Or it didn't get done.'

'Not always. You have to learn to look after yourself when you're a soldier. Harry gazed stupefied at his father. 'And I'll do the sheets,' he added. 'Elsie, your job is to take turns washing the rest of the clothes, but you only iron yours. No one else's. Understand?'

'But Aunty Win said . . .'

'I don't care what Aunty Win said.'

'She says that's what she gives us her money for,' interrupted Harry.

'Shush, Harry,' whispered Elsie. 'Dad, I don't want Mum upset.'

'And I don't want two of my family done in. Now you'll have to prepare the veggies for supper because you're 'ome first.'

'I'll 'elp,' said Harry eagerly.

'Good lad,' he said.

Harry beamed.

'But, Dad,' stammered Elsie. 'If they cause us any trouble . . .'

'Tell 'em.' He paused. 'No, I'll tell 'em meself.' And he made for the door.

'Dad, can I go up and see Mum?' Ralph asked.

His father nodded and flung open the door.

'Come in.'

Ralph peered round the bedroom door. His mother was propped up against the pillows, a cardigan and scarf wrapped round her.

The fire in the grate had not penetrated the iciness of the room yet and through the window Ralph could see nothing but snow.

Magazines and books lay on the table. Ralph quickly looked away. Her pretence at reading still embarrassed him.

He came and sat at the end of the bed. His mother looked pale, but relaxed. ''Ow are things downstairs,' she asked hoarsely.

'We're managing fine,' he said. 'You should get a cup of tea soon.'

'Lovely.' She smiled. 'I didn't think you'd be 'ere. I thought you'd have stayed at Mrs Egerton-Smythe's. You should 'ave.'

'Too nosy,' he said.

'About what?'

'You.'

'Oh.' She laughed and waved his remark away with her hand.

He glanced back at the books. 'Shall I bring the wireless up?'

'Nah. I got these,' she said. 'I'm 'oping Elsie or your aunt will come up and read to me. It hurts me eyes too much if I try.'

'Do you want me to?'

'Nah. You got to get to work, haven't you?'

'Yes.'

'I do feel sorry for you, havin' to go on a Sunday.'

'It's not so bad. She's been kind enough to let me have five afternoons off, six if you include Saturday.'

He didn't know what it was that made him decide that this was the moment to tell her that he knew she was illiterate. He didn't want to upset her. He just wanted her to know that it was all right with him, which he felt it was now.

'Mum,' he said awkwardly, glancing at the books. 'I know.'

His mother's face went scarlet. 'But you can't,' she whispered. 'Did Dad tell you?'

'No. I guessed.'

'Oh.'

She looked towards the window looking acutely embarrassed. ''Ow d'you feel about it, then?' she stammered.

'I was a bit upset at first, but I feel fine about it now. Is that why you've kept it a secret, because you're ashamed about it?'

She turned and looked oddly at him. 'I'm not ashamed,' she said. 'Why should I be?'

'Well,' he said, 'you know people might think it a bit odd, a woman of your age.'

'I ain't that old,' she said.

'I didn't mean that,' said Ralph quickly. 'But with Elsie being so bright, does she know?'

She shook her head. 'We thought she was a bit young. We'll tell her later.'

'Who else knows?'

'Your aunt. That's all. And your dad and the doctor, of course.'

'The doctor? Oh, is that because of reading prescriptions?'

'No,' said his mother looking puzzled. 'It's because he asked me questions and had a look at me.'

'Mum,' said Ralph paternally. 'Honestly you don't have to pretend there's something wrong with your eyes. I told you I know you can't read. And it doesn't matter. I'll teach you if you like.'

His mother stared at him completely perplexed. 'What's my eyes got to do with the doctor?'

'That's what I'm asking you.'

'Ralphie, what are you on about? There is something wrong with my eyes, but the doctor . . .' She paused. 'Wait a sec. Is this what you're on about? Me not reading?'

'Yes,' said Ralph, whose turn it was to be puzzled.

'And you think I can't?'

'Mum, there's no need to cover up any longer.'

Suddenly his mother flung her head back into the pillows and dissolved into laughter. Ralph watched astonished as she shook and gasped till the tears ran helplessly down her face. Eventually she grabbed a handkerchief from the table and wiped her face, still bursting into fits of giggles. 'Oh, Ralphie, you're so funny sometimes. You think you know it all and you go round with your eyes shut.'

'What do you mean?'

His mother took a deep breath.

'I was an *early* reader, Ralphie, but I'm like Elsie – terrible eyesight. When I was at school, the school loaned me glasses, but when I left I had to leave 'em behind.'

'Is this true?' Ralph asked, stunned.

She nodded. 'The teachers thought I was so bright they even told Mum and Dad I ought to train to be a teacher.'

'Why didn't you?'

She laughed. 'It was out of the question for us. We couldn't afford it. That's why it's been nice having your aunt living 'ere. I couldn't keep asking Elsie to read to me.'

'So all that's stopping you from reading is a pair of spectacles.'

'Yeah.'

Ralph suddenly felt a hatred for his father so intense, he thought he would scream. Instead he clenched his fists together. 'Surely with all of the wages here you could buy some?' he began.

'That money's for groceries, and clothes and soap.' She gave a short laugh. 'If there is any,' she added. 'It's not for me to buy myself luxuries.'

'And you say Dad knows about this?'

'Everyone knows about it.'

'Except me,' he added, embarrassed.

'I'm sorry, love. I would have said but it never even crossed my mind that you thought that.'

'Well, I better go and see how tea's doing.'

He noticed a mound at the end of the bed. 'The doctor says I've got to keep me feet raised,' she said noticing.

'Did he say how long?'

'Couple of weeks at least. I hope I remember how to use me legs when I get up.' And she smiled. 'Mind you, I'm getting much more sleep now that your aunt's not 'ere.' She hesitated and her face looked flushed again for a moment.

'I'll see you tonight, then,' said Ralph, and he kissed her awkwardly on her forehead.

As soon as he reached the kitchen he had a strong desire to grab hold of his father by the neck and smash his fist right into his face. Instead he avoided looking at him.

'Can I take it up?' asked Elsie.

'I want to go up,' protested Harry.

'Why not both of you,' said Ralph. As soon as he heard their footsteps in the room above, he leaned his hands on the table. His father passed him a cup of tea. 'You best let their ladyships know tea's up,' he said. 'That's if they'll deign to come in 'ere now.'

'Not yet,' said Ralph curtly.

His father looked quickly at him. 'What's up with you?'

'I've been having quite an interesting chat with Mum,' he said.

'Oh?' said his father, evasively.

'How could you be so insensitive? How could you let this go on?'

His father blushed crimson. 'You'll understand when you're older, lad.'

'I know about her feelings. That's enough.'

'She's happy about it,' he said awkwardly.

'That's because she's so unselfish. I just don't understand you, Dad.'

'No,' said his father, quietly. 'You don't.'

'When I think of all all the money you used to spend on beer and you couldn't even put enough aside for a pair of spectacles.'

'Spectacles!' his father exclaimed. 'What's spectacles got to do with it?'

Ralph gave an exasperated snort. 'You must know how much she loves reading. And all this time I thought she was illiterate.'

'Is that what all this is about?' laughed his father.

'Don't you start laughing too,' said Ralph incensed.

'I've got a lot more important things to think about than ruddy glasses,' his dad said. 'If she'd been so keen on havin' glasses she would have bought them when she was workin' in a factory.'

'With Kitty and Joan to feed as well? On your army pay?'

'She managed.'

'You selfish pig.'

'Don't you go speaking to me like that. You ain't too old for a hiding.'

'You're jealous, aren't you?'

'Don't raise your voice. Your mum will hear.'

'You're jealous,' Ralph whispered. 'Because Mum's got a brain.'

'Don't talk daft. Look, she's not complained.'

'She's too busy listening to everyone else's complaints.'

At that moment, they heard Elsie's voice coming from above them. It was her reading voice.

'She didn't waste much time, did she?' said Ralph bitterly. 'She loves reading and she's got to depend on other people to read to her.'

'She manages. I don't know what you're makin' all the fuss about.'

Ralph shook his head in disbelief. 'She's too good for you.'

'Mebbe she is,' said his father.

There was silence for a moment.

'The irony is,' said Ralph, 'that if you'd got her some glasses, she wouldn't have needed Aunty Win so much. You've made a rod for your own back.'

'And you don't know what you're talkin' about.'

'Well, I'm going to find out how much glasses cost, and buy her a pair with what I've saved.'

'Please yerself. Now are you gonna eat breakfast before we get the copper goin' or after?'

'You can change the subject, Dad, but I won't forget this,' he said bitterly, his cup of humiliation brimming over. 'Believe me, I won't forget.'

'So, she still only wants you mornings, even after the Pantomime,' said Elsie, in the kitchen.

'Yes. With all this snow, all I can really do is to keep the path clear and break any dangerous-looking icicles.'

Elsie was laying the table and looking more cheerful. The week's washing hung above their heads and on a clothes-horse in front of the range. She had ironed her uniform while it had still been damp and had even done a shirt for Ralph and Harry and her father.

'I'll take Mum's supper up to her,' Ralph volunteered.

'If you want. Can you tell Joan and Aunty Win it's ready?'

'I don't know how they can spend so long in that room. You'd think they'd want to be in the warmth.'

'Pride can make you act daft,' commented his father.

Ralph stood outside the front bedroom with his mother's plate and knocked on the door. A mournful voice whined, 'Come in.'

He peered round the door. Joan was sitting in bed with scarf, hat and gloves on.

'Supper's ready,' he said. 'Where's Aunty Win?'

'Upstairs,' she intoned. 'Is that for me?'

'No. It's Mum's. We're eating in the kitchen. You're mad staying in here.'

'Uncle John's cross with me.'

'No, he isn't. He's just worried sick about Mum and he wants everyone to pull their weight, that's all.'

'But I'm always so tired,' she moaned. 'I can't do more than I am already.'

Not too tired to go to the cinema three times a week and read magazines and write to Kay, Ralph thought.

'Got to go,' he said briskly. 'Otherwise this will get cold.'

He walked slowly up the stairs so he wouldn't spill any of the gravy. He had nearly reached the landing when he heard Aunty Win's voice. She sounded harsh and angry. 'How could you at your age?' she said. 'What kind of example is that to set Elsie and Harry?'

'There's nothing wrong with it, Winnie,' he heard his mother say. 'John's my husband.'

'In name, yes, but all that sort of thing should have stopped long ago. Is he bothering you now?'

'He's a kind man.'

'Well, he hasn't been lately, has he?'

177

'We're both very happy about it.'

'We're burstin' at the seams already,' said his aunt. 'There ain't no room for a baby as well.'

Ralph froze, horrified. So that's what all the red faces were about!

'If I was you, Ellen, I'd get up and scrub floors and let nature take its course.'

'I want this baby,' Ralph heard his mother say, in a voice which was steady and quietly defiant.

'I s'pose the next thing you'll be sayin' is you like all that sort of nonsense men get up to?'

'With John, yes,' she said simply.

There was a gasp. 'You little slut!'

'We love each other, Winnie . . .' By now her voice had begun to tremble.

Ralph stood, unsure what to do. If he barged in and told Aunty Win supper was ready downstairs, she would ignore him and his mother would know he had overheard. He crept quickly down to the kitchen.

'Didn't she want it?' asked his father.

'I haven't been in there. Would you take it? Aunty Win's up there and I think she's upsetting Mum. She'd take more notice of you.'

But his father was already out of the door with the plate.

As voices were raised upstairs, Elsie and Harry stared miserably at their plates on the table.

'Mum will never get better with her around,' said Elsie.

'Why don't she leave her be?' said Harry.

'We'll protect her from the old dragon,' Ralph said. 'Don't you worry. Anyway I've got some good news for you, Elsie.'

'Is it about school?'

'No, but I'll need your help, Harry'

'Yeah?' Harry said suddenly interested.

'I know going to the theatre is a bit sissy for you.'

'Yeah, it is. Pansy stuff.'

'But I was wondering whether you would escort Elsie into the theatre to see *Cinderella* for the Tuesday matinée. I've managed to get two tickets. You'd have to take time off school, but since they keep sending you home such a lot in this weather, I'm sure you won't miss much.'

'Harry?' asked Elsie.

Harry played to the gallery for all he was worth, humming and ha-ing. Ralph knew he would love to see the panto, but wild horses wouldn't drag the truth from him.

'All right,' he said, and Ralph almost exploded with laughter, for unbeknown to Harry he had virtually given a perfect imitation of their father.

Just then, Joan walked in, sat wearily at the table, slumped her cheek into the palm of her hand and gave a deep sigh. 'I'm not feeling too 'ungry,' she murmured. 'But I thought I ought to try and eat something to keep me strength up.'

'Heard from Kay yet?' asked Elsie kindly.

Suddenly Joan's head shot up. 'You shut up about Kay.'

'I was only trying to cheer you up,' said Elsie.

'Yeah, well nothing's goin' cheer me up at the moment.'

'If it's Aunty Ellen you're worried about . . .' began Ralph.

'It's me,' she said, slamming a forefinger into her chest. 'My life. My life on the shelf, a spinster! *And* I ain't getting much sleep. Aunty Win keeps wakin' me up in the night. She says I snore!'

They heard footsteps coming down the stairs and it was Ralph's turn to feel depressed. He dreaded facing his father, knowing what he had done to his mother. And he was disgusted with his mother for allowing him to have done it to her. He ached to go upstairs and pour it all out in a letter to Jessica. Instead he moved to where the stew was beginning to congeal in the saucepan, and hastily began to stir it.

And it was all over. Ralph steadied the light to hit upstage centre. The chorus had lined up in two groups on either side of the stage. The supporting cast, Baron de Broke and Grab and Grope, the broker's men, ran down the elaborate staircase to applause. Then there was a rousing cheer for Buttons and boos and laughs for the two ugly sisters who were now wearing massive wigs with birds' nests in them.

After Dandini's entrance and bow, the cast turned upstage. There was a drum roll, a crescendo of music and the Prince and Cinderella appeared in dazzling blue and white and silver clothes. Slowly they made their way down the red-carpeted stairway to more cheers and applause.

Then the whole stage was swaying with gusto from side to side.

'*Cast your troubles away,*' they sang,
'*This is the happiest day,*
For we have celebrated,
We feel rejuvenated
On this royal wedding day.'

They all held the last note and slowly raised their arms. Ralph felt a lump in his throat.

Underneath him, the audience was stamping and clapping and still cheering. The cast bowed and bowed again and Buttons and the ugly sisters and the Prince and Cinderella took more bows and then the whole cast took another one and the musicians stood and bowed.

The actress playing the fairy godmother stepped forward and raised her hand for silence:

'Ladies and gentlemen, we thank you for being such a receptive audience. It has made our last night a truly memorable occasion.'

Ralph gazed around the auditorium drinking in every sensation. He was eventually thrown out of his reverie by the strains of 'God Save the King' and countless seats slapping back as the audience stood.

The curtain fell and families laughed and talked their way up the steps towards the exits. Ralph rested his chin in his hands and looked down at the pit. The musicians had gone. Behind the curtain, Ralph knew that the stage hands, who would have been waiting in the wings, had probably already removed all traces of the panto. The fly-men would be lowering woodland scenes and palace backdrops and they would be untied, rolled up and carried off into the scene dock.

He was glad Elsie and Harry had seen the show. The day they had come he had actually seen their heads when the lights went up in the interval, and, to his amusement, saw that Harry was just as excited as Elsie.

The arrangement had caused a minor row with Joan and his Aunty Win, but he had eventually persuaded them to stay on in Winford an extra half-hour after work and take them home.

He still hadn't mentioned the row he had overheard in his parents' bedroom to anyone, not even in a letter, but he made it a point not to talk to his father, by being absorbed in domestic tasks when he was at home. His mother, however, had noticed that he seemed more 'thoughtful' when he went up to see her, but she assumed that it was because it was his last week working the lime.

That week, he had found out the name and address of an optician but had only got as far as standing outside it and peering in. As soon as he stepped near the door, his face would grow hot and he would walk hurriedly away. He felt so ashamed of himself. One minute he was lording it over his father, about how he would go and buy spectacles for his mother, and the next moment he didn't have the nerve to go in because he knew he would have to ask the optician to make a house-call to test her eyes and he was sure the optician would ask what was wrong with her and he would be unable to tell him without blushing, which was stupid, since he had discovered that she really was suffering from exhaustion. Her expecting a baby probably only added to her tiredness.

The auditorium was quiet now. Ralph climbed down the ladder and ran up the steps.

He found Isla and Helena moving like whirlwinds across the stage. Helena was unplugging and coiling up cables. Isla waved to him.

'I need to roll this up,' she said, and she indicated the cloth which had been the marble palace floor.

Behind them, the stage-hands were manoeuvring the large winding staircase to the back of the stage. Ralph leapt to the side of the floorcloth and began to roll it sausage-like with Isla. 'Where's the new ASM?' he asked.

'Don't mention her,' she muttered.

They carried the roll into the scene dock.

Seated at the prop table looking mumchance sat a slim, delicate-looking girl, with pretty chocolate-box features. Her short blonde hair hung in bouncy waves on either side of her face. She gave a sweet smile to them as they passed her by. Putting two and two together Ralph realised that this was her.

He and Isla dumped the roll in the corner designated for panto cast-offs.

As he turned, he was amazed to find about twenty flats already painted. Sam Williams and Judy were there, still painting, but Ralph observed they seemed to have achieved nothing short of a miracle.

'Is that all for *Dear Octopus?*' he asked astounded.

'Yes. It's a nightmare. Three acts, each with a different set. A country house hall, a nursery and a dining room, and masses of props. At least we'll only have two matinées a week now. On less, pay of course,' she added wryly. She hurried back towards the stage, Ralph following. The girl at the prop table was still sitting there, looking enraptured. Gazing into the distance, she appeared to be breathing in some exotic stage perfume. Ralph had a sudden desire to laugh, for the scene dock stank of size, the glutinous wash which was applied to new canvases.

As Ralph and Isla reached the stage, Helena walked towards them, glancing over their shoulders.

'Any change?' Ralph heard her say to Isla.

Isla shook her head.

Ralph joined them hesitantly. It was such a long time since the Saturday strike that he felt an intruder all over again.

'Can you stay?' said Isla swinging round.

Ralph's heart leapt a thousand feet. 'Yes, of course.' And every night if I could, he thought.

She smiled with relief. 'After we've swept the stage and marked up the canvas, could you help Helena remove the red carpet from the staircase?'

'Yes, of course. But I thought you were leaving,' he said to Helena, puzzled.

'I am,' she said. 'So's Robin, but I thought I'd help Isla set up. I'm afraid she needs all the help she can get.'

'Isn't the new ASM very good?' he asked quietly.

'She's a millstone,' said Isla bluntly. 'She has to be told to dot every 'i' and cross every 't'. She has no initiative whatsoever.' She lowered her voice. 'I've sent her out with lists of props and where she might find them, and at the end of the day, I'd meet her to check them off, only to find she's hardly any props at all! All she does is smile sweetly and say, "I didn't have much luck I'm afraid." She doesn't seem to realise that she's not supposed to come back until she's got everything. And I'd say, "But did you ask so-and-so?" I get another sweet smile, a blush, and a "Well, I didn't like to." or "I didn't think I should intrude." And then I've had to go running round the town like a lunatic after removing the rehearsal furniture and props for *Dear Octopus*, to the scene dock, until it's time for me to get ready for the matinée.'

'But have you complained?'

'Oh, yes. But Jack and Mr Johnson say, "Oh it's only her first week," or "She's probably a bit shy," and all she has to do is flutter those little-girl-lost eyelashes of hers and that's that. Now that I'm the stage manager, how I'm going to manage next week without Helena, and a replacement ASM, I don't know!'

It was later, when he and Helena had removed the red carpet and were fixing brass stair rods over painted canvas, that Ralph sounded Helena out.

'But you wouldn't get paid,' she said.

'I know, but I'd still be doing something for the theatre. Learning the ropes, that sort of thing.'

Helena gave an amused smile. 'I bet you'd do anything for Isla.'

He felt himself redden.

'Go on,' she said. 'Ask her.' He stepped down the staircase. She and Robin were laying out rugs on canvas which had been painted to look like a wooden floor.

'Oh, Ralph,' said Robin, pronouncing it Rayfe, like everyone in the theatre. 'Will you take over?' Ralph nodded.

'Marking up,' said Isla next.

'Shall I make tea?' asked Helena.

'Ask Jane to do it,' said Isla gaily between gritted teeth. 'And could you see if she's sorted out the Act One props? She might not have had time to do it yet,' she added, forcing a smile again.

'Point taken,' and Helena headed for the scene dock.

By the time Jane had arrived with a tray of tea, the stage resembled the hall of a Victorian-cum-Georgian country house. Isla was up a ladder fixing a pelmet above long curtains at the upstage right windows. She climbed down and moved the ladder downstage past the door which was supposed to lead to the porch and carried it to another tall window. Ralph stood by, holding the curtains in his arms, ready to hand them to her.

Robin was holding another ladder steady on the staircase while Helena hung a painting on the stripy wallpaper at the side of it.

Jane made her entrance through the double doors on the right side of the back wall, headed to a sofa below an open fireplace and placed the tray on a fender stool.

Isla, Robin, Helena and Ralph stared dumbstruck at her.

'Tea's ready,' she announced.

'Jane,' Isla asked shakily. 'Where did you find that tea-set?'

'In the *Dear Octopus* props. Don't you recognise them?'

Isla nodded.

'Shall I be mother?' Jane asked brightly.

'No,' said Isla. 'I'd like you to pour the tea into the mugs in the kitchen and then wash and dry that china extremely carefully.'

'But I could only find old stained mugs in the kitchen.'

'That's what we use, Jane, and the stage-hands don't come to you. You take tea to them. They haven't time to have a tea party.'

'I thought you'd be pleased,' she said, her voice quivering.

'I'll come with you,' said Helena quickly and she climbed down the ladder.

'I wanted to make it nice, you see,' Jane said.

'It's just that giving good bone china, which someone has lent us, to people who are messing about with hammers and paint is a bit risky,' Isla said in a clipped voice.

'Oh.'

'Pass those curtains up, will you?' Isla said briskly to Ralph, and Ralph, in heaven, in spite of the young ASM, gladly passed her the end with the hooks on it.

Later, when Ralph had a chance to look through the prop list, he understood why Isla had been so bad-tempered. There was a phenomenal amount for each act, with striking and resetting mid-act, and many personal props that certain characters in the play needed.

In the last act, in addition to having to strike the Act Two set, and erect a dining-room set, a huge table had to be laid with a dinner service for fifteen with folded napkins, champagne bottles, candelabras, lace mats, finger bowls, glasses, and so on. It was mind-boggling. He stared at the chaos on and around the prop table, hardly knowing where to start. Out of the corner of his eye, he saw Jane approach him with a mug of tea.

'Thanks,' he said.

'Are you a student?' she enquired.

'Not yet,' said Ralph. 'I hope to be.'

'I'm here for a year.'

'Lucky thing,' said Ralph.

'Yes, aren't I?' she sighed.

'I'll help you get this sorted out.'

'Oh, would you?' she exclaimed, wide-eyed. For some reason she made Ralph feel uncomfortable. 'Have you any idea what to do?' she added.

'Looking at this, you need to find the Act Three props and then set backwards ready for each act.'

'Why backwards?'

'So that the ones you need first are at the front of the prop table.'

She smiled nervously. 'There's such a lot to learn.'

'You'll pick it up soon enough,' said Ralph reassuringly. He flicked through the lists. 'These are the Act Three props,' he said, finding the paper and holding it up to her. 'We need to select them out of that lot,' he said, indicating the crowded table. 'How about if you find the sideboard props and I find the cupboard props?'

'All right. This is fun, isn't it?'

Helena had set up two trestle tables in the wings, for the second- and third- act props. She was already setting the Act Two props while Isla was setting the props for Act One on stage. Ralph surveyed the pile he had put on the Act Three table and ticked them off.

It was dawn when he, Isla and Helena emerged into the street.

'Ralph, have you asked her yet?' said Helena.

'Asked me what?' yawned Isla.

'Ralph wants to know if you'd like him to go round with Jane to help with the props.'

'Oh Ralph,' she said disappointed. 'You haven't got a crush on her too, have you? There are enough people going gooey-eyed over her already.'

'Of course I haven't,' he stammered. 'I don't mind going on my own. It'd probably be easier.'

Isla bit her lip and went quiet for a moment. 'Can I think about it? It is tempting. Where can I reach you?'

'Leave a message with Wilfred and I'll pop in on Monday morning.'

On Monday, there were two messages waiting for him. One from Isla telling him to pop backstage, and another from Mr Neville.

He went up immediately to the wings where he found Isla sitting in the prompt corner, a single light bulb above her prompt book.

'Cue number two is when Fenny comes in and turns on the lamp at the desk,' he heard the producer yelling from the auditorium. 'Bring up the straws on five, eight, eleven and thirteen.'

Isla glanced aside and waved to indicate he should wait.

'Cue three. It's when Fenny goes right to turn up the paraffin lamp on the bookcase. Nice. Cue four. The lamp left of the sofa. All right, hold it here.'

Isla turned swiftly round.

'I've sent Jane out with a prop list,' she whispered. She drew out a piece of paper from under the prompt book. 'This is a furniture list. I've ticked off what we have in stock and I've written down the names of the shops and people who might be willing to lend us the rest. Some will deliver, others we'll pick up.'

'That's fine!' yelled the producer. 'All right, let's keep it for the remainder of the act. Isla?'

'I've got an audition on Thursday with Mr Neville.'

'Wonderful!'

'Have you got that, Isla?'

'Yes, Sir. Sorry, Sir!' Isla yelled back.

She waved at Ralph and returned to check the next lighting cue.

That afternoon, his cheekiness had surprised even himself. Without hesitation he had walked boldly into antique and junk shops and asked them to lend furniture to the theatre. He had even persuaded a rector to lend them his study curtains. Because he was doing it for Isla, his shyness seemed to evaporate.

He was still high on adrenalin when he returned home. He packed Elsie off to the end of the table to do her homework, while he and Harry stirred the stew and laid the table. He took some wood up to his mother's bedroom and a warm brick wrapped in a cloth for her feet.

She was asleep when he tiptoed over to her fireplace. It was still glowing, sending shadows across the bleak unlit room. Glancing at her curtainless window he could see more snow falling. As he put the wood on to the fire it began to crackle loudly. His mother stirred. 'Is that you, love?' she asked sleepily.

Ralph came over to her bed. 'Yes.'

She opened her eyes. 'Oh, Ralphie, it's you. I thought it were yer dad.'

He turned away hurriedly, conscious of feeling uncomfortable.

'What time is it?' she asked.

'Supper time.'

She pushed herself into a sitting position.

'Here,' he said, and he plumped up her pillows for her.

'I can't stop sleepin'.' She smiled. 'The doc says he reckons I got seven years of it to make up for. He says lots of people are taking to their beds, 'cos they're so tired. That and the cold weather. I dunno. I think it's all this rest that's makin' me tired.'

'If you're sleeping, you must need it,' said Ralph.

'How's it going downstairs?'

'Fine.'

'I hope Elsie's not doin' too much.'

'Dad's made sure of that.'

'I thought he would. He's a good man.'

'Huh,' said Ralph.

'Oh, Ralphie.'

'Let's not talk about him,' said Ralph. 'Oh, I forgot, I've a warm brick for you.'

He lifted up the covers and came face to face with her legs. They were like a young girl's legs. He rooted around for the other brick and replaced it with the warm one.

'That's lovely,' she said. 'Now, tell me about the outside world. What's been goin' on?'

'Miners are still on strike, lorry drivers are still on strike. I saw soldiers delivering meat to a butcher's today.'

'Which one's that?'

'Featherstone and Sons.'

'That'll be horsemeat, then.'

'But there were queues outside.'

'There would be.'

'And it's still snowing.'

186

'I can see that from me window. I mean other news. Your news. Something good's happened. I can tell.'

'I've got an audition on Thursday.'

'Oh, Ralphie!'

'Only snag is, I haven't got anything decent to wear.'

'You could borrow yer dad's demob suit.'

'He'd never let me,' said Ralph.

'He needn't know. It's over there,' she said, pointing to the suitcase in the corner. 'Borrow the suit Thursday morning and return it Thursday night.'

'What if he happens to look in the case?'

'He won't.'

'Thanks, Mum.' He sighed. 'Now I just need to brush up my speeches.'

'You'll do them famously. And the garden? 'Ow's that comin' along?'

'Still no gardening. Just more shovelling. Half-pay, too.'

'Why?'

'There isn't enough to do.'

'Can't you get other shovelling work?'

'Oh, yes, but I'm helping out at the theatre this week. They're in a bit of a fix at the moment.'

'They?' said his mother looking amused. 'Sure it ain't *she*?'

'Mum,' said Ralph reddening.

His mother laughed. 'You better tell me, I'll only tease it out of you.'

'The new ASM isn't very good. Robin's leaving too for a job in London, so Isla is now the stage manager. She's on the book for the show and for the rehearsals.'

'On the book? What's that?'

'She prompts during rehearsals, if people forget their lines. And writes down all their moves in a book, plus she has to set up and reset for the evening or matinée performances.'

'I see.'

'So I helped find furniture for the next play today, and if the new ASM is having trouble finding props, I thought I'd help with that too. Luckily the next play is not too bad. It's only one set and they have some of the furniture in stock.'

'So when are you going to practise for your audition?'

'Midday, in Mrs Egerton-Smythe's garden shed,' said Ralph. 'Unless I can use one of the top dressing rooms.'

There was a sound of heavy footsteps coming up the stairs. The door swung open revealing his father, a plate of vegetable stew with a slab of bread on top balanced in one hand, and a cup of tea in the other.

Ralph quickly slid off the bed and picked up the cold brick. 'I better go and help downstairs,' he said quickly. He gave his mother a wave, but avoided looking at his father.

As soon as he had closed the door behind him, he heard his mother say warmly, 'Hello, love.' This was followed by the sound of a kiss.

Feeling sick, he headed swiftly for the stairs.

FIVE

'*I*t *is in the bells I hear my voices. Not today, when they all rang: that was nothing but jangling. But here in this corner, where the bells come down from heaven, and the echoes linger, or in the fields, where they come from a distance through the quiet of the countryside, my voices are in them.*'

He shifted around on his knees. It was such a strain speaking in falsetto. He had worked so hard on the speech in the cold he was afraid he might damage his voice if he worked on it any longer.

He hummed the quarter chimes of a clock.

'*Hark! Do you hear? "Dear-child-of-God": just what you said. At the half-hour they will say "Be-brave-go-on." At the three-quarters they will say "I-am-thy-Help." But it is at the hour, when the great bell goes after "God-will-save-France": it is then that St Margaret and St Catherine, and sometimes even the blessed Michael will say things that I cannot tell beforehand.*'

He stood up and brushed the dust from his trousers. His throat felt dry and sore. He swallowed and then found he had lost the ability to breathe. He tried to take in some deep gulps, but nothing happened. For a moment he panicked. Outside there was the sound of crunching. He opened the door to find Queenie creeping away. She had obviously been spying on him. He sighed. Was there no privacy?

'Queenie?'

She froze and then turned round looking embarrassed.

'What time is it?' he asked.

188

'Comin' up to half-twelve,' and she blushed. 'That's what I come to tell you, but I didn't like to interrupt you, like.'

'I wasn't talking to myself,' said Ralph. 'I was rehearsing.'

'Oh,' she said, feigning disinterest, and she ran back through the snow towards the kitchen.

Wilfred gave him the key to the top dressing room. Nobody was using it. Only one mirror had bulbs round it. Staring at his face by their light, Ralph wondered if it was that which made him appear so pale, or sheer terror.

He had discovered when putting on the collar he had hired from the second-hand clothes shop that, instead of lying neatly to the side of his cravat if left undone at the top, it flapped on either side of his neck like two starched wings. To his dismay he realised that he would have to go collarless as he had no tie with him to wear if he did the collar up to the neck. He also found that he needed braces for the trousers. He tied a piece of string round them, hoping that he would be able to untie the knot after the audition. At least his shoes looked smart. They were blackened with the blacking Queenie used for the fireplaces.

He put the jacket on, plumped up the cravat and dipped his hand in the new pot of hair cream he had bought that morning. He smoothed back his springy brown hair and was about to do his buttons up when he realised that his hand was still greasy. He looked round wildly for something to wipe it with but could find nothing. In the end he used the back of the shirt he had taken off. He took a last look at himself in the mirror from every angle. Dark red dots had suddenly appeared in the middle of his cheeks giving the impression of someone with consumption. He gave himself a good luck 'thumbs up' and then swiftly left the dressing room, locking the door behind him.

'What do you think?' he asked Wilfred when he handed him the key.

'Smart, very smart, sir.'

'Not too staid, though?'

'No. And if I may say so, a definite air of originality.'

Ralph took a deep breath, but he was still finding trouble breathing.

'I suppose I had better go up, then,' said Ralph nervously.

'Good luck.'

'Thank you, Wilfred.'

With trembling legs he ascended the stone steps. He thrust the

189

door on the small landing aside and walked past the dressing rooms and kitchen. The doors were open and he could hear voices. He lowered his head, raised his shoulders and headed quickly towards the safe haven of the door, leading to the privacy of the stage-left wings, or so he thought.

Standing in the wings were two men whispering to one another. One of them was a tall white-haired man in his seventies, Leon Beauchamp. He was the actor he had heard scraped brick dust off walls with a penknife to use as rouge. The other was an elegantly dressed actor in his twenties called Felix Venning, who had always been very friendly to him during the pantomime. From on-stage Ralph could hear two women and a boy reading from a script.

'Yes, Nan,' he heard the actress Geraldine Maclaren say. 'The government want him for some very important post. He's going up with Sir Ernest this evening.'

'Will it be abroad?' said the other woman and then Ralph recognised who it was – Elspeth Harding who had played Ellen Creed in *Ladies in Retirement!* He began to feel a thumping in his chest. To think he was standing only yards from her.

'There needs to be a tray there, Isla,' he heard Mr Neville say.

'There should be one there,' Isla remarked. 'Sorry about that. I'll get one.'

'Don't worry about it now. Just make sure it's there tomorrow for the run. Mime it, will you, Elspeth?'

'Will it be abroad?' Elspeth Harding repeated. 'Picks up tray,' she added to herself.

'I'm afraid so.'

'Ralph.'

Ralph turned to find Felix staring at him, amazed. 'What are you doing here, dressed like that?'

'I've got an audition,' Ralph whispered. 'How do I look?'

There was a pause. 'When is it?' asked Felix thoughtfully.

'After your rehearsal finishes.'

'That soon,' he stated.

'Is it?' gulped Ralph.

Felix gave his shoulders a squeeze. 'You look wonderful,' he said. 'What are you doing?'

'A speech from *Othello* and one from *Saint Joan.*'

'I'm sure you'll be fine.'

'I hope so.'

'It's just on nine. Shall I turn on the wireless?' Elspeth Harding asked.

'Yes, ma'am,' answered Geraldine Maclaren.

'And the wireless will be where?' asked Elspeth Harding.

'On the cabinet,' Ralph heard Mr Neville say.

'So I go over here,' she said, 'switch it on and we have the last two notes of Big Ben.'

Felix hastily moved near the prompt corner. 'This is London,' he read in a plummy BBC voice. 'His Majesty King George VI.'

This was greeted with howls of laughter on-stage and Felix disappeared from view.

'Sorry, old chap,' said the producer. 'It doesn't work. Isla, we're going to need a proper recording. Wonderful imitation though, Felix.'

There was a sound of a young boy still laughing hysterically.

'I didn't think it was that funny,' protested Felix from the stage.

'You weren't us three, all facing the wireless stage right, hearing your voice coming from stage left,' gasped Elspeth Harding.

'Couldn't I use a megaphone?'

'It'll sound like the Oxford and Cambridge boat race if you do,' said the producer. 'Right, everyone. That'll do. Run through first thing tomorrow morning. Usual thing. DLP.'

'DLP?' muttered Ralph puzzled.

'Dead letter perfect,' said a voice from behind. It was Leon Beauchamp. 'I hear you're auditioning?' he said softly, in a voice which had the rich timbre of someone who had used it for fifty or more years.

'Yes, sir.'

'Have you been sent by a stage school?'

'No. I live locally.'

'Ah.'

'And I've been helping out a bit.'

'How old are you?'

'Seventeen, almost.'

The man looked as if he was about to say something, hesitated, then smiled. 'Good luck.'

'Thank you, sir.'

'He's waiting for you now,' he heard Felix say on-stage.

Ralph suddenly felt violently sick. The white-haired actor had gone and he could hear the other members of the cast heading for the wings. And then there they were. Felix, Geraldine Maclaren, Elspeth Harding and a young boy. The boy stared, mouth open at his suit, until Elspeth Harding yanked him smartly to the door.

'Did you see what he was wearing?' Ralph heard the boy exclaim.

'Yes. And very nice too,' Elspeth Harding added firmly.

'Good luck,' said Geraldine Maclaren as she headed for the door. Felix stayed.

'You're not going to watch, are you?' Ralph asked.

'Not if you don't want me to.'

'I'd rather you didn't, if you don't mind.'

'Of course. I just need to check some of my personal props for tonight,' he said, indicating the prop table, 'and then I'll be gone.'

'Ralph!' said a voice from behind.

He turned. It was Isla. She stood looking at him up and down, clutching the prompt book to her chest.

'You look – ' she paused, 'so different.'

'Older?' he asked hopefully.

She nodded vigorously.

'That's good,' he said relieved.

'I'm to announce you when Mr Neville's ready.' And with that she made a hasty retreat back on to the stage.

To his dismay he noticed the door to the corridor opening. Two men and a woman peered round and stared at him. Realising they had been seen, they gave a nod and a smile and disappeared rapidly.

By now Ralph was tempted to run for it. Then he heard Isla announcing in her deep ringing tones, 'Mr Ralph Hollis.' And she suddenly appeared in the wings.

'You're on,' she said. 'I should enter by the upstage left doors. They're already open. Good luck.'

Ralph nodded his thanks and headed straight for them. Later he wished he had closed them behind him.

As masterfully as he could, he strode through them and downstage only to find that the auditorium lights had been darkened and the overhead lights were affecting his vision. It was so quiet he wondered if there was anyone there.

'Good afternoon, Mr Hollis!' said a disembodied voice suddenly from the darkness. 'We have met already, I believe.'

Ralph cleared his throat and peered into the gloom, shading his eyes with his hand.

'Uh . . . Yes, sir.'

'I hear good reports of you from Mr Walker.'

Ralph reddened. He was still trying to find out where the producer was sitting.

'Now what have you got to show me this afternoon?'

'A speech from *Othello* and one from *Saint Joan*.'

'Good. A classic and a modern classic. Good contrasting plays. What would you like to start with first?'

'The Shakespeare.'

'And you'll be playing?'

'Iago, sir.'

'Wonderful character. Perhaps you could set the scene for me.'

'Oi have't; – it is engender'd. Hell and noight
Must bring this monstrous birth to the world's loight.'

He glanced stealthily from side to side, threw his imaginary cloak over his shoulders, walked briskly upstage, froze for a moment and then came downstage again.

He heard the producer clear his throat. 'An interesting interpretation,' the voice boomed out. 'I've never heard Iago done with a Devonshire accent.'

'It's Cornish actually,' Ralph said, and immediately regretted it. 'But they are similar,' he stammered. 'It's supposed to show him as someone moving up the ranks.'

'I see. Well, your voice isn't bad.'

Ralph's spirits soared.

'It lacks colour, but it's early days.'

'Lacks colour?' asked Ralph devastated.

'Range. But technique can give you that. What have you got for me next?'

'*Saint Joan*, by George Bernard Shaw.'

'I know that, but which scene?'

'It's when she's praying in the cathedral at Rheims and explaining to Jack Dunois about her visionary voices and her need to pray.'

'Ah, yes. I know the scene well.'

'Shall I start?'

'Please do.'

Ralph clasped his hands together and crashed down on to his knees.

'Jack. The world is too wicked for me. If the goddams and the
Burgundians do not make an end of me, the French will.'

He fought down a strong desire to cough. His voice had gone so high he was terrified of it giving out altogether. He swallowed quickly.

'Only for my voices I should lose all heart. That is why I had to
steal away to pray here alone after the coronation.'

As he knelt there he could hear the bells chiming in the distance, see the sunlight streaming through the stained glass-windows, feel the presence of the saints overwhelming him with their messages.

When he had finished he stood up quickly and blinked, still awash with emotion. He waited for a response, but there seemed to be no signs of life from the auditorium. He wondered if the producer was as moved as he was, and too stunned to speak.

'A fascinating rendition, Mr Hollis,' boomed the producer, eventually.

'Really, sir!' Ralph said eagerly.

'Unforgettable. Was it your idea to play Saint Joan?'

Ralph wavered and then he decided to tell the truth. 'No. I'm afraid I can't take any credit for it. It was a teacher at my old school, sir.'

'Where the boys played all the female parts, I presume.'

'Yes, sir.'

'As in Shakespeare's day, of course.'

'Yes, sir.'

And then Ralph saw him. He had stood up in the middle of the stalls and was heading for the aisle to the right of the stage. Nervously Ralph watched him approach.

'Well, Mr Hollis, it was a brave attempt, but we no longer live in Shakespearean England. This is 1947 and we employ actresses to play our female roles.'

Suddenly Ralph felt his whole life crumbling before him. Why, oh why, hadn't he trusted his instinct?

'I'm going to be brutal with you because I think in the long run it will be a kindness. Do you have a job?'

'Yes, sir.'

'Don't give it up.'

'No, sir,' said Ralph huskily.

'If you *still* want to be an actor,' and he sighed despairingly, 'as I said, apply for drama school. There are scholarships, you know, but if you do audition, don't, whatever you do, ask advice from your old English teacher. Go to someone else.'

'Yes, sir.'

'And now, if you'll excuse me, I've rather a lot of plays to read.'

'Yes, sir. Thank you, sir,' Ralph choked out.

He stumbled towards the upstage doors and into the wings, looking for some consolation from Isla, but the wings were empty. As he pushed open the door into the corridor he noticed that all the doors were closed. He was sure he could hear stifled laughter coming from behind them.

He walked past them, his skin stinging as fiercely as though a swarm of bees had savagely attacked him. In a blur he headed for the door and down the steps to the stage door area to collect the key. Wilfred glanced up from his newspaper. 'It weren't that bad, were it?' he commented.

Ralph nodded, not daring to speak for fear of crying.

Wilfred handed him the key to the top dressing room. 'I believe it's all part of the business,' he said comfortingly.

Ralph numbed, stared at him uncomprehending. 'What is?'

''Umiliation.'

Up in the dressing room he found that his father's trousers were covered in chalk dust from the markings Isla must have put on the stage for the *The Years Between* rehearsals. He brushed them frantically with his hands and folded them neatly over the back of a chair. He dressed as quickly as he could, folded his father's suit with painstaking care, took a farewell look at the dressing room, and locked the door.

Wilfred had a hot cup of sweet tea waiting for him. 'Get that down you, lad.'

He was halfway through drinking it when he heard footsteps coming down the steps. It was Isla. She froze on the middle of them, red-faced. 'Oh,' she said awkwardly. 'I thought you'd gone. I'm glad I didn't miss you though,' she added hurriedly.

'It's all right,' said Ralph. 'I know I messed it up.'

'Did you?' she said innocently. 'I'm afraid I wasn't able to watch you. There was an emergency with the props and I had to see to it. Sorry.'

Ralph felt sure she was lying yet he wanted so terribly to believe her. 'Well, I may be lousy at acting, but I can still help with props, if you can bear to see me around,' he said bleakly.

'Thanks. I do still need help. Will you be available for the strike?'

He nodded.

'Didn't Mr Neville say anything encouraging?'

'Only that if I want to audition for drama school to get someone else to advise me.'

'And will you?'

'No,' he said bluntly.

'So you've given up the idea of being an actor?' interrupted Wilfred.

'No,' said Ralph, and he was surprised by his response, for in spite of feeling lower than the Equator, he couldn't bear the thought of a life not acting.

'I mean I won't get advice. I'll damned well choose what speeches

I want to do, and then at least if I fail . . .' He sighed.

'Don't worry,' said Isla quickly. 'Some drama schools give you a choice of speeches they've selected anyway.'

'Do they?' asked Ralph interested.

'Look, I must go and get a bite of something or I'll never get through the rest of the day. Can you pop in tomorrow afternoon, after the run?'

'Yes, of course.'

'I wouldn't wait in the wings, if I were you.'

He knew why. In case he bumped into some of the cast who he guessed had watched his audition from there.

'Where then?'

'In the kitchen. 'Bout two?'

'Do you want me to look for a tray this afternoon?'

'No. We've several in stock, but thanks for asking,' and she gave his arm a squeeze and hurried out of the stage door, leaving Ralph dazed and trembling.

His mother was asleep when he slipped the demob suit back into his father's suitcase. Downstairs he found a list of jobs which needed doing, in Elsie's handwriting. The range was almost out. He stoked up the fire, and dug out the eyes and sprouting stalks from a pile of wrinkled and filthy potatoes and then went out for a walk.

For the next few days he functioned in a miserable haze. When he woke he had to force himself out of bed. It was as though all the light in his life had been snuffed out. The goal, which had helped him endure his father and the endless digging of snow, had evaporated. He missed Jessica desperately. He longed to talk to her, yet felt too depressed and tired to write her a letter.

His salvation came from an unexpected source. Cousin Joan.

On the Saturday night, the strike had been easier than he had anticipated. He realised that none of the backstage staff knew about his audition or if they did, they weren't letting on. It was a relief to roll up his sleeves and do something practical. He had even left on his ankle boots and stuffed his cravat in his pocket. He couldn't be bothered about the outward impression he was making any more.

But once he stepped out into the night in his greatcoat and began the long tramp home through the snow, the heaviness in his chest returned. His head bowed, the snow fell into the inside of his collar down his neck and he didn't care. Back in the yard he shoved his bike into the coalshed, stepped into the outside lavatory where he relieved himself standing in the three inches of snow which had blown in under the door, and walked wearily into the scullery.

He knew there was an electricity cut, so like an automaton he lit a candle in the kitchen and knelt down in front of the range. He had just shovelled ash into a newspaper and was tearing and screwing another piece into several small balls, when a voice called out his name. He jumped so violently that he sent the poker clattering to the floor.

'Who's that?' he blurted out.

'It's only me, Ralphie,' said a shadow in the corner.

'Joan! What are you doing here? You scared me out of my wits.'

'Aunty Win said she couldn't take my snorin' any longer. She told me to sleep in 'ere,' she sniffed. 'Anyway what are you doin'?'

'Making up the fire for Elsie.'

'Do you do that every night?'

'No. Just tonight because it's Saturday. I do it in the morning. Early.'

'Oh!' said Joan, surprised.

'Well, I better get on,' he said.

He was about to turn back to the range when there was a loud sob. 'Oh, Ralphie,' she said. 'I can't go on any more!'

He felt a flicker of irritation. 'I don't suppose it'll be for long,' said Ralph through gritted teeth. 'I expect Mum will be up and being treated like a slave again soon.'

'It's not that,' she gulped. 'It's somethin' else. I've got to talk to someone about it. I got to!' And she burst into tears.

He walked over to the bed where she was sitting with the blanket pulled up to her neck, shivering.

'You still got your coat on,' she observed.

'I'd put it round your shoulders, but I think it would make your bed wet.'

'That's all right,' she hiccuped.

He sat at the end of the bed. 'So, what's it about?' he asked gently.

'Don't laugh at me, will yer?'

'I promise.'

'It's about Kay.'

'Oh,' said Ralph, beginning to lose interest.

'No. Listen. Please.' She paused. 'Got a hankie? My nose is running.'

Ralph dragged out a grey clump of material from his pocket and handed it to her. 'Don't look at it too closely,' he said. 'I've been cleaning props with it.'

She gave a small laugh and blew her nose. 'It's about her letters,'

197

she began falteringly. 'You know how I told you she went on about the central heatin', and refrigerators and beautiful clothes, and that? Well it's all a pack o' lies, except I'm not supposed to say anythin'. She don't want her mum and dad findin' out.'

'Why?'

'Because they were so against her marrying a GI. Her being so young and everything.'

'Did she tell you what it's really like out there?'

Joan nodded. 'She said, when she first arrived in New York, it really was luxurious, and Chip, her husband, really did buy her the biggest steak and ice-cream she'd ever seen. And it was true that she bought these American magazines. But you know what our ones are like. So thin. The ones out there are really thick.'

'I think I'm getting the picture,' said Ralph. 'She's been describing what she saw in the magazines.'

'Yeah. Ralph, she's living in the middle of nowhere in an old shack! When she arrived wearing lipstick and a pretty dress the family just gawped at her. She said she lives in boots, hardly sees anyone all day. Her husband is really poor and his family are all a bit touched. Well, so she says. She's really unhappy!' She buried her face into the handkerchief again and began crying.

'Why doesn't she come back to England?' Ralph said.

Joan's head sprang up. 'You can't leave your husband,' she said horrified. 'And anyway she ain't got no money.'

'But if she told her parents, perhaps they could get her out. After all, he did marry her under false pretences.'

She shook her head wildly. 'No, she wants her mum and dad to think she's having a better life than them. She thinks her mum will just gloat and say it serves her right, and her dad will be all upset. She says she's got to make the best of it.'

'Well, it's good she can confide in you, isn't it?'

'I wish she 'adn't,' she wept. 'I've got nothing to live for now.'

'Joan! Of course you have. You can send her things.'

'Why did she tell me?' she wailed.

'Shush,' said Ralph. 'You'll wake everyone up.' He paused. 'Look, Joan, you have everything to live for.'

'No, I ain't. The thing that's kept me going is her letters. To know that maybe I'd live in a comfy warm place one day. A lovely house of me own. That's bright and colourful and modern. It's been like a dream that's been smashed to bits. But I don't suppose you know what that feels like?'

'Oh, I do,' said Ralph.

'Oh, I know you had to leave school, but – '

'It's not that. Last Thursday I auditioned at the theatre and it was a total disaster.'

'Oh, Ralphie,' she breathed.

'I stood on the stage on my own, lights on me, actors eavesdropping in the wings, and I made a total ass of myself.'

'But you're good!' she exclaimed.

'What makes you say that?'

'We listen to you on the stairs when you're practising.'

'You don't!' said Ralph horrified.

'We do. Sometimes you sound just like a film star.'

He smiled.

'You won't give up, will you?' she said.

He shook his head. 'There's another thing. I don't know whether I ought to tell you, but . . .' At this tears began to run swiftly down her face again.

He took hold of her hands. 'You might as well,' he said.

'It's your mum,' she whispered.

'What about her? Has she got worse?'

'I dunno. I'm sure they're keeping somethin' back from us. Uncle John knows and I'm sure Aunty Win knows. She's been so bad-tempered and miserable about it. And I hear them talking in low voices and when I walk into the room they change the subject. Oh, Ralphie, if anything happened to her, I don't know what I'd do.'

'But you're always quarrelling.'

'I know. And I don't mean to.' She swallowed. 'If she dies, who's going to look after me. Oh, I wish me mum were 'ere.' And at that she burst into a fresh bout of sobbing.

'Joan,' said Ralph slowly, 'I know what's wrong with her.'

She gasped. 'But you can't do. They wouldn't tell you and not me, surely?' she cried indignantly.

'They have no idea I know. If I tell you, will you promise to keep it a secret? They're going to tell us all later.'

'But how . . .'

'I overheard Mum and Aunty Win talking about it.'

'Is it serious?'

'Depends how you look at it.'

'Well, go on.'

'First of all, she really is suffering from exhaustion. It's quite common apparently. The doctor said he's seen a lot of it. People have been carrying on for six years of war and then coping with post-war problems and then . . .'

'Ralph!' she said impatiently. 'What's the other thing?'

He took a deep breath. 'She's going to have a baby.'

'A baby? Here?'

'Well, not in Timbuktu.'

'I don't believe it.'

'Yes, that's how I felt,' he said.

But before he could continue he found her arms around him. 'Oh, Ralphie. Thanks for letting on.'

'Hey, I can't breathe,' he choked.

She let go of him. 'A baby!' she said rapturously.

'You're pleased?' asked Ralph astounded.

'Ain't you?'

'Yes. Of course,' he lied.

'I wonder why Aunty Win ain't, then?'

'She thinks Mum is too old.'

'A baby!' she repeated. 'Here.' And she laughed.

'Remember you promised to keep it a secret.'

'Course I will. I 'ope she tells me soon though, then I can start knittin'.'

'Oh, Joan, you are funny.'

'Why?'

'One minute you're going through a major drama. The next moment you're ecstatic.'

'I could tell Kay. That'd be all right.'

'It might get back to her parents.'

'Not if I tell her to keep it a secret. Maybe having a baby will give us more chance of moving out of here into one of them new prefabs.'

'Oh, Joanie,' he laughed. 'You never give up.'

'They have running hot water in them.'

'Joan, at least this isn't like our old place in London. I can remember having to share a tap and lavatory with neighbours. And me, Harry and Elsie sleeping in the same bed as Mum and Dad. Here, we've a scullery with our own water, a yard with our own lavatory, and four beds between seven of us,' he pointed out. 'We're much better off then a lot of people.'

'I s'pose. We're a lot better off than Kay,' she added quietly.

He stood up. 'I must lay this range before my hands freeze up.'

'All right.' And she sank back on her pillow. 'I wish it would stop snowin',' she yawned.

Ralph returned to the range.

'Ralph,' she said after a while.

'Yes.'

'Do you really want to be an actor?'

'Yes, but keep it a secret, won't you?'

'Course I will.'

He began laying the lumps of used coke on a pyramid of dried twigs.

'Ralph?'

'Yes?'

'You promise you won't tell anyone about Kay?'

'Yes, of course. I told you I would.'

'Did you? Oh,' she said sleepily.

Within seconds the room shook with loud trumpeting snores. Ralph finished laying the range and glanced at the noisy mound in the corner which was now visibly shaking.

'But that's something even I can't keep a secret,' he said quietly to himself, and he leaned over the table and blew out the candle.

SIX

*I*t was midday on Tuesday when Ralph saw Mrs Egerton-Smythe. On the Monday he had fled immediately out into the snow, begun shovelling for all he was worth, never once glancing towards the house, and had run from the house as soon as he was finished to search for props. He was in the kitchen eating bread with a rather nondescript soup and a slice of heated-up vegetable pie, scrutinising a long prop list for the play which would open the following Monday, when Mrs Egerton-Smythe flung open the door. 'Good afternoon, Mrs Egerton-Smythe,' he said rising.

'Ah. The power of speech has returned,' she commented. 'This is a good sign. Sit down.' She turned. 'Queenie, I hear there's going to be a delivery of meat at Featherstone and Sons.'

Queenie looked alert.

'Did you bring your ration book with you?'

'No, ma'am.'

'Well, if you manage to get any meat with my coupons, I'll give you half of my ration today and we can do a swap next time.'

'Thank you, ma'am.' And she rushed quickly to her hat, coat and boots which were hanging on the back door.

As soon as she was gone, Mrs Egerton-Smythe sat down at the table.

Ralph looked up from his soup to find her staring intently at him. 'I have a feeling I'm going to be interrogated,' he remarked.

'I received a letter from Jessica this morning, frantic with curiosity about your audition. She can't understand why she hasn't received a letter from you, giving a detailed account of it.'

'It was only five days ago.'

'You know Jessica, she wants to know everything immediately. She would assume that you would walk off-stage, write her a letter on the instant and post it.'

'Even if I had, it probably wouldn't have reached her in this snow.'

'You still haven't written, then?'

'No.'

'I presume it went badly, then?'

He lowered his head and gazed into his soup. 'Yes.'

'Are you sure?'

'Yes.'

'Do you know why?'

'I didn't trust my instinct. I should have chosen my own speeches.'

'That's a good lesson to learn.'

'But I've learnt it too late.'

'Ralph?'

Ralph looked up startled. It always surprised him when she called him by his Christian name.

'You're not seventeen yet.'

'Almost.'

'Oh, when?'

'April.'

'Anyway I think you have a good few years yet,' she said wryly.

'But some of the actors watched me from the wings. It's so embarrassing.'

'They'll forget.'

'I won't.

'So you're going to give up?'

'No!' he said angrily, and then realised this was his employer. 'Sorry, it's just everyone keeps thinking that.'

'Might it be because you're walking round like an undertaker's mute?'

'Probably.'

'What's that?' she said, glancing at the papers on the table.

'The prop list for the next play.'

'Still helping out, eh?'

'Yes. The new ASM is very sweet but slow, and a bit shy.'

'May I?'

He slid it across to her.

'*Something in the Air*. Good lord. Laurie and I went to see this on his last leave. It's great fun. It's about two young women who live with their widowed father, who's an eccentric inventor, and their desperate attempts to get a maid who won't leave within a fortnight. Oh, sorry. Now I've spoilt it for you.'

'It doesn't matter.' he said glumly.

'Quite a list of crockery, I see. Ah yes. I remember, now. They're trying to impress their aunt. Look, I think I can help you with this. Would I have this returned to me?'

Ralph stared amazed at her. 'Of course you would.'

'I think you need a bit of a helping hand in making a good impression?'

'Mrs Egerton-Smythe, I don't know how to thank you.'

'I do. You can stop walking round like a wet weekend. And anyway, I had better do it for Jessica. She'd be furious if I didn't help cheer you up. Now let's see,' and she scrutinised the list. She looked up. 'I don't have to provide port in this decanter, do I?'

'No. I expect they'll mix something up that looks like it.'

'Four sherry glasses, silver salver.' She sat back. 'Let's go for a walk around the house before Queenie arrives,' she said. 'Now eat up quickly. As my daughter would say, there's not a moment to lose.'

After they had stored the props in the garden room, Ralph called into the theatre. Isla had gone to a café. Wilfred gave him the directions.

He spotted her smoking at a corner table in a fug of other people's cigarette smoke. He raced down the aisle towards it, only to discover Felix, Basil Duke and Geraldine and Raymond Maclaren sitting with her. It was too late to turn back. He hurriedly took out the list and put it on the table beside her.

'I've got these,' he said, attempting to sound casual. 'We'll need boxes to carry them to the theatre, but we can collect them any afternoon we like.'

Isla glanced down at the ticks and to his relief she gave him a rapturous smile.

'This is splendid!' she said. 'I needed something to cheer me up.'

'But you don't need it. You've got a part in *Something in the Air*.'

'How do you know?'

'I read the cast list.'

'Seems you have a fan, Isla,' said Raymond Maclaren.

'No,' said Ralph quickly. 'I looked at everyone's names.' He glanced at Basil Duke. 'You're playing Uncle Cecil. Mrs Maclaren, you're playing Jennifer.'

'And I'm playing Mrs Mulligatawny,' interrupted Isla dismally.

'Which is a gem of a part,' said Basil.

'He's trying to be kind,' said Isla. 'It's a walk-on.'

'A walk-on?' asked Ralph puzzled.

'Well, almost. I hardly speak a word, and when I do, no one understands me.'

'She has adenoidal trouble,' said Basil. 'She'll steal the show.'

'How did the audition go?' asked Felix casually.

Ralph suspected he knew, but he decided to play along with it. 'I was terrible.'

'No,' said Felix in disbelief, puffing at his cigarette.

'And you know it,' added Ralph.

Felix opened his eyes wide with innocence.

'It's all right,' said Ralph. 'I'm going to let the memory fade, and then see if I can persuade Mr Neville to give me another audition.'

'Only this time he'll choose his material,' added Isla quickly.

'I see,' said Felix. 'May I give you some advice?'

'If it's about speeches, no,' said Ralph with false joviality.

'No. It's about your appearance.'

'What's wrong with his appearance?' said Basil. 'He looks fine to me.'

'That's not how he was dressed for the audition.'

'Oh,' said Basil. 'How was he?'

'Shall I tell him?' said Felix gently.

'Why not?' Ralph mumbled.

'A demob suit and cravat.'

'And I played Saint Joan in it,' added Ralph. 'Falsetto.'

There was a long silence, and much vigorous puffing of cigarettes. And then Ralph found his stomach quivering violently and he collapsed with laughter. He suddenly realised how absurd he must have looked and all around him the cast were exploding uncontrollably. They laughed for at least half an hour, and they and Ralph kept on laughing, not just at him, but at each other, as they exchanged horror audition stories, how they had fallen into the pit, or discovered that their flies had been undone. And Ralph listened and fell apart with them. Wilfred was right, humiliation was part of the job, but what he had neglected to mention was that a sense of humour was necessary in combating it.

After they had recovered, he and Isla called in at the scene dock and picked up two boxes. They found Jane cleaning the kitchen. Isla gazed at it in disbelief.

'I thought I'd give everyone a surprise. What do you think?' she trilled, throwing her arms out. 'I thought maybe I could cut out pictures from *The Stage* and *Plays and Players* and put them round the walls.'

Isla nodded like a mandarin statue.

'Very nice,' said Ralph attempting to fill the awkward silence.

'What props did you manage to get this morning?' Isla asked lightly.

'I thought I'd start looking for them after lunch. I've been working so hard, I haven't got round to eating any. Still, that's one way of keeping my figure,' she laughed. 'Oh, I feel so happy. I really feel part of the company now.'

'Um,' began Isla, her voice quivering.

'Isla,' said Ralph, 'perhaps Jane would like to take one of these boxes and you could get another one and we could meet at the stage door.'

Isla nodded tight-lipped and strode off.

'Oh?' said Jane puzzled. 'What's going on?'

'I found some props. We just need to collect them.'

'When?'

'Now.'

'But I haven't finished tidying up in here yet.'

'Jane,' said Ralph lowering his voice. 'Isla isn't in the best of moods.'

'Oh dear, is it that fiancé of hers?'

'No,' said Ralph. 'She has rather a lot to do.'

'I can join you after lunch,' she said brightly.

'I think you had better drop everything and come now.'

'Oh,' she said, looking suddenly alarmed. 'Oh, I see.'

Ralph and Isla walked in silence down the High Street with their boxes, while Jane chattered non-stop about West End plays she had seen, film stars she admired, school productions she had been in and what the local papers had said about her performances.

'Have you seen *Gone with the Wind*?' she had asked at one point. And Isla and Ralph had hardly time to glance at each other when she proceeded to tell them the whole plot. She was recounting Scarlet O'Hara giving birth when they arrived at Mrs Egerton-Smythe's.

'There's the front door,' Jane pointed out when they opened the small gate.

'We go in the side entrance,' said Ralph.

'No, we don't,' she laughed. 'That's for the servants.'

205

'We do,' said Ralph curtly.

'Mrs Egerton-Smythe told me to expect you,' said Queenie at the kitchen door, disapproval stamped all over her face. 'Come with me.'

They carried the boxes into the kitchen and into the hall.

Mrs Egerton-Smythe appeared on the stairs carrying several pairs of spectacles. 'These any use?' she asked. 'Some belonged to my husband, others were early ones of mine.'

'But how did you know?' Ralph asked amazed.

'I looked at your prop list, remember?'

'Oh, the prop list! I thought they were for my mother.'

'Your mother? She's not in the play, is she?' she asked bemused.

'No. It's just she needs . . .' He stopped. 'It's nothing. It doesn't matter. Oh, wait a minute though. When I bring them back, could I buy them?'

'Whatever for? Oh, for disguises?'

'No. For my mother. She needs glasses desperately.'

There was a tinkling laugh behind him. It was Jane. 'She can buy a pair at an opticians,' she laughed. 'You can't wear someone else's glasses.'

'My mother can't afford to buy them.'

'Why ever not?' asked Jane innocently.

'You can have them with pleasure,' said Mrs Egerton-Smythe, coming down the stairs. 'They're useless here. And the optician could always use the frames. Perhaps you could agree to some kind of exchange.'

'Thanks.'

As he and Isla walked ahead into the garden room, he heard Mrs Egerton-Smythe say to Jane, 'You must be the new ASM.'

'Yes,' she gushed. 'How do you know that?'

'Well, you're a bit slow on the uptake, aren't you, dear?'

Ralph grinned. Out of the corner of his eye, he saw Isla's mouth twitch. Every cloud has a silver lining, he thought. If Jane hadn't been employed at the theatre, he and Isla wouldn't have been drawn so close together.

It was when they were wrapping china and putting fire tongs and a coffee jar into the boxes that Isla suddenly said, 'If I can arrange it, would you be interested in seeing the run-through on Friday?'

'Would I?' he said eagerly. 'I'll say.'

'What about your job here?'

'Do you work here?' asked Jane, astounded.

'Yes,' said Ralph. 'I'll ask Mrs Egerton-Smythe if I can shovel in the afternoon instead. I'm sure she won't mind.'

'You'll have to hide up in the stalls before we start and stay there until I come up and give you the all clear.'

'That'd be wonderful,' breathed Jane. 'It'll be like having one's own private show, won't it, Ralph? Something for us to remember,' she added dreamily.

'Jane,' began Isla, 'you'll be backstage ready to change the rehearsal props between acts. You'll need all the practice you can get.'

'But how am I going to be an actress if I can't watch any of the rehearsals?'

'If you were quicker finding props you could.'

'I don't think that's fair,' Jane whispered, her lower lip trembling. Her huge blue eyes began to well up.

'Look, Jane, I know you're finding it hard. We've all been through it. But at least you've got Ralph helping, and he's not even being paid.'

'Exactly,' she sniffed. 'That makes me a professional and him an amateur, and yet he's being given the experience I should have. It's not right.'

'He's earned it,' said Isla. 'He's been here longer than you have.'

Ralph watched in amazement as they quarrelled over him.

The door was flung open. It was Mrs Egerton-Smythe. 'How are you managing?'

'We're all packed,' said Ralph.

'Are you sure you can carry all that lot?'

'Well, we wouldn't mind accepting a lift, would we?' said Jane, brightening up again.

'I'm afraid the only car Mrs Egerton-Smythe has is in her garage up on chocks,' said Ralph.

'Minus petrol,' added Mrs Egerton-Smythe.

'Oh,' said Jane, disappointed.

'I'll open the front door,' said Mrs Egerton-Smythe. 'You can go out that way. It's a bit congested in the kitchen.'

'Oh, no,' wailed Jane. 'I've just broken one of my nails.'

There was a moment's silence.

'See you tomorrow, then,' said Mrs Egerton-Smythe, slipping several pairs of spectacles into Ralph's jacket pockets. 'You only need two pairs for the play, so you might as well take the ones they won't be using now and keep the others afterwards.'

Ralph was so happy, his eyes began to sting.

'No need to get soppy,' said Mrs Egerton-Smythe shortly. 'Now be off with you.'

'Curtain,' yelled Isla. She was seated at the front of the stage with the prompt book.

The producer stood up in the stalls.

'Right. On to Act Three.'

It was a different producer. Ralph recognised him from past productions as an actor. He was medium height and in his forties with sleeked-back raven-black hair. His name was Arnold Swann.

'Jane!' yelled Isla.

Jane appeared with a note book. 'Yes?' she answered.

'Act Three,' said Isla.

'Strike the newspaper?' she asked gaily.

'And the breakfast crockery.'

Jane looked round blankly. 'I'm sorry, Isla, but I've forgotten which vase is supposed to have the fish in it.'

'The blue one. It needs to go stage left on the mantelpiece. The table there is supposed to be the mantelpiece.'

'Oh, yes.'

'Jane?'

'Yes.'

'Get on with it.'

'Yes, of course. Sorry.'

Ralph stared in disbelief that someone so hopeless could get away with it. But then having a hundred pounds laid down for her might have had something to do with it, he thought sardonically. He longed to leap down and help Isla. Instead he sat lower in his seat, praying that one of the cleaners wouldn't discover him, and watched Jane make a meal of every single change she had to make.

'Isla, I think you'd better label the rehearsal props for her.'

'Yes, Sir.'

At that point one of the actors appeared. 'Isla, I can't find the tray with our personal props for this scene.'

'It's on the chair by the prompt corner.'

'There is no chair there. I've looked.'

Jane had gone a deep crimson colour.

'Jane,' said Isla exasperated. 'Where is it?'

'I tidied them away.'

'You tidied them away,' repeated Isla slowly. 'Why?'

'I thought I was helping.'

'We'd better take a break,' said the producer. 'Isla, I hope this will be sorted out by Monday.'

'Yes, Sir.'

'Ten minutes, everyone!'

Isla rose and walked over to Jane. 'Here is the list of personal props for this act,' she said. 'You know where they are. Return them, please.'

Jane nodded and dashed off.

The awful thing was that Isla, with her robust forthright manner, was made to look like the big bad wolf, and the demure hapless Jane, the victimised Red Riding Hood.

'We all make mistakes when we start,' said Raymond Maclaren who was playing a young lab assistant called Bill. 'Don't be too hard on her.'

Isla nodded and gave a tight smile. She moved the armchair nearer the fireplace, checking her marks on the floor, and set the furniture and props for the next act.

Eventually the producer returned. Suddenly he gazed upwards. Ralph shrank even lower and held his breath.

Geraldine Maclaren, Basil Duke, and Eloise Neville, wrapped in overcoats, hats, scarves and gloves, walked onstage, volumes of steam erupting from their mouths. They stamped their feet as if attempting to get the blood supply to return to them and then, to Ralph's amazement, they hugged each other for warmth.

'Do you realise we "gels" have to wear evening dresses in Act One?' said Geraldine to Basil. 'We'll die!'

'Isla,' yelled the producer from the stalls, 'are we ready yet?'

Isla reappeared. 'Yes, Sir.'

'Right. Let's get started.'

Isla took her place on the chair at the downstage left corner, and faced the actors with her prompt book. The actors dived into the wings.

'Curtain up,' said Isla. 'Sound of rain from offstage. Fire blazing in the grate.'

As the act progressed, Ralph waited expectantly for Isla to put down her prompt book and get ready for her first entrance. It came later in the act. Aunt Vera and Uncle Cecil had been shown into the drawing room. Disappointed that their elder niece Biddie had managed to employ a maid, but overcome by the all-consuming smell of fish which her son Archie has caused by hiding a haddock in a vase of flowers, Aunt Vera prepares to 'rescue' another pretty young thing from this hell hole of ghastly smells and explosions.

Ralph listened expectantly as Aunt Vera asked for the maid to be called to put more coal on the fire. If, in fact, she existed.

The actress playing Biddie mimed pulling the bell pull. Any

minute now, thought Ralph, and he could feel himself trembling with excitement.

'Oh, she exists,' Biddie announced gaily.

'Knock, knock, knock,' said Isla.

At this point Isla dropped her book, ran up the side of the set and promptly walked downstage, speaking in a Cockney accent.

'Still too young,' yelled Arnold Swann. 'Much older.'

Isla nodded, hunched herself over and carried on talking.

Basil was right, thought Ralph. It was a gem of a part, but Isla was not picking up the comic elements at all. It was obvious that Biddie had employed the oldest, plainest, most eccentric maid she could find, to ensure that there was no possibility of Archie taking a shine to her, and persuading his mother to entice her away with an offer of a higher salary.

If Isla had just spoken nasally it would have been far funnier, the point being that Mrs Mulligatawny had no sense of smell. Suddenly aware that he was judging her so critically he felt disloyal.

Isla had exited and was standing by for her next entrance. The vase meanwhile was being moved from place to place, everyone except Archie unaware of its contents. Ralph had to look away hurriedly and pinch himself to prevent himself from laughing.

Isla made her next entrance.

Already she had forgotten that she was supposed to be middle-aged. She was still a radiant, beautiful twenty-year-old.

'Shuffle, Isla, shuffle,' yelled the producer. Isla nodded and shuffled towards a small table, but Ralph could tell that her heart wasn't in it. And then it occurred to him that comedy wasn't her forte. She had mostly played *ingénues* with different accents.

In his mind, Ralph pictured how he saw Mrs Mulligatawny's legs bulging with varicose veins, the only person oblivious to haddock mixed with Eau de Something.

'Padding,' he murmured to himself. Padding to make her look plumper.

Isla gave a bob and began to stride off.

'Shuffle,' yelled the producer.

Isla immediately slowed down and then sprinted downstage to the prompt book again, and the play continued.

'Curtain!' yelled Isla.

As the cast gathered together in the centre of the stage, the producer rose from the stalls and headed for the stage.

'Isla!'

Isla walked downstage.

'Yes, sir?'

'You must find some way of staying in your character, some key thing about her which you can switch into once you leave the prompt book.'

'Yes, I realise that.'

'Remember, she's delighted to have this job. And don't forget to smile at the end.'

'It feels so false.'

'She's smiling because no one has employed her for years and she still hasn't been fired. She has no idea the sisters are amazed and delighted she wants to stay. Does that help?'

'A bit.'

'If you're still having difficulties, perhaps Jane could be on the book for part of Act Three.'

'I'm sure I can manage, it's only a little part,' she said.

'Small parts are always the hardest. Remember all the other characters have a good run. They have time to establish themselves. You haven't. You have to be that person with a life of their own before you even walk on to that set.'

He turned to the rest of the cast. 'Notes in dressing room three,' he announced.

'Isla, you've had yours. You can carry on striking the props. I know you have a lot to do.'

Isla gave a relieved smile, a smile so wonderful that Ralph loved her even more deeply.

As soon as the cast and producer had left the stage, she glanced up towards the upper circle and waved.

Ralph stood up and waved back and then dived back behind the seating. Eventually she disappeared and minutes later he heard footsteps coming down the aisle. Anxiously he peered round. It was her. He leapt up.

'It was wonderful! You too!' he lied.

'I was terrible. I'm not very good at comic roles. Look,' she added, 'can I have a word in confidence?'

'Of course.'

'Let's get out of here first.'

She waited until they were out of the theatre and half-way down the High Street. She pulled him into a side street and headed for a small café. She peered quickly in through the window. 'There's no one from the theatre in here. Come on,' she urged. 'Quick!'

Puzzled, Ralph followed her in. She insisted on paying for their cups of tea and found a secluded corner.

'Why are you being so mysterious?' he asked.

'Because no one must know what I'm about to tell you.' She paused. 'Well, they'll know eventually, but I want to tell you first.'

'Jane's going to get the sack?' Ralph proffered.

'No such luck. Her father's got buckets of money and he's hinted that he might donate a sum of money to the theatre to replace the archaic lighting with new electrics. So we're stuck with her. Anyway that's not what I want to talk about.' She fiddled awkwardly with the spoon. 'This is going to be difficult.' She cleared her throat. 'Philip has been sent back on compassionate leave. His mother is seriously ill. He arrived this morning. He'd phoned the stage door. Anyway I rang him.'

'Is he coming here?' asked Ralph nonchalantly, feeling his stomach lurch.

'He can't. He needs to be near his mother.' She glanced away and then back to him. 'Here comes the difficult bit. I've decided to go and see him. I'll leave tonight, after the show.'

Ralph stared at her in disbelief. 'What about *Something in the Air*?'

'I shall be back before it opens. If I leave straight after tonight's show, I can catch the same London train as most of the cast do. Then, with any luck, I can get on a milk train, arrive there on Saturday and see Philip for twenty-four hours before coming back on Sunday. I'll leave notes for various people, apologising and explaining that my aunt is seriously ill, that I had to leave suddenly and I'll be back on Sunday.'

'Why did you want me to know first?'

'I was wondering if you would sort of hang around.'

'In case Jane panics,' he finished for her.

'Something like that. Yes. All she has to do in the morning is sit with the book during the run.'

'And play Mrs Mulligatawny,' he reminded her.

'The cast can cover me being there. It's the marking up and laying out of rehearsal props which is going to cause problems. Would you?' she pleaded.

How could he turn her down? She needed him. She had come to him for help. He was her knight in shining armour. For a moment he imagined her seeing her Philip and after so many years' separation she would suddenly realise who she really loved and would return and look at him with new eyes, and then he remembered something else.

'Isla. Cuts. It's Saturday tomorrow.'

'But that was when there were three shows. With two shows, if there are any cuts, they'll only be minuscule, and anyway the cast will have them marked down in the script. And they never take prompts.' She suddenly clasped his hands. 'It'd mean you'd have to cope with a strike, virtually on your own. I'm sure Jack will help you, but you'll probably have to mark up for the first act unaided.'

'Don't worry,' he said squeezing her fingers. 'I'll be fine.' And then he glanced outside. 'Isla,' he said ominously. 'It's snowing again.'

She swung round. 'Oh, it can't snow any more,' she said in a choked voice. 'It mustn't.'

'Do you think it's safe to travel in this?'

'That's why I'm coming back Sunday and not on Monday morning, in case there are any problems.'

'It's a hell of a risk.'

'I know, but I've got to see him before he has to go back. What if he gets killed before he's demobbed?'

Ralph looked away. 'Where does his mother live?' he asked casually.

She hesitated. 'Salisbury.'

That afternoon Ralph arranged to go back to helping out on Sunday at Mrs Egerton-Smythe's to make up for the Saturday morning he would be missing. To keep Isla's secret, he made out it was because he was needed at home. He stayed late doing odd jobs and went on from there to the eight o'clock performance of Daphne du Maurier's *The Years Between*.

Seeing the actors on stage, it took him a while to forget they were the same ones who had eavesdropped on his horrendous audition.

As soon as everyone began filing out of the auditorium, Ralph moved swiftly, leaping up the steps of the gallery to the passage which led to the stairway. Impatient to get out, he pushed his way with several 'Excuse me's' to the exit, through the foyer and out of the door, bolted round the corner and ran up the street towards the stage door. He leaned against the wall, panting. He had hardly caught his breath and stepped inside when Isla came tearing down the stairs with her coat and hat on, armed with a suitcase.

'Hello!' said Ralph with feigned surprise.

'No time to stop,' she said breathlessly and she pulled several envelopes from her pocket and dumped them on Wilfred's shelf. 'I've explained everything in a letter,' she said winking, and ran out of the door.

'Where's she going in such a rush?' asked Wilfred amazed.

'Don't know,' said Ralph innocently.

Wilfred glanced down at the envelopes and proceeded to sling

213

them into the appropriate pigeonholes.

'There's one for you,' he said. And he held it out for him to take.

'Oh?' Ralph said. He opened it trying not to let his fingers tremble. 'Oh, dear,' said Ralph. 'Seems her aunt is terribly ill. She's off to see her. Says she'll be back Sunday.'

'Blimey! That'll put the cat among the pigeons.'

'I wonder if Jane knows?' Ralph said.

'Can't do. One of these letters is fer 'er.'

'It'll be a terrible shock. Perhaps I should stay.'

'Come to think of it,' asked Wilfred, 'why are you 'ere? It ent Saturdee.'

'I've been helping out with furniture and props. I just wanted to know if there was anything else I needed to hunt for.'

'Oh.'

Ralph wandered over to the notice board and remained in the background as Geraldine Maclaren, Felix Venning, the boy and his chaperone, and the rest of the cast came down the steps and said their goodnights to Wilfred. Eventually there was the sound of light footsteps. It was Jane.

'Wilfred,' she said anxiously, 'I can't find Isla. Have you seen her?'

Wilfred reached out towards her pigeonhole and handed her an envelope.

'What's this?'

'Open it and you'll find out.'

She was halfway through reading it when she gave a cry of alarm. Ralph stepped forward. 'I've got one too.'

'But she can't do this!' she exclaimed. 'There's a run-through tomorrow morning and lunch to collect for the cast and two shows. Oh, no. There's no other ASM. I'll have to be on the book. And there's changes during the show,' she wailed.

'Can I be of any help?' he suggested.

She stared at him astonished. 'You?'

'I could remove and set the props Isla does and you could just carry on as normal.'

'You best ask Mr Johnson first,' interrupted Wilfred.

'Yes, of course,' said Jane.

'I could still pop in early to help you set up for the *Something in the Air* run.'

'Oh, no! It's got to be marked up!' she gasped. 'I don't know how to do it. Isla always does that. And she wakes me up in the morning.'

'I know how to mark up,' said Ralph. 'Show me where the

214

rehearsal props are and I'll set those up too.'

'Oh, Ralph!' she breathed, her eyelids fluttering. 'Would you really do all that? Just for me?'

Ralph felt acutely embarrassed. 'It's no trouble.'

'He likes any excuse to be in the theatre,' said Wilfred, rescuing him.

'Yes,' he said relieved. 'Yes, I do. And anyway I'll be around in case Mr Johnson wants to see me.'

He turned to the cubby-hole. 'Wilfred, can I come in early? I think it would be best if I was out of the way before the cast come in.'

'You mean before Mr Neville comes in?'

'In a nutshell, yes. Will you be in?'

'Oh, yes.'

'Will you be walking me home?' asked Jane softly.

'Oh, I'm sure you'll be fine,' stammered Ralph. 'It's stopped snowing.'

'I just wondered if you'd like to,' she added smiling.

'Yes, I would,' said Ralph quickly, 'but my mother is very ill.'

'Not dying too?' asked Jane alarmed.

'No. But I have to get the range laid ready for my sister in the morning.'

'Range?' she asked, puzzled.

Ralph felt his face growing crimson. 'My mother prefers old-fashioned methods of cooking,' he lied. 'She thinks food tastes better cooked slowly.' He neglected to mention that they rarely had anything to put in the oven.

'You'd best get going, lad,' said Wilfred, giving him a meaningful look.

'Yes, I best. Cheerio!' And with that he fled out of the door like a startled rabbit.

The bed in the kitchen was empty, although the covers had been thrown aside. At first he assumed Joan must have returned to the front room, but the screaming from upstairs made him fling aside the chairs and dash for the door. He found her standing in the hallway, shivering in an old nightdress and cardigan holding a candle. On the tiny landing above, clinging on to each other were Harry in his underwear and Elsie in a cut-down woman's nightdress and socks. The screams were coming from his mother. Terrified screams.

'What's he doing to her?' he asked.

'I don't know,' stammered Joan, white-faced.

'I'll stop him, the bastard!' he muttered and he leapt up the stairs, fists clenched. He had hardly reached the landing when Elsie grabbed his coat sleeve and yanked him back.

'No!' she whispered.

It was then that he heard what his mother was shouting. 'The street's on fire! There's nowhere to go! Where's Elsie? Harry, where's Elsie? Joan! Joan! Oh, lord, I dunno know where to go. We'll be burnt alive under these stairs. All the houses are gone. They're on fire both sides. The street's going. It's a V-2! It's a V-2! Stop where you are. Don't panic! Stay together! The yard! Try the yard! We can't get out! We can't get out! There's flames everywhere. Keep calm! Keep calm! Oh, God, we're going to be burnt alive.'

'It's all right, love,' said a deep soothing voice. 'It's all right, love. It was his father. 'Hold on to me. Hold on tight. Everything's all right now. The war's over. We're all 'ere. We're all safe. We're together now. I'm back. I'll take care of you.'

'Oh, John,' he heard his mother crying. 'I'm so frightened! I'm so frightened!'

'I know, love.'

'I didn't mean to wake you.'

'I'm glad you did.'

Elsie led Harry back to the bedroom. Ralph stayed for a moment on the landing, listening to his father comforting his mother. When he turned to come downstairs, his aunt was standing in the hallway.

'She never used to have nightmares before *he* moved in up there.'

'Kitty had nightmares when she and Frank were together,' said Joan.

'That's what men do to you,' said his aunt. 'Remember that.'

'Frank loves Kitty.'

'I expect that's why she had the nightmares then,' said Ralph, coming down the stairs.

'Are you trying to be funny?' Joan snapped.

'No. I'm just saying that perhaps Kitty or Mum needed to be with someone they felt safe with before they could let themselves remember something they'd buried.'

'Oh, Mr Know-it-all,' said his aunt and slammed the front-room door, leaving Joan and Ralph together.

'I have to clean the range,' said Ralph at last.

They trooped into the kitchen. There was no electricity. Joan put the candlestick on the table. Someone had already been clearing the grate.

'Who poked this through?' he asked.

'Uncle John. It was still warm so he left it there to smoulder,' she said, climbing into bed. 'Ralph,' she said, shivering violently. 'What did you mean then? About them nightmares.'

'After the war, the rector noticed some people cracking up. Especially women who had kept their worries to themselves. They didn't think they had any right to make a fuss. They worried about their children and husbands, and homes, and rationing and carried on even when they were widowed, trying to keep the families together. It happened to some men too, when they got home.'

'I was buried too,' said Joan. 'Do you think I'll get nightmares when I get married?'

'You might.'

'Yeah, it'd be awful 'aving them alone with no one to 'old you.'

Ralph imagined his father doing just that to his mother and he felt such conflicting feelings. He loved his mother, and he realised that, even though she loved him, she loved his father too. He was grateful that his father was with her, yet couldn't stand the thought of him touching her. It was all so confusing.

'Yes,' he said, at last, but Joan had already begun her late night trumpeting.

Ralph shovelled the ash from under the grate on to a sheet of newspaper. For his father's allotment.

EIGHT

'I've done it!' he whispered, gazing at the furniture and props he had set. He put a chair and table downstage left, facing upstage with the *Something in the Air* prompt book, and then he heard voices. He listened to see if one of them was Jane's. With horror he recognised Mr Neville's. He froze, not knowing whether to leap into the pit or stumble over the furniture into the opposite wings.

Before he could move, Mr Neville walked on-stage with his wife Eloise. 'If we play our cards right,' she said, 'we might be able to persuade Wilfred to make some tea before the others arrive.'

'That Isla is good, isn't she?' commented Mr Neville. 'She must have got here even earlier today. Oh, hello, Arnold!' he said looking off into the wings.

Ralph stood downstage left in the shadows, waiting for an opportunity to dive into oblivion. He watched Eloise Neville attempting to blow some warmth into her hands as Mr Neville

217

headed for the wings. Suddenly Mr Neville stopped, turned round slowly and stared at Ralph. 'What the devil!' he began.

Arnold Swann walked on-stage opening an envelope. 'Oh, hell!' he exclaimed. 'Isla left last night. Her aunt is dying.' He spotted Ralph. 'Hello? Who are you?'

'Master Ralph Hollis,' announced Mr Neville. 'I thought you had other work.'

'I did. I do,' stammered Ralph.

'What are you doing here?' asked Arnold Swann.

'Helping Jane set the props for the run,' said Ralph.

'Where is she?'

'She hasn't arrived yet. At least I don't think she has. Anyway I've finished, so I'd better go.'

'How did you know how to set them up?' asked Mr Swann.

Ralph was about to tell him about the run-through he had seen, but remembered in time that he wasn't supposed to be in the auditorium. He indicated the prompt book. 'Isla set it out quite clearly,' he explained.

'Did you mark this up too?' asked Mr Neville, astonished.

'Yes. I picked it up from Isla during the set-up after the Saturday strike.'

'How did you know Isla wasn't going to be around?' asked Mr Swann.

'I see the Friday shows and I pop in at the stage door to check if I can be around for the Saturday strikes. Because of the insurance business,' he burbled on, feeling his face growing hot. 'And she left me a letter.'

'How very convenient.'

'Yes, wasn't it,' gulped Ralph. He was about to leave when he remembered something. 'Er, depending how many chalk marks are rubbed off, I might need to help Jane mark up *The Years Between* set for the matinée. He looked from one man to another as if at a tennis match.

'Doesn't Jane know how to mark up?' asked Mr Neville.

'I don't think Isla has had time to show her yet.'

'I suppose so,' he sighed. 'But only because it's an emergency. Don't go getting any ideas.'

'No, sir,' said Ralph.

In the wings he heard Geraldine Maclaren and Felix talking.

'Oh, Mr Swann.'

'Yes?'

'If Jane hasn't arrived yet, would you like me to make tea?'

'Tea?' said Geraldine Maclaren, bursting on. 'Did someone say tea? Oh,' she said spotting him. 'Hello, Ralph.'

'Hello!' joined in Felix.

'You know each other?' said Mr Neville, surprised.

'Oh yes' said Felix. 'He had us in fits the other day.'

'Oh, what about?'

There was an awkward silence.

'My audition,' said Ralph, and he looked away quickly and glanced at Mr Swann.

'Yes,' said Mr Swann. 'Tea might help thaw us out before she arrives.'

Jane did not arrive until Act Two was well under way. To Ralph's surprise, Mr Swann had asked him to be on the book until she did. Having seen a run-through of the play he knew where people paused. At first he was terrified to look up to see if someone had dried when there was a silence, in case he lost his place, but after a while he learned how to follow the dialogue, and let his finger drift down the side of the script and hold it there while he glanced up.

He was so involved with Act One that the time passed quickly. The cast, seemed, to his amazement, a little nervous at first, with an audience, but then began playing it for all their worth so that his smile soon dissolved into laughter.

And then suddenly the end of Act One was drawing to a close. Eloise Neville as Aunt Vera had swept out after having given her ultimatum that her two young nieces were to have found a housekeeper or maid by the following week or they would have to live with her and be moulded into shape.

'We must find someone!' the youngest niece, played by Geraldine Maclaren, had wailed in despair, which was Raymond Maclaren's cue to burst in through the french windows as Bill, with a fish he had caught, too late, for the dinner.

'I've solved your problem,' he announced, waving the prop fish. 'Will this do?'

Annie Duncan and Geraldine Maclaren stared at him in exasperation.

'Not unless it can use a feather duster,' quipped Geraldine Maclaren.

'Curtain,' said Ralph. He leapt up from his chair, and in his haste to re-arrange the furniture, he forgot his shyness. It was only when he turned to walk off-stage with the crockery and noticed the cast peering at him from the wings that he could feel his face burning.

'Nearly done,' he panted.

'You're a lovely audience,' said Geraldine.

Ralph smiled. 'You're all so good.'

'More! More!' beamed Felix.

Ralph staggered towards him with the plates and glasses and placed them on the floor near the scene dock. He grabbed the tray with the breakfast crockery on it and brought it back on stage, where he met the producer.

'No sign of Jane yet?' Mr Swann asked.

'I haven't looked, sir. I thought I'd better get on.'

The producer nodded. 'Yes, please do that.'

They were in the middle of a scene between Bill and the two sisters when Jane arrived. Ralph, his finger glued to the page, was absorbed in watching them play swiftly off one another. Suddenly she appeared upstage, crimson-faced. 'I'm terribly sorry,' she stammered. 'I overslept. Isla took the clock and Mrs McGee didn't realise I was working today.' She stared out at the auditorium. 'Shall I . . .?' she began.

Ralph turned to find the producer standing and waving her off stage. 'Wait till Act Three,' he said.

'Oh,' said Jane crestfallen, and she scuttled off.

'Carry on,' he yelled, but Ralph could see that Raymond Maclaren was thrown. By sheer luck he had glanced at the next line so that he said immediately, 'Rather than give you fish, I thought I'd invent a new perfume.'

Raymond picked it up, immediately. It was the way a prompt should be taken, Ralph realised, because there seemed to be no gap in the scene and he knew it was another skill worth learning.

'Why?' asked Biddie, the elder sister.

Raymond Maclaren cleared his throat. 'For you,' he explained awkwardly. 'For a change. I think it's turned out quite well, if I say so myself. It definitely has a flowery smell. I haven't thought of a name for it yet. Perhaps you could help me out there. I'm not very well clued up on flowers.'

'Laburnum?' suggested Jennifer, the younger one, sardonically.

'Laburnum! Yes, that has a nice ring to it.'

'Laburnum's a poison,' said Biddie.

'Is it? Oh, I see. Very droll. How about Eau de Something?'

'*Eau de Chou*,' said Jennifer.

'*Chou*?'

'It's French for cabbage,' said Biddie. 'Do be quiet, Jenny.'

'What about Eau de Cauliflower,' added her sister crossly. 'Or better still, instead of Eau de Something, have Something Odour. Execrable Odour.'

'Jenny, you're being cruel!'

'Well, why today of all days does he have to invent the worst smell of the year? Just when you're about to interview a potential housekeeper.'

'Knock! Knock!' said Ralph.

'I'm sorry,' said Bill. 'I really was trying to cover up the smell of haddock.'

'It's all right. Take no notice of her. She's overwrought,' said Biddie.

'So would you be if your hopes of not living with Aunt Vera, Uncle Cecil and the awful Archie were dashed.'

'Knock! Knock!' said Ralph.

'I'll go and answer that,' said Biddie. 'Where's Father, by the way?'

'Loud explosion,' said Ralph.

Mr Neville mimed staggering through the upstage door. 'Did I hear someone at the door?' he choked.

To his embarrassment, Ralph found that he was clapping. Quickly he recovered himself.

'Curtain,' he said.

He turned and rose. Jane appeared on stage.

'I'll talk to you in a minute,' yelled the producer from the stalls. 'After the changeover.'

Ralph glanced at what Isla had written and he and Jane proceeded to set up for the last act. When they had finished they came downstage together.

'I'm awfully sorry,' began Jane.

'Can't be helped,' said the producer. 'But don't be late again.'

'No, sir,' and she sat down nervously with the prompt book.

The producer beckoned to Ralph. 'Come and sit down here,' he commanded. 'You might as well see how the play ends.

'Thank you, sir,' began Ralph, amazed.

'But he has,' said Jane from the stage, and then she gasped and threw her hand ostentatiously over her mouth.

Ralph froze, wishing the floor would open up and swallow him.

The producer was staring at him. 'I didn't hear that. Did you?' he commented.

Ralph smiled gratefully. 'No, sir,' and he made his way down the steps to the auditorium and sat next to him.

'Everyone ready?' called out the producer.

'Yes!' came several voices from the wings.

'Curtain up!' said Jane sweetly, now appearing to be in her element.

Annie Duncan entered as Biddie. She had hardly been on-stage

221

when Jane prompted her.

'So far, so good,' she said in a bright voice.

'That's Archie's line,' said Annie.

'Oh, is it? I'm sorry.'

'Start again,' said the producer.

'I'm terribly sorry, sir,' said Jane.

'Relax. I know it's your first time on the book.'

Jane gave a shy smile. She really was extraordinarily pretty, thought Ralph, but it was a prettiness which didn't attract him one little bit. It was too sugary for him.

'Curtain up,' said Jane again.

Annie reappeared. This time there were no mishaps. Annie placed a vase of flowers on a low table and opened the french windows in an attempt to erase the smell and exited to open the front door. Felix came bounding on as Archie, rubbing his hands together in glee.

Jane fed the line again.

Felix looked at her. 'Not yet, darling,' he said kindly. 'I say it after I've found dust on the mantelpiece.'

'Oh, I'm sorry, I thought you'd dried.'

'No. I'm just acting.'

'It looks terribly good,' said Jane.

Ralph felt acutely embarrassed by this display of amateurishness. He wanted Jane to do a good job so that Isla wouldn't be missed too much.

'Thank you, Jane,' said Mr Swann. 'Keep going.'

The play continued until it came to the dialogue leading to the entrance of Mrs Mulligatawny.

'Jane, stand in for Mrs Mulligatawny,' said the producer.

Jane visibly glowed. She walked demurely upstage holding the prompt book, playing the consummate actress.

'Knock! Knock!' went the cast for her.

Ralph grinned.

Jane gave them all a stunning smile, read the words beautifully, gave a curtsy and another sweet smile and moved upstage where she remained with the prompt book until her next entrance.

Thank goodness she wouldn't be playing Mrs Mulligatawny, Ralph thought. She had completely misinterpreted the part, playing it for all it was worth as the young petite juvenile lead.

'Well done everyone!' said the producer at the end of the run.

'Notes in the kitchen. Jane, put the kettle on, will you?' He turned to Ralph. 'Thanks for stepping in. But you shouldn't really be here, should you?'

222

'No but . . .' he hesitated. 'Jane's only just started and she doesn't know how to mark up yet. And with no Stage Manager she's terribly nervous about being on the book for the two performances.'

'I think Mr Neville will get Mr Johnson to stand in today. Look, I'll get Jane to bring you a cuppa on-stage and perhaps you could show her how it's done.'

'Yes, of course. Could you mention it to Mr Neville though?'

'Bad, was it?'

'He told me not to give up my job.'

The producer let out a whistle. 'Well, for what it's worth, I thought you handled the rehearsals very professionally.'

'Thank you, sir!'

Ralph followed him up the steps to the stage, his heart soaring. Professionally! That's what he had said. Professionally! He swiftly removed the rehearsal furniture.

Jane soon appeared carrying two mugs of tea, looking miffed. 'The first chance I have to get to know the cast and he sends me back here!' she complained.

Ralph said nothing. He carried on looking for the chalk marks which had survived the run through and then she said something which made him rocket his head upwards. 'Why didn't you wake me?'

'Pardon?' he said in disbelief.

'You must have realised I'd overslept.'

'I don't even know where your digs are.'

'Mm,' she said in disbelief. 'Sure you didn't do it on purpose?'

'Do what on purpose?' asked Ralph astounded.

'Make sure you had all the glory and attention. It's quite obvious that you've been trying your best to get your foot in the door. I bet you couldn't believe your luck when I didn't turn up.'

Poor Isla, having to share a room with her, he thought. 'Jane,' he said slowly, 'do you want me to show you how to mark up or what?'

'How come Isla knows?'

'Because she's the one who has to get here early and do it.'

'While I get given the miserable job of hunting for props.'

'That's what being an ASM is all about,' muttered Ralph, kneeling down with the tape measure and chalk. 'Are you watching?'

'Don't give me orders,' she snapped. 'I'm employed here, you know. You aren't.'

'The producer asked me to show you.'

'There's no point. Isla will be back tomorrow.'

'It's worth learning,' he said. 'You'll have to do it in the future when you're on the book.'

'I shall be acting only by then,' she said.

'Oh,' said Ralph and he hastily got on with the measuring.

But Jane was like a dog with a bone. 'If you're so interested in the theatre, why aren't you doing my job?'

He was about to snap out, 'I already am,' or 'Because I don't have anyone who has paid the theatre a hundred pounds,' when he remembered Isla. He took a deep breath and carried the furniture from *The Years Between* set and placed it on the marks.

'Let's get on with this,' he said politely. 'Now, do you want me to explain what I've done?'

'No, thanks,' she said huffily.

'I'll help you set up the props for the matinée, shall I?'

'I've got the mugs to wash up in the kitchen,' she said sulkily.

'I'll do that if you want.'

'So you can get a chance to fraternise with the cast.'

'After they've gone,' said Ralph exasperated.

'I'll do it.'

Ralph picked up his mug of tea and watched Jane flounce into the wings where he heard her give a sudden 'Oh!'

'Just picking up my script. I'd left it back here.' It was Felix. 'All set for the matinée?'

'Almost,' he heard her say brightly. 'I've marked it up. Just thought I'd see if people needed extra tea before setting up the props.'

Ralph stood with his mug in mid-air. Well, he had to give her her due. She was a good little actress.

And then Felix was on-stage and they stared at one another.

'Well!' Felix said, his eyes twinkling. 'She's one of the prettiest, lying little bitches I've ever met!'

For a fraction of a second, Ralph was shocked and then he burst out laughing.

'If I were you I would leave the props to her,' Felix added.

'I can't,' said Ralph. 'You'd be the ones to suffer, and then Isla would be in more trouble.'

'Mr Johnson is going to be on the book for today's performances and he'll be helping her with the set changes.' He glanced quickly into the wings and then back conspiratorially at Ralph. 'I think he's looking forward to it. He thinks she's going to be a future star.'

'She probably will be,' said Ralph dismally.

'Not a hope,' said Felix and he tapped his chest. 'No heart.'

As soon as Ralph had set up the props, he replaced *The Years Between* book in the prompt corner, left the theatre as quickly as he could and headed for Mrs Egerton-Smythe's. After shovelling snow all afternoon, he dashed home to help Elsie. He still hadn't found the right moment to give his mother the spectacles. Embarrassed at having made such a fool of himself, they remained in his jacket pocket. He got as far as the landing outside her room but, when he heard his father's voice, he ran down the stairs and trudged back into the theatre ready for the strike. To his surprise Wilfred offered him a hot drink as soon as he appeared.

He took it to the notice board – where the cast list for *Watch on the Rhine* by Lillian Hellman was pinned.

Wilfred called him over. 'There's a message for you,' he said casually, 'from Jack Walker. He wants to have a word with you before the strike. Somethin' 'bout insurance. Seems Mr Johnson will be 'elping out tonight.'

'Oh, no,' Ralph breathed.

'Bad, is it?'

Ralph nodded. 'I'm not allowed on stage during a strike because I'm not employed and therefore not covered by insurance. Mr Johnson has said I can observe and do things in the scene dock, but Jack Walker has been turning a blind eye to me helping on-stage.'

'Don't worry. Mr Johnson won't make a habit of it. He likes his tipple too much on a Saturdee.' He paused. 'Well, on most days, come to think of it.'

Ralph had guessed right. Jack told him to stay around the prop table. What made it even worse was that Mr Johnson and Jane did everything together, Jane waxing lyrical over everything he did, fluttering her huge eyelashes at him, and smiling at him in her most engaging way. They even did the marking up together, Jane going on about what a wonderful teacher Mr Johnson was, how she had longed to learn how to mark up, but Isla had kept it a secret (bright laugh), and she thought it was such a good idea for when she went on the book, not that she was ready for it yet (gush gush). It was nauseating.

Later, when he was about to leave the kitchen with the tray of tea, Jack walked in. To Ralph's dismay, he closed the door swiftly behind him.

'She's spilled the beans, hasn't she?' said Ralph. 'No more strikes.'

'What makes you say that?' asked Jack.

'I think she's got it in for me.'

'Ah,' said Jack. 'You ent succumbed to her charms.'

'But I thought you liked her.'

'I pretend to,' Jack said. 'Types like her can cause a lot of trouble. They can swing from sugar to venom in seconds if you don't play their game.'

'I know,' said Ralph. 'She tells lies too, brilliantly. It's incredible to watch.'

'Don't worry lad, once Isla is back this will just be an unpleasant episode.' He took the tray. 'I'll tell Mr Johnson we sent you home.'

He was out shovelling snow from Mrs Egerton-Smythe's veranda on Sunday afternoon when she came dashing out of the french windows.

'Someone on the phone for you!'

Ralph threw down the shovel and hurriedly took off his boots. 'Is it Jessica?'

Mrs Egerton-Smythe looked bemused. 'Jessica? No. She's not allowed to make phone calls.'

'Oh,' said Ralph puzzled. 'Who is it, then?'

'Isla.'

Ralph picked up the receiver.

'Hello, Ralph.'

'Isla! It's such a relief to hear you,' he said. 'Jane has been a real . . .'

'I can guess.'

'When did you get back to your digs?'

'I'm not back there yet. I'm at Philip's.'

'What! Oh, you're just about to leave?'

'No.' She paused. 'Ralph, I'm stuck. There are twenty-foot snowdrifts round here, and the ferries aren't running.'

'Sorry,' laughed Ralph. 'I thought you said ferries.'

'I did.' There was a pause. 'Ralph?'

'Yes, I'm still here. I think,' he said dazed.

'I'm awfully sorry, I'm afraid I told you a small fib. I'm at a place forbidden by anyone who has a contract with a theatre.'

'Where?' he asked impatiently.

'The Isle of Wight.'

'The Isle of Wight!'

'I'm ringing you because I won't be able to get back by Monday.'

'Don't panic,' said Ralph. 'Mr Johnson will be delighted to be on the book for the opening night. He and Jane are as thick as thieves.'

'It's not the book that's worrying me. I want you to take down my digs' address and go round there today. You must warn Jane.'

'But I told you Mr Johnson will deal with everything.'

226

'Mr Johnson's a man,' she interrupted. 'That's why you have to see her as soon as possible. Ralph, she'll have to play Mrs Mulligatawny.'

'**Y**ou're looking browned-off,' commented his father, who was sitting in his overcoat, carving a piece of wood when Ralph walked into the kitchen.

'Just tired,' he said. 'How's Mum?'

'Looking much better. She's even a bit bored, which is a good sign.' He cleared his throat. 'By the way,' he said. 'I just 'appened to be passing by the opticians and I popped in and asked about spectacles. It's out of the question. He said they could be anything from thirty bob to three quid or more.'

It was the opportunity Ralph had been waiting for. Hurriedly he took out the handful of spectacles from his pocket. 'Why not take these up to her and let her try them on? There are two other pairs at the theatre. Mrs Egerton-Smythe said they could choose which ones they want for the next play, and we could have them afterwards.'

He shoved them across the table. 'This ain't Mrs Egerton-Smythe playing Lady Bountiful, is it?' his father asked frowning.

'No. The ladies' ones are too weak for her now and her husband's are too strong.'

'You best take them up, then.'

'No, Dad. I want you to take them up.'

'You ain't doin' me no favours, you know,' snapped his father suddenly.

'If you take them up and say you were given them, she'll know you approve of her reading. If I take them up, she might not use them for fear of upsetting you.'

His father opened one of the cases. 'Blimey! These are good 'uns,' he exclaimed. 'You'd get a tidy bob for these.'

'Dad!' said Ralph angrily.

His father grinned. 'Just pulling your leg.' He gave a sigh. 'I still don't see why she wants to read though.'

'It'll be like a tonic. And she won't be so dependent on Aunty Win, will she?'

'You're a sly one,' his father said. 'Oh by the way, there's a thermos of tea made up for you and a slice of bread and dripping. I couldn't keep the range going because of the fuel. That's why everyone's gone to bed already. To keep warm.'

'Thanks, Dad.'

Ralph began eating while his dad opened the other spectacle cases. He gazed up at the washing hanging from the rack. Immediately he spotted two large corsets and several pairs of thick lisle stockings. Mrs Mulligatawny, he thought.

'So that young Jane has stepped in to play Mrs Mulligatawny,' said Wilfred.

'I wonder if they'll need extra help for the scene changes,' said Ralph casually.

'No harm in askin',' said Wilfred. 'Good job you popped in.'

He glanced at the small suitcase Ralph was carrying up. 'Not eloping, are you?' he said winking.

'No. Could I leave it with you?''

Wilfred moved from his chair and unlocked the door. 'Bring it in.'

Ralph found Mr Johnson in the kitchen.

'Yes?' he said on seeing Ralph.

'I just happened to hear about Isla. So I was wondering if you needed any help with the set changes. With props.'

Mr Johnson gazed at him thoughtfully. And then gave a sigh. 'Just for the dress and tonight. Until Isla gets back tomorrow.'

'Thank you, sir.'

'But only because it's an emergency. Understand?'

'Yes, sir.'

Ralph collected his suitcase from Wilfred and ran as fast as he could upstairs. He knew which dressing room she was in. The one he had changed in for his horrendous audition. He knocked on the door.

'Come in!' said a bright voice.

He peered his head round the door. Jane was sitting in front of one of the mirrors, her make-up spread out neatly on a towel.

'What do you think?' she said indicating it.

'Very professional.'

Ralph produced his suitcase. 'It's some of my aunt's things, just in case you want to borrow them.'

'I don't,' said Jane firmly.

'Don't you want to see what's inside?'

She sighed and smiled, as if he was a little boy. 'Go on, then.'

He placed the case beside her make-up and snapped it open. He might as well display the worst first, he thought. He lifted out a large boned corset.

'Ralph,' she said, 'that's for a woman twice my size.'

'Exactly,' he said eagerly. 'I thought you could pad it out.'

'So that the dress would fit?'

Ralph nodded.

'Not very flattering to Isla,' she said simpering, 'is it?'

'I think Isla was going to pad herself out too. The other thing I thought of was this,' he said, and he brought out a couple of rolls of old crêpe bandages.

'What's that for?' she cried.

'Wrapping round your legs. You see,' Ralph explained, 'you have such young pretty legs. If you wrapped these round them, then put the stockings over the top, it would make you look like you had varicose veins.'

Jane by this time was looking at him aghast. 'Ralph, I will play this part my way. I'm having enough trouble with that costume as it is,' she said indicating the black maid's outfit, hanging from a rail. 'If I was doing it for the week I'd put darts in it.'

It was then that Ralph noticed a neat pair of attractive low-heeled shoes, black court shoes. He realised that it was a lost cause. He returned the corsets and bandages to the case and snapped it shut. 'Of course,' he said, 'but do you mind if I leave it here, and then I'll take it home tonight.'

'I suppose so,' she began slowly.

'Thank you, Jane, I really appreciate it.'

The dress rehearsal began at 2.30 p.m. Aside from a few hiccups with lighting cues, the first act seemed to go smoothly, though it had lost the spark it had had on the Saturday.

'Well, I have to hand it to you, lad,' Mr Johnson commented, when Act Three had been set. 'You're fast. Have you checked the personal props?'

'They're on a tray at the end of the prop table.'

Jane, by now, had disappeared to change into her costume.

They were half-way through the act when he caught sight of Mr Johnson indicating to him. He moved swiftly to the prompt corner.

'You'd best give Miss Jefferson a call.'

'Yes, sir,' Ralph whispered.

He met her on the stairs.

'Well?' she said. 'How do I look?'

'Um,' began Ralph. 'I'm speechless.'

She looked dazzling, perfect for another play, but totally wrong for Mrs Mulligatawny. Her little white lacy headband was perched neatly behind her waved hair, and she was heavily made up with dark eyes and red lipstick. She looked more like an usherette at a grand cinema than a plain housemaid.

'Mr Johnson asked me to give you your call.'

'Oh, thank you. I'm not late, am I?'

'No,' said Ralph.

He walked briskly to the welcome darkness of the wings and watched her from the scene dock, standing upright, her hands planted over her trim hips, her head flung back, occasionally smacking her lips together, and then suddenly remembering to be demure.

Basil Duke entered the wings. At first he was too intent with concentration to notice Jane and then he caught sight of her and did a double-take. He gaped at her in disbelief and then, suddenly hearing his cue, he dashed on-stage. Jane followed on behind him. And the scene continued.

Ralph picked up the tray with the teapot and scones ready to hand to her. When she appeared backstage she took it from him and gave him a paternal nod. She appeared triumphant.

Ralph returned to the wings, and listened to the rest of the play.

'All right, everyone, let's stop there,' Arnold Swann called out. 'Bit flat, but that's to be expected. Can I have everyone on stage, please?'

Ralph began to sort the props out on the prop table, ready for the evening show. Anything to eavesdrop.

'Annie?' Mr Swann said. 'Have you still got that mousy grey wig you wore for Emily in *Ladies in Retirement* and Nanny Patching in *Dear Octopus*?'

'Yes.'

'Would you lend it to Jane?'

Ralph looked hastily down at the table, trying desperately not to laugh.

'And perhaps we can get a bigger dress that you can pad out a bit. 'Do you mean for me?' she asked, a tremor in her voice.

'Yes, I'm sorry, dear. You've made a great effort, and I appreciate it, but you've obviously had no chance to read the whole play. It's not your fault. Mrs Mulligatawny has been employed because she's so awful-looking,' he explained. 'Now, you're very pretty, so you need to flatten your face a bit and powder your mouth. Perhaps a bit of carmine on the inside of your lips to make them look thinner.'

Ralph headed for the kitchen. The kettle had just boiled when Jane burst in. Ralph could see she was close to tears.

'Mr Swann has asked me to make tea,' she said shakily.

'All done.' He was going to ask her how it went, but decided against it.

She lifted the tray but her hands were shaking so uncontrollably that the mugs were wobbling.

'I'll carry them as far as the wings for you,' he said gently.

She nodded.

He met the cast coming off-stage in the wings. Quickly he handed the tray to her and backed towards the prompt corner where Mr Johnson was jotting something down in the prompt book.

'That was quick,' he heard the producer say.

Mr Johnson glanced up. 'I'd like you to do a job for me,' he said.

'Yes, sir.'

'Go to dressing room three on the first floor and get the key to Annie Duncan's flat. She'll give you the directions. We need the wig she wore for . . . Oh, you wouldn't know.'

'I do, sir. I saw both productions.'

As Ralph left he heard the producer say, 'Now before we start, Jane, go and find some lace-up shoes from somewhere. I expect Florrie has a stock. I always find that if I can get the right shoes it helps me get into the character.'

'Yes, sir,' he heard Jane say miserably.

'And perhaps a towel to wrap round your middle, just to give you a feeling of weight there.'

Ralph made a hasty exit.

Annie Duncan's flat was in a huge decrepit house, with drab peeling wallpaper and well-trodden linoleum on the stairs. A black coin telephone stood in the hallway beside a notice with a list of do's and don'ts beside it.

Ralph nipped swiftly up the stairs.

Number six was more of a bed-sitting room than a flat. A flimsy partition separated a tiny kitchen with a screened-off bath in it. Dyed garments dripped over the bath into colourful icicles. The furniture, including a small divan bed, was draped in rich oriental covers with numerous cushions heaped on to it. Stacked on shelves were books, a wireless, a gramophone and copies of *The Stage*. A long rail with jackets, evening dresses, skirts, smart afternoon dresses and aprons hanging from it was pushed up against them. Wedged into a corner near by was a large treadle sewing machine surrounded by boxes of material and old shoes. Ralph stumbled over a gramophone case towards a shelf above a small chest of drawers, piled high with wigs, hats, gloves and spectacles. He spotted the grey wig and folded it carefully into his pocket.

As soon as he reached the theatre, he ran up to Jane's dressing room.

He knocked tentatively on the door. To his surprise he heard Mr Johnson's voice calling out, 'Who is it?'

'Hollis, sir.'

The door was flung open by him. Behind him, reflected in the mirror sat Jane, red-faced and swollen-eyed. Ralph brought out the wig. Jane immediately broke into a howl, blubbering, 'I can't do it. It's so humiliating. I'm an *ingénue*, not a character actress!'

She said 'character' as if it was a demeaning thing to be.

'You'd best set up, lad,' said Mr Johnson quietly.

Alone on stage Ralph happily set the furniture on the marks and checked the props for all three acts and picked up the personal props.

He knocked on dressing room two. Luckily for him it was empty, since it was Mr Neville's. He had just delivered personal props on the first floor, when he met the trio, in evening suits so shiny with age he could almost see his reflection in them. Their hair was slicked back and they had cigarettes dangling from their mouths. Two of them were carrying a violin and a cello. They gave him a peremptory wave.

Ralph had a strong desire to run to the lavatory and to stay there for a very long time. The show must be starting soon, yet he had heard none of the calls.

Ralph raced down the stairs to the stage door. Wilfred was in his usual place reading his newspaper.

'Wilfred, do you know what time it is?'

'It's nearly the quarter,' said a voice behind him. It was Mr Johnson. 'Do you know how to give calls?'

'Yes, sir.'

'Start giving them.'

He was half-way down the corridor after having knocked on the doors of dressing rooms one and two to give Mr and Mrs Neville their quarter calls, when he heard the door behind him being flung open.

'Ralph Hollis!' boomed a voice. Ralph turned to find Mr Neville in his shirt-sleeves, a stick of greasepaint in his hand.

'What are you doing giving calls? It's Jane's job.'

'Mr Johnson asked me to.'

Mr Neville gave a weary sigh. 'Go on with you, then.'

He met Jane in the wings after giving the quarter to the first-floor dressing rooms. She looked far more cheerful, but to Ralph's surprise she was made up as normal and still looked pretty.

232

'The producer made a special point of wishing me luck,' she whispered. 'Isn't that wonderful? He said I was a very courageous young woman and thanked me for stepping in at such short notice.'

Suddenly there was the sound of the trio playing in the pit. He and Jane stepped on to the stage. From beyond the curtain they could hear the distant murmur of the audience, filtering into the auditorium.

'It's actually happening,' whispered Ralph.

'My première,' breathed Jane.

Smiling, Ralph listened to the audience laugh their way through Act One. As the stage hands changed the set, Ralph hung back near the prompt corner so that he wouldn't be in the way. Before he knew it, Act Two was drawing to a close.

There was a huge laugh from the audience followed by loud applause, the sound of the curtain dropping and music. With sweating hands he strode swiftly on to the set, shifting furniture with Mr Johnson. Behind a screen in the wings, Annie Duncan was stepping out of her slacks and jersey and into an afternoon dress, helped by Florrie.

Ralph hastily picked up the tea tray and walked over to her. She glanced briefly at him, took it and murmured, 'Thanks.' Ralph stepped back, not wanting to interrupt the silent world that seemed to inhabit her. She stood quietly, concentrating.

The door flew open again and Raymond Maclaren entered the wings, dripping in sou'wester and mackintosh, holding a fish, followed by Felix in plus-fours and a monocle. Mr Neville followed swiftly afterwards, carrying a wad of papers.

The music ended. Over Mr Johnson's shoulder Ralph could see him give the lighting cue for the firelight and the cue to the fly-man for curtain-up. Ralph picked up a tray of peas and began rattling it to make the sound of the rain. It was after he had put it down that he realised he hadn't seen Jane. She had had all of Act Two to make up and change. Knowing how excited she was, he imagined she would have been down already.

'Mr Johnson?'

Mr Johnson glanced briefly aside at him.

'Shall I give Jane her call?' whispered Ralph.

Mr Johnson nodded.

Ralph fled up the stairs to the top floor and knocked at the door. 'Miss Jefferson, Miss Jefferson.'

From behind the door he heard a strange whimpering sound.

'Jane?'

233

There was no answer. He opened the door. Jane was sitting in an armchair, tears streaming down her face. Her costume was still hanging on the rail. A massive brassière and padding lay untouched on the dressing table. The wig was lying lopsided beside them.

'I can't do it! I can't do it!' she moaned.

'Oh, hell!' whispered Ralph. He knelt down and took hold of her shoulders, but she couldn't seem to focus on him.

'I can't make myself look that awful. I'll be a laughing stock,' she wept.

'That's the whole idea,' pointed out Ralph.

'I feel sick,' she said.

'It's only nerves.'

'The medicine has made me feel dizzy,' she slurred.

'Medicine? What medicine?'

She pointed at a green bottle and glass. Ralph leapt over to it and pulled out the cork. It smelled of alcohol. He spotted a large glass tumbler on the floor by her feet.

'Jane, how much have you drunk of this?'

'Just a glass,' she mumbled. 'Mr Johnson said one glass would steady me.'

'A whole glass?' he asked. 'Neat?'

'Neat?'

'Without water.'

'There isn't any up here. Oh, I'm going to be sick. Oh.'

Ralph spotted a fire bucket in the corner filled with cigarette butts and paper. He grabbed it and reached her in the nick of time. Within seconds she was vomiting violently into it. Ralph grabbed her towel and wiped her face with it. She sank back in the chair, ashen.

'At least you look the part now,' he said lightly. He paused. 'Jane?'

She did not answer. She was slumped to one side, her eyes closed.

'Jane!' he said, shaking her. 'Jane! Wake up! Wake up!' But Ralph could see she was unreachable.

He stood up and glanced wildly at the dressing table. With an awful realisation he knew there was only one thing left to do.

He threw open his suitcase, dragged out the corset and stockings, pulled off his lace-ups and trousers and began winding a crêpe bandage round one leg.

TEN

B lind hysterical terror he had heard about. Icy calm terror he
had not.

By the time he had slipped into the shadows of the wings, and
had moved behind the set, the awful memory of gazing in the
mirror at his face with his thin lips and red spots in the corners of
his eyes, under a grey wig and a maid's lacy cap perked lopsidedly
on top, had thankfully begun to evaporate.

Standing behind the door, listening to the scene on-stage, he
found himself swallowing great gulps of air, his mouth so dry it
reached his throat. How was he going to get away without
sounding male? For one moment he panicked. His throat was so
sore it felt as though it had been sandpapered. And then he had a
brain-wave. He would pretend to have a touch of laryngitis and
speak huskily. He gathered his wits together and sank himself into
his character.

He noticed the two small light bulbs on the flat nearest him.
When the red light was on it meant 'warn', the green light meant
'go' and wouldn't go off until 'Archie' had stepped off-stage. To his
dismay, he saw Raymond Maclaren coming towards him. He
turned hastily away.

'You look marvellous, Jane,' he heard him say, to the back of his
head. 'Good luck.'

Ralph gave a shy nod. Out of the corner of his eye, the red light
flashed for 'Bill's' entrance. Ralph listened to the next bit of
dialogue intently.

It was then that he realised with an awful shock, that Geraldine
Maclaren was standing by his side, staring at him.

'What the hell!' she whispered.

Ralph saw Mr. and Mrs. Neville approaching. 'Tell me later,' she
said. 'Concentrate!'

Ralph nodded.

Basil appeared. Ralph quickly got out of the way so that Basil
could make his entrance with Mrs Neville. Avoiding Mr Neville he
stepped to the side and turned away from him.

Mrs Neville thrust open the door.

'Where's the new maid?' he heard her demand.

'Haven't you seen her?' Geraldine Maclaren asked with more
than a *double entendre* in the question.

Ralph listened to the ensuing dialogue, his heart plummeting into
his belly and back up to his mouth.

'Well done, Jane,' he heard Mr Neville say from behind.

'I like the legs, a good touch.' And then it was time for Mr Neville to go on, leaving Ralph alone to listen to the complaints over the pungent smell of fish.

'Oh, she exists,' he heard Biddie announce gaily. The red light flashed on. He took a deep breath, made himself as middle-aged and friendly as he could and pushed open the door. With bandy legs he walked downstage conscious of what appeared to be searchlights searing down on him. To his relief, there was a wave of laughter. He gazed at Annie Duncan who was gaping at him transfixed as he delivered his lines in an adenoidal croak. He waited for some response, feeling the eagerness of wanting to be a good maid oozing from every pore.

'Oh, yes, I see,' she said clearing her throat, 'I think. Would you put some more coal on the fire, Mrs. Mulligatawny, and bring in the tea and scones.'

'Yes, madam,' he mumbled and he gave a neat little bob and exited, closing the upstage door behind him.

'One entrance down. Two to go,' he whispered to himself.

He stumbled backstage towards the prop table, only to be faced by Mr Johnson holding the tray with the teapot and scones out for him.

'I hope you have a good explanation for this, lad,' he said grimly.

'Yes, sir,' whispered Ralph as he hurried back with the tray.

'She'll have left by this evening. No one could put up with this smell,' he heard as he opened the door somewhat clumsily, and emerged into the glaring light again.

'Thank you, Mrs Mulligatawny.'

Ralph left the tray on the card table.

'Well, Mrs Mulligatawny,' said Aunt Vera stiffly, 'and how are you liking it here?'

'Oh, I feel so fortunate, badam, that I'm in such a lubbly home,' he said nasally. 'I'be nebber seen such a lot of carbet. Not that I'm complaining, you understand. I enjoy carbet sweeping.'

Although he was vaguely aware of laughter coming from somewhere, all he was really taking in was Eloise Neville's expression, which was one of dumb disbelief.

'The other places I'be worked in didn't eben stretch to linoleum. Though they do make such lubbly linoleum nowadays.'

'Yes, thank you, Mrs Mulligatawny,' Biddie interrupted. 'That will be all.'

Ralph gave her his bob and exited up-centre. He was just closing the door behind him when he heard a burst of applause. Obviously

236

Mrs Neville had done something after he had left which had amused the audience. One more entrance to go, Ralph thought, and it would soon be all over.

Suddenly, he realised he was supposed to make the sound of the explosion and he raced backstage. To his relief he discovered Mr Johnson was by the panatrope and there was the sound of an explosion as he placed the needle on the appropriate spot on the gramophone record.

Ralph rushed back to the doors, trying to catch his breath.

By now there would be general racing round on-stage. And then he heard his cue to open the door and stagger on.

'So glad that one didn't have our nubber on it, badam. Bore tea?'

'Yes, thank you, Mrs Mulligatawny.'

Ralph lumbered over to the tray which now had the vase placed on it.

'So you see, we won't need to move in with you, Aunt Vera,' said Biddie.

It was at this moment that Mrs Mulligatawny was supposed to notice something strange in the vase. Puzzled, Ralph slowly pulled out the haddock, and then for some reason or other, he found himself glancing quickly at the ceiling.

Aunt Vera looked triumphant.

'Spoken too soon, my dear, I think you're about to lose her.'

'Well, Mrs Mulligatawny,' began Biddie shakily, 'I can't think how that got there.'

'But I have my suspicions,' said Jennifer, glancing at Archie.

'Probidence, that's what it is. Ebery cloud has a silber lining,' wheezed Ralph. 'This'll bake a nice bish subber!' And he beamed happily at everyone.

At this point the characters, Jennifer and Biddie were supposed to laugh uncontrollably, which they did with more than usual gusto.

From above, Ralph heard the welcome sound of the curtain making its downward journey as he continued to gaze at the two sisters' hysteria. The audience, who were also rolling around with laughter, broke into thunderous applause.

As soon as the curtain hit the deck, Ralph found someone dragging him downstage by the hand. It was Felix. 'The curtain call,' he said urgently.

'My wig will fall off if I bow,' said Ralph alarmed.

'Look up at the audience. Chin up and smile.'

The curtain sprang upwards again.

'Take the bow from Mr Neville,' Felix whispered out of the side of his mouth. 'Keep your eyes on him when he makes the announcement for next week's production.'

And then he was bowing and the applause went on and on and it suddenly hit him that there were hundreds of people sitting out there, clapping for them all, and he was one of them, only he was too terrified to enjoy it.

Then Mr Neville stepped forward and Ralph kept his eyes riveted on him.

'Ladies and gentlemen, we thank you for your splendid reception tonight for this rollicking family comedy. Next Monday we will open again with a searing thought-provoking play set in America, called *Watch on the Rhine*. If you have enjoyed tonight's performance, please tell your friends.' This was followed by more applause. 'And now,' he added as the applause began to die down, 'God bless and goodnight'. He stepped back and Ralph watched the entire audience rise to their feet as the strains of 'God Save the King' came from the pit. Ralph kept his eyes focused on the dress circle, his heart thumping.

Hardly had the curtain hit the deck when he found Mr Neville towering over him in a rage. 'Well! Jane told me you were trying to take over her job, but never in my wildest imagination did I think you would stoop to this.'

Ralph, stunned by this extraordinary accusation, was rendered speechless.

'Hang on a minute,' burst out Felix, 'Where is Jane?'

They crowded round the dressing-room door. Jane was still slumped unconscious in the armchair with Ralph's greatcoat draped around her. Mr Neville lifted her hand. It fell back limply.

Raymond Maclaren picked up the glass from the side of her feet and smelled it. 'Whisky,' he said.

'You gave her whisky?' said Mr Neville. 'How much?'

'I didn't,' said Ralph, feeling his face growing red.

'He can't afford to buy whisky,' said Felix, 'not on his salary, or rather his lack of salary.'

At that moment Ralph spotted Mr Johnson appearing from behind the crowd.

'Where did she get it?' said Raymond Maclaren.

'She didn't say,' said Ralph avoiding the question. 'But I'm positive she thought it was medicine,' he added brightly.

'Would someone mind telling me what the hell's going on?'

It was Arnold Swann.

He spotted Jane.

'I'm terribly sorry, sir,' said Ralph. 'I had to do something. There

238

was no time . . .' His voice dwindled away.

'When did this happen?'

'In Act Three'

There was a sudden silence as everyone stared at him.

Ralph cleared his throat awkwardly. 'Would you like me to put the kettle on, sir, and make some tea?'

He didn't know why he said it. It was such an incredibly stupid question. Suddenly Felix collapsed into laughter, followed very quickly by the rest of the cast, including Mr Neville. Even Mr Johnson was smiling and looking a little relieved.

'I should get changed first,' choked Felix.

'Changed?' asked Ralph. And then he remembered, He turned to see a pale face and a grey wig with a maid's hat perched skew-whiff on top, with a black dress drawn over a large bosom and hips. And he grinned.

'Oh, my goodness!' said Felix suddenly. 'I've a train to catch!' And he disappeared.

'What shall we do about Jane?' asked Ralph when everyone had caught their breath. 'She can't go home by herself.'

'You could put her in my car,' suggested Basil. 'If it's still functioning. I'll need help carrying her though.'

'I think there'd better be a woman with you,' said Ralph. 'Because of her landlady.'

'Eloise and I will come with you, Basil,' said Mr Neville.

Eventually they left Ralph to change in privacy.

He was back in his street clothes and using Jane's Crow's Cremine to remove the last vestiges of make-up when there was a knock at the door. It was Mr Johnson. He slipped in and closed it. 'Thanks for not telling.'

'Do you think she'll blab?' Ralph asked.

'It's a possibility. I'll have a word with her.'

He was about to leave when Ralph called him back.

'What is it now?' said Mr Johnson.

'My make-up. Is it all off? My father will kill me if he spots any on me.'

Ralph was suddenly conscious of the soup travelling towards him. He sat up with a jolt. A combination of a morning of shovelling snow after a late night and the warmth of the kitchen was making him drowsy.

Queenie was rolling out pastry at the other end of the table. Ralph yawned.

'Work too 'ard fer you?' she commented.

The door opened. It was Mrs Egerton-Smythe. He went to stand but she waved him back into his seat.

'So,' she said, standing in front of him, 'how was the opening night? I gather from the bags under your eyes you went to see it.'

'I helped backstage,' he said.

'How did you manage that?' she asked impressed.

'Jane was nervous so I offered to help set up Act Three to give her more time to change.'

'And how was she?'

'Um.'

'Not very good?'

'In a manner of speaking.'

Mrs Egerton-Smythe looked at him puzzled and then glanced quickly aside at Queenie. At that moment the telephone rang.

'Oh dear,' said Mrs Egerton-Smythe, 'if that's another person wanting to use my Aga . . .'

'I'll tell 'em we're fully booked,' said Queenie. 'You're too soft hearted, ma'am.' And she wiped her hands on a tea towel and left the room.

'Quickly!' Mrs Egerton-Smythe whispered urgently.

'She got drunk and passed out.'

'So what happened?'

'Someone else had to play her part at very short notice.'

'Who?'

'Me.'

Mrs Egerton-Smythe opened her mouth in silent laughter.

'I'd love to tell Jessica, but it might be a bit tricky,' said Ralph. 'One of the mistresses might read it. Could you tell her that her friend Ruth . . .'

The door was flung open. 'It's for you,' Queenie snapped out at Ralph. 'A Mr Johnson from the Palace Theatre.'

He was waiting for Ralph in a tiny box-like office, eating

240

sandwiches and reading a racing paper. He peered over it, and beckoned Ralph to sit on a chair.

'What did your employer say?'

'I can start work for her a little later tomorrow morning, so I can give Jane a call. I can make it up in the afternoon. Unless you want me to go hunting for props.'

Mr Johnson looked at him puzzled. 'That's Jane's job,' he said.

'Yes, of course.'

'Have you ever helped in that way?' he asked suddenly alert.

Ralph felt his face growing hot. He didn't want to get Isla into trouble.

'Sometimes I've known where a couple of things have been,' he said nonchalantly, 'and happened to have mentioned them to Isla.'

'Mm,' said Mr Johnson suspiciously.

'Have you heard from her?'

'Yes. She's completely snowed in.' He stared hard at him. 'I hadn't realised things were so bad around Salisbury,' he said leaning heavily on the last word.

Ralph swallowed. 'Well, it's pretty bad here as well,' he said quickly. 'There's talk of my father being sent home from work, what with the fuel shortage.'

'Where does he work, then?'

'At the paper mill.'

'What does he think about you hanging round here?'

Ralph decided to be honest. 'Like Mr Neville, sir, not a lot.'

A flicker of a smile appeared on Mr Johnson's face. 'You're not going to give up, are you,' he stated.

'Of course not,' said Ralph surprised.

He sighed. 'Another one wanting to be an actor.'

'Not want to be, sir. Going to be.'

'It's a hard life.'

'It's the one I want.'

Mr Johnson threw his paper aside. 'I take it you can help tonight.'

'Yes, sir.'

At least Ralph hoped so. Mrs Egerton-Smythe had let him phone his Uncle Ted's house. His Aunty Grace had taken the message that he would be working late that night, but Ralph doubted the message would be passed on. They disliked him and they were bone lazy. Ralph had discovered that before her illness his mother had been doing his aunt's shopping.

'Do you need Act Three props and furniture to be cleared?'

Mr Johnson nodded. Ralph could see a 'but' forming.

'If you gave me enough for a bag of chips and a cup of tea, since I haven't had time to prepare food for tonight, wouldn't that put me temporarily on the payroll and have me covered by insurance?'

Mr Johnson gave a weary sigh. 'I must say I could do with the help.'

'I could do it now sir,' said Ralph eagerly. 'I know where everything goes. Then I could put the Act One furniture and props for tonight downstage ready for setting once the Act One set is put up.'

'Anything else you'd like to do?' asked Mr Johnson wryly.

'Well, naturally I'd mark up and set Act One,' he said.

Mr Johnson smiled. 'Want one?' he said, indicating the sandwiches.

It was later in the afternoon that Jane came in. Ralph had been chatting to Wilfred in his cubby-hole. He leaned out of the window.

'How are you? he asked.

She turned briskly at the foot of the staircase. 'As well as can be expected,' she said bitterly, 'in the circumstances.'

'Mr Johnson's letting me help again tonight,' he said reassuringly.

But she seemed indifferent and with a slight nod of the head retreated upstairs.

Gradually the cast began to filter in for the evening show. Ralph gave the calls. Then it was 'overture and beginners', curtain-up, and the performance had begun. Once when Ralph was smiling in the wings at something which was happening on-stage, he was startled by an angry whisper. It was Jane.

'What's the point of staying?' she hissed. 'You can't see anything.'

Ralph looked at her amazed. He assumed she was joking.

'You can hear their delivery. And their timing is so good. I like to hear the audience too, don't you?'

'Yes, of course,' she said hurriedly.

'Feeling better about tonight?'

'I think all this is going a bit to your head, you know.'

But Ralph was surrounded by a wall of happiness so deep that she couldn't penetrate it. He didn't even hold back when it was time to change the props for Act Two and Mr Johnson didn't show any signs of objecting. As soon as Act Two had begun, Jane disappeared to get changed.

Act Two came and went. The audience laughed and applauded and he could see by the way the cast came off-stage that they were relieved. There was nothing so awful as trying to make people laugh and being greeted by a stony silence.

Halfway through Act Three Ralph asked Mr Johnson if he ought to see how Jane was doing. Mr Johnson hesitated at first, and then nodded. Leaping up the stairs Ralph almost began to whistle when he remembered it was bad luck in a theatre.

He reached the top dressing room and knocked on the door. 'Miss Jefferson!' There was no reply. 'Miss Jefferson?'

The silence made him freeze. He opened the door. The room was empty. At first he assumed she must have nipped out to the lavatory until he noticed the maid's uniform hanging on the rail. Her make-up was still laid out on the dressing table. It was then that he saw the note, propped up against the mirror.

'It's no good,' it said. 'I'm too unwell.'

He didn't read the rest. He could see that her overcoat was missing.

'Enough is enough!' spluttered Mr Neville, hovering over him. 'From now on I do not want you within five miles of this establishment.'

Beyond the curtain, Ralph could hear the audience leaving the auditorium. He had a feeling it would be for the last time.

'I'm sure there's a good explanation,' said Felix, coming again to the rescue.

'Did you give her her call?' Mr Neville asked.

'Yes, sir. That's when I found out she wasn't there. She left a note. She said she was ill. I didn't know what else to do.'

It was then that Arnold Swann walked on-stage. 'Is this some sort of joke?' he thundered, and he swept through the band of actors surrounding Ralph.

'I wish it was,' said Ralph glumly.

'Where's Jane?'

'Gone back to her digs. She's not well.'

'Not well, my foot!' He turned to Mr Neville. 'She should be sacked.'

'That's not quite so easy,' said Mr Neville awkwardly. 'Anyway now is not the time. We've got to think who can play Mrs Mulligatawny for the rest of the week.'

Ralph was now out of the picture. Gradually he moved away from the crowd and sat despondently on the settee. Female names of various actresses came floating through the air, and then, to Ralph's astonishment, he heard Basil Duke say, 'Did anyone realise he wasn't a woman?'

243

There was a sudden silence.

'No,' said the producer.

'Why not let him keep doing it? His timing is good. I thought it was a fluke last night but he was still getting laughs tonight and not ruining our laughs either.'

Ralph couldn't believe his ears. This was Basil Duke praising him.

'He's an amateur,' exploded Mr Neville.

There was then a loud babble of arguments.

'This is ridiculous!' he heard Mr Neville say.

'But Basil has a point,' said Mr Swann, 'and the audience has been none the wiser.' This was followed by a further babble of voices, and then he heard Geraldine Maclaren say, 'It would be cheaper if you let him do it.'

That seemed to hit home. There was more conversation, and then Felix ran off for his train and the other actors dwindled off-stage.

The two producers walked towards him. Ralph rose to his feet.

'What do you think of this part, then?' said Arnold Swann smiling.

'It's a gem,' stammered Ralph. 'I knew it as soon as I saw the run-through last week.'

'Well, Mr Neville and I have decided to let you play the role.'

'On one condition,' added Mr Neville.

'I don't get in the way?' put in Ralph.

'No. You let Geraldine Maclaren do your make-up.'

To Ralph's embarrassment he felt a fierce stinging sensation in his eyes.

'I take it you're happy with that?' said Arnold Swann.

Ralph nodded.

'You'll be paid a week's salary on Friday,' added Mr Neville. 'It won't be much as you're not doing ASM duties.' Arnold Swann gave Mr Neville a surprised glance 'Well, many ASM duties.'

Upstairs Ralph drank in every inch of the dressing room. It was the shabbiest room in the theatre, yet to him it had a glamour which was indescribable. It was to be his workplace. His preparation room for a week. He had hardly got into his street clothes and removed the grey wig when there was a knock at the door. It was Mr Neville. Ralph stood to his feet.

'I think I'd better take Jane's note,' he said quietly.

Ralph picked it up from the dressing table and handed it to him.

'I'm sure she'll get her nerve back, sir.'

Mr Neville made a gesture to silence him. 'Last night I found out quite a lot of information from Jane's landlady.'

'Oh?' gulped Ralph, trying to appear casual.

'It appears that you knew that Isla wasn't returning on Sunday. Why didn't you inform me immediately? In fact, why didn't she?'

'She wanted to cause you the least amount of trouble. If Jane knew the part then you wouldn't have had to ring round for another actress to travel down.'

'I had been under the assumption that Jane did it all at the last minute. She was very impressive in the dress rehearsal. Wrong, but polished, albeit slightly stilted. But you played the part in a totally different way. Why didn't you tell her about the character?'

'I did. But she wanted to do it her way, and anyway I'm an amateur.'

'Ah,' said Mr Neville. 'Hoist by my own petard.'

'I didn't mean . . .' began Ralph apologetically.

'You *are* an amateur, as an actor. You still need training, but in every other aspect, in your attitude and dedication, you are the professional and I am afraid young Jane Jefferson is the amateur.' He paused for a moment at the door. 'By the way, when you did that audition for me, why didn't you do a comic piece, since it is obviously what you're best at?'

'My English teacher didn't think you would take me seriously.'

'You can tell your English teacher that comedy is a very serious business. The more seriously it's played . . . On second thoughts, time to forget your English teacher, eh?'

'Yes, sir.'

'Goodnight.'

'Goodnight, sir.'

Ralph sat down at the mirror and surveyed his made-up face. Reflected in the mirror on a rail behind him, he observed his maid's outfit swinging from the draught of the door. He smiled happily at himself, stuck his fingers in Jane's removing cream and larded his face with it.

TWELVE

'Completely blocked,' said Felix. 'They said I'd freeze to death if I slept in the station waiting room because they had to cut down on fuel for the fire in there.'

'I'm stranded too,' said Annie Duncan, 'and I only live a mile

245

away.' She sighed. 'Even if I managed to find a taxi to take us there, all I can offer is some cushions on a cold floor and a nosy landlady.'

'Basil is taking me to his place. I'll be fine,' said Felix.

'Do you think he'd give me a lift?'

'Of course he would, darling.'

Ralph slipped through the cast and over to Wilfred. 'What's going on?' he asked.

'Railway line to London's blocked,' Wilfred explained. 'That's going to muck up rehearsals tomorrow.'

Basil Duke appeared at the stage door, covered in snow. 'More bad news, I'm afraid. My car won't start. I'm stranded too.'

'Oh, no!' said Annie.

'Where the hell can we stay?' exclaimed Felix.

Before he could stop himself, Ralph heard himself say, 'I know somewhere.'

Suddenly he found himself the centre of attention. 'It's the lady I work for. I'll need to ring her first, of course.'

'Do you think there's really any chance? I mean, there's three of us.'

'Four including me,' said Ralph. 'I can only ask.'

While Ralph was using the phone with a pile of pennies donated to him by the cast, he cupped a hand over one ear to block out the hubbub behind him. The phone rang and rang. It was 10.30p.m. She might already be asleep. Everyone went to bed so early nowadays to save on fuel, he remembered. To his relief he heard it give a click.

'Hello, Winford 236.'

'Hello, Mrs Egerton-Smythe. It's me.'

'Yes, you can,' she interrupted. 'I've just been making up your bed. I took one look at the blizzard outside and I didn't think you'd be such an ass as to attempt to go home tonight.'

'Thank you, but I'm ringing up to ask you another favour.'

'Oh, yes?'

He took a deep breath. 'Three of the cast are stranded. Is there any possibility you could put them up too? One of them could have my bed and I could sleep on the settee.'

There was a silence. 'How many ladies?'

'One,' said Ralph quickly.

'And three chaps,' she said to herself. 'Well, if they all pitch in and help.'

'Oh, I'm sure they will,' said Ralph.

'And they're all thespians, you say?'

'Thespians?'

'In the acting profession.'

'Yes.'

'So how soon are you coming?'

'Now. It'll take us a bit of time.'

'I know, I've seen what it's like,' she said. 'I'll hunt around for some jimjams.'

'Jimjams?'

She gave a laugh. 'Pyjamas. Oh, Jessica would love this,' she exclaimed and hung up.

When he turned, he found Felix, Basil and Annie, standing expectantly behind him.

'Well?' Felix asked.

'No problem,' Ralph said airily, 'providing we all help out.'

Felix gave him a hug.

Ten minutes later, remembering his 'no problem' remark, Ralph almost laughed at the absurdity of that statement. As they staggered down the main street, the blizzard blew directly into their faces, piercing their eyes and pricking their faces with its icy blast. Reeling, the four of them lowered their heads and stumbled through snowdrifts. Glancing aside at his companions' hunched bodies, Ralph saw snow piling up on their hats and lying thickly on their shoulders like white epaulettes. From the knees down their legs were hidden, except when they lifted them up high in order to step into the next mound. They didn't talk much. All their concentration was absorbed in taking the next few steps forward. Shyly, Ralph hung back while Basil and Felix took Annie Duncan's arms and lifted her over each drift.

Basil shouted something to Ralph over his shoulder. 'How far?' Ralph made out.

'Second turning on the right,' he yelled back.

They leaned against the whirling flurry of whiteness, half blinded. When they turned off the main street into the road which led to Mrs Egerton-Smythe's avenue, the relief was immense. The wind no longer hit them full in the face, and the narrowness of the road with its houses gave them some protection.

'Not long now!' yelled Ralph.

Having grown used to a respite they were nearly knocked senseless when they turned into the wide avenue with its enormous well-spaced houses.

'We must be near the river,' shouted Basil.

'We are,' cried Ralph. 'Mrs Egerton-Smythe's garden runs down to it.'

They staggered, clutching one another, as the wind cut into their eardrums.

'Stop!' yelled Ralph as they stumbled past Mrs Egerton-Smythe's large ornate gate. 'This is it.'

'No light,' observed Annie Duncan dismally. 'She must have gone to bed.'

'There's an electricity cut,' Felix reminded her.

They tramped up the long path to the front door, Ralph feeling a little awkward at not approaching the tradesmen's entrance. He pulled the bell-pull. Within minutes of it clanging he could see a flickering light approaching him, and the door swung open revealing Mrs Egerton-Smythe in an overcoat, trousers and jersey, holding a lighted candelabra aloft.

'Ralph, take everyone to the kitchen,' she said.

Ralph was mortified with embarrassment. Basil Duke not being let through the front door! This really was rogues-and-vagabonds treatment.

'It's warm there,' she continued. 'And I've laid out dry clothes.' And with that she closed the door.

On entering the kitchen, Ralph realised he had misread Mrs Egerton-Smythe's behaviour. Their boots were completely covered in snow, as were their coats. The floor in the kitchen was tiled and easy to swab down.

On the draining board and kitchen table were two candelabras. Men's jumpers and pyjamas were laid out across the backs of the chairs.

'Oh, my God!' exclaimed Felix. 'Warmth.'

Mrs Egerton-Smythe was putting plates out onto the table. Two empty clothes horses were standing near by.

'Ralph, I've put out your usual pyjamas. I thought you'd like to lend the dressing-gown to one of the chaps and have a pullover instead. I haven't any slippers. You'll all have to make do with woolly socks.'

She turned to Annie Duncan. 'If you'd like to dump your boots and coat in here, I'll take you to the garden room. You can change in privacy there.' And with that she swept Annie out of the room.

'She's marvellous,' said Basil.

'She doesn't waste words,' Felix commented. 'Does she?'

Ralph laughed. 'Never,' he said. 'Her daughter's just the same.'

'Is she here too?' Basil asked.

'No. Boarding school. It should be her half-term soon.'

Ralph felt too wet and cold to be embarrassed at peeling off his clothes in front of Felix and Basil and it was obvious that they had done it so often, they weren't embarrassed either.

Felix took the dressing gown as he was the tallest and it fitted him the best. Ralph and Basil wore thick jerseys over pyjamas and thick socks. They had just stood their boots in a row in front of the range when there was· a knock at the door. It was Mrs Egerton-Smythe with a candelabra and Annie's clothes draped over one arm.

'You can go into the garden room now. Ralph, you can take them. Oh and come back straight away, I'll need a hand with the food.'

'Food!' chorused Felix and Basil.

'All actors are starving, so I've heard,' she said. 'You're not any different, are you?'

'No,' said Basil laughing. 'This is awfully kind of you, Mrs Egerton-Smythe.'

'No, it isn't. I'm enjoying myself. Now shut up and go and make yourself warm.'

Basil smiled.

The fire had been lit in the garden room. Annie was crouched in front of it in a pair of Jessica's pyjamas and jersey and socks, with bread on the end of a toasting fork.

'She's got me working already,' she smiled.

Their eyes were drawn to the dusty wine bottles and several glasses on the mantelpiece.

'I think I've walked into paradise,' said Felix quietly.

In the kitchen, Ralph found Mrs Egerton-Smythe cutting up a pie into slabs.

'Give those spuds a prod,' she said, handing Ralph a fork.

'Oh, by the way, I thought you were very good.'

Ralph swung round. 'Pardon?' he said.

'In *Something in the Air*. I saw it last night.' She looked up from the pie at him. 'You got a lovely review in the Winford Observer today. Only they refer to the ASM who took over. They must have been in on Monday. A new comic talent, it says.'

'Are you sure?' he stammered.

'You can read it for yourself. I still have a copy of it in the garden room. I thought I'd send the cutting to Jessica. Might be worth you buying several copies tomorrow on your way to work.'

Ralph stared at her in disbelief.

'If you don't close your mouth soon,' she observed, 'you'll catch a fly.'

Ralph shut it.

'I thought it might be useful to have up your sleeve when you next approach the producer of the theatre for an audition.'

'Yes. Thanks!'

'Here,' she said, handing him two plates. 'Hold these.' She lifted the saucepan off the Aga with a cloth and with a large spoon with holes in it she took some potatoes from the pan and piled them onto the plates.

'Tell them to eat it while it's hot.'

'Have you ever played Rough?' said Basil.

'No,' said Felix, 'but an actor friend of mine has.'

'It's a nightmare,' said Basil.

'Rough? Is that a style of playing?' asked Mrs Egerton-Smythe.

'No,' laughed Basil. 'Ex-Detective Rough in *Gaslight*. He has these endless monologues, mostly questions, and the heroine of the piece has mainly to intersperse with "Mmm" and "Oh", etc. It's hell to learn.'

In spite of wanting to listen, Ralph felt himself drifting off. The wine, a full stomach, the firelight and the general feeling of happiness were making him feel drowsy. He felt a hand on his shoulder. Standing over him was Mrs Egerton-Smythe.

'Bed, young man!' and she pointed to the camp bed by the settee.

Ralph had to give in. His head had hardly touched the pillow when he drifted off into instant sleep, only to be woken by an intense discussion about the Third Programme.

'It's often the only chance I have to listen to classical music and decent plays,' Felix was saying with passion. 'It would be lunatic to cut those.'

'I think they'd ration air, if they could,' he heard Mrs Egerton-Smythe sigh.

Ralph fell asleep again. He later woke up to hear Basil Duke say, 'He has the determination and stamina.'

'And the talent, don't you think?'

'Oh, yes, but talent without staying power is nothing. I've seen people who have little talent but through sheer perseverance improve. That, and getting on in a company, and liking the way of life.'

'But you still think drama school is the best option for him?'

'Yes. He'd have a chance of doing the classics then. Shakespeare, Restoration comedy, Greek tragedy, voice production and movement. Of course he might have to postpone everything within the year.'

'Oh, you mean with this National Service rumour,' said Mrs Egerton-Smythe.

Ralph fought to stay awake, but when he opened his eyes next, light was coming in through the windows. He sat up quickly and stared round the room. Felix was sleeping in another camp bed. Quietly he hopped out of bed and made his way to the hall. As soon as he saw the time he panicked.

He found Queenie in the kitchen busily ironing their clothes. She looked up at him disapprovingly.

'Queenie! You're a gem.'

'I am not a gem,' she said, pursing up her lips. 'Mrs Egerton-Smythe left instructions in that note over there,' she said, waving at a piece of paper propped on the draining-board. 'Such goings-on,' she snapped.

'We were stranded,' Ralph explained.

'But theatre types,' she said, ignoring him. 'Treating this place no better than a brothel.'

Ralph burst out laughing.

'I don't see what's so funny.'

'You, Queenie. Oh, hell!' he exclaimed. 'I'm late.'

'Your trousers are over there, I recognised them. There's towels in the bathroom. Tea'll be waiting for you when you comes down.'

'Oh, Queenie, you're a . . .'

She glared at him.

'Thanks.'

In five minutes he was dressed, had gulped down a mug of tea and was racing down the path with a slab of bread and dripping in his hand.

'How did you get on with Queenie?' Ralph asked.

'Bit dour at first,' said Felix. 'But Basil won her round.'

'She even took to me!' said Annie, smiling.

'Mrs Egerton-Smythe says we can stay again tonight if we're stranded,' said Felix. 'Will you be coming?'

'I'm helping with the strike and my mother's not too well. I haven't seen her properly for nearly a week, so I'll see.'

'We're going to Rosie's Café after notes,' said Annie Duncan. 'Coming?'

Ralph grinned.

It was while he was waiting for them by the stage door, that Wilfred waved a note at him. 'Mr Neville wants a word with you, lad,' he said. 'He's in his office.'

Ralph's heart fell. 'I'm supposed to be going out with the others to the café. Will you tell them to go on and I'll meet them later?'

Wilfred nodded.

Ralph found Mr Neville's office on the other side of the building. It was a room off one of the passages at the back of the auditorium.

From outside the door, he could hear Mr Neville in the middle of a telephone conversation.

'I realise that,' he was saying. 'But the leads! We've a very experienced company here. Surely they'll show off your play to better advantage than amateurs . . . of course we'd like to put it on . . . Yes. The money for doing it here arrived today. May I suggest that you send any future backers to see it later on in the week, when it's had time to run in . . . Two matinées. Yes . . . I'll expect the actors to be at the theatre ready for moving Act One on Tuesday morning prompt. I'm sure it will be . . . Goodbye.'

Ralph heard the receiver clunk on to its cradle. It was followed by a loud sigh.

He knocked at the door.

'Yes!' a voice said impatiently.

Ralph opened it and peered round.

'Bring the rest of you in, lad,' he commanded.

Ralph stepped in, closed the door behind him and stood waiting for a barrage of criticism.

'I know you can speak French. What standard?'

'School Cert standard,' said Ralph surprised.

'Accent good?'

'I think so.'

'Think is not good enough in this business.'

'It's good, sir.'

'Can you sing? I don't mean choirboy stuff, I mean loudly. Raucously.'

'Yes, sir.'

'I'm offering you a part in the play next week. It's set during the French Revolution. New play. Having a try-out here. You'll have to come on and sing the 'Marseillaise' every now and again, plus be in a small scene at the end where you fall to pieces and then recover enough to go to the guillotine with dignity. I shall be producing it. Think you can do a serious part?'

'Yes, Mr Neville.'

'Without a Cornish accent?'

Ralph smiled. 'Without a Cornish accent.'

'We don't pay rehearsal money. And since you're an amateur – '

'Sir, I must have something.'

'Oh?' he said frowning.

'To give my mother.'

'I see. Well, I haven't much to give.'

'I realise that, sir, but I don't want to be a burden on my parents.'

He sighed. 'You'll get one and sixpence a performance. That's twelve shillings'

Ralph stood there speechless, astonished that he could win him round without a major battle. Mr Neville, obviously misinterpreting his silence, suddenly said, 'All right, I'll give you sixteen shillings. But no more! That's my last offer.'

'Yes, Mr Neville. Thank you, sir.'

'And, Ralph,' he said as Ralph made for the door, 'don't go getting any ideas that this is going to be a regular occurrence.'

'No, sir,' smiled Ralph, but nothing could burst the bubble of laughter that he could feel welling up into his throat.

The response in the café from Felix and Basil and even Annie Duncan and the Maclarens touched him. All he said was, 'I've been offered a part,' and they leapt from their chairs and hugged him.

'It's only a small part,' he added, sitting down with them.

'Always the hardest to play,' said Basil. 'With a small part it is even more important for you to be living it in the wings before you come on and, if you're bobbing on and off, you have to really concentrate to keep that world going.'

Ralph decided from that moment he would read anything he could on the French Revolution. As if reading his mind, Basil said, '*A Tale of Two Cities*. Dickens gives a marvellous account of the revolution in that.'

'He doesn't need that,' said Raymond Maclaren.

'True,' said Basil, 'but it might spark off an idea or two.'

'You'll be getting him to read Stanislavski next.'

'Who's Stanislavski?' asked Ralph.

'He was an acting teacher in Moscow,' said Felix. 'He encouraged actors to resist playing roles artificially. He got them to concentrate on the inner life of the characters they were playing rather than indulge in histrionics.'

'Useful for some. Not for others,' remarked Basil. 'I find he gives long-winded intellectual explanations for things I picked up when I was ten.'

'Yes, but you're an instinctive actor,' remarked Felix. 'Not everyone is. I agree with his idea that you should leave the outside world at the stage door, once you enter into a theatre, don't you?'

'Yes, but many actors do that anyway,' said Basil.

'I don't,' said Raymond Maclaren.

'Could be you can concentrate faster,' observed Basil. He turned to Felix, 'All that drawing from your own experiences, I find limiting. To me, observing other people, reading novels and books on psychology, is more interesting. I'd much rather draw from those.'

'Yes, but don't you draw from yourself when you act?'

'If I do, I'm not aware of it. Things start to happen spontaneously when I get under the skin of the part. I want to forget myself.'

'I heard Mr Swann say that the right shoes can sometimes help,' said Ralph, eagerly joining in the discussion.

'Yes, I find that too,' said Annie Duncan. 'I once had to play a tramp in *Major Barbara*,' she said, 'and I got hold of a huge pair of ankle boots which I held together with string. Then I wrapped all sorts of things around me. I couldn't walk without shuffling and I found as soon as I had the character's walk, her voice came.'

'Costumes are just the icing on the cake for me,' said Felix, 'on the dress rehearsal.'

'I like to be in disguise,' said Basil. 'I love it if people in the audience don't know it's me playing a certain part.'

'Funny that,' said Felix thoughtfully. 'Some like to put on layers, I like to peel them off. It's terrifying sometimes, but tremendously exciting.'

Ralph listened enraptured. The cast bought him pie and peas and tea and he returned to the theatre feeling cock-a-hoop. He sneaked into the wings and came face to face with Mr Johnson. 'I'm so sorry, sir,' he began.

He noticed that the Act One set of *Something in the Air* was up. He cleared his throat. 'Am I still allowed to set up?'

Mr Johnson shifted from one foot to the other looking vaguely embarrassed. He nodded.

'Thanks.'

'Can you be here for the strike tonight?' he asked casually.

'Yes, sir.'

'I'd like you to concentrate on props,' he said.

'Yes, of course,' said Ralph, concealing his disappointment at still not being allowed on to the stage.

'I'd particularly like you to mark which props are not on the list.'

Not on the list!' Ralph exclaimed.

'That's what I said. Are you free on Monday morning?'

'I can be, sir.'

'I want you to get the rest of the props by the dress.'

Ralph was conscious of his mouth falling into the flycatching position. He closed it quickly.

'Yes, sir. Can I take the list home with me on Sunday after the strike? I might be able to find a few things tomorrow.'

He nodded again.

Ralph headed towards the prop table in a daze. He felt a mixture of terror and an enormous sense of being needed. He knew that if he managed to find the rest of the props by Monday, he could get into Mr Johnson's good books. He would then be in a stronger position for applying for an ASM job in the future. He was so excited he was trembling. 'Chalk,' he suddenly said to himself. When he turned he found Mr Johnson by his side with a prompt book, chalk and tape measure. He said nothing, but Ralph had the distinct feeling that Mr Johnson had been observing him.

And it was all over. Mr Neville had stepped forward and announced the following production. Ralph stared fixedly at him at the end of the line, a lump in his throat the size of a fist. To him it had been the most important week of his life. To the cast it was just another week.

Mr Neville stepped back. The trio played the opening strains of 'God Save the King' and the audience rose to their feet.

As soon as the curtain hit the deck the cast ran off into the wings, and stage hands instantly appeared to carry away the set. Later it would be turned into a set for some other production. Noticing one of the stage hands staring oddly at him, Ralph suddenly remembered he was dressed as a woman, quickly lowered his head and made for the wings.

He changed and took off his make-up as fast as he could, leapt down the stairs and knocked at dressing room three with Annie Duncan's wig. She already had her coat and hat on, a script under her arm.

'Your wig,' said Ralph.

'Oh, thanks! Leave it on my dressing-room table. Must fly. I want to see if the trams are running tonight. 'Bye.'

Ralph was about to leave when he noticed two lace handkerchiefs stuck to the mirrors.

'Saves us from ironing them if they dry there,' said a voice.

It was Geraldine Maclaren. Before he could comment he found himself being dragged into the dressing room and plumped on a chair.

'If you don't want your father to throw you on to the streets, we had better get that slap off.'

'I thought I had done,' he protested.

'Chin up,' she commanded. 'Close your eyes.'

Ralph saw her come towards him with a great dollop of removing cream. Hastily he closed them.

'It's those nooks and crannies,' she said massaging the cream in.

'Thanks for letting me borrow the greasepaint,' he said.

'Keep them. I just cut off some stubs at the end. You can add them to your collection for when you next play a woman.' She laughed and began wiping the cream off his face.

'Ah, a rival,' he heard. It was her husband.

'You can open your eyes now,' said Geraldine Maclaren. 'Darling, what do you think?' she said, twisting him round.

'Not a trace. No one would even guess that you'd been within miles of this den of iniquity, except of course for the smell.'

'What smell?' said Ralph alarmed.

'A mixture of greasepaint and Crow's Cremine. You'd better put some powder on him.'

'Powder?' Ralph cried in alarm.

'All the men put it on,' said Raymond Maclaren. 'It takes the shine off.'

'No, thank you,' said Ralph hurriedly. 'It might get on the bolster. But what about the smell of the greasepaint?'

'Don't worry,' said Raymond smiling. 'Only us lot would know what it was.' He handed a script to his wife. 'The cast list is up for next week.'

Ralph sprang to his feet. 'Am I on it?'

Raymond nodded.

He sprinted out on to the landing, leaping down the steps to the stage-door area. The list was where it normally was on a Saturday night, on the notice board, opposite Wilfred's cubby-hole.

'*Vive La Liberté*,' he read, 'by Rupert Armitage.' He scanned down the names. He was the last on the list.

'French Youth,' he read. 'Ralph Hollis. French Youth,' he repeated.

'Mr Hollis?'

He turned to find Wilfred waving a script.

Ralph moved towards him as if in a dream, and then the script was in his hands and he was hugging it to his chest.

He wondered if a sculptor felt like this when he was suddenly given a hunk of untouched clay to work on.

'I take it yer pleased?' said Wilfred, grinning.

'Pleased! Wilfred, this is the best day of my entire life!'

'Oh, yes. Well, before you get carried away, let me remind you there's a strike going on.'

'Oh, lor'. Yes. Thanks!' and he raced back up the steps.

Half the props for *Watch on the Rhine* were missing. There needed to be more nineteenth-century vases and ornaments. Jane had been sent home early and Mr Johnson was monosyllabic with tiredness. In the last week, since Isla's absence and because of Jane's ineptitude he had worked harder than he had for a year.

Ralph made tea for everyone and left for Mrs Egerton-Smythe's house with the prop list, his stubs of greasepaint, his aunt's stockings and corset packed in his suitcase. When he arrived, there were no lights on. He trudged through the snow to the kitchen door. It was in darkness too. When he stood back he could see light falling on the snow-covered lawn. Relieved he walked on to it and looked into the garden room from the darkness. There were only two people in the room and they were talking with great animation around the fire. Mrs Egerton-Smythe was seated at the armchair facing outward. Sitting cross-legged on the floor with his back to Ralph was Basil Duke.

Mrs Egerton-Smythe was talking to him at breakneck speed. Ralph watched mesmerised. He had never seen her so relaxed and talkative. She waved her hands in the air and gave a shrug as if to say, 'You see my predicament.'

Basil Duke leaned forward and Mrs Egerton-Smythe listened intently to what he was saying. Whatever it was, it was short and to the point. At first she stared amazed at him and then threw back her head and collapsed into the armchair laughing. The firelight and candlelight sent shadows and lights across her face, making her appear strangely beautiful. It startled Ralph. He suddenly knew he couldn't knock on the door. There was an intimacy coming from the room that he did not want to invade.

He edged back into the shadows and crept stealthily towards the side of the house. Snow had begun to fall again. He moved quickly down the path towards the avenue.

'Come in.' He pushed open the door, the tray perched precariously on one arm.

His mother was sitting in bed, propped up against pillows, wearing two cardigans, a woolly hat and a scarf. The fire had only just been lit. Perched on the rim of her nose were an enormous pair of men's spectacles with tortoiseshell rims. He presumed Mr Egerton-Smythe's.

'What do you think?' she said, indicating them and beaming.

257

'Your dad brought in a load of 'em, and insisted,' she paused, 'yes, *insisted* I try 'em on. These are the best ones,' she said. 'How do I look?'

Comic and lovely, he thought. 'Splendid,' he said.

'Do you know what I read last night? A story in one of Joan's magazines. A whole story. On me own. I've asked your aunt to borrow some books from the library for me.'

'Not her sort, I hope.'

'Her sort?'

'You know Aunty Win. She'd probably get something about a bigamist in the carpet trade who murders his first wife, smuggles her out in one of his rolled-up rugs, and then commits suicide. Hideously.'

'Poor Win. How's she copin'?'

Ralph struck a martyrish stance and toppled over on to the eiderdown.

'Oh, stop it, Ralphie. She ain't that bad.'

'Worse. But at least she's forgiven me for borrowing her corset and stockings.'

'That were a terrible thing to do, love.'

'I was desperate. Luckily the review won her round,' he said, hastily picking up her mug of tea and handing it to her.

'Oh, yes. Elsie read that out to me. Your new ASM done ever so well, didn't she?'

Ralph nodded. 'I was able to say, the person who got that review was helped by borrowing your corset, Aunty Win.'

'What did she say?'

'She just made humphing noises. Are you going to drink that?'

'Yes, Mr Bossyboots.'

'But Joan's a changed person. She smiles now. Sometimes she even looks quite decent.'

'Ralph!' She glanced out of the window. 'The sun's out. Good, eh? I've never known a winter with so much snow,' she remarked. 'Has your friend got back yet?'

'Isla? No. She's still stranded. They think she's in Salisbury. They'd have a fit if they knew she was in the Isle of Wight.'

'Uncle Ted had a call from Kitty and Frank in Kent yesterday. They're havin' an awful time in them Nissen huts. They've got stoves, but the Kent miners are on strike so they ent got no fuel.'

'Do you think they'll move back here?' said Ralph.

'Nah. I think they're stuck. Also Frank has been given a chance to retrain. You'll never guess what at.'

'What?'

'A carpentry teacher! I can't get over it. They're ever so short of teachers and a lot of ex-servicemen . . .' She stopped. 'Ever thought of being a teacher?'

'No,' said Ralph firmly. 'Actually I've been offered a small part in the next play.'

'As an actor?'

'Yes.'

'Oh, Ralphie,' she breathed.

'It's only a tiny part, but it's a start.'

'There you are. You can't have done so badly in that audition thing, can you?'

Ralph nearly mentioned playing Mrs Mulligatawny but stopped himself in time. It was going to be bad enough trying to tell his father he was going to be on-stage, let alone that he'd already done so dressed as a woman.

'There's something else,' said his mother casually. 'I mean, there was another reason why Kitty and Frank was phonin'.'

'Oh, yes.'

'Kitty is going to have a baby.'

'That's nice,' he said, watching his mother turn red.

'Yeah. That's what I thought. I think that's what cheered Joan up. She's already begun knitting.' His mother looked awkward again. 'Do you have to go to work today?'

'Afraid so. And prop hunting. The new ASM hasn't been able to find half of them.'

'Well. I expect she's been busy with this part she had to take over.'

Now Ralph felt himself reddening. 'Anyway that's what I'll be doing,' and he slid off the bed. 'Do you think I should tell Dad about the part?'

She looked thoughtfully at him.

'Play it by ear,' she said at last.

It was crisp and sunny outside, but still too deep to risk taking his bike out. In the streets people were out walking as if hungry for the sudden influx of sunshine. Children were dragging old trays and wooden boxes behind them, searching for slopes to slide down. For a moment he stopped and stared at them, thinking of Elsie and Harry. He wondered if his father would make a sledge for them. He hoped he would. He didn't want them to miss out, like him.

'The rest of the props have been found,' Mr Johnson yelled.

'Thank God.'

'Can they be put out now?'

'Certainly. Send her on.'

'Him as a matter of fact, Mr Neville.'

Ralph heard footsteps coming back to the wings. Mesmerised he watched Mr Johnson stride to the prompt corner, pick up a piece of paper and walk back to where Ralph was standing. 'This tells you what goes where.' And he thrust the paper into his hand. 'I think it's about time you got the credit.'

And to Ralph's amazement he returned to the stool.

Shaking, Ralph picked up one of the boxes he had carried to the theatre. Mr Johnson had accepted him. More than that, he wanted Mr Neville to know that he had a good opinion of him. He took a deep breath and entered upstage centre to a blaze of lights. Suddenly he felt shy at such exposure. He lowered his head, placed the box by the french windows and took out an ornate Louis XVI clock.

In the background he heard Mr Neville talking electrics while he turned his back on the auditorium and quietly took out the ornaments and vases and placed them round the set.

When he returned with a second box, he found Mr Neville on stage holding a French newspaper and a vase.

'These are remarkable,' he commented. 'Where did you find them?'

'A French woman called Madame Dugon. She's a friend of my employer. She's a music teacher. She's teaching me the 'Marseillaise'.

'Is she now?' He smiled. 'Good. Carry on.'

'Thank you, Mr Johnson,' whispered Ralph as he watched Mr Neville returning to the auditorium.

Before the cast of *Watch on the Rhine* came in for the dress rehearsal, Wilfred let him have the key to the top dressing room. Walking up and down Ralph went through the 'Marseillaise' over and over again and stopped as soon as his throat began to tickle. He then sat down to read the play.

He discovered that the French Revolution was merely a backdrop to a story about love and revenge. As the play progressed, numerous people were guillotined willy-nilly, and in the last scene Ralph's character found himself awaiting execution. It was very melodramatic stuff and to Ralph somewhat overblown and unclear in parts. The love scenes all seemed very similar, but he was pleased with his scene at the end, and although there was no information about the youth, he decided to make up a background for him.

FOURTEEN

T he following morning he arrived early for his first rehearsal. Wilfred let him go on stage and switched on the lights. Ralph stared out at the auditorium, doing humming exercises until he could feel his lips buzzing. Then he did a few scales. Footsteps in the wings suddenly made him feel self-conscious. He turned to find Basil emerging from the wings.

'Who taught you those exercises?' he said.

'The teacher who lent me the French props.'

'They're good. Especially the humming. I can give you some diction exercises too, if you like.'

'Thanks. I would.'

'Did you bring a pencil? You'll need one to write down your moves.'

'Damn. I didn't think.'

'I did,' he said, and handed him one.

'Thanks.'

'How are you feeling?'

'Nervous. Look, I haven't learnt my part yet.'

'Good. It's best not to tackle lines till you know your moves. They stick better if you learn them with the moves. Also it's an advantage to know roughly how the other actor is going to respond to you. If you learn them before then, you'll be reacting to the responses you imagined instead of what's really happening. It's useful for long speeches, but otherwise no.'

'Thank goodness.'

'You need to learn them after rehearsals though. Don't procrastinate, there isn't time.'

'I won't.'

Basil glanced around. 'I wonder who's setting up for rehearsals.'

Ralph gave a gasp. 'I forgot to call Jane! And I've just got into Mr Johnson's good books.'

The sound of voices came from the wings, and Felix and an older actor walked in with Annie Duncan. 'I must have had the end of the carbon,' he heard her comment, as she looked at her copy.

'At least it's not a cue sheet,' laughed Felix.

'What's a cue sheet?' Ralph asked Basil quietly.

'It's when nobody gets a copy of the whole play. Just the few words somebody says before it's your turn to speak. It's horrendous! I was in a new detective play once and we all had cue sheets, and I remember this elderly actress, who got murdered in the first act, came up to me and said, "Who did murder me. darling?"'

Mr Neville's voice was heard in the wings. He walked on-stage with the playwright, a young man in a tweed jacket, cravat, corduroy trousers and longish hair. Following them were a middle-aged man and a woman in her late thirties. They were talking in extremely animated tones and waving their arms around. Ralph guessed they were the amateur leads he had heard the cast gossiping about. Apparently, they were friends of the playwright.

Mr Neville quickly looked around at the stage. Spotting Ralph, he excused himself to the man in corduroys and approached him.

'Where's Jane?' he asked.

'I expect she's on her way, sir.'

'You'll have to be on the book to take down the moves and measure up where the furniture goes until she arrives.'

'Yes, sir.' He ran over to fetch the prompt book, but it was missing.

'This is the last straw,' Mr Neville muttered quietly when Ralph told him.

'I could mark the moves in my copy,' Ralph suggested, 'and write them in the book later.'

'All right. I'll need you to take a list of furniture and props as we go too.'

'I've a note-book with me.'

'Good. I like a man who comes prepared. Right, let's get started.'

As Mr Neville rejoined the man in corduroys, Basil gave Ralph a wink.

'Do your best,' he whispered. 'Having no one from stage management turn up on the first rehearsal with the playwright here has left Mr Neville with egg on his face. The less you apologise the more professional everything will seem.'

Ralph nodded and ran off to get chairs set up for the producer, playwright and himself.

'Will everyone who's in this opening scene stay on stage. The rest wait in the wings.'

The opening scene was in the drawing room of a member of the aristocracy at some soirée. During it, the fair Antoinette rejected the baron's forceful attentions and was rescued by the count. The baron left vowing revenge. Odd bits of humour were thrust in by a handkerchief-waving fop played by Felix. The baron was played by Basil.

The two romantic leads, Claude and Margaret, had obviously learned their roles together and announced every line out front. They had no idea how to respond to anyone else, and were so thrown when Mr Neville gave them a move, that they forgot their lines and became brow-beatingly histrionic. It was acutely embarrassing to watch. The cast politely got on with their jobs, holding the scripts in their hands and marking down their moves.

Someone proclaimed that the peasants were revolting. And the fop remarked that he agreed. It was a terrible old gag, but everyone was too polite to groan with the playwright present.

Suddenly Annie Duncan ran on looking distraught. 'They're dragging people on to the street and hanging them from the lamp posts,' she screamed.

Chérie, I must get you out of here,' said the male romantic lead out front as he clasped the female lead's hands fervently.

'No, I must stay with you,' she replied, also out front, with no reaction to the hysteria going on behind them as people ran around in terror, scripts in hand.

As Mr Neville gave them their moves Ralph hurriedly wrote them down. 'There's a secret panel!' announced the hero. 'We must escape quickly.'

'Hold it!' said Mr Neville as the two leads went upstage. 'We can't have the secret panel up there.'

'But that's how we've rehearsed it,' protested the woman.

'That's the outside wall,' pointed out Mr Neville. 'You'd plunge to certain death if you went that way. Our designer, Mr Williams, has the secret panel downstage right. As the panel closes, Nigel, you'll be given a cue light from the prompt side and then you and Ralph will enter by the upstage-right door.'

Downstage right. Exit all, scribbled Ralph. Enter upstage right.

'Let's try that. Take your script upstage, Ralph.'

Ralph rose silently and walked past everyone, his legs feeling like jelly.

He met the actor called Nigel in the wings.

Everyone was fleeing off-stage.

'Panel closed,' yelled Mr Neville. 'Cue light green!'

Then, to Ralph's amazement, he watched Nigel transform himself into a belligerent angry peasant. Ralph swallowed and ran on-stage with him.

'Down with the aristocracy!' yelled Nigel. 'Off with their aristocratic little heads.' There was a pause. 'They're gone.' He turned to Ralph. 'Find 'em. They must be here somewhere.'

'Yes, sir,' said Ralph.

'No more 'sirs' now, lad. This is the revolution. Yes, *camarade*.'

'Yes, *camarade*!' repeated Ralph.

'Huh!' said Nigel, picking up some little trinket. He looked downstage at Mr Neville. 'Where will the snuffbox be, sir?' Ralph held his pencil poised.

'The small down-centre table. Ralph, I want you to be stage left over by the fireplace when he picks this up and I want you to notice him take it. Nigel, you realise that he notices and then say your line. Ralph, your motivation for opening the left stage-door is to look for the people who have escaped. The reason you turn is to tell him there's a corridor out there.'

Ralph nodded.

'Let's try that out, then.'

Swiftly Nigel looked at the small table and glanced stage left and stopped. Ralph was still stage right, writing down the moves.

'Ralph!' said Mr Neville. 'You need to move stage left as soon as you say, "Yes, sir".'

Ralph nodded again.

'Take that entrance again, the two of you.'

They exited.

'Panel closed. Green light.' Nigel moved on swiftly.

'Down with the aristocracy! Off with their aristocratic little heads. They're gone. Find them. They must be 'ere somewhere.'

'Yes, sir,' said Ralph, moving swiftly stage left.

'No "sirs" now. This is the revolution. Yes, *camarade*.'

'Yes, *camarade*,' Ralph repeated as he opened an imaginary door stage left, and turned to find his compatriot stealing a trinket.

Nigel, noticing, looked guilty for a second and then raised his hand and laughed. 'Spoils for the Revolution!' And Ralph beamed.

'For the revolution,' Ralph yelled.

'Curtain,' said Mr Neville. 'Let's get on with scene two, night-time.'

As Ralph approached his chair and table, he found to his embarrassment that Mr Neville was looking at one of the pages in his notebook.

'I was going to put down the snuffbox on your prop list.' He indicated the page. 'Is this background to your character?'

Ralph nodded, his face still burning. 'It's just to make him seem more real. I thought I'd invent what he does in the periods when he's off-stage too.' He swallowed. 'It helps me.'

'Best way to tackle a small part,' Mr Neville said, thrusting it at him. 'Now, some of this furniture must be cleared. The rest needs to have old blankets thrown over them and wine bottles, flasks and flagons around the place. That sort of thing. To show it's been taken over.'

Ralph scribbled like mad.

'And any pictures on the walls and ornaments will need to be removed too.' Mr Neville looked up at the rest of the cast. 'Be back in ten minutes prompt.'

To Ralph's amazement, Mr Neville held the other end of the tape for him, while Ralph measured and marked where the furniture was set. Ralph realised that it was because he wanted to get on. Once the centre line was down, measuring off from the downstage right and left was relatively easy with Mr Neville's help. He then asked Ralph to shift the furniture while he stood and observed from the front.

'Left a bit,' he said. 'Hold it. Down a fraction. That's it!'

Within minutes he was seated again and Ralph was sent to tell the playwright that scene two was about to begin. Ralph found him in the wings, his arm around the female lead's waist, extolling her acting talents.

As scene two progressed, intrigue followed intrigue in the plot. The baron cunningly avoided execution by guile and by making himself part of the proletariat, sending spies and informers everywhere and stirring up trouble. As the youth, Ralph had to be as keen as mustard to take orders, trusting every new leader. The only lines he had were 'Death to the bourgeoisie!' and *Vive La France!*' but he was so absorbed in watching what was going on around him in his character, that he felt he had much more to do.

As soon as he had made his exit he returned quickly downstage to write down more moves. It was as the rehearsal came to an end that Jane suddenly appeared on-stage carrying a tray filled with mugs of tea.

'Who is this apparition?' Ralph heard the playwright exclaim under his breath.

Ralph glanced across at Mr Neville. He could see his face flinch, and he realised that he couldn't cause a scene in front of the playwright, otherwise it would blow the gaff about Jane's tardy entrance.

Jane looked stunning and fresh-faced as usual. Ralph had to hand it to her. She certainly knew how to make a good entrance. Everyone was freezing so the hot tea was a real blessing. She had even made a mug of tea for him. Ralph heard her compliment the playwright on his wonderful play and he visibly grew in stature. Out of the corner of his eye, he spotted the female lead observing Jane and the playwright with nervousness.

Ralph continued measuring.

After lunch Ralph found Mr Johnson sitting in his office nursing a hangover.

'Yes?' he said, his forehead propped into the cup of his hand.

'Can I have the prompt book,' asked Ralph.

'You'll need to make it up yourself. I'd also like you to do this week's Saturday strike as a paid helper. I'll inform Jack Walker.'

'So I'll be allowed to help on-stage?' asked Ralph eagerly.

'That's right, now come on in and I'll show you a prompt copy.'

By the time Ralph had run round to Mrs Egerton-Smythe's to shovel snow and Madame Dugon's to rehearse the 'Marseillaise' and shovel even more snow, it had been dark for some time. He arrived home, his face numb with cold and tiredness, his stomach aching. Harry, Elsie and Joan had already gone to bed, and his aunt was ironing a blouse with the look of a martyr about her. Ralph stumbled wearily to the range and lifted the lid of a saucepan. It was empty.

'If you don't come, you don't get,' sniffed his aunt.

'I've been working,' he protested.

'So have we all, and we manage to get here on time.'

Ralph had hardly collapsed into a chair with the large book Mr Johnson had given him and two scripts when he heard heavy footsteps. He could sense a row coming, but didn't have the strength to muster his defences.

The door swung open and his father swiftly closed it behind him, strode across the room, picked up a cloth and opened the oven door.

'Lift your chin up, lad,' he said abruptly.

To Ralph's surprise a plate of pie and potatoes was shoved in front of him, and the next thing he knew his father was pouring him a mug of tea from a stewing pot on the range.

'Thanks, Dad,' he exclaimed.

'You look done in,' he remarked, and he poured himself a mug. 'Want one, Win?'

'No, thank you,' she snapped, and she folded up her blouse, slammed the iron back on the range and left the room.

His father sat opposite him. Ralph was aware of him observing him. At one point he leaned over the table, grabbed one of his hands and turned it over.

'She's working you 'ard,' he commented, looking at his skin.

'I've been helping someone else too.'

'Oh? Pay you well?'

'In kind,' Ralph said evasively.

'Oh, yeah?'

'The stage manager is still trapped by snow. The stage director asked me to help find things for this week's play. This woman's agreed to lend some of her antiques in exchange for me doing a spot of shovelling.'

'And the theatre's still not paying you?' he asked.

'Mr Neville, he's the producer of the theatre, is going to give me some pay next week, because I'm helping out. And Mr Johnson, he's the stage director, he's going to pay me for the Saturday strike. It should make up for Mrs Egerton-Smythe not being able to pay me so much,' he added quickly.

His father sighed. 'I dunno,' he said. 'It's a mug's game to me. Where's it all going to get you?'

Ralph shrugged. He still couldn't bring himself to tell his father about the part he'd been given. He suspected it would be his last chance of acting with professionals and he couldn't risk his father preventing him.

'You'd best get to bed as soon as you've finished that,' he commented.

'I can't, I've work to do for the producer, before tomorrow morning.'

'What sort of work can you do 'ere?' he exclaimed.

'I've got to make up a prompt book. I've got some glue. I need scissors. Do you think Aunty Win would let me borrow hers?'

'Not ruddy likely.'

'Is she still browned off with me borrowing her corset and stockings?'

His father nodded. 'Mind you, she's browned off with everything at the moment. I'll sharpen up one of our knives. That do?'

'Yes. Thanks, Dad.'

To Ralph's relief, his father didn't ask any more questions.

'How's Mum?' Ralph asked.

'Aching to get out of bed. I'll see how she is and if I'm still off work I'll go with her to the doctor's next week.'

'Do you think she'll start working again like she used to?'

'No. Everyone's got to pull their weight now.'

'But you know Mum.'

'Doctor says she mustn't lift anythin' heavy,' he said. 'Or hang curtains,' he said grinning. 'Curtains! Chance'd be a fine thing.'

Ralph laughed. 'Do you think she'll take any notice?'

'Yeah. This time she will. She's too much to lose,' he added quietly.

Ralph arrived at the stage door early again and set up. This was the morning he was going to have to sing the 'Marseillaise' in front of everyone.

Jane was on the book. The first scene took place between the lovers and went on and on and on. The second scene took place in a law court.

Mr Johnson and Jane were to be part of the crowd. Ralph noted that Jane kept gazing at the playwright and indicating how even more wonderful she thought the play.

The trial was a fiasco. After much heckling from the revolutionaries the prisoners, including the romantic lead, were condemned by their lily white hands. Ralph was then supposed to step forward, stand on a bench and sing the 'Marseillaise'. As this moment came nearer, he remembered what the music teacher had advised. 'Go for the freedom not the anger' she had said. 'Because you are not trained, anger will tense you up. Think liberty. Open your chest. Let the song expand you. You are a banner.'

Before he had time to lose courage he climbed up on to a chair, and began singing, letting the words surge through him in a great torrent of belief in a better, juster world. When he had finished he suddenly remembered where he was, and found everyone gazing up at him. Suddenly all the cast burst into applause. Mr Neville was staring at him.

'With a voice like that you'd better book him for the annual revue,' said a familiar voice.

'Thank you, Felix,' Mr Neville said wryly. 'Carry on, everyone.'

The scene ended with the prisoners being taken away to certain death.

As soon as the rehearsals came to an end, Ralph found Jane by his side. She gave him a dazzling smile. 'That was tremendous, Ralph, especially for an amateur!' she exclaimed.

'Thanks,' said Ralph, fighting down a smile.

'Look,' she said, taking his arm, 'could you do me an enormous favour?'

'If I can,' he said, dreading what she was going to say next.

'I'd like to discuss my part with the playwright. And Rupert has suggested we do it over lunch. So I was wondering – '. She paused. 'It would be so kind if you could, um, mark up. Could you?' she pleaded, her large blue eyes misting over.

'Delighted to,' said Ralph with relief.

He was on his knees, measuring up, when the female lead appeared. She looked anxious, her hands fluttering around her neck. 'Oh, hello,' she said nervously. 'I was looking for Mr Armitage. 'You wouldn't happen to know where he is?'

'There's a café where the cast eat,' he began.

'I can't go there,' she protested. 'I'm the lead.'

Sadly Ralph watched her leave. Little did she know that the professionals looked down their noses at her and the other amateur playing the male lead. Not only were they far too old for the parts, but they were so mannered as to be embarrassing.

The following morning Ralph woke to the sound of running water. He leapt out of bed and jigged up and down in his bare feet on the floorboards by the window. The first signs of a thaw were turning the streets into a mush of moving snow. He grabbed his clothes, broke the ice in the jug on his chest of drawers, and left Harry to sleep. Harry, like Elsie, had been sent home from school for the week. To his surprise, he found Elsie already up and in the kitchen in an old jumper and skirt, black baggy stockings and ankle boots.

'I told you, you didn't have to get up,' he protested.

'Couldn't stand stayin' in that bedroom any longer,' she whispered. 'Aunty Win is getting worse. She keeps going on and on about how she helped me with the school uniform.'

'Not again,' said Ralph wearily. He glanced at the range. 'You've done a lovely job,' he said.

'I only lit it,' she remarked. 'You laid it. That's for you,' she said pointing to a hunk of bread and dripping on a plate.

'Splendid,' he exclaimed.

'You're getting posher and posher.'

Ralph's mouth was too full to comment. He stood with the bread in his hand and gazed out at the dripping, streaming pipes outside the window. He decided, there and then to cycle into town. It would be the first time he hadn't walked since Isla had left.

Once outside, sitting up high on his bike, his greatcoat flapping behind him, there was an air of spring. It was sunny and the long icicles which had formed over the last few weeks seemed even starker and more noticeable in the sunlight. As he hit the High Street, gushing water from the rooftops resembled the sound of a river. It was as though the winter was streaming away. He felt buoyant. He had survived two rehearsals and had gone over every note and move Mr Neville had given him, read bits of A *Tale of Two Cities*, invented in his mind what he had been doing off-stage and had written down his feelings about the Revolution. He had also given himself a name, Jean-Pierre Dubois. It made him feel more real. He decided that his mother was widowed and he had two sisters. He knew that costumes would be provided for the cast, but for the last scene he would make himself some shoes out of strips of rags to show his gradual decline.

He left his bicycle leaning on the wall outside the stage door, said a brief hello to Wilfred and headed upstairs.

He stayed on-stage after clearing back the *Watch on the Rhine* set. The last act took place in a bare cell with one bed in it, the hero's bed. Ralph guessed it would be upstage centre and quickly he did some of Madame Dugon's humming exercises and scales before the others arrived. To his surprise, Jane and Rupert Armitage arrived first, he chatting in animated fashion, she acting riveted by his every word.

Not being able to bear looking at them, he flicked open his script and read through his part. Throughout the act, various prisoners were led to the guillotine. Twice Ralph had to ask the guards if Camarade Jaques had been in touch. The third time he is told that he has been, and it has been he who has condemned him. Ralph, as the youth, realises that it is because he has seen too many trinkets being stolen by the man. Devastated and confused he cries out, 'But I can't go to the guillotine! I believe in the Revolution!' He is to die at dawn. He cries out to his mother. The hero gives a long speech about dying with dignity till Ralph is convinced. As he is led away he turns and thanks the hero. Upstage he is heard to sing the 'Marseillaise'. There is a swish of a guillotine and silence.

As he reread the end of the act he was aware of chatter around him. He looked up. Felix and Basil were deep in conversation. Annie Duncan came up to him. She would be in the prison cell with him too. 'Hello!' she said brightly. 'How are you getting on?'

'I'm not very good at reading and acting at the same time,' he confided. 'Don't worry,' she said. 'Mr Neville won't be expecting a performance from you today, but if you don't mind me giving you a piece of advice, be word perfect by the run tomorrow morning.'

'Don't worry,' he said, 'I will be.'

Mr Neville was in conference with the playwright. He was shaking his head vigorously and glancing at Ralph. Near by, Jane was standing in a demure pose looking even prettier, as if butter wouldn't melt. Felix was standing near by with his script.

Ralph felt acutely uneasy. There was some disagreement going on and he sensed that it involved him. Eventually the playwright handed over two newly typed sheets. Mr Neville glanced down at them and began reading.

Felix came up to Ralph. 'Keep acting your socks off this morning,' he whispered.

'What's going on?' Ralph asked.

'I'm not sure, but whatever it is, I suspect it stinks.' And he left him.

He watched Mr Neville look up at the playwright and frown. A heated discussion was going on. The two men went over to the prompt table and, with a pencil, Mr Neville prodded the pages and pointed something out. The playwright nodded. Mr Neville then crossed some of the new dialogue out and appeared to put in arrows. Ralph pretended to study his script again. Eventually the two men agreed and the playwright walked over to Jane and handed her the two edited pages. Jane pretended to be surprised and delighted, but Ralph saw an angry flicker appear at the side of her mouth.

Then he realised Mr Neville was beckoning him over.

Ralph moved hastily towards him feeling slightly sick.

'I know you're in the cell for most of this act, but I'd like you to be on the book this morning.'

'Yes, Mr Neville,' and he sank into the chair, still wondering whether his part had been cut and given to Jane.

He was nearly right. Jane was given an extra little scene in the cell in which she played a shy pretty creature who is bewildered by what was happening to her. The gaoler attempts to flirt with her, hinting that by granting him a few favours she can escape the guillotine.

'No, not that!' she cries, shrinking back, when she realises what he is implying, and she goes heroically to her death. It was a little vignette and didn't really seem to fit into the rest of the play. Even pruned it was too long.

Mr Neville seemed short-tempered that morning. With disappointment Ralph realised that he was not going to do any acting at all on-stage. The two times he begged the gaoler to get in touch with Camarade Jaques he had to read the lines from where he was sitting, with Mr Neville telling him to jot down his moves. It was only when he came to his breakdown scene with the count that Mr Neville told him to go upstage with his script.

Surging up every ounce of concentration, he stood with his pencil poised and attempted to convey despair while reading and writing down moves at the same time and he felt useless.

The actor playing the count grabbed him and began his long speech with one hand on Ralph's shoulder and his face out front, and it looked as though he was about to stay in that position for the duration.

Mr Neville had other ideas and, throughout the speech, he had Ralph first of all attempting not to listen, then being moved, and then finally being filled with courage, so that Ralph found himself marking the speech with his own moves. He realised he would need to know the lead's speech back to front.

As the gaoler came to take him away, he turned. 'Merci *camarade*. No. Merci, Monsieur le Comte,' and he began to walk towards the wings, then tore back to the prompt book. There was a monologue from the count which was interrupted by Ralph singing his section of the 'Marseillaise'. From his seat Ralph began:

'Allons enfants de la patrie
Le jour de gloire est arrivé
Contre nous de la tyrannie
L'étendard sanglant est -

(swish, clunk!)'

Suddenly everyone on stage and in the wings collapsed with laughter. Swaying helplessly they tottered downstage. Bewildered, Ralph gazed up at them.

'I don't think we need the sound effects of the guillotine!' Mr Neville remarked wryly.

'Oh,' said Ralph.

To his relief he realised that people needed desperately to laugh. The atmosphere on-stage had been strangely tense that morning. 'Do you want me to do it again?' he asked.

'You might as well. It's Antoinette's cue.'

Ralph began singing again, and then stopped. More laughter. Even Mr Neville was laughing now. He turned to the playwright. 'I'm awfully sorry, Rupert, but it is funny. I think it'll get a laugh from the audience too.'

Rupert looked slightly ruffled, but because of the sound of continuous stifled laughter from the wings, he finally nodded in agreement. For a fraction of a second, Ralph could have sworn he heard a familiar laugh, a laugh he hadn't heard for some time, but he had no time to think, for they were moving on into the rest of the scene. There was a matinée of *Watch on the Rhine* that afternoon and they had to keep the momentum going.

The gaoler let in Antoinette. She did her farewell scene with her lover, which was much the same as the other farewell scene and slipped him a phial of poison. There were more hand-claspings and looks out front. Mr Neville had to keep breaking them apart and moving them around the set as they appeared to have their feet glued to the spot.

The gaoler returned. Antoinette's visiting time was over. She exited and, after a long farewell, the male lead took the poison.

'No Lunaire will ever die by public execution. *Vive La France!*' he screamed. The actor then staggered over to the bed where he proceeded to drape himself decorously over it and die.

'Right. Break, everyone,' said Mr Neville.

Without thinking, Ralph immediately grabbed two chairs and marched off-stage to get the tape measure and *Watch on the Rhine* script. Standing in the wings was a young woman in green, with large brown eyes. She smiled.

'Hello,' she said quietly.

Ralph stood there, the chairs swinging from his hands, and he laughed.

'Isla!'

FIFTEEN

'The Isle of Wight? How was it? I mean did you see your fiancé?' He had waited till they were alone before he had dared to ask.

Her face softened, and she smiled in a way Ralph had never seen her smile before. She opened her mouth to speak and then simply nodded.

He was glad he had asked. It had been foolish to think he had any hope, but that simple look had removed the last vestiges of it. He felt saddened, yet touched that she had exposed her feelings in such a direct way.

When he arrived home that evening he was surprised to hear laughter coming from the kitchen. He opened the door.

'Mum!' he yelled.

She was sitting at the table, Elsie and Harry at either side of her, talking ten to the dozen. She looked pale and tired but serene. He wanted to throw his arms around her and give her a hug, but felt too shy to do so. Instead he just laughed with pleasure. Joan was smiling and knitting. She caught his eye and held up a small sleeve.

'For Kitty's baby,' she said, but the look she gave him said that it was for his mother's and for the first time since he had overheard the news he felt a strange flutter of excitement. As he watched Joan knitting the tiny garment, he realised that the coming baby would be his brother or sister. Auntie Win was rattling on about yet another carpet sale but Ralph saw his father gazing at the knitting too and he looked flushed. Suddenly his mother glanced quickly at his Dad and they gave each other a look so tender it was embarrassing.

'Can I borrow your scissors, Aunty Win?' he said hurriedly.

She stared suspiciously at him. 'What for?'

'To use on this,' he said. And he held up a dirty old piece of sacking.

'You're jokin'. My good scissors on that!'

'What are you going to do with it?' asked Elsie, suddenly.

'Cut it into strips, join it up and then use it for binding my feet.' He blushed. 'Not *my* feet,' he added hastily. 'I'm making it for one of the actors. He won't have any shoes for the last act. He wants to show that he's got poorer by the end of the play. I said I'd make them for him.'

'Well you ain't borrowing my scissors on that. It'll damage 'em.'

'Use the knife again,' said his father. 'It'll look more real. If this bloke's supposed to be poor he'd 'ardly make himself shoes with a nice pair of scissors. He would have sold them or pawned them for food.'

'Of course,' said Ralph surprised. And he looked at his father with new eyes. He had forgotten his father would be an expert on poverty. That was why he wanted security for his children.

'I was going to sew the strips together too, but I suppose he wouldn't have a needle and thread either. Knots would be better wouldn't they?'

His father nodded. 'Elsie!' he said, 'Lay the table for supper.'

Ralph's mother rose to her feet.

'Sit!' yelled Ralph and his father.

She sat down with a bump and laughed. 'I feel like a dog!' she exclaimed.

'One step at a time,' said Joan in a motherly fashion.

Everyone stared amazed at her. It was such an un-Joan-like remark. She blinked at everyone. 'Well, that's *my* opinion,' she said.

'Mine too, love,' said Ralph's dad, and Joan glowed.

'Supper!' said Elsie, leaping to her feet.

It was difficult to find a private place to learn his lines. If he did it in his bedroom, Harry would find out and spill the beans. In the end he put on his greatcoat and wellies and sat outside in the lavatory with a candle. He imagined the moves as he learned his lines for Act Three and then slowly went through his lines for Act One and Act Two, thinking through what had happened off stage. It helped him get a feel of his *first* line and made it feel less of a first line.

Then he read through the long rallying speech the romantic lead gave him in the prison, over and over again, with the moves. He knew that he had to change from feeling sheer terror to a numb, but burning sense of courage which would carry him, head unbowed, to the guillotine.

'You bin pipped at the post,' Wilfred remarked when Ralph entered the stage door. 'Isla's already 'ere. So's Jane.'

'Oh!' said Ralph, trying to hide his disappointment.

He found Isla sitting downstage with a prompt book. She looked up. 'You've done a nice job,' she commented, indicating the book.

He shrugged. 'I enjoyed it,' he said.

'Have you been setting up and marking up too?'

He nodded.

'Sly old cow. She never said.'

Ralph looked around. 'Where is she?'

'In the kitchen washing up the mugs. Come here,' she said. 'I've been finding out quite a lot about you. Did you really play Mrs Mulligatawny?'

'Yes.'

'I thought the others were pulling my leg.' She gave a gleeful laugh. 'And did Jane really vomit in the fire bucket and pass out?'

'Yes.'

'Oh, I'd love to have seen that. Aren't I a bitch?'

Ralph smiled.

'Nervous about the run?' she asked.

'How did you guess?'

'Your hands.'

He looked down and found he was wringing them.

'Don't worry.'

'But if I dry?'

'Pick up the prompt as though nothing has happened.'

He remembered how Raymond Maclaren had picked his up in *Something in the Air* and it made him feel better.

Gradually the cast filtered in. As soon as Nigel appeared, Ralph went up to him. 'Excuse me,' he said, hesitantly. 'I hope you don't think I'm being presumptuous but I've given myself a name.'

'Good. It means I can call across to you in the crowd scenes. What is it?'

'Jean-Pierre Dubois.'

'All right, everyone,' said Mr Neville. 'For those who are new to the company I would like to introduce you to Isla Leighton. She hasn't been able to be with us for the last fortnight, because she's been stranded in the snow. If you have any problems, please go to her and she'll help. Oh, and before we start, please, I beg of you, don't any of you go to the Isle of Wight before opening night.'

This was greeted with laughter. Isla was smiling. She had obviously been forgiven.

Act One came and went. Ralph remembered his lines and his moves but he felt depressed. He had concentrated so hard on remembering, that he could see the script in front of his eyes. He even knew which page he was on. He felt both self-conscious and yet struggling hard not to be.

The two leads were word-perfect, but remembered hardly any of the moves Mr Neville had given them, throwing other members of the cast, who occasionally dried because of the leads' inadequacies. Ralph understood the wisdom of learning the lines after working on the scenes. He managed to remember what he had to do in Act Two as well, which involved mostly listening and responding and he sung the Marseillaise adequately, but again he felt he was observing himself from the outside, and he didn't like it.

Then came Act Three. Jane gave an almost identical performance to the one she gave during the dress rehearsal as Mrs Mulligatawny. It was a sigh one minute, coy, then shy again the next, with posed looks and fluttering eyelids, but because her voice was so clear and she was so pretty she looked good. Then it came to his moment with the romantic lead. To Ralph's dismay, the actor began playing his speech out front again. There was no eye contact between him and Ralph at all and Ralph realised that if he moved too much he would distract attention from him. All he could do was allow his words to sink in and respond accordingly. When the gaoler came to take him to the guillotine and Ralph turned to say a farewell thank you, the actor was still staring out at the auditorium, so that Ralph had to say it to his back. He waited for some response and seeing that there was to be none, he threw his head back and marched off into the wings.

At the end of the run, Mr Neville told everyone to meet in dressing room three for notes. First he gave notes to everyone except Ralph, Jane and the two leads, and having done so, dismissed them, leaving him to stare at the remaining four.

'Now,' he said quietly, 'when I give moves, I do not give them for my own pleasure. I give them to be kept.'

Ralph felt himself grow hot.

Mr Neville turned to the two leads. 'You were the worst offenders.'

The female lead began visibly to pout.

'If you both insist on standing like the Rock of Ages every time you open your mouth, or indeed set foot on stage, the audience will fall asleep. Also this play has other people in it who you should be responding to.

'But I can't remember my lines if I do your moves,' protested the female lead, her lower lip quivering.

'I realise that you had to do some work on the speeches before you came because they are so . . .' He paused. 'Substantial. But if you could give yourselves a reason why you make those moves, it would help you remember them.'

He turned to Jane. 'And you are coming over as a flapper.'

Jane looked mortified.

'Too much posing. Get a long skirt from Florrie for the run tomorrow if you haven't one. You'll find you can't pose so much then. Ralph!'

Ralph swallowed. 'I know,' he said. 'I was lousy.'

'I didn't say that, did I?'

'No, sir.'

'I've asked you to stay because of Act Three. Now it's the last scene of the play and it's vitally important.' He turned to the male lead. 'You must involve Ralph. Otherwise he's stuck upstage like a lemon. If he reacts to you, he'll be upstaging you, so all he can do is sit still. The audience doesn't want to watch two immobile people. It's not a radio play. And remember you are French. More passion please.'

He turned to Isla. 'Go over Act Three with them sometime this afternoon and stop them if they get the moves wrong. Then do all the love scenes between Claude and Margaret,' he said indicating the romantic leads. 'Jane, you can do any prop hunting and set up for *Watch on the Rhine*.'

'But don't you need me for rehearsals too?'

'No.' He turned to the two leads. 'I know this is hard for you, but I'm doing it for your sakes too.'

Ralph could see that they had been deeply offended and that it was a wise tactical move not to give them their notes in front of the rest of the cast.

While the female lead sat in the auditorium in her coat, sipping tea, Isla took the male lead and Ralph through his speech. Ralph's admiration for her grew. In spite of a lot of stamping and shouting from the male lead, Isla patiently corrected him. Gradually he began to make eye contact with Ralph and Ralph was able to respond, albeit briefly, to these brief flashes of communication.

It was slow, long and painstaking, but eventually Ralph was sent away and Isla began rehearsing the scenes between the two leads. Ralph didn't envy her.

Outside, the spring feeling of the previous day had disappeared and a frost seemed to be slowly descending. He pushed his bike towards the High Street. Today was the day Mrs Egerton-Smythe paid him, but he knew it wouldn't be much as he had done so little for her. For the first time he knew he couldn't see the show on his usual Friday night, so it came as a great surprise when his father returned enough for a seat in the gallery and told him to go. 'Load of nonsense,' he had grunted after he had handed it over. 'But if you want to waste your money, it's your funeral.'

He was enormously grateful. Up in the gods staring down at the props he had collected and losing himself in *Watch on the Rhine*, he felt a fire in his belly again and it lifted the mild depression he had been feeling since Isla's return.

On the Saturday run, he was Jean-Pierre again instead of Ralph Hollis looking at Jean-Pierre. The lead still forgot half the moves in his rousing speech, but what he did remember gave Ralph something to respond to.

There were no notes. Everyone had to flee to catch a train, buy make-up or get something to eat before the matinée. Ralph cycled through roads slippery with frost to Mrs Egerton-Smythe's to break up ice and clear sludge.

That night he helped out on stage during the Saturday strike. It was as though another wall had been removed. And he had been paid. Before he set off to work at Mrs Egerton-Smythe's again the following afternoon he was able to hand over more money to his father.

It was bitterly cold working outside and the frost bit into his hands and cheeks making them red raw. He shovelled and swept the path leading to her front door and cleared the veranda. He was glad to be working though. He felt sick with nerves for the opening night and it took his mind off it. He decided not to mention to his family that Isla had returned, otherwise his father might wonder what he was doing still helping out at night, and he felt mildly guilty about it after his father's sudden kindness.

On Monday he cycled into the theatre early. 'Your dressing room's already open,' Wilfred said when he arrived. 'You're sharing with Mr Nigel Healy and Mr John Forsyth, in dressing room five.'

Ralph leapt up the steps. He found the door ajar. Shrill humming was coming from inside. Florrie was hanging clothes on a rail and singing. 'Has my costume arrived?' Ralph asked.

'Oh, yes. And your wig.'

'Wig!'

She pointed to three wigs on the dressing room table, each had a paper label pinned on to it. Ralph picked the one with 'Hollis' on it and put it on. It was dark brown, long but tied at the back.

'You'll need some glue,' she said, indicating the net.

Under the costume rail were a row of shoes. 'They didn't have size eight in stock, so you'll have to stuff them with something.'

They were black with square buckles on the front.

'Got garters?' she asked.

'No.'

'I got some upstairs. You'll need 'em to keep your stockings up.'

It was then that Ralph noticed several pairs of thick dark stockings hanging over the end of the rail and heavy leather belts. He found his breeches, and shirt and jerkin hanging on a hanger. He fingered them, trembling.

'Excited?' commented Florrie.

'Terrified,' he admitted.

'Ain't exactly your debut, is it?'

'Feels like it. I didn't know I was going to play Mrs Mulligatawny when *Something in the Air* started so I didn't have time to think.'

She looked at him searchingly. 'You'll do,' she said at last, and left the room with a bundle of costumes for dressing room four.

Stepping on to the set in costume and full 'slap' was the best part of the dress rehearsal. Ralph walked through his Act One moves and then stood centre stage and breathed in deeply. He was pumping around such adrenalin it seemed there was no breath left in his body. 'Don't forget to breathe out,' said a voice from behind. It was Basil Duke, in a white wig, crimson jacket and ornate waistcoat, ruffles emerging at the neck and sleeves, red breeches, white stockings and black shoes with heels.

'I just wanted to get a feel of the set,' said Ralph embarrassed at being caught out.

'Yes, I like to do that too,' he said. 'Who helped you with your make-up?'

'Nigel. He's been so kind. He's let me borrow sticks of his greasepaint, and I know it's expensive.' He breathed out and relaxed his shoulders. 'Do you still get nervous on a first night?'

Basil nodded. 'By the way, don't get upset if you start forgetting things in the dress. There's a lot to readjust to, props, costume, lighting. And sometimes Mr Neville will stop to correct lighting or go back on a sound cue. Sometimes the dress can run straight into the first performance. I hope you've brought sandwiches.'

'No.'

'Don't worry, we'll share ours with you. Next first night, remember.'

Ralph laughed. Basil's confidence in him always cheered him.

He stepped out into the corridor. Jane, in a long floral dress with panniers on either side, was giving beginners calls to dressing rooms one and two. As Claude and Margaret were the leads, they had the best dressing rooms but sadly it only separated them more from the professionals, who still looked down on them and never mixed. Being extremely aware of his amateur status, Ralph was flattered to be put in a dressing room with two professionals.

He returned to the wings and watched Isla from the shadows. Gradually the cast appeared, dressed as the aristocracy in ornate costumes, and ruffles and white wigs, or peasants in baggy breeches and stronger, more sombre colours with dark wigs. The two leads were in blues and white.

Felix looked magnificent. Lace exuded from every portion of his costume and his fingers were covered in rings. His white wig towered above the other men's wigs and in the middle of his elaborate make-up was a beauty spot.

Isla announced, 'Overture and beginners', even though the Billy Dixon Trio were not there for the dress. And then she was giving a signal to the man in the flies and Ralph heard the curtain rising.

'*Ma chérie*,' he heard Felix say on stage, 'I couldn't possibly lift that. I might damage my nails.'

There was polite laughter. The play had begun.

The dress was disappointing. Ralph didn't forget his lines or moves, but he felt flat. Most of the cast stumbled around him, taking the odd prompt, but the two leads forgot nearly every move Mr Neville had given them so that in the prison scene Ralph was left acting on his own, while the leads continued to pose and speechify down centre.

One good thing that did come out of the rehearsal was the sacking shoes. They slowed his movements down which felt right.

There were notes in dressing room three while stage hands reset Act One and Jane was left to reset the props, much to her chagrin. Ralph sat, pencil poised. His notes were short.

'Lift your chin up a bit more, Ralph,' Mr Neville said. 'There are people in the gods who have paid to get in. They don't want to see the top of your head. Oh, and the sack shoes work well in the cell scene. Keep them in. Lose the jacket too. And put some white powder on. You look too healthy.'

In the break which followed, Felix, Basil and the men in the

280

dressing room, broke some of their sandwiches up and left them on his section of the dressing table but Ralph was too nervous to eat. They seemed to understand, but insisted he keep them.

'You'll be ravenous by Act Two,' they said.

Ralph sat in front of the mirror and stared at his made-up face.

He took a deep breath. '*Vive Le Courage*,' he whispered to himself.

To his surprise, Basil and Felix and other members of the cast popped their heads round the door to wish him luck for his first official opening night. Soon after this there was a knock on the door. It was Jane.

'Mr Healy, Mr Forsyth, Mr Hollis, this is your five-minute call. Your five minute call, please,' she announced.

'Ten minutes to go,' he muttered, and he stood up.

'We're not on for ages,' said Nigel.

'I know, but I feel safer if I'm in the wings.'

'In case you lose your way later on?'

Ralph laughed. 'Something like that.'

'Remember we're on the OP side.'

He was glad he went down early. He needed the darkness of the wings to collect his thoughts and he understood now why Basil stood quietly backstage long before he was needed. From the pit he heard the trio playing French music and the chatter of excited first nighters from the auditorium. His chest felt taut and he found himself fighting for breath again.

He discovered his shoulders had been raised. He concentrated on breathing out and soon felt a rush of air filling his lungs again and the panic receding.

Not long after this, Nigel joined him. He gave Ralph a smile, and then Ralph watched him go into himself.

The music stopped and the curtain rose.

'*Ma chérie*, I can't possibly lift that,' they heard Felix crow. 'I might damage my nails.'

The soirée had begun. Antoinette Le Breton spurned the baron's advances and was rescued by the count. The baron exited, threatening revenge. The soirée continued. Annie Duncan was standing near them by now, listening intently to what was going on on stage, and watching the cue lights on the flat near the door.

As if in tune with one another, Ralph and Nigel suddenly gave each other a glance and moved nearer the door and then Annie Duncan's green light flashed on and she threw aside the door and disappeared.

'They're dragging people out of their houses and hanging them

281

from the lampposts,' they heard her shriek.

Ralph looked at Nigel. He was already standing differently, and his face had a hard belligerent look to it. This was the man Jean-Pierre looked up to. From above the door they could see a red light. It would change to green as soon as the last person had gone through the secret panel, though Ralph could see members of the cast already coming through it and off-stage into the wings. The green light flashed on. Ralph gritted his teeth and ran behind Nigel on to the set. He ran over to the stage left door as directed, turned to see his boss pocketing a trinket and before they knew it the curtain had come down and the trio was playing yet another French tune.

Because Ralph was not officially allowed to help with the props, he had to disappear into the wings again while Jane and Isla gathered them up, took them off-stage, and threw rough covers over the rest of the furniture. The music finished and the curtain rose again. It seemed only seconds later that the curtain was down again, and applause was heard through the next lot of music. Stage hands appeared to remove the Act One set and the court scene was put up with Isla and Jane running off and on with props.

Remembering that this was the act when he sang, the roof of Ralph's mouth suddenly felt like glue. On-stage it grew quiet. Actors took their places silently. The music came to an end and the curtain rose. When it came to the court scene, Ralph's only way of coping was to be Jean-Pierre as if his life depended on it.

He listened avidly to everything which was going on with approval or disapproval, bewilderment or triumph, so that when he had to sing the 'Marseillaise' it felt natural. And then Act Two was over and he was starving. He was about to run upstairs for his sandwiches, when he decided to use the hunger in the prison scene.

He sat in a corner by the prompt table, removed his shoes and wound the sacking round his feet. He stood up and hung his jacket over the back of a chair and stood beside Jane and the male lead, dabbing white powder on his face with cotton wool while the stage hands whisked off the courtroom and brought back the painted flats for the cell scene. He shuffled on behind the male lead, Jane and Annie Duncan following, and took his place under the cell window. The lights above them grew dimmer.

A range of thoughts and feelings flooded him. Hunger, cold, despair. Longing for mother and sisters. Bewilderment that he was in the cell at all. And fear. Terrible, terrorising fear. The music came to an end. Ralph bowed his head and listened to the curtain rise. The last act had begun. Annie Duncan was taken away. Jane did her little scene with poignancy and then it was the scene between Ralph and the male lead. Gradually he felt his body unbend and his courage returning. When it was time to be led away, a new feeling of defiance swept through him. His 'thank you' came out roughly as the gaoler pushed him through the door.

It was all over for him now. Quietly he joined the rest of the cast in the wings as the duet between the two leads was acted out on stage and the male lead was left to commit suicide. As he yelled '*Vive La France!*' there was the sound of the curtain descending. Everyone looked in Isla's direction.

'Now!' she whispered urgently.

They moved swiftly on-stage and joined hands in the order Mr Neville had put them in. The curtain sprang upwards and Ralph found himself staring out at the auditorium to an applauding house. He looked up at the gods, keeping an eye on the male lead who was leading the bows. Then, as the applause began to die down, Basil Duke stepped forward.

'Ladies and gentlemen, thank you for your appreciative response to this remarkable new play. If you have enjoyed it, which by your applause you certainly have done, I do invite you attend next week's show, a light-hearted modern comedy entitled *Fit for Heroes*. The performances will be at the usual time, 7.30 p.m. Matinées Thursdays and Saturdays. Goodnight and God bless.'

As he stepped back, the first strains of 'God Save the King' began. The opening night was over.

The make-up was taking longer to remove than he had anticipated. His eyes were causing the most trouble. He closed one and spread the cream into every crevice of the other, but by the time he had wiped it a great smear of carmine and brown seemed to cover the top half of his face. His eyeballs were also beginning to look pink and bloodshot. He was battling with his other eye when a familiar voice made him glance up into the mirror.

'Might be an idea to bring a thermos of hot water tomorrow.'

Mrs Egerton-Smythe was standing behind him. She was made up and looked surprisingly attractive. From the morning after she and Jessica had looked through Laurie Egerton-Smythe's belongings, he had noticed a dramatic change in her. She looked younger and frowned less. He gazed at her, wanting to ask her what she thought, but not quite daring.

She leaned over him. 'Basil Duke is very good, isn't he?'

'Tremendous,' whispered Ralph.

'Are villains his speciality?'

'No. He can play anything.'

'Powerful too.'

'And he can be funny.'

'I'll have to come again.'

'Did you enjoy the play?' he asked casually.

'I enjoyed some of it,' she said warily. 'The two leads leave something to be desired and the dialogue is a little stilted.' She smiled, a twinkle in her eyes. 'But I thought your performance was a fairly reasonable one.'

He beamed. This was praise coming from Mrs Egerton-Smythe. She squeezed his shoulders. 'I'll see you tomorrow afternoon, then.'

'Morning. Now that Isla's back, I'm not needed any more. The next play only has one set.'

SIXTEEN

'What's it like living at Mrs Egerton-Smythe's now?' Ralph asked.

Ever since he had overheard her announce to Queenie in the kitchen that she was to become a theatrical landlady and that she quite understood if Queenie wanted to hand in her notice, Ralph had been bursting to ask Basil.

It was Friday night and Ralph had been removing his make-up when Basil made his surprise visit to his dressing room.

'Isn't it freezing?' he went on.

'Yes. But it always is in digs.'

'But is it nicer than where you were staying before?'

'Ten times nicer.'

'Even with Queenie there?'

'Even with Queenie. Her bark is worse than her bite.' He smiled. 'I hear you were paid today.'

Ralph flushed with pleasure. 'Yes.' He hesitated. 'Actually, there's something I've been wanting to ask you about that. I notice people giving Wilfred something.'

'Ah. Everyone gives him a shilling on Saturday night. It's the custom.'

It was then Ralph noticed he was carrying a newspaper.

'It's the *Winford Observer*,' said Basil, handing it to him. 'You've got a nice mention. I didn't tell you earlier in case it made you self-conscious on stage.'

Ralph picked it up and scanned it rapidly. The production and scenery had a good mention and both Felix and Basil's performances were praised, as was Annie Duncan's. The supporting cast, it commented, did the best they could with a stilted script. 'Special mention must be given to a young newcomer, Ralph Hollis, whose acting abilities drove through in spite of his lack of vocal technique,' read Ralph aloud. 'His singing voice is a clear tenor, a must for the Rep's next review. His face seemed somewhat familiar, but I can find no mention of him in earlier productions.'

It added that pretty young Jane Jefferson, who played a cameo role in Act Three would have been better cast as the female lead.

Ralph let out a whistle. 'That's tough on Margaret,' he remarked.

'Yes,' said Basil. 'And the backers are in tomorrow afternoon. I hope a good night's sleep will put it out of her mind.'

'Not if Jane has anything to do with it,' Ralph said. 'She'll probably offer to give her acting lessons.'

Cycling home, Ralph had the sensation of flying and swimming at the same time. Still euphoric, he left his bike in the yard, crept into the scullery and opened the door into the kitchen. He had just finished lighting a candle when he found Joan sitting up in bed with her coat wrapped round her shoulders. He jumped. 'You gave me a fright!' he whispered.

'I had to warn you,' she said urgently.

'Warn me? About what?'

'That,' she said pointing to a newspaper on the table. 'There's been a terrible row.'

'Oh no!' he said, the penny beginning to drop. He sank down into a chair. 'My name.'

Joan nodded. 'Aunty Win was readin' about this murder case – you know the one about the mysterious string bag found in the bushes – when she spots this bit with your name in it.'

'She would.'

'She read it out,' Joan continued, 'at supper.'

'In front of Dad?'

'Yeah. First thing he wanted to know was who knew. Aunty Ellen went bright red. The rest of us was as surprised as he was. He was so cut up about it. The thing is, he's going to keep you in tomorrer.'

'But I've got two shows. There's backers coming.'

'It won't make no difference. He's determined.'

'Hell!'

'What are you going to do?'

'Leave before he wakes up. If it wasn't so cold I'd sleep out.' He knelt down in front of the range. 'I hope he doesn't hear us,' he whispered. 'Joan?'

'Yeah?'

'Are you any good at lying?'

'Sometimes. Why?'

'Then you'd better say you were asleep when I came in. I don't want you to get into trouble.'

'I'll go red, I know I will. He scares me when he's riled.'

'You better go back to your room and make your bed before morning.'

'Will you wake me before you go?'

'Yes. Joan?'

'Yeah?'

'Was Mum . . . Was she very upset?'

'She were crying.'

'Oh, hell. Why does he make life so difficult?'

'He kept saying "Why didn't you tell me?" and "Got any other secrets?" It were awful.'

'I think I better stay the night at Mrs Egerton-Smythe's tomorrow. It might give him time to cool down.'

'But what if he goes to the theatre tomorrer to get you?'

'He wouldn't be seen dead within a hundred yards of a theatre, let alone in it. He'd be afraid someone might see him and think he was a pansy.'

There was a creak from upstairs. They stared at each other in horror. For the next few minutes they kept silent.

Eventually Ralph pointed to the range. Joan nodded and lay down.

Gingerly Ralph cleared out the grate and relaid the fire. He then blew out the candle and lay across three of the chairs, but every time he began to doze off, he woke up terrified he would oversleep. Eventually he gave up and sat at the table staring out the window. Gradually a pinkness suffused the sky so that the bombed buildings, stark and black in their base of white snow, appeared almost beautiful. Chilled he crept over to Joan.

After vigorous shaking, he eventually managed to wake her.

'Quickly,' he urged. 'Go back to your room. I'll make up the bed.'

She stumbled shivering across the room. Ralph ran to the door and opened it for her, easing it gently to a close behind her. He then made up the bed swiftly, took a last look at the room, and tiptoed hurriedly towards the scullery.

It was too early to go to Mrs Egerton-Smythe's. To kill time he wandered through the High Street staring into windows. A strange display caught his attention in a stationery shop. Frozen bottles of black, blue-black, and royal and red ink had exploded. Every shred of paper on display was now covered in colours. Outside the windows, huge icicles hung down like different length organ pipes.

Eventually he hovered outside her house, longing for a light to appear at the window. And then he saw a familiar figure walking towards him.

'Queenie!' he yelled, waving.

She gave her usual disapproving frown and he laughed.

'What you doin' 'ere?' she called out suspiciously.

'I thought I'd come early.'

''Ad breakfast?'

'Not yet.'

'She gave a snort. 'Looking for a free one, I s'pose.'

'I'll lay the Aga for you, if you like.'

'No, thanks. You can get some wood and coal in.' She paused. 'Know how to lay a table?'

'Of course.'

'You can do that as well, in the dining room.' And then to Ralph's amazement, she added, 'for the artistes.'

They walked up the side path to the tradesman's entrance, Ralph talking non-stop, relieved at not being alone any more, and at being in a friendly environment again. Queenie who was being her usual reticent self, walked silently beside him giving the odd grunt. He opened the kitchen door for her and she waved her hand roughly at this gentlemanly gesture, but he could see that she liked it. Ralph let her in and then raced down to the woodshed for some kindling. He took large buckets down to the coal cellar, but when he saw how little was left, he realised he would be lucky to fill one. If the miners' strike didn't end soon, and the fuel shortage didn't improve, Mrs Egerton-Smythe would soon be living on a diet of rationed sandwiches.

'There's hardly anything left,' he told Queenie.

'I could have told you that.'

'But how have you been able to cook with the extra mouths to feed?'

'They bring in driftwood when they gets 'ome,' she said nonchalantly. 'And a couple of them 'ave queued up for coal somewhere with a shovel. Dunno where. Didn't ask.'

'So they're not totally horrendous?' Ralph said teasingly.

She glanced at him out of the corner of her eye and gave a short shrug.

'Not my business to comment. I do what I'm told and that's that.' She peered down at his wellingtons. 'On second thoughts you'd best not lay the table. You start clearing away the path again. I'll call you when breakfast is ready. You'd best have it in 'ere before the ladies and gentlemen come down.'

In front of the house Ralph suddenly found himself looking anxiously over his shoulder. Every footstep in the snow brought him out in a sweat. He realised that it had been stupid to come to Mrs Egerton-Smythe's. His father was bound to know where to find him. He shovelled rapidly. If he could finish his work quickly, perhaps he could leave early and escape to the theatre.

It was while he was sitting at the kitchen table that he first saw Mrs Egerton-Smythe. She had popped in to see Queenie.

'I hear you have potential West End backers coming in this afternoon.' She peered at him closely. 'You're as white as a sheet. Did you get any sleep last night?'

'None.'

'You're not nervous, are you?'

'No. Home trouble.'

'Your mother?'

'Father. He didn't know I was in the play, and there was a review.'

'Oh, my lord!' she exclaimed. 'What did he say?'

'He was asleep when I got home. I was wondering, could I come back here tonight after the strike?'

'Yes, of course you can, but you're going to have to face him some time.'

'I thought tomorrow night would be soon enough.'

She nodded. 'Meanwhile you must get some sleep before this afternoon. For the sake of the play,' she added firmly. 'After the others have gone off to do their run of *Fit for Heroes*, I'll fill a hot water bottle and make you up a bed on the couch in the garden room.'

'I can take a nap at the theatre.'

'No, you can't. Those dressing rooms are damp and freezing.'

'But . . .'

'No buts. I'm the boss while you're here.'

Ralph smiled. It was useless to protest.

'By the way,' she said, 'you might be seeing more of me than usual if you're still frequenting the theatre. I noticed a post being advertised in the *Observer* and met your Mr Neville for an interview last Wednesday. I am to begin work as his assistant-cum-secretary on Monday.'

Queenie gave a gasp.

'You mean you're going to be doin' a *job*, ma'am?'

'Yes.'

'But what will Mr Egerton-Smythe say?'

Mrs Egerton-Smythe gave a wry smile. 'Do you really want to hear?'

'Perhaps not,' she said hastily.

'Now, Queenie, about supper.'

Ralph bit into his bread and dripping. As the steam from his cup of tea approached his mouth, he was aware of a strange heavy feeling and was relieved that Mrs Egerton-Smythe was so bossy.

He arrived at the theatre at 1 p.m., refreshed and armed with sandwiches and a jug-shaped Thermos Mrs Egerton-Smythe had lent him with warm water in it to wash his make-up off. As soon as he stepped over the threshold of the stage door he felt safe. He had cycled, head lowered, as fast as he could in case his father happened to be around.

He liked to be dressed and made up before the half. He was a nervous wreck once it had been called. His costume on he wrapped the old greatcoat Mrs Egerton-Smythe had given him round his shoulders and moved speedily towards the steps, down towards the door. As he passed dressing room one, he could hear a distressed female voice and Claude, the male lead, talking. He hovered in the corridor.

'It's only the local rag. Probably written by some seedy journalist. You wouldn't have been given the lead if the producer hadn't wanted you to play the part.'

If only he knew, thought Ralph.

'And I know that Rupert particularly asked for you to play it.'

At this there was a fresh bout of sobbing. 'He's been avoiding me for days,' she wept. 'I'll die if he leaves me.'

'He won't. He's just very busy with getting people in to see the play.'

'I can't do it! I can't.'

Then Ralph heard an exasperated snort. 'If you don't, you can bet sweet little Jane will step into your shoes at a moment's notice. Do you want to give her that chance?'

'No.'

'Then pull yourself together. This could be the most important day of your life.' There was a pause. 'You're wonderful. You know you are.'

At this point, Ralph decided to make a move.

He slipped into the wings and laid his strips of sacking, white powder and cotton wool, near the Act Three cell props. He wandered on to the Act One set, breathed it in and then decided to look for Isla. He found her in the kitchen.

'Hello,' she said cheerily. 'You had a lovely write-up in the *Observer*. Did you see?'

'Basil showed me last night.'

'I didn't say anything when I gave you your calls, because Nigel and John weren't mentioned.'

'Has Jane seen it?'

'Yes!' she said, her voice lowered. 'And she's been unbearable.'

'I overheard Margaret crying in her dressing room.'

'Me too. If that Rupert has got any gumption, he'll come and flatter her like mad, but I think he's got such a dose of Jane-fluttering-eyelashitis, that he's avoiding her. He's such a fool. There's not only West End Managements coming, there's a rumour that someone from Gainsborough Films will be in the audience.'

'I heard Claude persuading her to go on.'

'Oh, she'll do that all right. It's what she does when she goes on that worries me. She's an amateur. She's got no technique to fall back on.'

Ralph suddenly felt depressed. 'Neither have I,' he said, quietly.

'But you're picking things up,' she said encouragingly. 'You're not set in your ways. And your singing voice is better than anyone's in the company.'

'Don't exaggerate, Isla.'

'Well, it's better than mine,' she said beaming, and they both burst into laughter. 'Mine sounds like one of those vaudeville spots where a man plays tunes on a saw!' She glanced at her watch. 'Must go. It's time to give the quarter.'

Ralph headed for the wings. His stomach seemed to dissolve into his chest and vice versa. Once backstage he felt more at ease. And then everything took on a momentum again and Isla was sitting in the prompt corner, music emerged from the pit and beyond them was the chatter of the matinée audience.

Members of the cast appeared in the shadows and made their way on-stage. The music finished and the curtain rose.

Ringing clear as a bell was Felix's voice as the aristocratic fop.

As Ralph listened to the play he was aware of something different. The pauses were longer, and when the female lead spoke, she appeared to be paraphrasing. Nigel appeared and stood quietly, lost in his own thoughts. Then Ralph noticed him raise his head and listen, riveted. He turned and gave Ralph a nod. Ralph joined him.

Annie Duncan came off-stage.

'What's happening?' whispered Nigel.

'Margaret is going to pieces and Claude is acting with face out front and no moves.'

'We'd better be prepared in case she jumps and they leave through the secret door earlier. At least Isla can see and give us our cues.'

Annie nodded, and they listened acutely. 'Hell!' they heard her whisper.

There was a jumble of words, followed by a pause, and then Felix threw in a line about needing to get his hanky re-ironed and what was keeping Lady Charlotte.

'Thank you, Felix!' she sighed. Her face took on a terrified look and she fled on screaming about people being hanged from lampposts.

From then on Nigel and Ralph didn't take their eyes off the cue lights. The scene hiccuped along. Members of the cast appeared backstage from the secret panel downstage right, their hands and eyes thrown upward.

Now only the two leads were left on stage. The red warn light was already on. Ralph was aware of Nigel getting himself prepared.

'Give it everything you got. Bags of energy. We need to lift the end of this scene. Don't gabble, but pick up the cues fast.'

Ralph nodded.

From behind they heard the two leads walking backstage. The green light was on and Nigel ran on like a starved animal hunting its prey, quivering with anger and violence. The scene between them had an extra charge. Ralph swiftly obeyed orders and tore across to the stage left door. Then he turned to find his comrade not only picking up some trinket, but staring at him with such venom that it alarmed him. Then there was the smile, the swagger, the cover-up. 'For the Revolution!'

And Ralph felt relief flooding him, and he flung his arm up with exuberance.

'For the Revolution!' As soon as the curtain hit the deck, Isla and Jane rushed on, removed pictures and ornaments and threw old covers over the furniture and it was scene two.

Somehow the rest of the play staggered along with the two leads giving ever more wooden and paraphrased speeches while the rest of the cast fought to keep any excitement in the piece bubbling. Ralph had never had so much concentrated attention and response when he sang the 'Marseillaise' in Act Two and he threw himself into it with such gusto that he felt a lump in his throat.

There was an all-round sense of relief when Act Two ended. The female lead had only a little scene at the end of Act Three. Ralph ran into the wings, slipped his shoes off, quickly wrapped the strips of sacking round his feet, threw off his jacket and hat while the set was being changed and dabbed white powder on his face. As soon as the stage hands were in the wings and on their way to the scene dock, Ralph, Jane, Annie and Claude headed for the stage and threw themselves among the ragged blankets on the floor. Ralph half closed his eyes. The music was coming to an end. The curtain was rising. He concentrated on the image of the guillotine.

The scene moved with pace and power. Annie was taken off. Jane wrenched every drop of emotion from her scene and was taken soon after. To Ralph's surprise the male lead remembered his moves and clasped Ralph with a new intensity. Ralph realised he must be relieved at acting with someone he felt safe with and Ralph went with him, responding as spontaneously as he could within the confines of their moves. He felt his courage over facing death returning and as he turned for the last time, his thank-you was really heartfelt.

To his surprise he heard a round of applause as he hit the wings. Facing him was the female lead, waxen-faced. At least it would fit the scene thought Ralph.

The actor playing the gaoler was standing nearby. There was the cue to go on and the two lovers were left on stage for the last time. By now the rest of the cast were gathered in a group, crossing their fingers. Suddenly they heard her make her farewell speech. Everyone stared at Isla who was rapidly flicking pages. A huge chunk of the script had obviously been cut. They could hear the gaoler being called.

'I'm ready!' she was shouting. 'I'm ready to leave.'

Before the cast could stop him, the man playing the gaoler had opened the cell door and escorted her out. As soon as she reached the wings she dissolved into sobs. Felix took hold of her by the shoulders. 'You've forgotten to give him the poison,' he said.

'Oh no!' she gasped. She saw Ralph. '*You'll* have to take it on.'

'I can't,' said Ralph. 'I'm dead.'

'The gaoler!' she said desperately. 'Couldn't he?'

'No,' said Felix. 'He wants to see him guillotined.'

'I can't go on again.'

'Perhaps you could pretend she got the key from me,' said the gaoler.

'Shush,' interrupted Basil.

Everyone listened. 'He's making his death speech.'

'How the hell is he going to die?' put in Nigel. Now all eyes were back on Isla, bar Margaret who was weeping inconsolably into a corner.

Isla wasn't looking at the prompt book any longer. She was staring mouth open at what was going on downstage. Without speaking, the cast moved gradually nearer her.

'You'll never get me to die by the guillotine,' the lead was shrieking. 'Never will a Lunaire be executed in public!'

This was followed by a gagging noise.

'What's he doing?' whispered Felix.

'Strangling himself,' she whispered mesmerised. There was a thump. Hurriedly Isla gave the cue to the man in the flies and the curtain came down.

'Quick!' she said. 'Bow before the audience laugh.'

At that point everyone sprinted towards the gaol door which was now open.

'I can't face them,' Margaret wept. 'Look, I'm crying.'

'They'll think it's emotion,' snapped Felix. 'Smile through your tears,' and he grabbed one of her hands. To her amazement Basil grabbed the other and she found she had to run with them or be dragged.

It wasn't until the bows and the National Anthem were over, and the curtain was down again, that the cast stared at one another like shell-shocked victims.

Isla appeared suddenly. 'Dressing rooms, please,' she said. 'Jane and I have to reset Act One.'

And at that point everyone except the leads, fled through the corridor, leapt up the steps and dived *en masse* into dressing room three where they promptly collapsed into laughter.

It was only when they had begun to gather breath that Nigel suddenly said, 'I hate to sober up this get-together, but do you realise we have another perf. to get through?'

But it didn't sober them up. It only made them hiccup helplessly into another bout of hysteria.

Eventually when they had calmed down, Felix said, 'Poor thing. She's gone through hell this afternoon.'

'So have we,' said Nigel.

'I know, but we'll be involved in another play next week. This is a pinnacle for her. Seriously do you think we should see if she's all right?'

'The trouble is,' said Basil, 'she might take offence. I'm afraid she's a bit high and mighty.'

'I don't think so,' said John quietly. 'I wonder if Mr Neville will pop in to see her, or Rupert?'

'I doubt it,' said Felix. 'They'll probably be talking to the guests.'

'Poor Claude,' said Basil. 'Fancy having to commit suicide by self-asphyxiation.'

'Better than kicking himself to death,' reflected Nigel.

'What shall we do?' said Annie.

'Have something to eat, take a rest and play it by ear,' said John.

'I'll help Isla make tea,' said Ralph.

'And pick up any gossip?' suggested Felix.

'Well, I might,' Ralph said nonchalantly, but he couldn't help smiling at being found out.

After the excitement of the matinée, the evening performance was somewhat of an anticlimax. The male lead did his best, though he was as wooden as ever, and the female lead managed to remember her lines, but almost on a monotone, her eyes glazed as though someone had slipped her a Mickey Finn during the break.

The rest of the cast tried to pull out the stops again, but it was the end of the week and half of them had done a run-through of another play in the morning. Ralph felt tense, as though he was trying too hard to compensate for his tiredness and the knowledge that it was his last performance.

As the cast made their way to the wings after curtain down, the stage hands, Jack Walker, the chief electrician and his assistant were already waiting in the wings to take away the set and dismantle the lights.

Isla was removing props. Ralph grabbed his greatcoat, jacket and shoes, and headed swiftly out of the door. Florrie was out in the corridor with a list.

'Do you want your garters now?' Ralph asked, rolling them off his breeches.

'Leave 'em in yer dressing room, love. I'll pick 'em up later.'

On the steps above him, everyone was ahead of him in a whirl of long dresses, frock coats and wigs.

By the time Ralph had changed out of his costume, Nigel and John were already out of the door.

'Have a good weekend,' they yelled over their shoulders.

'You too,' Ralph yelled back.

The door closed and he felt overwhelmingly sad. They hadn't even said goodbye. To them it was just another week. To him, it was his last performance at the rep. The write-up in the *Observer* had only confirmed what Mr Neville had told him, that he needed training.

He thrust his fingers into some cocoa butter Nigel had left for him and rubbed it into his skin. Icy blasts whistled through the dressing-room. He put the cocoa butter round his face and neck with a rag, the skin on his arms rising into enormous goose-pimples. His eyes were still a mess. He poured the warm water from the flask into a tiny bowl and washed them. It annoyed him that he was taking so long. He knew Isla and Jane needed help on-stage. He would have to finish cleaning off at Mrs Egerton-Smythe's.

He replaced the cocoa butter in front of Nigel's mirror, neatly put his garters beside his wig in front of his mirror and pulled on a jersey, and then, taking a last look at the room, he shut the door. There was one thing he needed to do before going on stage. He made his way to the stage door area clasping a shilling in his hand. Basil and Annie were standing at Wilfred's cubby-hole. Ralph hung back and read the notice next to the cast list for the following week's play, *Robert's Wife*.

DIGS IN LARGE DRAUGHTY HOUSE.
BREAKFAST PROVIDED. LATE SUPPER
TO BE COOKED BY ARTISTES ON ARRIVAL
HOME IF DESIRED.
LONG-TERM OR ONE-NIGHTLY, SHOULD WEATHER
HAMPER TRANSPORT. PLEASE CONTACT
MRS EGERTON-SMYTHE. WINFORD 236

Noticing that Basil and Annie had left, he went up casually to Wilfred, his face hot, his palm sweating round the shilling.

'In case I don't see you before you go, Wilfred,' he stammered, shyly, 'I'll say my goodbyes now.'

Wilfred's hand was ready. 'Thank you, sir!' he said smiling. 'And a very good weekend to you too. Would you do something for me?'

'Yes, of course.'

He turned and took an envelope from one of the pigeonholes. 'I think it might be quite important. So if you could give it to her as soon as possible.'

For some reason he thought it would be for Jane, but there in small scrawly writing on the envelope was the word 'Isla'.

'Of course.'

He raced up the steps, his ordeal over, a spring in his heels. Wilfred had treated him like a professional.

Isla was on-stage with one of the large brooms, looking harassed. 'Thank goodness the cell scene was an easy one to clear,' she said. 'Jane still isn't down.'

'Sorry I was so long,' he said guiltily. 'I still haven't got the knack of taking off my make-up fast.'

'Can you get a broom?'

'Of course. Oh, this came for you,' and he gave her the envelope.

By the time he returned with the broom, she looked stunned.

'Isla?' he said gently. 'What is it? Is it bad news?'

Isla raised her head slowly, and held out the letter for him to read. 'It's from Jane,' she said in disbelief. 'She's eloped. With Rupert Armitage.'

SEVENTEEN

'Gretna Green?' he said staring at the contents of the letter. 'Where's that?'

'Scotland. You can get married at any age there without your parents' permission.'

'Isla,' he said slowly, 'I think she wants you to spill the beans.'

'What!'

'If you were going to marry anyone in secret, would you tell?'

To Ralph's surprise she reddened. 'No, I wouldn't.'

'Neither would I, unless I wasn't sure.'

'Or wanted to have a big dramatic scene with my father up in Gretna Green,' added Isla.

'That's possible.'

She shook her head. 'No. I might be the only person she's told and that might be because of sharing a room with her and needing to let Mrs McGee know so that she doesn't have the police looking for her.'

'Isla, you'll have to either tell someone or pretend you never received the letter. You can't do that, because Wilfred knows and he might say something.'

'And if I don't tell, my landlady will call the police on Monday.'

'Is Mr Neville *in loco parentis*?'

'I don't think so. Oh, hell, if I mention it on Monday and he knows that I've known since tonight . . .'

'He's not going to be very popular with her father.'

'Oh, lor', I'd forgotten about him. What shall I do?'

'You must let Mr Neville know. Tonight.'

'But I can't leave here. I need to mark up.'

'I'll go if you think you can cope without me.'

'Jack will help me carry the furniture,' she said. 'And the props don't get set till Act One scene two. Oh, no!' she cried. 'The props! The set only has a beer crate on it to begin with, and when the curtain comes down on Act One scene one, the ASMs have to fill the stage with props in minutes. It's all got to be rehearsed on Monday morning and timed!'

'All the more reason Mr Neville needs to know tonight. If we leave it, he'll think it's a plot cooked up by us to present me as an ASM.'

'The air will be blue. It's no joke being the bearer of bad tidings.'

Ralph shrugged. 'Now the play's over, I've nothing to lose, have I?

Mr Neville was still awake, reading and scribbling notes in a copy of *Robert's Wife*, by a tall black paraffin heater in the sitting-room, surrounded by shelves heaving with plays and scripts, theatre memoirs and gramophone records.

He lived with his wife in an upstairs flat two doors away from the theatre. Ralph stood outside the hall door, frantically rehearsing what he would say, but when Mr Neville towered above him in his spectacles a cigarette dangling from his lips, Ralph just thrust the envelope into his hands and said, 'I think you ought to read this. Isla couldn't come herself. She's setting up for *Fit for Heroes*.'

Mr Neville had scanned the contents of the letter, beckoned him to follow him up the stairs and indicated his armchair by the heater. Then he had silently flicked through his address book and had begun dialling.

He seemed to stand there for an eternity until finally he heard Mr Neville say, 'Mr Jefferson, it's Adrian Neville from the Palace phoning. I'm sorry to disturb you so late at night, but I felt it my duty to tell you about your daughter as soon as possible . . . No. I had no idea . . . A playwright. Of sorts . . . I suspect they caught the 10.30 train to London and will catch a night train, if there is one, up north. I can't see him trying to get there in a car in this weather. It might be worth finding out which stations the trains for Scotland leave from. You might discover them sitting on the platform together.'

Eventually, after apologies and 'not at alls' and 'my pleasure!', Mr Neville put the receiver down and gave a sigh. 'Next time I take on an ASM to train, it'll be the son or daughter of someone in the business.'

Ralph froze. 'I'd better get back and help Isla,' he said quietly.

297

'You're quick off the mark to step into Jane's shoes,' he said sarcastically.

Ralph reddened. 'Mr Johnson employed me long before tonight.'

'And I suppose you're now trying to take her place. Hence this,' he said waving the letter.

This was the last straw, thought Ralph. It was bad enough finishing the show, but to have his actions misinterpreted! He sprang angrily to his feet.

'No! Actually I heard a rumour that Jane's father might be donating new lighting equipment to the theatre and if he didn't know soon enough he might not feel so generous. Also, I thought Jane wanted people to know! If I'd wanted her bloody job I would have told Isla to keep quiet until Monday when it was too late for you to phone round and get a new ASM. Preferably one of the sons or daughters of someone you know in the business, and of course with money!' He strode towards the door, remembering the words of Charles Egerton-Smythe. 'Don't bother seeing me out,' he yelled. 'I'll find my own way, thank you!' and he flung the door open only to find he had stepped into a cupboard.

'The door out is over there,' said Mr Neville sardonically, pointing to one on the opposite wall.

Hot with fury, Ralph refused to look at or speak to him. He marched past, yanked the door open and slammed it so hard behind him he hoped it would knock every single play script off the shelves.

He stormed out into the night and ran to the exit door at the side of the foyer. It had slammed shut in the wind. Cursing, he ran round to the stage door. Luckily it was still open. A huge open skip stood under the notice-board, filled with the costumes of *Vive La Liberte*. Florrie was having a cup of tea and a chat with Wilfred in his cubby-hole. They immediately looked up at him.

'Anythin' wrong?' asked Wilfred.

'Everything!' he said dramatically. 'Every bloody thing!' And he leapt up the steps, his greatcoat flapping behind him.

Isla had just finished marking up. 'That was quick,' she remarked.

'He didn't waste any time. He phoned her father immediately. God I can't *stand* him!' Ralph said, pounding his thighs with clenched fists. 'He thought I was trying to step into Jane's shoes. Oh, to hell with him. What do you want me to do?'

'Sort out the *Vive* props while I set the *Heroes* props back here. I just have to put a beer crate on the set.'

It was later, while they were in the kitchen, that Isla let him into her confidence. They were talking about Jane again.

'Does Jack know?' Ralph had asked.

'Yes.'

'And Mr Johnson?'

'No.'

'He's not going to be pleased to be helping backstage again.'

'He already is. With only one ASM we need all hands for the quick change in Act One. Mr Neville will probably tell him tomorrow to hire an extra stage hand.'

'I see.'

'I'm sorry. It's so unfair.' She looked thoughtful for a moment. 'How good are you at keeping secrets?'

'Very. Why?'

'Because I have something to tell you, but it mustn't get out.' She took a deep breath. 'When I was in the Isle of Wight, I wasn't just trying to get through snowdrifts. I was taking steps to wear this,' and she pulled on a piece of string hidden under her jersey and drew out a gold ring.

'Is that what I think it is?' gasped Ralph.

Isla flushed and nodded. 'My father doesn't know. If he had, he would have done everything he could to have prevented it. I'm twenty-one now and I don't need his permission.'

'But why the hurry?'

'Philip's mother is dying. She's very fond of me. Philip and I wanted her to be at our wedding and for it to be a happy occasion.'

'But didn't she think it was a bit funny your parents not being there?'

'I lied. I said my father had a film engagement in Ireland and my mother had gone with him. I don't know whether she believed me. But it didn't matter. She was so happy. We got married in a tiny church on the island and a friend of the family gave me away. Philip and I thought we would just have a day together, but when we were snowed in, it seemed like it was meant. Philip's mother insisted we stay on our own and only visit her when we really wanted to.'

She tucked the ring hurriedly down her jumper. 'If Mr Neville found out, I'd be for the high jump and my father would go thundering after Philip.'

'But won't he eventually?'

'Yes, but as long as it happens after my mother-in-law's death, I don't care.'

'Is he still there?'

'Yes. He can stay till . . .' She paused. 'Until the funeral is over.'

'And then will you tell your father?'

'No. Philip will have to rejoin his regiment, but as soon as he's

299

demobbed, I'm leaving the theatre for good, and we're going to get a smallholding. I'm going to be a farmer's wife. And I'm going to walk dogs and have loads of plump rosy-cheeked children.'

Ralph stared at her. She was smiling so broadly he hadn't the heart to feel jealous of her Philip. But to leave the theatre!

'You think I'm mad giving it up, don't you?'

'Yes.'

'I never really chose it, you see. And I'll never be any good at it in my father's eyes.'

'But surely his opinion doesn't matter?'

'No, but mine does and I know my limitations.'

Ralph suddenly realised as he observed her glowing what being married meant. She had made love. Perhaps that's why she looked so soft when she came back. Perhaps that's what making love did to you. She reminded him of someone else. And then it came to him. It was the look on his mother's face, the morning she had had her lie-in. And his father too.

'May I kiss the bride?' he asked shyly.

'Of course,' she laughed.

He kissed her on the cheek and then before he realised what he was doing he had his arms around her and was hugging her tightly.

'I'm so pleased for you, Isla, I really am.' And he was. He never thought he would hear himself saying it, but he wanted more than anything for her to be happy.

He stretched his legs and moved them around. There were no feet bumping into his knees, no knees colliding into his feet. He opened his eyes to find himself in a huge room. A shaft of cold white light filtered through a chink in the curtains. He struggled on to his elbow, yawned and fell back against the pillows. A waft of steam rose from his mouth. He pulled the blankets up over his nose and lay there savouring the warmth of the bed and the silence, while he had the chance.

This was the day he would have to see his father. He could no longer flee to the theatre for sanctuary. The thought filled him with dread. It wasn't his father's rage that he couldn't face, it was his father's authority over him. Authority to remove him from school. Authority to push him into an apprenticeship he didn't want. And now authority to forbid him to go near a theatre again.

If he disobeyed, it would mean everyone in his family living in an atmosphere of tension and continual rows. But life without the theatre was no life. It would be like living without half one's blood supply. Nothing else had the magic, the excitement, the challenge and satisfaction.

Eventually he hopped out of bed in a pair of enormous pyjamas on to a tatty carpet and drew back the curtains. 'Snow. Snow. Snow and more snow.'

It was freezing in the bedroom so he pulled on his clothes as quickly as possible. He was about to leave when he noticed some orange marks on the pillow.

He found Mrs Egerton-Smythe and Basil Duke, a woman in her fifties, and a very young man sitting round the kitchen table over a pot of tea.

'Kettle's just boiled,' Mrs Egerton-Smythe announced, 'if you want to use it for washing in the bathroom.'

'Thanks,' said Ralph. 'I'm afraid I've left make-up on your pillow.'

'Bring it down later. I'll boil it.'

After he had washed, he came and joined the others for tea.

'What time is it?' he asked.

'Quarter to twelve,' Basil answered.

Ralph sprang to his feet. 'I'm so sorry. I never realised. I'll get to work straight away.'

'No, you won't,' said Mrs Egerton-Smythe. 'Eat that,' she said, pushing some dry toast in his direction. 'Sorry there's no butter.'

As he munched through the toast he discovered that the young man, who was called Timothy Trenton, was only three years older than him. He had been to drama school and he had come early so that he could see the cast in action on the opening of *Fit for Heroes*. He had a copy of *Robert's Wife* on the table. He was playing a young working class lad called Dick, who had got a girl into trouble and wanted to do the right thing by her, but was being prevented from doing so by his mother.

Listening to the young man's account of his part, Ralph was ashamed to feel a twinge of jealousy. Afraid that his silence would give it away, he raced through his breakfast and gulped down the tea as fast as he could.

'Don't bother about the front today,' said Mrs Egerton-Smythe. 'I think it would be rather nice to get wood ready for the garden room fire. Could you chop some up for me?'

'Yes, of course.'

'I'll go down to the river and pick up any driftwood,' offered Basil.

'If you bring it to the woodshed I'll show you where I stack it,' said Ralph. 'I have a sodden section, a semi-damp pile and a ready-for-chopping pile.'

'I'll clear out the grate,' said Mrs Egerton-Smythe.

'No I'll do that,' protested Ralph.

'Nonsense. I want to.'

'I'll give you a hand when I've finished reading this,' Timothy said indicating the play. 'I like to read it several times before I start thinking about how I want to play the part,' he added eagerly.

The young man's happiness was beginning to grate. Ralph carried his cup and plate over to the sink, grabbed his coat and flew out.

He could take out his anger and frustration on the wood. He started on the kindling wood first. As he chopped away at it, with wood leaping in all directions, he listened to Basil dragging or wheeling up timber from the river. The door would fling open and Basil would stagger in with his latest find and stack it up in the sodden section.

Ralph rested the axe for a while and stacked up a pile of wood in his arms ready to take it into the house. It was nicely stacked up to his chin when he realised that he couldn't open the door without most of the wood falling. Hearing footsteps approaching he waited expectantly for Basil to open the door. But instead he appeared to stop outside.

'Can you open the door?' he yelled. 'I've a full load.' He heard the footsteps go to the door and then it was swung open. 'Thanks,' he said gratefully and staggered towards it.

He had hardly stepped outside when two hands gripped the lapels of his greatcoat, lifted him almost off his feet and slammed him against the door sending the dry wood falling into the snow. Poised only inches from his nose was his father's furious face.

'Don't think you can hide here, my lad,' he rasped.

'They'll get wet,' Ralph cried, looking at all the kindling in the snow.

'Let them! Have you any idea what you've done?'

'I was trying to find a right time to tell you,' he gasped, feeling his father's hands pulling his jacket up to his throat. 'But it never seemed to be a good moment.'

'So why did you tell your mum? You made her deceive me, you good-for-nothing little sod.'

He drew him away from the shed wall and then flung him against it again. ''Ave you got any idea what they're goin' say at work? They'll think I've a Nancy-boy for a son when they find out.'

'How will they?' Ralph choked. 'If they think like that they won't read a theatre review, will they?'

'Pray for your sake they don't. Meanwhile you give your notice to Mrs Egerton-Smythe today and tomorrow morning you go to the Labour Exchange and you get a proper job. One that leaves you no time for playing around.'

'But I can't leave Mrs Egerton-Smythe's like that. I'll have to give her at least a week's notice to give her time to find someone else.'

He tightened his grip again. 'Give your week's notice, then, but that's it. If I ever, ever find you anywhere near that ruddy building . . .'

'Hey,' yelled a voice. 'What's going on?' Basil, who had been dragging a huge piece of timber, was running towards them. 'Leave him alone.'

Ralph's father whirled round, ready to do battle. Ralph groaned inwardly. This was worse than his worst nightmare. Then, to Ralph's astonishment, Basil gave a cry and dropped the wood and his father stood and stared at Basil, white-faced.

'Digger!' exclaimed Basil.

'Toff!' cried his father.

Then to Ralph's utter amazement, they suddenly ran laughing towards each other and embraced.

Eventually they broke apart, slamming each other on the back, until they stood hands on hips, gazing at one another.

'What the hell are you doing here?' asked Basil.

'I live in Braxley,' said Ralph's father. 'I come in to see my son.'

Ralph, his face burning with humiliation, hastily began picking up the wood from the snow. 'Your son!' Basil said, astounded. 'Ralph is your son!'

'Rayfe?' said his father, repeating Basil's pronunciation of his name.

'I had no idea. I mean, I knew he had the same surname but he doesn't look anything like you.'

''E don't sound nothin' like me neither,' added his father dryly.

'So how?' began Basil perplexed. 'Oh, your wife!'

'She don't talk like him neither.'

'You mean it's self-taught?'

'He stayed with a rector during the war and went to a grammar school. He lost his accent there.'

'So what's the row about?' asked Basil. 'I thought you were going to strangle him.'

'I dunno 'ow to tell you.'

'Come on.'

'I only discover he's been acting on a bleedin' stage, just like a ruddy pansy!'

At this juncture Ralph walked rapidly up the garden towards the kitchen. Behind him he could hear Basil roaring with laughter. Timothy opened the door for him and after wiping his boots, Ralph moved swiftly towards the hall.

'Where's Mrs Egerton-Smythe?' Ralph panted.

Timothy shrugged. 'Don't know. Sorry.'

She was in the garden room, peering out of the french windows. 'What on earth is going on out there? Who's that man with Basil?'

'My dad, I'm afraid.'

She glanced at him, alarmed. 'Your mother hasn't taken a turn for the worse, has she?'

'No. He has. He wants me to give you a week's notice, go to the Labour Exchange tomorrow and find some proper work.'

'Basil seems to be chatting in a very friendly manner.'

'They know each other.'

How?'

'I don't know. I didn't wait to find out. As soon as my father started on his all-men-in-the-theatre-are-pansies, I made a dash for it.'

'So he obviously doesn't know that Basil acts?'

'Hell. They're coming this way!' Ralph exclaimed. 'What'll I do?'

'Look busy. Lay the fire.'

'I hope this is going to burn. I dropped it in the snow.'

'They're heading for the kitchen. I'll go and see what's going on,' and she walked briskly out of the room.

Ralph concentrated on the fire. After he had laid the smaller wood in a pyramid, he realised that he needed to bring in more wood from the shed. Not wanting to walk through the kitchen, he opened the french windows and ran down to the woodshed. It was after his third trip back with an armful of logs that he found Mrs Egerton-Smythe waiting for him.

'Mystery solved,' she announced. 'They were in the same unit.'

'I didn't know Basil was in the army.'

'Why should you, the war is over.'

'That's what you think.'

'Let's get this fire going and leave them in here to talk about old times.'

'But I've talked about Basil at home,' said Ralph perplexed. 'And he's never said anything.'

'Basil Duke is his stage name.'

'Does Dad know what he does?' Ralph enquired.

'Now he does. The men thought he was an English teacher. He left them none the wiser. There's a great deal of leg-pulling going on in the kitchen. I wouldn't worry about it. They're chalk and cheese of course, but they obviously like and respect each other.' She looked thoughtful for a moment. 'It must be hard for men to leave a unit where their companions have been through situations that aren't always easy to talk about with people outside.'

Ralph lit the fire, and blew it into life, adding more wood until there was a good blaze going. There was a slam of the kitchen door and raised voices.

'He's a damn hard worker,' he could hear Basil saying. 'You should be proud of him.'

'That's no excuse for deceit,' his father said. 'Why didn't he tell me?'

'Would you have let him do it if you had known?'

'No.'

'There you are then. You didn't leave him much choice.'

The door opened. Ralph kept his back turned. He heard them move onto the settee and the sound of china behind. He glanced aside. Mrs Egerton-Smythe was carrying a tray of tea things and sandwiches. There were two cups and saucers, Ralph noted. He sprang to his feet.

'If you'll excuse me,' he said quietly, and then made for the door.

'I say,' said Timothy. 'Is he really working class?'

'Yes,' Ralph said.

'Do you think he'd lend me some of his clothes for the play?'

'Not in a million years. And anyway he hasn't enough to lend.'

The middle-aged woman, who he had learned was called Martha, leant over the kitchen table. 'I don't understand, if he's your father . . .'

Ralph knew what was coming and he suddenly felt a wave of fatigue sweeping through him. He was so fed up with explaining.

'Mrs Egerton-Smythe will explain,' he said. 'I've got chopping to do.'

In the woodshed he felt at peace. No more friction, no more answering awkward questions.

'Logs first,' he muttered to himself, and he dragged a long branch over a makeshift stool and picked up a saw. He had been sawing and chopping for some time and was just beginning to forget that he had any problems when he heard footsteps running through the snow. 'I thought it was too good to last,' he groaned.

The door swung open. It was Timothy. If he had come to watch

305

Ralph carrying out some working class activity to help him with his part he would be sorely tempted to behead him and shout, '*Vive La France!*'

'Yes?' he said with feigned indifference.

'Mr Neville. He wants to speak to you,' he said breathlessly.

Puzzled, Ralph ran back up with him.

Mrs Egerton-Smythe was chatting on the phone when he arrived in the hall.

'Ah, here he is!' she exclaimed. 'All yours,' she said to Ralph.

Ralph watched her go upstairs. He could hear his father and Basil still arguing in the garden room.

'Hello, Ralph speaking.'

'Ah, good. I'm glad I caught you. Cooled down a bit, have we?'

'A little,' said Ralph stiffly.

'Still interested in working for the theatre?'

Ralph's heart fell. 'Yes, but I'm having a few problems with my father.'

'You don't want to hear what it is, then?'

'Yes, of course, sir.'

Ralph listened to his proposal.

'Interested?'

'Very, but I need to ask my father.'

'When will you see him next? I know you're helping all day there.'

'He's here. I'll ask him now.'

Ralph put down the phone and walked towards the garden room, rather like Jean Pierre to the guillotine. Basil and his father were sitting on the settee eating sandwiches and talking about men Ralph had never heard of. Ralph walked towards the fireplace and stood in front of them.

Eventually they looked up.

'Dad,' began Ralph firmly. 'Mr Neville, from the Palace Theatre is on the telephone. He's offered me work for this week. No acting,' he added hurriedly. 'Just moving furniture and props about. What do you say?'

*I*t was a strange week. Once inside the theatre doors, there was order. Ralph checked furniture and props, chatted to Isla and members of the cast as they drifted in, ran from dressing room to dressing room giving the half, the quarter, the five minutes and Overture and Beginners calls, and then stood in the wings listening to the Billy Dixon Trio. Everything rolled forward in a stable framework and within that framework the adrenalin flowed.

Outside the theatre, there was drama and chaos. Ralph's father returned to the paper mill, but there was still not enough electricity for a full working day and in the time it had closed, because of the fuel crisis, many pipes had burst.

In the North of England there were blizzards so that any coal from the few mines which were functioning still could not reach the South.

Around Winford the snow continued to fall, followed by thaw and rain which solidified into ice and brought with it howling winds.

There was now meat in stock but vegetables were scarce. Market gardens lay buried in snow, potato pits were frozen, and the roads continued to be blocked. Thick slush even prevented milk being delivered.

A thaw began bringing with it floods, fog and landslides. By Friday there were fears of the river bursting its banks, as it began to pour with rain, snow and more rain.

At home, Auntie Win announced that she couldn't stand civvy life any more and that she had been for an interview at the ATS Office as they were asking for new recruits. Because of her outstandingly good war record with the Women's Auxiliary Air Force, she had a pretty high chance of being accepted. This had thrown Elsie into despair as she saw her chances of staying on at the Grammar dwindling, in spite of Ralph's assurances. Harry wasn't much help either, as he had heard that the school leaving age was being raised to 15 and unless his father could wangle an early apprenticeship at the Paper Mill and get the school authorities to turn a blind eye to the new regulations he would have to endure another year of elementary school.

The only good thing on the horizon was that his mother grew stronger by the day and seemed to accept Auntie Win's announcement philosophically.

To Ralph's surprise his father took up Ralph's suggestion of allowing Harry and Elsie to go to a cinema matinée at the Odeon, on the Saturday to see a new film for children which had only just been released, called 'Hue and Cry'. Ralph thought it might cheer them up.

Suddenly it was Saturday and Ralph was aware of it being yet again his final week's work at the theatre. He left early for the matinée performance and took Elsie and Harry with him. Because of the tremendous winds which were blowing, they were nearly kept at home, but they looked so devastated that the suggestion was put aside, especially since there were children going from the next street, which meant that they could travel back together, even though they were a rival gang.

Their father insisted that they wear wellies and his instinct had been right. As they began to draw closer to Winford, they could see that the streets nearest the river were flooded.

'Good eh?' Harry remarked excitedly, and Elsie had laughed and nearly lost her spectacles.

The High Street sloped upwards towards the cinema so that thankfully it was unaffected by the floods. Ralph left them at the box office and headed back to the theatre. He paddled through the stage door to find Wilfred attempting to mop water out.

'Waste of time,' grunted Wilfred, glancing up at him.

The stage door gave a loud slam. Ralph went to push it open, but the wind was so powerful that he had to lean his whole weight against it. Eventually he managed to open it.

'I need something to hold it back!' he yelled to Wilfred. 'Can you get something? I daren't let it go!'

'Hang on,' Wilfred shouted.

He reappeared with two stage weights, the kind Ralph had seen holding the wooden supports which were attached to stage flats.

They stared at the swirling river. There was no sign of a bank on either side. The houses on the other side had water creeping up their brickwork. Ralph hung on to his cap whilst Wilfred's white hair rose like waving seaweed.

They dashed inside. Ralph paddled to the notice board to see if the cast list for the next play had been put up. It hadn't. It was too early.

He stepped out of the water and onto the steps. 'I'll just check the props,' he said to Wilfred, 'and then come down and give you a hand.'

As soon as he saw Isla in the kitchen he asked her the usual daily question.

'Any news of Jane?'

'I'm sure there must be,' she said. 'But Mr Neville is keeping it close to his chest.'

'Do you think her father will insist that she comes back?'

'Knowing him, yes. From what I can make out, he has a reputation of always promising to deliver the goods.'

'What if Jane doesn't come back and they get a new ASM?'

'Don't think about it.'

Suddenly there was a loud howl. 'What on earth was that?'

'The wind,' said Ralph. 'It's really blowing a gale now outside.'

'I hope people from London have the sense to leave early. I hear the rails are flooded again.'

'Hello!' said a voice.

They looked up to find Basil in the doorway smiling. 'You're early,' Isla remarked.

'I heard the weather forecast. I thought I'd get here quick. The river's overflowed at the end of Mrs Egerton-Smythe's garden,' he added. 'It's creeping up the lawn. Luckily there's a bit of a slope, but if we get any more rain, I don't think there'll be much gardening for you, Ralph.'

'I have to go to the Labour Exchange on Monday anyway,' he said grimly.

'I know,' Basil said sadly. 'Still you've had this week.'

'Thanks to you,' said Ralph.

'Live for today, eh?'

'That's what I've been telling myself.'

There was a loud crash from somewhere upstairs. 'What the hell!' Basil exclaimed.

'It's the wind,' said Ralph.

'I'll go up and check the dressing rooms,' said Basil. 'Maybe one of the windows has blown open.'

Isla and Ralph retreated to the wings, set out the props and furniture ready for the quick change and checked that the personal props were in the dressing rooms. One by one, members of the cast drifted in in various states of dishevelment and wetness. To Isla's relief everyone made it and before Ralph realised, the lead up to another show had taken on its usual momentum.

The wind grew louder around the theatre during the performance and lights began to flicker. As soon as the matinée was over and they had set up for the evening show, Mr Johnson set oil lamps and candles backstage in case of an electricity cut.

In spite of the howling wind crashing round the building, Mr Johnson, the stagehand, Ralph and Isla managed to do the quick change from Act one scene one to scene two in one and a half minutes and the applause and laughter from the auditorium even penetrated the gales.

Once the curtain was down, it was all hands to the deck to clear furniture and props in an effort to beat a possible electricity cut.

Similarly the cast had fled into the wings to change, eager to find out if the trains were still running. Because of the flickering lights Mr Johnson stayed to help strike and set up the new scenery. Isla had just finished marking up where the furniture needed to be placed for *Robert's Wife* when they were suddenly thrown into total blackout.

After much shuffling, cursing and groping in the dark, an oil lamp was lit. Isla held it in the air while Mr Johnson and Ralph attempted to set the furniture, but it was taking so long that Mr Johnson suggested they all go home and return the next day.

Judith, Jack Walker, Sam and the stagehands had already left, so they were surprised to hear Wilfred's voice coming from the wings. They made their way towards him and held the lamp up. He had a script under one arm.

'Thought I'd better catch you before you two went home,' he announced to Isla and Ralph. He held the script up to Isla. 'You've got a part this week,' he said. 'And I've got a message for you, lad, from your Dad.'

'My Dad!'

'Yeah. He come in earlier.'

'To the stage door?' he asked incredulously.

'Are you going to let him give you the message?' butted in Isla.

'Yes of course. Sorry.'

'He said for you to stay at Mrs Egerton-summats, tonight, because of the weather, I suppose. He was pretty cut up about something. Asked for Mr Duke. They left together.'

'He and Basil Duke?'

'Yeh. You got a sister?'

'Yes. Elsie.'

'Seems she's in a spot of trouble. Your father wanted Mr Duke's help. Said something about Mrs Egerton-Summat lending a boat. Went on about ruddy civvy's. Or words to that effect. And how they was all useless. I didn't hear any more. Mr Duke just said "Tell me on the way", and they left in a hurry.'

'Thanks, Wilfred.'

'Mr Johnson,' interrupted Wilfred, 'I don't think Miss Isla should go home unaccompanied.'

'Oh, Wilfred, don't be daft,' Isla protested.

'I mean it. It's fierce enough to blow you over out there, and you'd better leave your bike 'ere for the same reason,' he said to Ralph.

The four of them made their way down the corridor, Mr Johnson carrying the oil lamp. As soon as they pushed open the door which led to the small landing above the steps, the howling from outside was alarming in its intensity. For a second they stood at the top of the steps and hovered motionless.

'I see what you mean,' shouted Mr Johnson.

By the time they reached the water which swirled round the stage door area, Ralph noticed Isla touch Mr Johnson's arm and though he couldn't hear what she was saying, he realised she had accepted his offer.

Ralph had never seen or heard anything so forceful in spite of his five years in Cornwall. It seemed more like a hurricane than a gale. They paddled towards the door. To their surprise they noticed a haze in the distance from some street lights. There was the sound of shattering glass and falling tiles.

'What about tomorrow?' shouted Isla to Mr Johnson.

'I'll phone you both then!' he yelled.

'I'll be staying at . . .' began Ralph.

'I know!' Mr Johnson bellowed. 'I have the number!'

It took the four of them to hold the stage door back so that it didn't slam itself shut into disintegration. They paddled towards the High Street, their arms linked.

Mr Johnson and Isla turned left. Ralph did not like the idea of Wilfred being on his own. Neither did Wilfred like the idea of Ralph being alone. They attempted to offer to accompany each other, both apologising at the same time, neither Ralph realised, wanting to offend the other.

Eventually after much arm waving and yelling, they separated and Ralph turned right into the High Street only to find himself almost knocked senseless. He staggered over to one of the shops and pinned himself against the building, his head and body bowed into the tremendous force of the wind.

As he inched his way piecemeal down the street, he was conscious of the tinkling of glass and he had to admit he was afraid, not of the storm, but of the heavy objects which were now flying through the air. He could easily be knocked unconscious if one hit him.

He inched his way along the shops, crawling on hands and knees when he had to pass an alleyway.

As he struggled down the tree-lined road which led to the avenue where Mrs Egerton-Smythe lived, he was startled to find trees

311

uprooted and stretched across the road. He glanced up at the ones still standing, ready to run for it if it seemed they were about to fall.

Buffeted and thrown by the gale, clinging to walls and gates, he ran the gauntlet of flying branches and slate tiles. He had been stumbling down the avenue for what seemed an hour when to his astonishment he saw a man pushing the gate of Mrs Egerton-Smythe's house open. It was so extraordinary to see another human being that it made him feel ridiculously safe, and then he noticed that he was carrying a bag. A doctor's bag.

He cried out to him, but it was obvious that the man could not hear him. Ralph watched him clinging to his Homburg, bent double as he pushed his way against the wind to his car.

He must be mad, thought Ralph, driving in this.

As he reached the path leading to the tradesmen's entrance, he noticed a tiny pool of light. With a sense of deep relief he staggered up the path, half drunk with exhaustion, and dived into the tiny conservatory outside the kitchen door. Glass crunched beneath his feet and a draught blowing across his face told him that several of the window panes had been blown in. The kitchen door was unlocked. To his surprise he saw that the electric light was on. The cuts had obviously not affected this part of Winford. A note with his name on it was leaning against a thermos. Next to it were pyjamas, woolly socks and a heavy jersey. The Aga was cold, but the kitchen still retained its warmth. As Ralph let it seep into him, a piercing pain shot into his ears. He pressed the palms of his hands against them for a second and then picked up the note.

'You'll find us in the garden room. Bring damp clothes with you.'

With numbed fingers, Ralph undid his boots.

Once changed, a heavy tiredness seemed to drag him down. He stepped into the cold hallway, clothes over one arm, thermos in the other. He had just shut the door when he was surprised to hear his father's voice coming from the garden room.

'Waste of time,' he was saying. 'Soon as they gets married they have to give up them sort of jobs.'

Ralph crept across the hall.

'Never a waste.' It was Mrs Egerton-Smythe speaking now. 'Suppose your daughter's husband was injured or became an invalid or died. If she had children she would have something to fall back on. And even if she didn't work again, surely her education would help your grandchildren.'

'But there's bus fares and uniform and glasses.'

'Uniforms you can get second-hand. I do for my daughter.'

'I dunno.'

312

'You could at least let her stay until she does her School Cert.'

'Ralph's got it and it got him sacked.'

'Then they're fools. Yes they are,' she said firmly. 'He's a hard worker.'

'Oh yes. I'll give him that.'

Ralph was surprised to hear such praise.

'But stubborn.'

'Sounds like he takes after his father.'

Ralph froze, waiting for his father's wrath to descend, but to his amazement he heard him give a laugh.

'Mebbe,' he commented.

Quickly Ralph retraced his steps, opened and closed the kitchen door noisily and thumped as loudly as he could in stockinged feet to the garden room.

Standing in the open doorway he found himself staring at a clothes horse and chairs arranged around the fireplace. Damp clothes were draped across them, steaming in front of the fire. Basil and his father were on the settee facing it and Mrs Egerton-Smythe was sitting on the edge of the armchair seat turning over a shirt. Behind the settee, asleep on a camp bed was Harry. His father was holding a small figure wrapped up in a blanket on his lap. It was Elsie, also asleep.

'Close the door,' Mrs Egerton-Smythe protested. 'You're bringing in the draught.'

Ralph quickly did so. He rushed over to the settee and gazed down at his sister. Her hair was still damp and she looked pale. On a low table in front of her lay a smashed pair of spectacles with only one ear piece.

'What's happened?' he asked, shakily.

'Pour yourself out some tea,' commanded Mrs Egerton-Smythe.

'I'll make him some toast,' said Basil, and he cut a piece from a loaf and sat on a pouffe in front of the fire with a toasting fork strategically placed between the clothing.

'She and Harry were mucking about on one of them bomb sites on the other side of the river,' his father said. 'Playin' cops and robbers, or something like that. It was all to do with this 'Hue and Cry' film. The gang from the next street were playing silly buggers, and started teasing Elsie for being a girl and when Harry stood up for her they took it further than they had intended. Anyway they starts pushin' this wall what was loose. Elsie's glasses got broke and she fell and got stuck under fallen rubble. The little bleeders ran off leaving Harry to try and free her. And all the time the river was risin'. When he couldn't get her out he ran for help but he couldn't

313

get back across the river.'

'But how had they got across in the first place?'

'They nicked a boat, didn't they?' he said fiercely. 'And they'd rowed back in it.' His voice began to shake uncontrollably. 'Someone spotted him yelling eventually and called the police but the weather was so bad they couldn't make it across to him.'

'To cut a long story short,' said Mrs Egerton-Smythe, 'your father and Basil borrowed my boat and took various ropes and tools and somehow managed to do what the police couldn't do.'

'I suppose the Army did us some good eh?' said Basil to Ralph's father.

His father gave a brief nod. 'We found her spectacles first,' he said quietly. 'They was floatin' in the water. I thought she'd bought it. The flood water was so high and it were freezing cold, but she'd managed to claw her way up to a sitting position.'

'We found her up to her chest in water,' said Basil, 'singing.'

Ralph smiled.

'We freed her, wrapped her up and put her in the boat.'

'But is she all right?' Ralph asked. 'I saw the doctor leaving.'

'Yeah,' said his father. 'Shock and exposure,' he said, 'but she's strong, he said. She don't look like it I know,' he added, smiling down at her. 'She's such a skinny little thing, but she's got a fire inside her.'

'Stubbornness perhaps?' said Mrs Egerton-Smythe pointedly.

He sighed.

'Yeah. I do seem to have strong willed nippers.'

'Very healthy I think,' said Mrs Egerton-Smythe. 'They'll be survivors.'

Ralph watched his father glance down with enormous fondness at his sister and in spite of being glad for her sake, he was alarmed to feel jealous. He sat down by him and unscrewed the thermos. As he poured out the tea, he was suddenly aware of the three separate areas in his life, all being together in the same room. He didn't know whether to be glad or sorry.

Outside, the wind swept under the veranda roof and rattled the French windows.

'Clocks go forward tonight,' he commented warming his hands around the cup. 'It's summertime now.'

Act Three
March – April 1947

ONE

*T*imothy was standing in the kitchen doorway, yelling his head off about something, but the wind which was bursting through the small smashed windows and threatening to shatter the remaining ones, drowned his voice.

Ralph crunched his way through the broken glass with a dustpan in his hand and leaned closer.

Timothy was pointing wildly behind him. 'The phone!' he shouted. 'For you!'

Ralph felt a firm hand on his shoulder. His dad had been trying to help him clear the debris in the tiny conservatory outside the kitchen. Between them they had attempted to block up the exposed frames but, as fast as they boarded up one, the wind only blew it back out again with ferocity. All they could do was chip away the broken bits and clear the floor until the next window was smashed in.

His father took the dustpan from him and waved him in. Ralph stepped into the kitchen where he hurriedly undid his bootlaces.

When he reached the hall, he found Mrs Egerton-Smythe deep in conversation. 'Plenty. They'll have to be cleared a bit, but with a few willing hands it shouldn't take too long. It'll be cold, of course.' There was a pause. 'I thought you might be. Why not use two. Or three, if you need. Now what about the scenery . . . Well, that's something, but if you have . . .' She laughed. 'Good lord! A week! You think it'll be that long? Yes, I can imagine. Is he? No! No, we haven't even thought about lunch yet.' She turned aside. 'He's here, by the way. Yes, I'll stay here and see what he says and then go and get his father if needed. Yes, it is, isn't it?' she said. 'Every cloud, as they say. I'll pass you to him now.' She handed him the receiver. 'It's Mr Johnson.'

'Hello, Mr Johnson. If it's about work this afternoon, I've warned my father I'll need to go back to the theatre today and he's agreed.'

'Good,' said the voice at the other end. 'But things are a little more complicated. It wasn't a government electricity cut last night. Our electricity has been flooded. It's pretty old anyway and this is the final straw. The theatre will be dark for at least a week by our reckoning.'

'A week! But what about *Robert's Wife*?'

'It'll have to be postponed till next week. The good news is that Jane's father has come up trumps. He's obviously cut up about what amounts to a breach of contract on his daughter's part and is going to foot half the bill and get some new equipment put in.'

'Splendid! So you want me to be available to finish setting up during the week?'

'More than that. I've been chatting to Mr Neville this morning. It seems that the producer of *Hobson's Choice* is none to keen on Isla playing a part her size *and* being on the book.'

'He's not going to take it away from her?' Ralph protested. 'No. Can you belt up a minute?'

'Sorry.'

'The producer is Arnold Swann. He wants someone else to be on the book for rehearsals *and* for performances, and has asked specifically for you.'

'Me?' Ralph yelled.

Out of the corner of his eye he caught Mrs Egerton-Smythe smiling. She shrugged as if to say it had nothing to do with her.

'But what about Mr Neville?'

'He's agreed.'

'I don't believe it.'

'Just this once, he said. But . . .'

Ralph laughed. 'I'm not to get any ideas that it'll lead to any more work?'

'In a nutshell.'

'On the book,' Ralph breathed.

'I take it you'll do it, then?'

'If my father agrees.'

'I'll have a chat with him.'

Ralph hesitated. He didn't want Mr Johnson to hear how working class his father sounded, and then he felt ashamed of his snobbery.

'Thanks,' he murmured.

'That's the good news. The bad news is that we can't rehearse *Hobson's Choice* or do runs of *Robert's Wife* to keep it up to scratch in the theatre, because there's no lighting. But Mrs Egerton-Smythe has kindly offered us rooms in her house. Tell me, are they big?'

'Enormous.'

'Good. If Mr Neville agrees I'll be contacting you and Isla this afternoon and we'll see what rehearsal props we can find for tomorrow. Now you better let Mrs Egerton-Smythe fetch your father.'

Ralph turned to her. 'Yes?' she asked.

'Yes,' he said. 'Thanks.'

While she was gone, Ralph decided to broach the subject of the new ASM.

'Any news about Jane?' he asked casually.

'No. Except that it looks highly unlikely that she'll be back.'

'So Mr Neville will be looking for a new ASM?'

'Yes. But not until this fiasco is over. Also it looks as if he'll be needing two now plus a stage manager because of Isla.'

'Why?' he asked alarmed.

'When Mr Neville gives an ASM or stage manager a biggish part, you know that he's thinking of making them an acting member of the company. If I'm reading the situation correctly, he'll be looking for someone to be ASM and play as cast, an ASM to replace Jane, and a stage manager to replace Isla. Isla's been with us for some time now and apart from the little hiccup in the Isle of Wight, she's made a good impression.'

'So at the most,' he said, 'I've two more weeks to go if my father lets me?'

'Three. If the cast agree, Mr Neville is going to rehearse *Hobson's Choice* for two weeks before the first performance.'

'That'll please them,' said Ralph.

'Not necessarily. Remember actors don't get paid during rehearsals, and if they're not performing *Robert's Wife*.'

'Oh, I see what you mean.'

At that moment, his father appeared, in the hall. 'Mr Johnson, my father is here.'

Presenting the receiver to his father he was conscious of his hand shaking. He casually sat at the foot of the staircase.

'John Hollis speakin'.'

Ralph held his breath. 'So when can he finish this set-up thing, then? . . . Well, he can't hang around, turnin' down work till it suits . . . Yeah. Till today. I'm packin' him off to the Labour Exchange tomorrer.' He gave a sigh. 'Seems to be quite a few of these emergencies . . . Yeah. Well, I take your point. But I won't have him setting foot on-stage . . . I suppose that's sumthin'. Just in the background, eh? . . . Three weeks! I dunno. Three weeks is a long time. Yeah. That's true. There ain't much at the moment.

Unless you fancy coal mining.'

He was smiling, observed Ralph. Actually smiling! His father glanced at him wearily.

'You really want to do this "book" business?' he asked Ralph. Ralph sprang to his feet.

'Yeah,' his father answered for him. He then made a placating gesture. 'That's all right, Mr Johnson. If it helps. Yeah. Yeah. Do you want to speak to him before he takes off?' And he handed the receiver back to Ralph.

'Thanks, Dad. You won't regret this!'

'I already am,' his dad grunted.

Hobson's Choice was a Victorian comedy in four acts, set in Lancashire in 1880, in which a timid and illiterate lad is persuaded under duress by his tyrannical boss's eldest daughter to marry her. She, unlike her two younger prettier sisters, looks after her father and runs his boot shop. In Willie Mossop she sees a great talent and a hard worker and she teaches him to read. Gradually through her, he grows in confidence and eventually takes over Hobson's boot shop and their marriage of convenience flowers into an affectionate sort of love.

Mr Neville was playing Hobson, Annie Duncan the eldest daughter, Maggie, and Basil, Willie Mossop. Geraldine Maclaren and Isla were playing the two younger sisters who were being courted by suitors, played by Raymond Maclaren and Felix. The smaller parts were being played by four other actors and Arnold Swann.

'Curtain-up,' said Ralph shakily. 'Alice and Victoria are behind the counter.'

It was Monday morning. Geraldine Maclaren and Isla stood in their long practice skirts behind the row of chairs which represented the counter.

'Oh, we should be knitting and reading,' said Geraldine.

'I put a book and some needles on that table over there,' Ralph said.

Annie Duncan as Maggie walked towards her sisters.

'Oh, it's you,' Geraldine remarked as Alice. 'I hoped it was Father going out.'

'It isn't,' said Annie as Maggie. She stopped and pointed to a table and chair set inside the shop front. 'I presume that's my desk,' she said to Ralph. Ralph nodded.

She crossed over to it, marking it in her script, as did Ralph in the book. 'He *is* late this morning,' said Geraldine.

'He got up late,' said Maggie and she proceeded to open the large book Ralph had set on the 'desk'.

'Has he had breakfast yet, Maggie?' said Isla, as Victoria, her nose still in her book.

'Breakfast! With a Masons' meeting last night?'

'He'll need reviving,' Isla commented.

'Then I wish he'd go and do it.'

'Are you expecting anyone, Alice?' asked Isla as Victoria.

'Yes, I am, and you know I am, and I'll thank you both to go when he comes.'

As the scene progressed, Felix came in as Alice's suitor, and Maggie, tired of him visiting the shop so often on the pretext of buying shoelaces, bossed him into buying a new pair of boots, and leaving his old ones to be mended. The producer gave the cast their moves and they scribbled them down.

Eventually Mr Neville tottered in from the living quarters as the bumptious Henry Horatio Hobson, suffering from a hangover. There ensued an argument between him and his daughters, mainly over the younger ones having been seen walking down the streets with 'humps' behind them, his name for bustles. Ralph, his finger on the script, couldn't help smiling. Mr Neville was playing the part magnificently already.

'Do you want us to dress like mill girls?' Isla exclaimed.

'No. Nor like French madams, neither,' growled Mr Neville. 'It's unEnglish, I say.'

'We shall continue to dress fashionably, Father.'

Ralph listened with amusement as Mr Neville launched into a tirade. 'You don't know when you're well off,' he yelled, coming to the end of his speech. 'But you'll learn it when I'm done with you. I'll choose a pair of husbands for you, my girls. That's what I'll do.'

'Can't we choose husbands for ourselves?'

'I've been telling you for the last five minutes that you're not even fit to choose dresses for yourselves.'

'You're talking a lot to Vicky and Alice, Father,' said Annie as Maggie. 'Where do I come in?'

Mr Neville swung round astonished. 'You?' he exclaimed.

'If you're dealing husbands round, don't I get one?'

'Geraldine, Isla,' interrupted the producer, 'I'd like you to stare at her as if she's said something in Swahili.'

They nodded and marked it quickly in their scripts.

'Carry on,' he said.

'Well, that's a good one!' and at this Mr Neville threw back his head and gave a roar of laughter. 'You with a husband!'

Ralph watched nervously as the scene was moved. He knew Basil Duke would be starting soon and he was keen to see what he was going to be like. So far the cast had been very impressive. Isla had positively sparkled. Her opening had terrific potential. Already she seemed to have her part ready for performance. Martha the actress who was staying at Mrs Egerton-Smythe's, was playing the rich Mrs Hepworth who insisted on knowing who had made her shoes. Mr Swann moved the actors around the area which was to be the trapdoor. Another actor who played the foreman, Tubby Wadlow, came and crouched in the square with Basil. Slowly Basil rose.

'Are you Mossop?' demanded Mrs Hepworth.

'Yes, mum,' murmured Basil almost incoherently in a northern accent.

'You made these boots?' Basil made as if to look at the prop boots Ralph had provided.

'Yes, I made them last week.'

'Take that.'

But instead of ducking as if about to be hit, as it was requested in the script, Basil spoke to himself. 'I duck and raise my head. Take visiting card.' And he went through the motion of taking it.

To Ralph's surprise, Basil appeared not to be acting at all. Instead he mumbled as he wrote down his moves. Perhaps it took him time to warm up, thought Ralph. He was off-stage soon after, having exited down the trap-door and the scene progressed. Ralph knew he would be back again for the scene where Maggie proposed to him. It was a lovely scene and he was looking forward to it.

There followed a scene, where Jim, a drinking pal of Hobson, arrived and the girls were waved away. Ralph took down the moves of the two men as they discussed what marrying the two younger daughters would entail. Having been told he would need to give a money settlement when they married, Hobson decided he would rather they were never married and left with his friend for a pub called the Moonrakers. The next scene was the one Ralph had been waiting for. Maggie was on her own now. Ralph watched her mime opening the trap-door. Basil was crouching in the square. 'Willie, come here.'

'Yes, Miss Maggie?'

'Come up, and put the trap down; I want to talk to you.'

Basil stood up, his eyes riveted to his script. 'We're very busy in the cellar,' he mumbled.

'Show me your hands, Willie,' she commanded.

'They're dirty,' said Basil, hardly looking up.

'Just step stage left of the trap-door nearest the door,' said Mr Swann.

Basil scribbled the moves down, as did Ralph in the book. 'I hold out my hands,' Basil stated, putting one hand out.

'Yes. They're dirty,' said Maggie, 'but they're clever. They can shape the leather like no other man's that ever came into the shop.'

To Ralph's embarrassment Basil continued to stumble and mumble his way through the moves. Annie Duncan was somewhere between Isla's standard and Basil's. Ralph glanced occasionally at the producer to see if he looked concerned, but he was acting as if there was nothing wrong. Perhaps he knew something Ralph didn't. A death in Basil's family or something.

They were coming up to the close of Act One where Hobson, informed by Maggie that Willie Mossop was going to marry her, took his the belt to him.

'You're making a great mistake, Mr Hobson, and – ' said Basil into his script.

'You'll put aside your weakness for my Maggie if you've a liking for a sound skin,' roared Hobson. 'You'll waste a gradely lot of brass at chemist's if I am at you for a week with this.'

Mr Neville then swung a belt strap. 'I'm none wanting thy Maggie,' read Basil, 'it's her that's after me, but I'll tell you this, Mr Hobson: if you touch me with that belt, I'll take her quick, aye, and stick to her like glue.'

They were wonderful lines, thought Ralph, and yet Basil was hardly giving them any expression at all, whereas Mr Neville was huffing, blowing and roaring as Mr Hobson and he didn't seem the least worried by Basil Duke's abominable performance. And then there was the strike of the belt, and Willie, his temper riled, defiantly kissed Maggie on the cheek. The act came to an end with Maggie flinging her arms round Willie and Mr Neville sitting staring at them, amazed and perplexed.

'Right,' said the producer. 'Act Two.'

It was in the dining-room, when the actors who lived outside Winford had gone to the café and the lodgers at Mrs Egerton-Smythe's had gone to the kitchen to have something to eat, that Ralph asked Isla about Basil. He was helping her set up for a run of *Robert's Wife*.

'Isla, you're brilliant as Vicky,' he exclaimed. 'You're mad to want to give it up.'

'It's just a facility I have,' she shrugged.

He picked up two of the chairs. 'Is anything worrying Basil?' he asked casually.

'Not that I know of,' she said. 'Why?'

'He seemed a bit subdued.'

'He's often like that when we do the moves. He feels his way in,' she explained.

'Oh.'

She smiled. 'It's your first time at a first rehearsal, isn't it?'

'I was at *Vive La Liberté*.'

'Yes, but they were mostly caricatures. Actors like Basil would much prefer fortnightly or three weekly rep. Come to think of it, most people would. Now,' she said, 'props.'

TWO

'*T*he girl in the aspidistra case has been freed,' said Ralph's mother over her huge spectacles.

'About time too,' Aunty Win commented. 'He had it coming to him.'

Ralph looked up from his prompt book where he had been ruling lines for lighting cues on the blank page on the left. It was late on Friday evening and his aunt was ironing a blouse for the morning while his mother read bits out to her from the latest *Winford Observer*.

'Had aspidistras coming to him?' Ralph commented, puzzled.

'He was drunk,' Elsie informed him.

'And it wasn't the first time,' interrupted his aunt. 'Huge fellow, he was.'

'Seventeen stone and six foot,' said Elsie, 'and he comes up the stairs saying 'ow he's goin' to cut everyone up into pieces. And she chucks this pot with an aspidistra in it and it knocks him down the stairs.'

'And he dies of fixation,' Harry said.

'Asphyxiation,' Elsie said.

'Which probably means that he choked on his own vomit,' Aunty Win added with relish.

'Win!' Ralph's mother exclaimed.

'It's all right. We've had supper. Now read me out the bits Kitty sent from the *Kent Messenger*.'

This produced groans. 'I don't know why you're making such a fuss,' she said.

'Because she'll have chosen all the bits you like,' Joan said.

'Of course she will. She wants me to give her a nice present for that baby of hers when it comes.'

'Win!' cried his mother again.

'Anyway,' she went on, 'you're just as interested in the string bag strangler case as I am, ain't you?'

Ralph's mother unfolded newspaper cuttings from a letter. '*Kent Messenger* picture led to strangler's arrest. Vital clue in Wrotham Hill Murder case. A small photograph on the front page of the *Kent Messenger* of the crocheted string bag was the means of bringing a murderer to book.'

At this point Ralph switched off and continued going through the prompt book, painstakingly rubbing out messy scrawls and rewriting moves and cues again neatly in pencil. He had nearly survived the first week of being on a book for a rehearsal period. The standing-in for Jane had paid off. It wasn't half as difficult as he thought it would be and the producer seemed willing for him to succeed.

The following morning there was to be a run of the whole play, followed in the afternoon by a run of *Robert's Wife*, on stage with electricity or oil lamps. The producer wanted them to get used to the acoustics of the theatre again.

'Oooo. Here's something that will really get your blood racing, Aunty Win,' cried Elsie. 'Right up your street.'

'Go on then!' Aunty Win said impatiently.

Ralph sighed and prepared himself for death by drowning, strangulation and stabbing by a suicidal bigamist.

Elsie took a deep breath. 'Flood-damaged carpets restored as new,' she announced dramatically. 'For drying and cleaning Axminster cotton, Wilton, Indian, three shillings and fourpence per square yard. Chinese or Turkish three shillings . . .'

But her voice was drowned with everyone collapsing with laughter. Even Aunty Win was smiling. 'Very funny,' she commented.

Things had certainly changed lately, observed Ralph. Joan was happier in the knowledge that two babies were coming into the world. Aunty Win had been accepted for the ATS and had given in her notice at the shop. Civvy street, she declared, was not her cup of tea. His mother appeared more relaxed and energetic, and Dad had managed to secure an apprenticeship for Harry as soon as he had reached his fourteenth birthday, which had the effect of lifting Elsie's spirits, so it was a surprise that his parents decided to put their fly in the ointment that night when everyone was at their happiest. They waited until everyone had their tea in front of them as if tannin might soothe the blow.

'Your father and I have got an announcement to make,' said Ralph's mother suddenly.

Ralph noticed a strange glow on his mother's face and, to his anguish, he felt his face burn. They were going to announce the coming infant. Joan was looking expectant. His aunt wary. Only Harry and Elsie didn't know what was coming. 'We've talked it over and we think that it's for the best.' And she indicated Ralph's father.

'We're going to apply for one of them new council houses they're building in these new towns.'

'Most of them have got three bedrooms *and* a bathroom and an indoor lav and a nice garden,' said his mother.

This was greeted by a stunned silence. Harry was the first to speak. 'But what about the paper mill, Dad?'

'I'll travel there and back but, if the worst comes to the worst, maybe I'll retrain for somethin' else.'

'But, Dad,' Ralph exclaimed, 'you're always going on about what a wonderful pension scheme they've got there.'

'I know.'

What about me apprenticeship?' cried Harry.

'And my job,' interrupted Joan.

'But you're always complaining about it,' Ralph's father said. 'You might find nicer work in a new town.'

'But they're out in the country, ain't they?'

'Yeah. That's just what your Aunt Ellen and I think is so good. Nice fresh air for us all. Pretty surroundings.'

'No cinemas or dances,' put in Joan.

'No gang in the next street,' said Harry.

'Dad,' said Elsie, quietly, 'does that mean I'll have to leave the grammar?'

'I'd see if there was one nearby you could go to. I'm sure it can be done. And that's another thing,' he said, 'your Ma and I have had a long chat about that too, and I have agreed to let you stay at school long enough to take the School Cert exam everyone keeps going on about.'

'Oh, Dad!' said Elsie, her face flushed, and she raced across to him and flung her arms around his neck.

'But you must leave after that. And no more borrowing glasses from your old school.'

'But, Dad, I won't be able to do the work.'

'Yes, you will. You're having proper ones of your own. I'm

taking you to an optician and you can get tested and measured, or whatever they do to eyes.'

'Oh, Dad!'

'But you're to wear string round 'em. I can't afford for you to lose 'em.'

'I think you've forgotten something,' said Aunty Win, ominously.

'What's that, Win?' said Ralph's mother.

'The small question of uniform,' she said with finality. 'If you moved her to a new grammar school she'd have to get a new uniform.'

Elsie's face fell.

'I've thought of that,' said Ralph's dad. 'You can get second-hand uniforms. Mrs Egerton-Smythe told me.'

'Huh!' said his aunt.

Ralph felt his whole world crumbling. He knew he only had two more weeks of work left at the theatre and he realised that, unconsciously, he had been hanging on to the hope that he might get more work if he just kept showing his face. If he lived away, there would be no chance of that.

'Joan,' said his mother, 'you're always going on about having a nice modern house. I thought you'd be pleased. You wouldn't have to have baths in a tin tub in here any more.'

'I know,' she said miserably.

'It wouldn't be immediate,' said Ralph's father, looking at everyone. 'But we've got to do something. This place is leaking like a sieve. These storms have blown half the tiles off the roof.'

'Can't you get the landlord to replace them?' said Ralph. 'He's charging enough.'

'He's old. He can't cope.'

'He's not too old to raise the rent.'

'That's true,' said his mother.

'It's only our room what's leaking Dad,' said Harry. 'And we don't mind, do we?'

'No,' said Ralph.

'Our bedroom's just started leaking too,' said his mother quietly. 'Couldn't we look for somewhere in Winford?'

'With the housing shortage!' his dad exclaimed. 'We're lucky to have this one as it is. Look at Kitty and Frank!'

'These things take time,' said his mother. 'So we're putting our names down now.'

There was a silence.

'Well, I don't know, love,' said Ralph's father. 'There's no pleasing them.'

Saturday and Sunday were taken up with two runs and moving the *Robert's Wife* props on the set, and setting aside boxes in the scene dock ready for *Hobson's Choice*. It was difficult to remember that they had another week to play with but, having three sets to dress, Sam Williams and Judith were relieved at having the extra time. The electricity was working. On the Monday, *Robert's Wife* had its dress rehearsal and opening night but it was decided to keep the *Hobson Choice* rehearsals at Mrs Egerton-Smythe's so that Sam and Judith could have the extra room for painting and drying the sets on stage as well as in the scene dock. They would be back in the theatre for Friday morning rehearsal. Pay-day.

It was on Wednesday morning that Basil Duke's performance changed. The producer had decided to rehearse the scenes, between Maggie and Willie Mossop, so that they could work on the changes which came over them before and during their marriage. As soon as the proposal scene began Ralph had the peculiar sensation of the hairs on his head prickling. Suddenly he was unaware of watching acting.

It was real, what Basil and Annie were doing. Imperceptibly, they had developed little mannerisms, different ways of holding themselves and walking naturally, as if they had gradually entered the characters' skins. Watching the two of them working together with the producer, he was conscious of witnessing something he would never forget. He watched Maggie soften, watched Willie Mossop grow in maturity and stature. And then it was the end of Act Four and Willie Mossop had successfully returned to Hobson's boot shop after successfully running his own with Maggie, and had taken over.

'What are you doing?' cried Maggie, as Willie took her hand. 'You leave my wedding ring alone,' and she pulled her hand away.

'You've worn a brass one long enough,' Willie said.

'I'll wear that ring for ever, Will.'

'I was for getting you a proper one, Maggie.'

'I'm not preventing you. I'll wear your gold for show, but that brass stays where you put it, Will, and if we get too rich and proud, we'll just sit down together quiet and take a long look at it, so as we'll not forget the truth about ourselves . . . Eh, lad?'

She very tenderly touched his arm and Willie turned to look at her. And it was obvious to Ralph that this unlikely pair had fallen in love with one another.

'Eh, lass!' he said, and he kissed her affectionately.

Suddenly Mr Neville as Hobson re-entered with a hat on and the intimacy was broken. Maggie broke away. 'Ready, Father,' she said in her old business-like manner. 'Come along to Albert's.'

And Hobson, gazing at her meekly, answered, 'Yes, Maggie.'

They crossed in front of Willie and moved to the off-stage door, leaving Willie alone. Ralph had long since left looking at the book. Mesmerised he stared at Willie coming down-stage in amazement, an expression of utter disbelief at being the new boss.

He was struggling, searching, grasping for something to convey what he was feeling and then it came. 'Well, by gum!' he exclaimed.

Ralph and Annie burst out laughing and Basil marched off to the door. It was magical. He was magical. He was no longer Basil Duke, but Willie Mossop, and through the play Ralph could see what Maggie had spotted in him. A gifted, broken, loveable man, who just needed someone to draw out what was already there.

On Thursday morning, Mr Swann concentrated again on particular scenes in the play, stopping and starting, going through them again and again, and then running them through and giving them notes. It was while Ralph had been sent to the kitchen to make tea, that they had an unexpected visitor. In the garden room the producer was rehearsing with Mr Neville and Hobson's drinking crony. In the dining room, Basil and Annie were going through their scenes, and in the library, Isla and Geraldine were going through their bits with Felix and Raymond.

Mrs Egerton-Smythe was in the kitchen, reading through a pile of play scripts, and writing comments about them. They were in three piles GA, PGIR, MHT, which translated meant, 'god awful', 'potentially good if rewritten' and 'must have it!' There was nothing in the 'must have it' pile yet, but there were five plays in the GAs and one PGIR.

Queenie was up to her hands in flour and Ralph was just about to take a tray of tea round when the front door bell rang.

'It would!' moaned Queenie, gazing at her hands.

'Mmm?' murmured Mrs Egerton-Smythe, her head in her hands and a leaking pen in her mouth as she ploughed through a period drama.

'Shall I answer it?'

'What?' said Mrs Egerton-Smythe absently.

'The door. I'll get it.'

'Oh, yes,' she said vaguely.

'It might be the rector with boxes of boots,' said Ralph, 'although I did say I'd pop round this afternoon.' He placed the tray on the hallstand table. From three rooms came loud vibrant voices all with northern accents. Ralph strode towards the door and flung it open, to find himself looking up at Charles Egerton-Smythe. Charles Egerton-Smythe opened his mouth to speak and then noticed the cacophony of voices coming from every direction.

'What on earth?' he began.

'*Hobson's Choice*,' Ralph paused 'Rehearsals.'

'Rehearsals? Here?'

'We'll be back in the theatre tomorrow,' Ralph added reassuringly.

'I don't believe I'm hearing this,' he muttered. 'Is Mrs Egerton-Smythe here?'

'Yes. Shall I ask if she can see you?'

Ralph watched him change from red to purple to puce and back to red again.

'Of course she'll see me!'

'Well, she's up to her ears in work,' Ralph began, and he felt his face reddening. He didn't know if Mrs Egerton-Smythe's son knew of her new job.

'What work would that be?' he asked slowly.

'Um,' said Ralph, and he attempted to wave his hand nonchalantly. 'I'll tell her you're here.'

'Yes, do that, will you?' he said with rising sarcasm. 'Don't worry about the door, I'll close it after myself.'

'Yes, of course,' Ralph stammered, and he backed towards the kitchen.

As Ralph opened the door, he found Mrs Egerton-Smythe mumbling into the manuscript. 'Frightful! Awful! Even I can tell this dialogue doesn't come off the page. If I come across another zounds or alack-a-day, I shall spit.'

'Mrs Egerton-Smythe,' Ralph began tentatively.

'Oh, here's something new; "Take that, thou varlet." Oh, no, here comes another alack-a-day.'

'Mrs Egerton-Smythe?' She looked up. 'You've got blue-black ink all down your chin.'

'Is that what you've interrupted me for?'

'No. Mr Egerton-Smythe is here.'

'Jolly good,' and she carried on reading. 'Oh!' she said startled. 'Zounds!'

'Cripes!' said Queenie.

'And alack-a-day,' added Ralph.

'What's he doing here?' said Mrs Egerton-Smythe.

'I don't know.'

'Where is he?'

'In the hall. He's not too happy. I think I may have put my foot in it.'

'How?'

'I said you were working, but I didn't say what on.'

At this juncture the door burst open and in he stormed. 'Am I to be left in that cold blustery hall . . .'

He stopped and stared at the mounds of play scripts on the table. Queenie was busily washing flour off her hands.

'I'd better take the tea around before it gets cold,' and Ralph backed out of the room closing the door behind him.

Within seconds, the entire cast of *Hobson's Choice* had crept out into the hall and were engaged in the ancient art of eavesdropping.

'Do you mind telling me what the hell is going on?' they heard Charles Egerton-Smythe roar.

'Didn't Ralph tell you?'

'Ralph? Do you mean Hollis the gardener's boy?'

'Ridiculous title, isn't it?' she said. 'He can't be the gardener's boy because I have no gardener. Come to that, I'm not sure whether I have a garden, it's so long since I've seen it.'

'Mother!'

'Would you like me to leave, ma'am?' they heard Queenie ask shakily.

'Who is he?' Ralph heard Mr Neville whisper.

'Her son,' whispered Basil, smiling.

'What's the problem?'

'His mother,' laughed Basil and he suddenly pressed his lips together to control himself.

Mr Neville looked perplexed.

'Charles, did you come about anything in particular?' they heard Mrs Egerton-Smythe remark. 'Only I've rather a lot to get through.'

'Where did all this come from?'

'The Palace Theatre.'

'What are they doing here?'

'I'm reading them.'

'What for?'

'Charles, I'm beginning to feel I'm in the witness box.'

'That boy said you had a job.'

'Yes.'

'You don't mean paid, do you?'

'Yes.'

There was a snuffling choking sound. 'Shall I put the kettle on, ma'am,' they heard Queenie say, falteringly.

'She'll be offering to make high tea soon,' commented Ralph.

'Have you any idea of the damage to Father's reputation . . .'

'Charles, your father is dead. I think you ought to accept that.'

'His memory is not dead, Mother. His library is . . . is a . . .'

'Shrine?' put in his mother.

'Mother.' There was a pause. 'There are people, theatre people rehearsing in there. Where are the law students?'

'They never came back.'

'What did you say to them?'

'Nothing. I just ran out of fuel. It appears they must only have come for the free heating. Once that had gone, the lure of your father's collection faded into insignificance.'

'Do you realise I could have you out of here?'

'I don't think so, Charles, not that it would bother me. It is rather ridiculous that one woman should be living in this huge house alone.'

'That's not what I've heard.'

'Oh, you mean my lodgers. Yes, it's been much better since they moved in.'

'You'll regret this.'

'Really? When? I've not felt this happy in years.'

'I wish I could write this down,' said Arnold Swann.

'Ah, the penny's dropped,' said Mrs Egerton-Smythe. 'You've called to check I've not been running a house of ill-repute.'

'No, I came to read Jessica's report.'

'She's still at school. She doesn't come back till tomorrow. At least give her the weekend before you home in on her.'

'Tomorrow,' thought Ralph. 'Whoopee!'

'Have you thought what this might do to her? It is my duty,' he began.

'No, it isn't. You're not her father. And all this will business has gone to your head.'

'How dare you speak to me like that?'

'Charles, I'm getting rather tired of your attempting to intimidate me. It might work with your employees, but just because you're the executor, it doesn't wash. I don't know whether you've noticed, but I am managing to pay the bills in spite of your behaviour.'

'I'll soon put a stop to that.'

'Your behaviour?'

'No. I shall have a word with your . . .' There was a pause. 'Your employer.'

'You'll have to make an appointment. He's a very busy man.'

'She's good, isn't she,' said Felix.

'Mmm,' said Basil fondly.

His comment had such warmth in it that it took Ralph by surprise. He glanced aside at him. He was beaming happily.

'And I think my appointment book will be full,' added Mr Neville amused. 'Since she is in charge of it.'

Suddenly Isla got a fit of the giggles, which sent Geraldine into convulsions. Hastily they bolted back into the library.

'We'll see,' thundered Charles.

'Will you be staying for tea, sir?' they heard Queenie ask politely.

'No, thank you, Queenie,' they heard him answer icily. 'Mother, don't think you've heard the last of this. Not by a long chalk.'

'Or by hook or by crook,' she added. 'Sorry, I've been reading so many clichés recently, it's catching.'

'Footsteps!' Ralph whispered urgently.

Everyone fled into the various rooms, leaving Ralph suddenly alone. The kitchen door opened. He looked around frantically for something to do. In a panic he grabbed a brush and vigorously began stroking the bear which had been standing by the hallstand ever since it had been returned. He heard Charles Egerton-Smythe walk past him.

'So nice to see you again, sir,' said Queenie, displaying the supposed deafness that all servants were supposed to acquire. And then the footsteps came to a sudden halt. 'Hollis!'

Ralph spun round startled. 'Yes, sir?'

'Why on earth are you cleaning that bear's fur with a clothes brush?'

'Oh, sorry,' Ralph stammered. 'Is there a special one for the bear?'

Mr Egerton-Smythe gave a squeak, turned on his heel and made for the door. As soon as Queenie had closed it after him there was a silence in which you could, as Mrs Egerton-Smythe might be tempted to say, have heard a pin drop. And then suddenly there was the sound of uncontrollable laughter from behind four doors. Queenie stared disdainfully at the tray on the hall table.

'Ralph!' she admonished. 'That tea will be stone cold by now!'

'Me? I shall go to a matinée this afternoon in town and then spend all evening listening to the Third Programme with a friend. There's a marvellous play on tonight. And I shall attempt to cook some *pièce de résistance* for us with a few resistant pieces of anything I can get hold of. Then I shall read *Cuckoo in the Nest*. You know, you really ought to listen to the Third Programme.'

'I'd like to,' said Ralph, 'but it wouldn't go down well with my family.'

'Save up for your own wireless,' he said. 'You don't know what you're missing.'

'I do. You keep telling me,' said Ralph. 'Thanks for the book.'

Felix had lent him his copy of *An Actor Prepares* by Constantin Stanislavsky.

'I'll try and finish it by next Saturday.'

'Take your time. I'm sure this won't be your last week,' he said encouragingly. 'And if it is you can use returning the book as an excuse to pop in and see us.'

Ralph smiled. 'See you Monday,' Felix said.

It was Saturday afternoon. They had just completed a run-through of *Hobson's Choice*. The extra week of rehearsal had taken the play into another dimension. There were nuances and a naturalness between the performers that gave it a sense of exciting immediacy. But it was Basil Duke who was the most breathtaking. Everyone in the rest of the cast stayed around to watch the scenes between him and Annie Duncan. They were riveting and as spontaneous as if the words had only just occurred to them. Observing the way they played off one another, Ralph learned something more about acting, that it wasn't just a case of giving out, it was as important to respond, to listen to what was being said to you as the character you were playing. He also noticed that Basil did not have the frenetic energy that some performers had. He remembered overhearing one of the actors say that as long as one kept talking onstage everything would be all right. Basil was the opposite. He wasn't afraid of silence. In fact, watching him, one wasn't aware of the silence, because one could read his thoughts. His face and his whole physique were so expressive that they appeared to have a language of their own. He even dared to turn his back, something the others wouldn't have dreamt of. Basil got away with it because one could see from the way he held himself, what emotion he was feeling, and Ralph yearned to be that kind of actor. He realised that an actor's voice wasn't his only tool. His whole being was his tool. It was terrifying, but incredibly exciting.

And when Basil was left alone on stage as Willie Mossop, fighting for the words which could express his extraordinary achievement, and he eventually said, 'Well by gum,' the cast broke into applause. And Ralph discovered that all the petty jealousies he had thought of as being normal in a theatre company were false. To be a member of a rep company everyone had to pull together as a unit. The play *was* the thing. People rooted for one another, helped one another, were pleased for one another, commiserated with one another, exposed their weaknesses and strengths and he wanted more than ever, with a yearning so painful, to be part of such a company.

He watched Felix raise his coat collar and pull down his trilby at a rakish angle, his long brolly with the carved handle at the ready. Outside there was another deluge of rain. He turned as footsteps came down the stairs and Geraldine and Raymond Maclaren came running down to meet him. They weren't in *Robert's Wife* either. Wilfred gave them their copies of *A Cuckoo in the Nest*. They had managed to get some film work during the afternoon that week and were travelling into town with Felix.

'What's up?' said Wilfred after they had left. 'You look browned off.'

'I've only one week to go,' said Ralph dismally. 'Isla will be joining the main company then, and there will be two new ASMs and a stage manager who won't know me.'

'You can show 'em the ropes.'

Ralph sighed.

'When did you last eat?' Wilfred asked.

'You sound like my mother.'

'A good meal will buck you up.'

'Too much to do. I promised to help pick up some props this afternoon. I was hoping to see a friend this evening, but they need help with the sets of *Hobson's Choice*' so I'm helping out a bit with the show tonight.'

'Nice, is she?'

'Who?'

'The friend you want to see.'

'It's not like that,' Ralph protested. 'She's just a kid.'

'Oh, yes?' Wilfred said, a twinkle in his eye.

Mr Johnson appeared at the stage door. 'Ready?' he asked.

Ralph moved swiftly out into the rain and ran with Mr Johnson to a rickety old van parked across the road.

He had hoped that Jessica would have stayed up to see him when he came in from the Saturday strike, but the house was dark and silent. A note for him was propped on the kitchen table, telling him to go to the garden room. On the draining board he noticed there was an empty bottle of wine and two glasses.

A camp bed had been made up for him in front of the fire in the garden room. Next to it was a thermos and a pair of pyjamas. Exhausted he changed into them and slid between the warm flannelette sheets.

When he awoke he found his damp clothes and the bowl and Thermos had been removed. He hopped out of bed. It was freezing. He drew aside the long faded velvet curtains at the french windows and was surprised to find, in spite of the wind, a patch of sunlight on the muddy waterlogged lawn.

Hugging himself he ran into the hall. The first thing he heard was laughter coming from the kitchen. He recognised Basil's voice, but he couldn't place the woman's laugh. Some instinct made him knock before entering.

'Come in!' they chorused.

To his surprise he found that the other woman was Mrs Egerton-Smythe. She and Basil were sitting opposite one another. To his surprise, Mrs Egerton-Smythe was wearing a man's jersey and slacks and her hair was tousled and loose. She was smiling. They both looked relaxed and dishevelled. 'Had a good sleep?'

'Yes. What time is it?'

'Nearly one o'clock. Your clothes are there,' she said, indicating the dry ironed clothes.

'Thanks! Um.'

'Yes?'

'Where's Jessica?'

'In the summerhouse. Trying to sweep the mud and water out. I don't know why. Looks like we're in for another deluge. It'll only fill up again.'

After Ralph dressed in the bathroom, he noticed he was trembling. He squeezed some toothpaste on his finger and rubbed his teeth vigorously, smoothing back his springy hair as fast as he could. Avoiding the kitchen for some reason, he raced back to the garden room, flung open the french windows and stepped into a large pair of wellingtons under the veranda. To his surprise he found himself running down the lawn into the wind, his heart pounding, his elbows pumping up and down like rivets.

He found her in the summerhouse, leaning on a shovel and staring out at the window at the river. She was wiping her forehead with a woolly hat. She had a vivid green jersey, slacks and wellingtons on, and her long red tangled hair was lying across her shoulders, coppery in the sunlight. She didn't notice him at first. Then suddenly she turned and her face broke into a smile and Ralph had an overwhelming desire to kiss every enormous freckle which was scattered across her face and hug her to himself so hard that he would be able to feel her heart beating too. He knew he was blushing and he watched her blush too, but it didn't matter because it was obvious she was as delighted to see him as he was to see her.

'So tell me what's been happening?' she said mischievously. 'I want to know it all. Every detail.'

And he knew he would do just that, and, he suspected, he always would.

'And are you sure there's no chance at all?'

He shook his head. 'I'm lucky to be on the book.'

'Are you nervous about being on it during the performance?'

'No. Just terrified.'

She gave him a playful punch. 'Silly. So what will you do?'

'I'm hoping Mr Johnson will still use me for the Saturday strikes, and with voice coaching and working on new audition pieces . . ..'

'Male audition pieces,' she teased.

'Definitely male,' he grinned. 'I shall audition for a drama school scholarship. It's my only hope.'

'Yes. Me too,' she murmured. She looked uneasy for a moment. 'If I tell you something, you promise not to say a word?'

'I promise.'

'Mother knows, but we don't want my brother to find out.'

'Find out what?'

'You know I told you he wants me to leave school at sixteen and go to finishing school?'

'Yes.'

'Well, I'm going to be allowed to take my School Cert this year,' she said. 'If I get it, it means I can spend more of next year building up a portfolio for art school. I won't be able to do life-class drawings, of course.'

'Those are people with no clothes on?'

'Yes. But some of the girls have said they'll pose for me in their swimsuits. So far it's only the ones with wonderful figures, but with a bit of flattery, I hope to persuade some of the girls with the more interesting figures.'

She looked at him thoughtfully. 'I suppose you wouldn't?' she began.

'Not in this weather!' he exclaimed.

'No.' She laughed. 'In the summer.'

For a moment they gazed at one another in silence. It sounded so wonderful, thought Ralph. Those three single words. In the summer. Just knowing that she would still be around and wanted to see him. He smiled shyly. 'In my swimming trunks,' he laughed. 'We can take a boat down the river.'

'Can you row?'

'Yes. And you?'

She nodded, and then she frowned. 'I suppose you'll be away the summer after that,' she added quietly.

'I haven't got into a drama school yet,' he said. 'And anyway they have holidays.'

'I didn't mean drama school. I meant conscription.'

'Conscription?'

'Or National Service, or whatever they're calling it now.'

'Jessica, what are you talking about?'

'Mother told me. It's been in the newspapers for the last fortnight. Everyone from eighteen to twenty-six has got to do eighteen months of National Service from next year, or five years part-time.'

Ralph felt the blood draining from his face. 'You're not serious, are you?'

'Yes. I thought you'd know already.'

'I haven't read any newspapers,' he murmured. 'I've had my mind on other things. Oh, hell, this is terrible. There's no point in me trying for a drama school for next year, then.'

'Mother said it can be postponed till after you've done your studies, although I think that's mainly for people at university.'

He sighed. 'Everything seems to be two steps forward and four steps back.'

'I'm sorry, I didn't mean to depress you. Come on,' she said, putting her arm in his. 'Let's lock up and go back into the warm.'

They found Mrs Egerton-Smythe alone in the kitchen humming. She took one look at Ralph and put her hands on her hips. 'What's up with you?' she exclaimed. 'I thought you'd be pleased to see Jessica.'

'He is,' she interrupted. 'He didn't know about this National Service thing. I've just told him.'

Ralph slumped into a chair, his head in his hands. 'I'll never be an actor at this rate,' he said. 'Never!' He looked up earnestly at Mrs Egerton-Smythe. 'I don't know what I'll do if I can't be. Life won't be worth living.'

'Oh, I expect you'll find something to keep you going,' commented Mrs Egerton-Smythe wryly.

'Mother,' said Jessica slowly. 'I know it's not his birthday until next Saturday, but couldn't we give him his present early?'

'You don't need to give me a present,' he protested.

'You don't have a choice,' said Mrs Egerton-Smythe. 'You can either like it or lump it.'

Ralph couldn't help but smile.

'What do you think?' said Jessica eagerly.

Her mother gazed at her bemused. 'I'm not sure it would cheer him up *that* much.'

'It would. I know it would. Please.'

Her mother stood wearily to her feet. 'Don't raise your hopes too much,' she said to Ralph.

'And don't follow us,' Jessica warned.

Ralph stayed alone at the kitchen table and stared miserably out of the window. Suddenly it grew dark and there was a rumble of thunder. Inside he felt as dismal as the lowering sky. All he had to look forward to were two and a half years of misery. One year doing a job his father approved of, followed by eighteen months' square-bashing. It wasn't a joyful prospect.

Hearing footsteps he sat up and tried to fix on a smile.

'Close your eyes!' he heard Jessica yell from the hall. 'No peeping,' she admonished. There were two loud thumps. 'You can look now.'

On the table were two large suitcases.

'Thanks,' he said, attempting to appear cheerful. 'Suitcases. Marvellous. I've always wanted suitcases.'

'It's what's inside the suitcases,' Jessica said exasperated. Ralph pushed aside the two brass locks on the one nearest him. They sprang open with a snap. He lifted the lid. Inside were piles of Laurie's clothes.

'Tremendous!' he said, attempting bravely to hide his disappointment. They were enormous. He would never grow into them in a million years.

'There's more in that one too,' she said.

Ralph was aware of Mrs Egerton-Smythe silently watching him. Like the first suitcase it was filled with more of his suits. An evening suit, a tweed jacket. 'Are you sure?' he asked Mrs Egerton-Smythe.

'Of course we are,' said Jessica. 'I thought I'd weep buckets when I saw them but we didn't, did we?' she added, turning to her mother. 'They cheered us up.'

'We can let go of them now,' said her mother. 'We're delighted

337

they can be of use.'

'I'll probably need to get them altered,' he said. 'I hope you don't mind.'

'Ass,' exclaimed Mrs Egerton-Smythe. 'They're not for you to wear!'

'They're for you to swap,' Jessica explained. 'At your second-hand clothing shop, for the equivalent in your size. You told me you needed certain clothes before you could get a contract as an actor. That is right, isn't it?'

Ralph laughed. He couldn't believe his luck. 'Yes, but actors in the rep use that shop. They might hire them and wear them on stage. How do you feel about that?'

Jessica looked at her mother and beamed. Her mother was smiling.

'He'd love it,' Jessica said.

'Will you come with me when I take them there?' he asked Jessica.

'I took it for granted I would!' she said, pretending to be affronted. And then she smiled. 'Let's go tomorrow morning.'

'I can't,' said Ralph. 'The lights have to be set up ready for the dress. I could go on Tuesday morning. I shall only be needed for the evenings from then.'

'Tuesday morning it is,' she said with satisfaction.

He picked up a pair of flannel trousers and brogues. 'My wardrobe,' he said grinning. 'What a start!' And he suddenly thought of a plan.

Just then the phone rang. As soon as Mrs Egerton-Smythe was out of the room, Jessica sprang up and sat near him.

'What's up? You're up to something. I can see it in your eyes.'

'It's just an idea, that's all.'

'So?' she urged.

He leaned eagerly towards her. 'I was wondering, once I get my wardrobe, whether to go along to Mr Neville, show him, and see if it might tempt him to give me another acting part. What do you think?'

'Oh, yes! Oh, you must.'

'Maybe I could see him after his rehearsals on Tuesday once we've been to the shop. It's probably hopeless, but I've got to do something. I've got to try.'

'Of course you have. Now,' she began firmly. 'There's something I've got to ask you before I burst.'

He reddened. 'Yes,' he blurted out. 'I do.'

'Do what?' she said.

'Like you. A lot.'

She smiled shyly. 'Thanks. But that wasn't what I was going to ask.'

'Oh? What then?'

She took a deep breath.

'How long has this romance been going on between Basil Duke and my mother?'

'Jessica, where on earth did you pick up such an absurd idea?'

'It's obvious,' she said. 'Haven't you noticed how relaxed and happy she is?'

'Maybe it's because she has lodgers to keep her company, and a job.'

'Haven't you seen the way they look at one another?'

'Jessica, they can't be.'

'Why?'

'I hate to be rude but your mother's so much older than him.'

'Eleven years.'

'How do you know?'

'I asked him.'

'And he told you?' said Ralph astounded.

'Yes.'

'How old is he?'

'Thirty-six, and mother is forty-seven.'

'Eleven years is still a big gap.'

'They couldn't get married anyway. They'll have to live in sin.'

'Jessica!'

'Shush! She'll hear you.'

'I'm sure you're imagining it,' he whispered.

'I'm sure I'm not.'

'Why can't they get married? He's not married already, is he?'

'No.'

'How do you know?'

'I asked him.'

'Didn't he think you were being a bit nosy?'

'Yes. Well, I was.'

'Wasn't he annoyed?'

'No. He didn't have to answer. It was up to him.'

'So why can't they get married? Not that they have any intention,' he added hurriedly.

'Because of the terms of Daddy's will. If Mother marries again she'd lose this house and her new husband would have to provide a home for her instead.'

'What would happen to the house?'

'It would go to Charles.'

'So it would be in his interest for her to marry again?'

'I never thought of it like that. I don't think he'd want that though,' she said after some thought. 'He couldn't take the scandal.'

They heard voices in the hall. Quickly Ralph leaned across the table. 'You haven't said,' he began urgently.

'Haven't said what?'

'Whether *you* like me,' he asked awkwardly. 'Do you?'

She nodded. 'Of course I do.'

Ralph reached out and held her hand.

'A lot,' she added.

FOUR

'Eh, lass!' he replied tenderly and he kissed her gently on the lips.

Ralph quickly pushed the switch down. He saw Maggie spring away from Will and straighten up.

'Ready, Father,' she said briskly. 'Come along to Albert's.'

'Yes, Maggie,' Ralph heard Mr Neville say, now obedient as a lamb.

Ralph watched them cross·in front of Will and head for the door which led out of the shop and then they were in the wings. They turned and watched Basil Duke. Ralph quickly looked back at Basil. He was downstage now, his mouth open. He shook his head, total disbelief on his face. And then with an exultant boyish smile he blurted out, 'Well, by gum!' and he turned on his heel and headed for the door.

Hardly had the words left his lips than the most tremendous explosion of laughter rocked through the auditorium and the applause which erupted was such that Ralph had never heard before. And he knew there was nothing to touch that night. That night everyone had seen something special.

He gave the curtain-down cue to the fly-man and to his relief it came down. As soon as it hit the deck, the cast leapt back on to the set and joined hands downstage and Ralph gave the cue for curtain-up. The audience were cheering now and then, to Ralph's utter amazement, people stood in the boxes and in the front of the stalls and there was the sound of hundreds of seats being flung back. The audience were giving them a standing ovation! He could see Annie clasping Basil's hand tightly as the cast beamed and bowed to shouts and yells.

Ralph sat back and noticed that not only was he drenched in perspiration but he was shaking from head to foot. He had done it! His first performance on the book of a play with three sets. Two stage hands had changed the scenery and once Isla had changed her costume she ran on-stage too and helped with the props. He closed the book, and watched the cast, their arms wrapped round each other's waists heading through the wings and back to the dressing rooms.

As he switched off the small light above the prompt corner, the old sadness returned. He had a sudden urge to escape before anyone could talk to him. He was running down the steps in his overcoat to the stage-door area when he heard two familiar voices chatting to Wilfred. Jessica and her mother were standing there, bundled up in coats, hats and scarves. They whirled round when they saw him and gave him a huge smile.

'It was wonderful!' laughed Jessica. 'They were all so good. But Basil Duke!'

'They're lucky to have him,' said Wilfred. 'See him while you can, I say.'

'You did awfully well too,' said Jessica.

He made a face.

'No, seriously. I know you couldn't be seen. But all those set changes. I mean, it all seemed to go off without a hitch.'

'Thanks'.

He took one look at her exuberant face and he couldn't help but laugh.

'Have I said something funny?' she asked bemused.

'No. You just cheer me up.'

'Good,' she announced. 'Now you haven't forgotten about tomorrow morning, have you?'

'No, Miss Bossyboots,' he said grinning, 'I'll pop round early to pick up the suitcases and we'll walk there together.'

'Made for you, sir. If you don't mind me saying so, there are not many young men who could wear that jacket with such distinction.'

Ralph was standing in front of the mirror in a russet and brown tweed jacket, grey flannels and a cravat tucked in an open-necked shirt. The transformation astounded him.

'Do I look like an actor?' he asked Jessica hopefully.

'Oh, yes,' she said.

'And a gentleman,' said Mr Gutman, beaming.

They had unpacked Laurie's clothes, and laid them across the counter. Mr Gutman had been impressed with the quality and had promised to do his best to match like for like. He picked up the list of clothing Ralph needed.

'Dinner jacket, two lounge suits, morning suit. I suggest we begin with the evening dress.'

Three dinner jackets were selected and Ralph emerged from a changing room three times to stand in front of the mirror under the scrutiny of Mr Gutman and Jessica. Mr Gutman insisted he wear a dress shirt, and a bow tie, to give the full effect.

'I wonder if I should grow a moustache,' Ralph said staring at himself wistfully.

Mr Gutman put a white silk scarf round his neck. Ralph grinned and gazed at Jessica who was staring rapturously at him.

By the time they left the shop, Ralph, in his new clothes, had his basic actor's wardrobe in one suitcase and in the other a striped blazer, white flannels, white V-neck cricket jersey, a long dressing-gown, corduroy trousers, corduroy jacket, ties, pocket handkerchiefs, shoes, a coat and raincoat, a trilby hat, a woollen scarf, collars, studs and a pair of cufflinks. As soon as he and Jessica were out of sight, Ralph dropped the suitcases on the pavement and they laughed and flung their arms around each other and Ralph felt such a mixture of tenderness and desire to get right inside the very skin of her that it overwhelmed him. Yet he felt fiercely protective of her too. They broke away and gazed at each other, flushed and happy.

'I wonder if Wilfred will let me keep these at the theatre,' he said at last. 'If I take them home, my father might sell them.'

'He wouldn't, would he?' she gasped.

'He might. No one in our family has ever had such a fine wardrobe.'

'Don't feel guilty,' she said, reading his thoughts. 'They're the tools of your trade.'

He smiled and drew her close to him again.

'Thanks for letting me come,' she said quietly.

'I'd have hated to have gone on my own,' Ralph said. 'I needed an audience.'

She poked him in the ribs. 'Show off!' she admonished.

When they came in the stage door Wilfred's eyes opened wide. 'Very nice, sir,' he said approvingly.

He agreed to let Ralph leave his suitcases in his cubby-hole and was about to open his door when Ralph stopped him. 'There's something I have to do first,' said Ralph, his heart thumping towards his mouth.

'It'll have to wait. There's a message from Mr Neville. He wants to have a word with you in his office.'

Jessica and Ralph glanced at one another.

'I want to have a word with him too,' Ralph told him. 'That's what I need the suitcases for.'

'You're not leaving, are you, sir?'

'No.'

'The opposite, he hopes. Good luck.'

'Where are you going?' Ralph asked.

'You don't want me hanging round your neck. You'll be better on your own.'

He nodded. She was right. And at least she wouldn't have a chance to see him terrified.

'I'll meet you in the actors' café,' she said. 'Then you can tell me all about it.'

'Every detail?'

'Every detail,' she laughed.

He watched her leave. As soon as she was out of sight he noticed that Wilfred was watching him.

'Lovely girl,' he observed. 'I'd hang on to her if I were you.'

'I intend to,' he said smiling.

Outside Mr Neville's office he could hear him talking on the telephone. He waited till the receiver had clunked and then hurriedly knocked at the door before his courage gave out.

'Come in!' Mr Neville yelled.

Ralph had intended throwing the door open with a flourish, which he could have done had he been carrying only one suitcase, but, with two, his wonderful bravura entrance disintegrated into a stumble and trip through the door.

'Going somewhere, are we?' remarked Mr Neville.

'I hope so,' stammered Ralph. 'Going places, that is, metaphorically speaking.'

Mr Neville opened his mouth to speak, but Ralph dropped one case and held up a hand imperiously. 'I need to speak first, if you don't mind, Mr Neville.'

To Ralph's annoyance, he looked amused. He decided to stay standing. 'Since I have no chance of being an ASM in this company, I have come to offer my services as an actor.'

Mr Neville moved slightly.

'No. Don't stop me. I know I have no training, but I'm doing voice exercises and I'll work hard and improve.' With a grand flourish he dumped one suitcase on to the chair in front of the desk and snapped it open. 'In here,' he said with authority, 'I have the basic requirements for an actor's wardrobe.' He glanced down and saw white flannels. It was the wrong case. He cleared his throat, shut it quickly and hauled the other suitcase on to the chair. 'As I said, in this case I have the wardrobe needed for an actor's contract which means I can play more parts.'

Mr Neville rose.

'I'm not finished yet.'

Mr Neville sat down again with a sigh.

'I can't go to drama school next year,' Ralph said, emotion welling up, 'because this government has seen fit to bring in conscription next year. This could be the last year of my life,' he added, feeling the tears well up into his eyes 'That is why I would like you to reconsider taking me into your company. Since I can't pay you to be an ASM, perhaps you can pay me to be an actor.'

He shut the case and picked it up firmly. 'I shall await your decision. I can be contacted at this address,' and he thrust a scrap of paper on to the desk.

Mr Neville sprang to his feet. 'Please!' he begged. 'Don't give me another grand exit, I couldn't bear it. Now sit down and shut up for a minute.'

To Ralph's dismay he found himself doing just that.

'First of all,' Mr Neville said, 'conscription doesn't start next year but in 1949, so you have two years to live. Also, I have been attempting to contact you all morning.'

'Oh!' began Ralph.

'Shush! You've had your speech. Now it's my turn. Remembering your original portrayal of Iago, I know you can do a Cornish accent, and a genuine one at that. I'd like you to play a small part in *A Cuckoo in the Nest*. Interested?'

Ralph was rendered speechless. He gave a nod. 'But my father,' he began.

'That's what I'm coming to. I need to speak to him. Can you tell him to come to my office after work?'

Ralph shook his head wildly. 'He wouldn't set foot in a theatre.'

'Do you think he'd come to my flat?'

'He might.'

'My flat it is, then. When does he finish work?'

'Six o'clock.'

'I'll meet him at six-thirty, prompt, today.'

Ralph hovered on the road near the paper mill. As soon as he spotted his father, he manoeuvred his bike through the maze of men and youths on bicycles who raced past him. He had changed back into his old clothes and hobnail boots so that he wouldn't look conspicuous. Head down, eyes up, he cycled after his father, who was riding with the foreman who had caused him to be sacked. As soon as the foreman pushed off in a different direction, Ralph peddled harder.

'Dad!' he yelled hoarsely. 'Dad!'

His father swung round, and braked hard. 'What is it? Is it Mum? Has she been taken poorly again?'

'No. It's Mr Neville. He wants to see you.'

'Belt up,' he said bluntly. 'Don't say another word.'

'But it's urgent.'

His father began cycling again. Swiftly Ralph followed him. Gritting his teeth, he wove in and out of the other bicycles and kept on his tail. To his surprise his father broke away from the crowd and took off down a road leading to Winford. Now there were only five of them going in the same direction. He saw his father glancing back over his shoulder. Gradually the other men cycled off in different directions. His father swerved round a corner. Ralph found him waiting for him by a kerb, red-faced and sweating.

'Never do that again!' he said angrily.

Ralph slowed down beside him.

'If any of me mates find out I have anything to do with that ruddy theatre,' he said looking furtively around, 'they'll think I'm one of them Nancy-boys.'

Ralph's spirits sank. It was hopeless. Mr Neville would never persuade his father to let him act.

'I had to catch you before you got home. He wants to see you at six-thirty.'

His father gave a short laugh. 'If you think I'm going to set foot in that building . . .' he began.

'At his flat,' Ralph interrupted.

'What for?'

'He has a couple more weeks' work to offer me,' said Ralph evasively. 'There should have been a new ASM today, but . . .' And he shrugged his shoulders.

His father sighed. 'When is this going to end?'

'It's work, Dad.'

'Not what I call work.'

They stood silently staring at one another.

'Two weeks?' he said.

'Yes,' said Ralph.

'I dunno,' he said wheeling his bike, and he shook his head.

'It's an emergency, Dad.'

'It's always an emergency.' He clambered back on to his bike.

'So what are you going to do?' Ralph asked.

'Don't worry,' he said grimly. 'I'll see him all right.'

'How will you let me know if it's yes or no? I won't be home till late.'

'I'll see you in the morning.'

'But, Dad.'

'Let's take one thing at a time, shall we?' and he pushed off.

Ralph rode with him to Mr Neville's flat and rang the bell. He heard footsteps coming down the stairs.

'He lives in the upstairs flat,' Ralph explained.

The door swung open and Mr Neville took one look at Ralph's father, gave a warm smile and stretched out his hand.

'Mr Hollis,' he enthused. 'I do appreciate you giving up your time to come and see me.'

They shook hands. Ralph noticed a hint of awkwardness in his father's manner. 'We don't need you, Ralph,' said Mr Neville.

'He was afraid I'd go AWOL before you opened the door.'

'Ah,' said Mr Neville and he ushered Ralph's father in and began to close the door behind him.

'I believe you and Mr Lord were in the same unit,' Ralph heard him say.

Once back in the theatre, Ralph was running around setting the props for Act One, checking the remaining and personal props and giving people their calls. And then it was curtain up.

When he returned home and slipped into the scullery, he could hear Joan snoring loudly from the kitchen. Stealthily he opened the door, lit a candle and pulled the ash-pan out of the range. It clattered noisily. Joan gave a grunt. 'Ralph?' she yawned sleepily.

'Yes. Sorry I woke you.'

He turned back to the range. To his surprise he found that the ash had been removed and the range fire laid.

'Uncle John did it for you,' she said.

Ralph walked over to the bed. 'Was he in a good mood then?' he asked, surprised.

'I dunno. He didn't say much all night. Him and your mum went to bed early. They was talkin' a lot upstairs about somethin'.'

346

Ralph sighed.

'What's up?' Joan asked.

'There's a chance of me doing another fortnight's work at the theatre. But don't say anything. He's a bit touchy about it.'

'Don't worry, I won't.'

He went over to the candle and blew it out. He had just opened the door to the hall when Joan whispered to him. 'Good luck.'

He smiled. 'Thanks.'

Breakfast was a noisy affair. Harry had turned the wireless on. Ralph had lit the range and put the kettle on, his mother was frying bread, and his aunt and Joan were arguing about some overpricing at Joan's shop. Elsie and Harry had broken up from school and were grumbling because they hadn't been allowed to lie in.

'We ain't got enough coal to go cooking all mornin', said their mother. 'We all got to eat together.'

Ralph's father moved silently among them and then disappeared into the scullery with some hot water to have a shave. Eventually Ralph couldn't stand the suspense any longer and he sauntered casually in after him. He took some cutlery from the draining-board. His father was squinting into a small cracked mirror, a cut-throat razor in his hand. Ralph lost courage and returned to the kitchen.

All through breakfast everyone sat round the table, chatting and laughing. Ralph didn't seem to hear a word they were saying and every now and then he noticed his father staring at him. With no appetite, Ralph slowly munched his way through his fried bread. 'Dad?' he said eventually.

His father, who had been gazing into the distance, glanced back at him.

'Can I or can I not?' Ralph blurted out.

'Can you what?' his father asked, dazed.

'Play the small part in *A Cuckoo in the Nest*?'

'Oh, that,' said his father vaguely. 'Yeah, yeah.'

Stupefied, Ralph stared at him. He didn't know whether to thank him or not. His father seemed in such a strange mood that he was afraid he might not have realised what he had said and that if Ralph spoke again and asked him to repeat the question he might give the opposite answer. He glanced up at his mother who was standing at the range listening. She gave him a gentle smile and then put her finger to her lips. Ralph gulped down his tea.

'I'd better get a move on, then,' he said quickly. 'Don't want to be late, do I?'

347

But his father just gazed silently at him.

It was a relief to reach the stage door. He raced up the steps and headed backstage. Isla was on stage marking up for the Act One run through and Act Two rehearsal of *Cuckoo in the Nest*.

'Can I help?' he asked.

She sprang to her feet. 'Ralph! Has your father let you?'

He laughed and nodded.

'Splendid!' she cried. 'I've written down all the Act One moves for you and I have a spare script.'

'You appear twice in scene two and are in another scene in Act Three with a dog.'

'A dog?'

'A dog. A real one. In fact, as soon as we start doing the moves for Act Two today, I was wondering if you could find one,' and she gave him a pleading look.

'I expect I could,' he said nonchalantly. He was in such high spirits he was beginning to feel he could do anything.

'Right,' she said, 'this is the parlour of the Stag and Hunt Inn. The bar is over there,' she said, indicating stage left. 'You come in up centre.' Ralph followed her with his script. 'I'll read the stage directions for you first,' she went on.

Ralph stood up-centre.

'Noony, an old villager, very disreputable, and looking like a tramp, makes a sudden dart and cautious entry from centre, crosses left to bar,' she read. 'Now you call out to Alfred. I'll read his and Peter's part.'

'"'Bain't no harm,"' he muttered. He exited.

'Now wait there,' said Isla. 'You'll have to time this during the dress for the door. But you close it and then open it again.'

'And yell, "Cat",' added Ralph looking at his script. 'That's to her, isn't it?'

'Yes.'

Ralph mimed opening a door. 'Cat!' he yelled and he mimed shutting the door.

Laughter from the wings caused him to swing round. Basil and Geraldine were there. Ralph blushed.

'Thanks for coming in early for your moves,' Basil said. 'It means we don't get held up.'

'Not that we'd mind,' said Geraldine.

'So your father let you play another role, eh?' he said smiling.

'Yes. And he didn't eat me. It's a real puzzle. Did you have anything to do with it?'

'No.'

Now more actors were arriving and chatting and Ralph suddenly began to feel nervous. Mr Neville arrived, gave Ralph a brief wave and took his place beside Isla downstage. As well as producing he was playing a small part in Act Three. Ralph sat in the auditorium and watched scene one which took place in the sitting-room of a flat in Kensington in 1925. As scene two drew nearer, Ralph made his way up the auditorium and, while Isla set it up, he noticed Mr Neville turn and beckon him.

'We'll move your two scenes and continue the run,' he said over the orchestra pit.

'I've got the moves down already.'

'Good,' said Mr Neville, surprised. 'Do you want to throw yourself straight into it?'

Ralph nodded, feeling sicker at every nod. He didn't remember much of the run. He was too conscious of waiting for his two scenes to come up and cursing himself for his ineptitude when they were over. His nose in the book, he stumbled awkwardly and red-faced across the stage, acutely self-conscious. When the run was over, Mr Neville waved him over, while Isla set up for Act Two. Ralph approached him with dread, expecting the sack.

'Let's discuss your character, shall we?'

Ralph nodded again.

'Try and get a picture of what this man is like. If he reminds you of anyone you met in the West Country, use it. Now about farce.' He paused. 'Do you remember me telling you that you must play comedy extremely seriously?'

'Yes, Mr Neville,' said Ralph.

'You must play farce four times as seriously. It's very tempting to make a lot of empty gestures, talk fast and do funny walks. That comes into it a bit, but if it doesn't come out of the character or the situation then all the audience will see and hear is a mess and a lot of gabble. It's quick responses which are important. Quick thinking. The truth is exaggerated. For example, Noony just doesn't like an odd drink now and then, a drink is an oasis in a desert, to him it's life and death, but obtaining one in this inn is like committing grand theft. See what I mean?'

Ralph smiled. 'Yes.'

'Don't worry if you haven't got him yet. Think about him when you learn the lines tonight.'

'Yes.'

Mr Neville turned and faced the cast. 'A little bit of hush, please.' There was silence.

Ralph left the stage quietly, leaving the producer to move Act Two and headed for the stage door. Once there he suddenly felt totally perplexed. Where was he going to find a dog? And it had to be a small one. He put on his mac and stepped out into the rain. For some reason he found himself heading for the rectory again. His visit there, however, was to help him in a way he had not envisaged. He was just going up the street when an old tramp pushed open the rectory gate and stepped onto the pavement. His scraggy hair and beard were white and he wore layers of clothes in different degrees of disintegration. He was wheeling an old bike, a raincoat over his arm and gazing at them with a gap-toothed smile on his face.

Watching him stop to feel the substance of the raincoat and glance with relish at the bicycle, Ralph wondered whether clergymen were the same the world over, for the rector in Cornwall was always giving away raincoats and bicycles to tramps.

'Noony!' Ralph whispered. Instead of going to the rectory, he followed him from a safe distance and observed his every movement. He noticed a vibrancy in the man, in spite of his age which made Ralph rethink his approach to Noony. Before, he had been thinking of playing him old and doddery. Then he remembered a comment which Arnold Swann and Annie Duncan had made about shoes. That often shoes gave you a clue to the person. The old man Ralph was following was shuffling because his boots, probably gifts, were not only too large for him, but were held together by two bits of string. He knew then that he must get some large ankle boots.

'The second-hand shop,' he whispered. 'And layers of clothing,' he muttered. 'And I must have slightly flushed skin, and veins on my face from too much drinking.'

Suddenly he found himself standing in the middle of the pavement daydreaming about Noony, so that when he next looked down the street the tramp was out of sight. But he had been daydreaming! That was a good sign. He began to think about what Noony might have been doing before he made his first entrance. 'Waiting for Mrs Stoker to disappear,' he said aloud, 'that's why he dives so rapidly through the door while he has the chance. Oh, lor',' he gasped, suddenly remembering, 'the dog!' He changed his mind about going to the rectory and decided instead to call in at Mrs Egerton-Smythe's. It would give him a chance to see Jessica again.

Mrs Egerton-Smythe was sitting in the kitchen surrounded by

manuscripts, her spectacles cock-eyed. Queenie was ironing silently, and Jessica was sketching her. They all looked delighted to see him. To Ralph's amazement Queenie remarked brightly, 'Fancy a cuppa!' The silence was obviously killing her. Jessica quickly drew a page down over her sketch. 'No peeking,' she said. 'I'm just keeping my hand in.'

'Well, how did rehearsals go?' asked Mrs Egerton-Smythe.

Ralph made a face. 'I was awful.'

'Is that what Mr Neville said?'

'No.'

'Belt up, then.'

'Is your mother always so rude?' he asked Jessica.

'Always,' she added.

'How's it going?' he said indicating the manuscripts.

'I have found a jewel amongst the dross,' she said picking up a pile of dog-eared exercise books and waving them at him. 'All handwritten and too long, but with tightening up, I think it would be very exciting to do.'

'I take it it's "yes"?' Queenie interrupted.

Ralph laughed. 'Yes. Please.'

Queenie lifted the lid of the Aga and slid the kettle over. 'So, what brings you here?' Mrs Egerton-Smythe asked. He could see Jessica looking shy, which he found extraordinary, yet endearing at the same time. 'I'm looking for something for the show.'

'My dining-room set by any chance?'

'No. Well, not yet,' he said smiling. 'A dog.'

'A dog?' everyone chorused.

'A real one?' asked Jessica, now springing up from her chair and returning to her old inquisitive self.

'Yes. And small. Got any ideas?'

By the time Mrs Egerton-Smythe had rung round her friends, had persuaded one of them to agree to lending him a chihuahua for the production and arranged for Ralph to spend Sunday afternoon with the dog so that he could get used to it, it was time to return to the theatre. On his way he dived into the second-hand clothes shop and arranged to hire a huge pair of boots with the money he had remaining from swapping and selling Laurie's clothes.

There was nothing awful enough for Noony's clothing, but Mr Gutman gave him the address of a WVS clothing depot where they sorted out everything from rags to almost-new clothes. He set up for *Hobson's Choice* as fast as he could, slipped on the boots and began learning his lines. He discovered that the best way to learn them was in character. So it took longer than he had anticipated, but at least he had an extra day, he consoled himself, before the next run of Act One on the Friday.

Hearing the door open, he turned to find Isla.

'Hello,' she said curiously. 'I wondered who was in here.'

'I was just learning my lines.'

'If you want to use one of the top dressing rooms, I'm sure Wilfred wouldn't mind giving you a key.'

'I'm afraid of losing track of the time up there.'

'Did you have any luck with finding a dog?'

'Yes. She wants to know who will be looking after it.'

'Well, since I'll be on the book,' she began awkwardly.

'Me?' Ralph suggested.

'It's either that or have the owner backstage and they have a tendency to chat to people during the show just as they are about to go on.'

'Don't worry,' said Ralph. 'I'll do it. Do you want me to help you with prop hunting tomorrow?'

'You can't. It's a matinée and you're on the book, remember? It's a bit of a shock having had two weeks for *Hobson* and being thrown back to one week. I think we'll have to do a lot of running around on Sunday. We've three sets to dress. Still it's furniture mostly and we've already got quite a lot from stock.'

Suddenly she looked down at his feet. 'What on earth are you wearing?'

'Noony's boots.' And he demonstrated how they made him shuffle. 'I seems to get the voice roight when I wears 'em like,' he said in a husky, rich West Country dialect.

She laughed. 'You're mad!' She glanced at her watch. 'You better get them off and get a move on. It's time to give the half.'

The next morning, while Act Two was being run, Ralph collected the dog from the owner, who unfortunately insisted on coming too. Remembering what Isla had said, Ralph took her into the kitchen while the Act Two run through was going on. As soon as it had finished, he went up to Mr Neville and explained the situation. To his relief, Mr Neville was delighted.

'Wonderful,' he said. 'It might hold things up a bit having it for the rehearsal period, but at least we'll know what we're letting ourselves in for before the dress. And she's agreed to allow us to borrow him for the rest of the week?'

'Yes. And he's a her. But I'm afraid she's come along too.'

'First class. She can show us how to handle her. Good lad.'

Ralph flushed. He nipped into the kitchen, made the woman a cup of tea and hared back to the wings where he put on his Noony boots. As soon as he heard the actors coming up to where he had to appear, carrying the dog, he asked the woman to stand in the wings beside him. It was difficult to concentrate because she kept asking him what they were doing and commenting about how 'dreadfully exciting it all was' which made it difficult to hear what was going on.

'I think you'd better hand her to me now,' he whispered. When he had practised holding the dog on the Sunday he had completely forgotten he would be handling a script at the same time.

He watched the young actor playing Alfred walk onto the set.

'Aye, Mrs Spoker?' he said.

'Come you here,' commanded the middle-aged actress who was playing Mrs Spoker. 'I am going to make the tea. When those two persons come down from dressing, make sure they don't go without they pay.'

'Aye, Mrs Spoker.'

'I'd like you to exit downstage left, Mrs Spoker,' said Mr Neville.

'What two persons?' said the actor playing a character called Stoley-J.

'Cross left centre,' said Mr Neville. 'That's right, on the line.'

The actor repeated his line. 'Surely she . . .'

'Sorry,' said Mr Neville. 'My fault. Move after that line. Bewildered.'

The actor smiled, walked backwards, repeated the line and then crept left, conspiratorially. 'Surely she doesn't mean the Hicketts?'

'Aye, there's trouble,' said Albert. 'In and out of his bed all night 'e were. 'E lost his dog, 'e lost his trousers, 'e grubbled up his room and 'e burst his jug.'

'Lost his dog? How did he come to lose his dog?'

A young actress walked on with her script, stage right, pencil poised.

'I don't see her yet, do I?' said Alfred.

'No,' said Mr Neville.

'It happened loike this – the dog were in the stables and it were howling so much that 'e thought – '

The actor turned to the producer. 'Then I see her and follow her out grinning?'

'Try seeing her after "howling". And you, Gladys,' he said turning to the young actress, 'take that as your cue to leave.'

'Right,' she said, noting it.

'So I start moving out on the next few words.'

'Yes,' said Mr Neville. 'Totally mesmerised. As if she's a magnet and you're a piece of iron filing.'

'It 'appened like this. The dog were in the stables – and it were howling.' Immediately his eyes glazed over and he shambled off after the young actress in a hypnotic trance as he spoke and disappeared off stage. There was laughter. 'Yes,' said Mr Neville. 'Something like that.'

'This was Ralph's cue to enter. He shuffled forward quickly, clinging to the dog with one hand and attempting to read the script with the other.

'Don't worry,' said Mr Neville. 'Once you have that script under your belt, it will be easier. Keep going. Isla, if he drops it, the script I mean, just yell out the words to him. On you go.'

''Ere! Mister! Oh,' said Ralph stopping. 'Who am I saying this line to, Alfred or the parson?'

'Alfred. And come downstage a bit.'

Ralph did so.

'Go ahead.'

'Oh, good day to ee, Parson.' Ralph turned to him again. 'It says I take off my hat.'

'We'll take that as read.'

'Um. I can't write any of the moves down. Isla.'

'I'll give them to you afterwards.'

'Thanks.'

He turned to the parson. 'I take off my hat,' he muttered.

'Shall I move up to him now?' said the actor playing the parson.

'Yes,' said Mr Neville.

'Hallo, by Christopher! You've found the dog!'

The scene continued with Mr Neville joining in. Eventually the dog was handed to him, wriggling and squirming, and then after being given half a crown, Ralph had to creep out up-centre.

While Ralph watched from the wings, the dog then had to be handed to the parson. He exited saying, 'Oh, dear, oh, dear, it spat on my chin!' to which Mr Neville commented, 'If that's all it does we'll be very lucky.'

The actor playing the parson looked for Ralph in the wings, went to hand it to him, the owner stepped forward, Ralph stepped back for her to take the dog but, misunderstanding, she backed too and the dog shot from the actor's arms.

There followed a wild chase across the stage and into the auditorium with the entire cast running up and down the aisles, attempting to coax the traumatised creature out of hiding.

Somehow she was caught. Rehearsals resumed. Ralph saw the

woman to the stage door and asked Wilfred if he could borrow a key so that he could rehearse Act Three lines and moves ready for the run the next day. He was too terrified to procrastinate.

The two performances of *Hobson's Choice* that day were received rapturously. Both times the auditorium were bursting at the seams.

Ralph returned home, laid the fire ready for the morning, whispered through all his lines sitting up in bed, so that he wouldn't fall asleep but he did.

To his relief the run-through went on without too many hitches, with Ralph helping Isla set up for each act and looking after the owner's maid and dog.

The dog behaved well. It was too terrified by the bright lights to do much else and the actors realised the more it squirmed, the funnier it was.

Ralph was about to rush off to hunt for a hat, clothes and props when Isla stopped him. 'Where are you going?' she called. 'You're supposed to go up to Mr Neville's office with the others.'

'No, I'm not,' he said. 'I'm only down as doing the part. He's never paid anyone for rehearsals before.'

'All I know is that he asked me to tell you to go up to his office.'

'I wasn't that bad, was I?' he groaned.

'Ralph, stop hitting yourself over the head and just get up there or I'm for the high jump. He was quite insistent. I meant to tell you earlier but I forgot.'

Outside the office, he paced up and down, trying to prepare himself mentally for the worst. First he told himself he couldn't get sacked at such a late date, but then he realised a small part like his would be a picnic to a trained actor.

Depressed, he hovered by the door and knocked. Mr Neville was sitting behind his desk. Mrs Egerton-Smythe was tucked behind a small table in a corner. Already there were signs of order amongst the disarray of papers. 'You wanted to see me, Mr Neville,' Ralph said.

He nodded, and beckoned him to take a seat. Ralph removed a pile of manuscripts from the only remaining chair, placed them on the floor and sat. Mr Neville clasped his hands together and leaned over the table. Here it comes, thought Ralph.

'As you know, I have had a word with your father,' he began.

'Yes,' said Ralph. 'Thank you. I never thought he'd allow me to set foot on-stage again. Oh,' he said. 'He hasn't changed his mind, has he?'

'On the contrary. He's given permission for you to take Jane's position for the next nine months.'

Stunned, Ralph stared at him in disbelief. 'Pardon?'

'It's quite simple. You are to be an ASM. Officially.'

'But he can't pay!' Ralph protested.

'No. But Jane's father has already put down his daughter's annual wages. To make amends for Jane's sudden desertion, he has agreed to leave the payment with me to do with what I wish. I need two ASMs. I want you to be one of them.'

'I think I'd better sit down,' said Ralph weakly.

'You are already,' Mr Neville pointed out. 'You will be paid two pounds a week. In addition to ASM duties you will be requested occasionally to play small parts. Obviously, since you have acquired a professional wardrobe, the parts might be more numerous. Mrs Egerton-Smythe?'

Mrs Egerton-Smythe held out an envelope. 'Your first pay packet,' she said, smiling.

'Inside you will also find a letter making an official contract between the theatre management and you. I take it you accept this "apprenticeship", as your father calls it?' added Mr Neville.

Ralph nodded, dazed. 'We will review the situation next January. Perhaps by then you will have decided whether to apply for a scholarship to drama school before doing your National Service or work until National Service and be a student later. If you still plan to go.'

'Oh, I do,' Ralph exclaimed. 'But do you mean I'm part of the company for nine months?'

'Yes.'

'And my dad has agreed?'

'Yes.'

'How did you convince him?'

'I didn't. You did. He thinks you're cuckoo, of course.'

'Open the envelope if you don't believe it,' said Mrs Egerton-Smythe.

'Oh, I believe it,' said Ralph, still feeling perplexed. 'I just can't take it in. I mean, I thought it was impossible.'

'Well, your face is around the building so often, we've grown used to you. Perhaps now I'll get some peace.'

Ralph rose, clutching the envelope. 'Thank you so much, Mr Neville. You won't regret it.'

'All right. All right. Now off you go. I expect you have a list of props a mile long to find before the show.'

Ralph was about to leave when he remembered something. 'Mrs Egerton-Smythe?' She looked up again. 'Does Jessica know?'

'No. I thought you might like to tell her yourself. You'll find her waiting for you at the café.'

SIX

'The extraordinary thing is that Charles has been so much nicer to us now. Maybe my mother standing up for herself has taken a weight off his shoulders.'

'Does he still think your father was a genius?'

'Yes.'

'Do you?'

'No. He was brilliant in a law court but in other ways he was really rather stupid.' She sighed. 'My mother thinks that once Sandra has the baby, Charles's memory of my father will fade into him being a normal human and the baby will be the genius then.' She laughed. 'And at least then, she says, being a proud grandmother, she can join in.'

'This is the place,' said Ralph suddenly.

'Do you want me to wait outside?' Jessica asked.

'No. Two pairs of eyes are better than one.'

They were standing outside a large house. They opened the gate and trudged up the rough path to a small porch. Ralph took hold of the heavy ornate ring on the door and knocked.

A small elderly woman opened it. Ralph looked down at her. Behind her were bags stacked up in a hall.

'Yes?' she said. 'Can I help?'

'I'm terribly sorry, I thought this was a WVS clothing depot.'

'That's right. Have you brought some clothing?'

'No. I want to buy or exchange.'

'You need to go to the clothing exchange shop for that.'

'I need clothes in a bad state. Rags. I'm from the Palace Theatre. I need to look like a tramp, you see. For a play.'

'You'd best come in, dear.'

'Can I bring my friend?'

Jessica, who had remained by the wall, peered round and smiled.

'Of course. This way.'

They stepped into the hall and she ushered them into a room at the front of the house where three women were busy sorting and sewing. Two walls were filled with shelves made of packing cases inside which were bundles of clothes with coloured labels with letters and numbers attached to them.

A middle-aged woman in a green overall was tying up folded garments into bundles. Another was hunched over a black sewing machine.

'You want to speak to Mrs Jenkins,' said the small elderly woman and she led them to a thin young woman who was standing at a trestle table, painstakingly sorting out one large pile of clothes into three piles. Underneath the table were three boxes. The young woman picked up a grubby pair of men's combinations. 'That can go in the nearly good pile,' said the middle-aged woman. 'It's good, but it needs washing and mending first.'

'What about this?' she said, lifting a filthy, ragged shirt.

'Take them buttons off and put it the salvage pile.'

It was perfect, thought Ralph. 'Could I have it, please?' he blurted out.

The two women stared at him. 'This young man is from the Palace Theatre,' the elderly woman explained. 'I'm sorry, I forgot to ask you your name.'

Ralph hesitated. He wasn't sure which pronunciation to use. The way they pronounced it in the theatre, or how his family pronounced it.

'Rayfe,' he said, choosing the theatre one. 'Rayfe Hollis.' Out of the corner of his eye he saw Jessica smile. 'I'm playing a tramp,' he added hurriedly, 'and I'm looking for layers of ragged clothes.'

'We've plenty of them,' said the middle-aged woman. 'You'll find the salvage in this box,' she said, drawing one out.

Between him and Jessica, they found enough to go under a shirt, but he had to pay for a pair of old trousers, since Jessica pointed out that if he wore ones with flies which didn't do up, the audience wouldn't be watching anything else. He even found a misshapen old trilby hat which had seen better days.

He and Jessica ran down the path, both exhilarated at his find.

'I need you to get the next thing for me at the chemist's,' he said. 'I'm afraid I'd be too embarrassed.'

'What is it?' she asked. 'It can't be lipstick.'

'Talcum powder.'

'What do you want with talcum powder?'

'It's for whitening my hair. Oh, and I want to make my face look as if it's got a few veins in it. Any ideas?'

'A sponge might work,' she said thoughtfully. 'I used a bit we have at home for making tiny patterns on paper with paint. Why don't you try it with greasepaint on and press it to your skin?'

She slid her arm into his. 'How does it feel to be a professional actor?'

'I'm not there yet,' he protested. 'I'm an acting ASM.'

'So? How does it feel?'

He laughed. 'Like I want to sing to the rooftops.'

'Why don't you, then?'

'All right. If you do it too.'

So they did.

There was such a queue for the performance that night that there were even members of the audience standing in the boxes. It was as exciting as the first night. Even more so, since most of the cast's performances had grown during the week, especially Basil's, Mr Neville's and Maggie's. Isla was still attractive and enchanting but exactly the same as she had been at the read-through and, for the first time, Ralph could see her limitations as an actress, at least as a character actress. At the end of the performance, there was not only cheering from the audience, but stamping, followed by a standing ovation and a curtain call which seemed to go on for ever. It was a heady night.

It was strange walking home, brimming with the night's performance and the knowledge that there was a contract in his jacket pocket, and yet be greeted by darkness and silence in his home. Joan wasn't sleeping in the bed in the kitchen, so he couldn't even share his news with her. He left most of his pay-packet on the mantelpiece and began raking out the fire.

In the morning he raced downstairs to see his father, but he had gone out early, which Ralph found rather strange since it was his seventeenth birthday. The family had saved up their weekly ration of bacon, butter and bread so that he could have a birthday breakfast. That was his present from them and he ate it with exaggerated relish for their benefit as they sat round the table watching him.

To his amazement, he discovered that no one knew about the theatre contract, not even his mother. As soon as he announced it she flushed with pleasure and everyone pored over the letter from the theatre with its stamp in the corner.

'Didn't you suspect at all?' he asked her.

'Oh, I knew Mr Neville had talked it over with him. He told me that much and we had quite a chat about it, but I left it up to him to decide, and he ain't said nothin' yet. Oh, Ralphie,' she said beaming, 'you're going to be a proper actor?

'Will you speak to us if you get famous?' said Harry.

359

'Course I will,' he laughed. 'Will you speak to me?'

'I might,' he said airily.

Elsie gave him a friendly thump.

'Happy seventeenth, love,' said his mother suddenly and she shyly stumbled over to his chair and gave him a hug.

Later as he clambered on to his bike, he kept whispering, 'seventeen', over and over again. Sixteen sounded babyish in comparison, so it seemed strange that no one in the theatre noticed or commented that he seemed older. Perhaps when he started growing more facial hair, that would be the final turning point.

Wilfred seemed unusually reserved that morning. And jumpy. When Ralph asked if he could leave his Noony clothes up in the dressing room he would be using the following week, Wilfred yelled out, 'No,' with such alarm that Ralph was quite taken aback. Then Wilfred backtracked nervously and offered to keep it in his cubby-hole for him, waving his hand and saying, 'Later, later.'

Mystified, Ralph leapt up the steps. No one commented on his birthday, not even Isla. But then, he hadn't told anyone and if he mentioned it, they might think he was after a present, so he decided to keep quiet about it. After helping Isla set up for Act One, scene one, he pulled on his boots and hat and found a quiet corner in the wings where he could quickly go over his lines again and do some of his voice exercises.

He wasn't pleased with his performance in the run and Mr Neville had to keep reminding him not to pull his chin down or turn too far away from the audience. He had hoped to have got it by Saturday and he felt cross with himself. The thought of the opening night a mere two days away made him feel sick, but he reminded himself he had the contract and that part of Mr Neville's job was to teach him, and that made him feel a little less gloomy.

After the run, Mr Neville asked everyone to meet in the kitchen where it was a little warmer, for notes. When the notes were finished, Mr Neville asked Ralph to fetch the key to dressing-room five. Apparently one of the new cast for the following week's play to be rehearsed, *Nine till Six*, had sent a skip in early. Mr Neville was curious to know who it was. It was an odd request, thought Ralph, but his was not to reason why, except he remembered Wilfred's funny behaviour. 'I don't know if Wilfred will let me have it,' said Ralph.

'Tell him Mr Neville sent you.'

With relief that his notes had been incorporated with the rest of the cast, and he wasn't made to feel like an outsider, Ralph pushed open the door to the corridor and headed down the steps. Mr

Neville had been pleased with the way his character was developing but he warned him he would be expecting him to speak up on Monday. Wilfred handed the key over readily at the sound of Mr Neville's name and appeared to be smiling at something.

'Oh, Wilfred,' he said, 'I might as well take my rags up with me.'

Suddenly Wilfred turned crimson and began to stammer. 'Did that for you already,' he stumbled out.

'Oh,' said Ralph surprised. 'Thanks.'

It was quiet, almost peaceful, in the corridor outside dressing-room five. He inserted the huge key and turned it. He couldn't wait to step back inside it again. The key gave a welcoming click. Ralph pushed open the door and fumbled towards the light switch to the nearest dressing room mirror. On the dressing-room table at the far end of the room he saw his Noony rags. A battered old skip was standing by the window near by. It obviously belonged to an experienced actress, he thought. This skip had done a lot of travelling. As he drew nearer he noticed that all the leather and buckles had been replaced with new ones. It would be good for another fifty years, Ralph reckoned. A label was hanging from one of the handles. He turned it over. It read: RALPH HOLLIS.

He stared at it, shaking. His skip? His own skip? Dazed he tried to undo the buckles but he was trembling so much that his fingers became uncoordinated. Eventually he managed it. He prised back the lid. Inside were all the clothes he had obtained at Mr Gutman's shop, laid out neatly, by Florrie, he guessed. Lying on top were parcels and envelopes and a cigar box.

Inside the parcels were sock suspenders. 'For those endless farces where you'll have to drop your trousers,' said the label, signed by Geraldine and Raymond Maclaren. From the rest of the cast there were braces, shirt garters, a dickie, a bow tie, a tin of removing cream, tins of different shades of powder, foundation cream, a roll of cotton wool, a pile of clean rags, a bottle of spirit gum and Happy Birthday cards, most of which were covered in hand-drawn cartoons of him playing Hamlet dressed as Mrs Mulligatawny, or carrying a dog dressed as a country yokel.

The cigar box he kept till last. Inside it were sticks of greasepaint. Some were new, others were stubs obviously donated by the company. Lying alongside them were different coloured lengths of thin plaited crêpe hair, ready to be teased out into beards, sideburns and moustaches. Shattered, he sank on to the floor and sat staring at the contents in the box, vaguely conscious of a whispering coming from somewhere over his shoulder. He looked up to find a blur of faces at the door.

'Oh darling,' he heard Geraldine Maclaren exclaim, 'he's crying!' and Basil said quietly, 'It's all right. He's just happy.'

SEVEN

Clomping down the steps of the stage door area, in boots too large with a would-be escapee bundle of dog was not easy. Wilfred gave him a broad grin.

'You looks like Ben Gunn in that white beard,' he commented.

'I hope I manage to keep it on till the curtain call,' Ralph remarked.

'It looks firmly glued on to me,' said Wilfred reassuringly.

'Oh, it's stuck on all right. It's just so unbearably itchy I'm tempted to tear it off. It feels like a colony of fleas are dancing a rumba round my chin.'

The maid peered out and giggled and then hurried out and took the dog. 'There, there,' she said comfortingly. The dog began licking her face frantically. She beamed and looked up at Ralph. ''Ow'd she do?'

'Stole the show.'

'And you?' said Wilfred.

'I got a round.'

'Ow d'you mean you got around?' said the maid puzzled. 'Around where?'

'A round of applause,' explained Wilfred. 'It's when the audience claps as someone makes an exit.'

'Oh.'

'First-night audiences are always generous,' said Ralph. 'Actually, if you want to know the truth I think it was Popsy who got the round.' And he tickled the dog behind the ear. He could see the maid was pleased. 'How are you getting home?' he asked.

'The chauffeur is picking me up.'

'Oh, very lah-di-dah,' chorused Wilfred and Ralph.

'Is your young lady in tonight?' Wilfred asked.

'No. I wanted to have a chance of several goes first. She's coming Friday.' He paused. 'And Saturday.'

'Got a part in the next one?'

'No. It's an all-female cast. It's set in a dress shop. I'm going to try to persuade my cousin Joan to see it. She works in one and she's never been to the theatre before.'

Wilfred opened his cubby-hole door for the maid to re-enter. Ralph made his goodbyes to her and quickly stumbled back up the steps. He felt uneasy being out of touch with the play. Someone might cut their lines as in *Vive La Liberté*. Once he reached the wings he felt safe again. Waves of laughter were coming from the auditorium. There was now a confrontation of misunderstandings between various spouses which would eventually untangle themselves by the close of the act.

Isla was sitting at the book, smiling. She looked so much happier these days that he had thought she had changed her mind about leaving, but she said she was happier because she knew it was temporary. It was her last but one week as a stage manager. The next day a new stage manager and ASM fresh from drama school would be on the book for the rehearsals of *Nine Till Six*, during the day, and Ralph would be official dogsbody and prop finder and occasional small parts. The following week Isla would be in the acting company on a contract of 'play as cast'. Every Saturday she would look at the cast list of the next play and take her script home at the end of the show. No more Saturday strikes for her. He would miss her.

He still hadn't seen his father to thank him and by Sunday night he realised that, although his father had given his permission, he wasn't comfortable with the decision and it saddened Ralph. He tried to get some information out of his mother, but all she had said was, 'You know your dad, he needs time.'

Another wave of laughter shook him out of his reverie.

He glanced at Isla again. She smiled and gave a nod. It was coming up to the end of the play. The other members of the cast were now in the wings. Ralph prepared himself for the dash to the front of the stage for the curtain call.

And then it was over. The thank-yous were given. The announcements for *Nine Till Six* were made for performances the following week and it was 'God Save the King', curtain down and a mad scramble to the dressing rooms for those who had a train to catch to London. And Ralph was part of the scramble and he loved it.

Upstairs in dressing room five he found himself alone. The two actors he shared the room with had already left. He stared at his talcumed hair, white eyebrows and powdered mouth, the purplish veins across his nose and the lines he had drawn into the creases where he had frowned for the purpose. Basil had helped to make up the beard from white crêpe hair. Beside him was a heavy Victorian volume, a tip he had picked up from Basil. Now all he had to do was peel the itchy beard gently from his face, in one piece, lay it flat in the middle of the book so that he could use it again the following night. He placed it as best he could and gingerly pressed it to a close. He hoped it wouldn't stick to the pages. He would have to come in early the next day to check.

Having achieved that, he rubbed the cream vigorously into his face, pushing it hard into the traces of spirit gum round his chin, and then grinned at the colourful mess. He made a grotesque face and then in a rasping voice said, 'Wanna kiss me?' Hastily he cleaned it off and rinsed with the warm water he had in the thermos Mrs Egerton-Smythe had now given him. He brushed as much talc out of his hair as he could, wound a cravat round his neck, tucking it in his shirt, and sprang up to grab his raincoat and trilby. Before switching off the light, he gazed at all the good-luck cards round his mirror. He would never throw them away.

'April 7th, 1947,' he whispered. A date he would remember all his life. He grabbed Felix's *An Actor Prepares* from the dressing table, gave the room a cheery wave and locked up.

'Wish I could lose years as quick as that,' Wilfred commented as Ralph handed over his key. 'I thought you'd be complaining over how long I took,' said Ralph.

'First to arrive, last to leave,' Wilfred remarked. 'Like Mr Duke.'

Ralph, taking it as a compliment, smiled. He picked up his bike which was leaning near the notice board and wheeled it to the stage door. 'Good night, Wilfred.'

'Good night, Mr Hollis.'

It wasn't until he was outside that Ralph took in Wilfred's 'Mr Hollis'. It was all he could do not to laugh with exhilaration. The street lights had been switched off. A half moon was hovering under lowering clouds. Ralph squinted to adjust his eyes to the sudden darkness. He pulled up his collar and wheeled his bike out on to the street. Before mounting it, he was conscious of a figure standing in the shadows on the far side of the road. It made him jump. He forced himself to look in case it was his imagination, but he picked out a man, his hands in his jacket pocket, shoulders hunched, a scarf wrapped round his mouth, the cap pulled down.

He pretended not to have noticed, and began to walk nonchalantly, afraid that if he moved too fast the man might be precipitated into action. To his alarm, he heard footsteps. The man was following him! A rush of adrenalin made his heart pound. He knew what some men thought of people who worked in the theatre, and how they felt they had every justification in bashing the hell out of them. He quickened his pace slightly. The footsteps also quickened. Fumbling with the handlebars, he threw himself on to the saddle and pushed off as fast as he could, the bicycle wobbling madly.

By now he could hear the man running. He gritted his teeth, willing the bike to stop swerving. He had just got going when a voice roared out, 'Ralph!' He squeezed on the brakes and swung round.

'Dad!' he gasped. 'What the hell are you doing?'

His father walked briskly up to him, looking furtively over his shoulder. 'You scared the wits out of me. What's with all this cloak and dagger business?'

'Didn't want no one to see me, did I? Now if anyone asks you,' he added nervously, 'you ain't seen me. I've told everyone I'm out for a drink with an old army mate. All right?'

'It's a bit late for a drink, isn't it?'

'I come out earlier.'

'Where have you been then?'

He shifted awkwardly. 'Checkin' up.'

'On what?'

'This apprenticeship of yours. I wanted to make sure you was gettin' a good deal.'

'Dad,' said Ralph, the light beginning to dawn, 'were you in tonight?'

'In?'

'To see the play?'

'Shush. Not so loud,' he snapped.

'Dad!'

He shrugged then nodded.

'So what did you think?'

'Had its amusin' moments, I s'pose. Toff was good. As usual.'

'What do you mean "as usual"?'

He began to squirm uneasily. 'I only saw him in the last one. *Hobson's Whatever*. That's all.'

'But what did you think of me?'

His father looked him squarely in the eye. 'You'll do,' he said.

Ralph smiled. That was praise, coming from his father.

'I expect that Mr Neville will help you speak up a bit. I could hear you though. From upstairs. You'll get by. He'll learn you.'

'I wanted to thank you, Dad.'

'Oh, yeah?'

'But you were never around.'

'I been busy.'

They stood looking at each other awkwardly. His father cleared

365

his throat. 'Now that we're alone, I thought I better tell you, well, your mother and I thought I better had. We thought.' He paused. 'See, things are going to be a bit different at home soon.'

'With Aunty Win going?'

'There's that too.'

Ralph watched his father look away and then he realised he was acutely embarrassed. He could see his father swallowing.

'Is it good news?' Ralph asked, probing.

'For your mum and me. And Elsie and Harry, I hope. Your ma is telling Joan tonight.'

'I see. But you think I might not feel the same way?'

'I dunno.' He hesitated. 'See, we'll have somebody movin' in, so to speak. Another mouth to feed.'

Ralph realised that, however much his father wanted to tell him, he couldn't. If he was any kind of actor this was his chance to use it to everyone's advantage.

'Dad,' he said, smiling, 'I wouldn't be about to have a brother or sister, would I?'

His father looked at him in amazement and then nodded.

'That's splendid!' Ralph said.

Relief flooded his father's face. 'You're pleased! You're really pleased!' he exclaimed.

And then Ralph realised he wasn't acting. 'Yes,' he laughed. 'I really am. It'd make a change having a real baby in the house, instead of a lot of adults behaving like babies.'

His father was grinning from ear to ear. 'I'm cock-a-hoop about it. It's the best thing that's happened to me since I got demobbed. I missed so much of you nippers, being away. Now I've got a second chance, see.'

Ralph nodded. 'Can I ask you something else?' Ralph said. 'It's not about this news. It's about me getting this ASM job. Why did you agree?'

'I gave up, didn't I,' he said evasively.

'And,' added Ralph, not believing him.

'Well, you stood up to me. I didn't like it, but I respected you for it. If you couldn't stand up to me you'd never last the course in a job like that,' he said, indicating the theatre. 'And there was all this National Service business. You'll be doing what you don't want to do soon enough. I don't like it, but there you are.' He looked at him searchingly. 'By the way, when you get called up and they asks you what your occupation is, have you thought of what you'll tell 'em?'

'I'll say I'm an actor.'

'Thought you might,' he groaned.

'At least I won't have to spend so long square-bashing as you, Dad.'

His father sighed. 'I thought I'd done enough for all of us. Still, I hope it won't be as bad gettin' out for you, as it's been for me.'

'Was it that bad? Coming back home?'

His father nodded. 'And I'd been looking forward to it, which was worse. I felt right out of it. Specially with so many females. Big and clumsy. A right cuckoo in the nest.'

'Like me?' suggested Ralph.

His father laughed. 'Like you.'

Ralph held out his hand. 'New beginnings, Dad?'

'New beginnings.'

They shook hands and then his father stood back for a moment and gazed at him. 'Sod this for a game of soldiers,' he blurted out. 'You're dead a long time,' and he threw his arms around him and hugged him fiercely.

Ralph let go of his bike and buried his head in his father's shoulders and they clung to each other silently.

Eventually they broke apart, his father sniffed and then gave Ralph two hearty slaps on the back.

'Come on, son,' he said hoarsely. 'Let's go 'ome.'

CURTAIN